rüffer & rub

Symphony of Dreams

The Conductor and Patron
Paul Sacher

Lesley Stephenson
with
Don Weed

Published by rüffer & rub Sachbuchverlag GmbH, Zurich, 2002
info@ruefferundrub.ch | www.ruefferundrub.ch
All rights reserved
Copyright © Lesley Stephenson 2002

Design: Diem & Partner AG, Zurich

Printed and bound by Books on Demand GmbH, Norderstedt
Paper: Cream white, 90 g/m^2

ISBN 978-3-907625-10-1

This book is dedicated to the men and women whose support and expertise led to my recovery from a long-term illness.

Dr Michael Awty
Mr André Cardinaux
Dr Harold Gelb
Dr Wayne Prigoff
Mrs Ursula Schmidt-Itschner
The late Dr Elsie (Pat) Stephenson
The late Dr Neville Stephenson
Dr Donald L. Weed

When Paul Sacher was a young boy,
his mother said to him,
'That which you want to do, you can do.'
He never forgot those words.

Contents

Acknowledgements 11
Introduction 13

Prelude: The Law of Stones 19

I The History
  1 Dreams in the Passage of Time 25
  2 On the Threshold of Freedom 29
  3 A House Divided 33
  4 City Bound 37

II The Dream
  5 'That Which You Must Do' 45
  6 'That Which You Want to Do' 63
  7 The Garden of Payerne 73
  8 As Silent as Graves 91
  9 A Will and a Way 103
  10 More than a Name 115

III The Reality
  11 The Price of the Dream 133
  12 The Lord of the Manor 149
  13 The Share Majority 165
  14 The Lemonade Years 177
  15 Uncle Paul 191
  16 The Catalyst 207
  17 Everything Flows 223

IV The Legacy
  18 Sunshine and Shadows 239
  19 The Crown of Dreams 251
  20 Solitude 263
  21 The Grand Old Man of Roche 273
  22 Nothing but Age 289

Coda: Con Grazia 307

Appendix
Notes 313
Sources and Bibliography
   Archives 317
   Correspondence 319
   Interviews 319
   Publications 321
   Photograph Sources 327
Index 329
List of Paul Sacher's Commissions 335
Paul Sacher's Family Tree 353

Acknowledgements

Over the years of working on this biography, I received considerable assistance from many individuals and institutions.

First, I would like to thank the hundreds of people, particularly Paul Sacher and his family, who granted me interviews. Many of them are named in the book; others may not have been quoted directly, but helped build up my picture of Sacher's world.

Many libraries and institutions gave me short- or long-term help during my research. I wish particularly to thank the staff of the council archives in Pratteln, Rheinfelden, Zuzgen and Payerne (in Switzerland), Mr Andreas Barth from the Canton of Basle City Archive, and Dr Matthias Manz-Tanner, former director of the Canton of Basle Country Archive in Liestal. My thanks also go to Mr Peter Bartók, who gave me access to many documents from the Béla Bartók archives during our lengthy interview in Florida.

I further wish to thank the Basle historian and author Mr René Teuteberg for his introduction to the history of Basle; the Pratteln historian Mrs Alice Bielser, who shared her own family research and helped me to decipher the early records of Paul Sacher's ancestors; the staff of the Paul Sacher Foundation; Mr Urs B. Roth for his transcriptions of Paul Sacher's letters to his mother, Mrs Lili Roth-Streiff; Mr Luc Boissonnas for his assistance and corrections in connection with the story of Sacher's work for Pro Helvetia; Mrs Joan Newby for her reading of the early manuscript and helpful suggestions; and Miss Marianne Majer for numerous conversations relating to the history of the Basle Chamber Orchestra.

I wish to thank my parents, the late Drs Neville and Elsie Stephenson, as well as André Cardinaux, for their reading and correction of the various versions of the book; Theresa Stefanidis of the Stefanidis Agency, Inc. for her representation and support; Thomas Baumann for his unstinting technical assistance, and Helen Simpson for her erudite editing of the final English manuscript.

Finally, and most importantly, my greatest thanks go to my long-standing collaborator and editor, Don Weed.

Introduction

In the summer of 1984, I was singing in Francesco Cavalli's opera *La Calisto* at the Bath Festival in England. During a break in the performances I visited my parents in Surrey, and at breakfast one Sunday morning the conversation turned to Paul Sacher, with whom I had established a close friendship since meeting him in Australia ten years earlier. My father asked, 'Who is writing his biography?' I had no idea. I had never heard Sacher mention a biographer, even when I worked with him on ghost-writing or translating his articles and speeches. A couple of hours later, Paul rang from Basle to ask me how the performances were going, and I asked him who was writing his biography. He replied, 'You.' He knew my work as a writer, and we had always worked well together. So I agreed, and the first of dozens of lengthy interviews was held in the following months.

From the beginning, I felt it was important that the project should be independent. Although Paul gave generously of his time in interviews, made suggestions about those to whom I should speak, and wrote letters on my behalf to the official archives in Basle and Pratteln in order to gain me access to his family and school records, I was never put on the payroll of any of his institutions. This enabled me to maintain sufficient distance from him and his entourage to remain objective, and to tell his story in the manner I felt best suited to the task.

There was sometimes a price to pay for my independence; for example, my discomfort when I was interrogated by the late Professor Edgar Bonjour in the front parlour of his home in Basle as to whether my intentions were serious and honourable. Bonjour, a retired professor of history from Basle University and a greatly respected author and historian, made it clear that I must fulfil my intention to complete the project, as I was stopping anyone else doing it. It was only when I had spoken to him at length about my work that he consented to grant me an interview.

Working on Paul Sacher's biography revealed a saga of size and complexity I had not anticipated. Perhaps even more fascinating than the stories in the book itself was the entwining of our personal histories while it was being written. During the fifteen years of our discussions, in both our lives there were deaths, marriages, divorces, illnesses, and all the other trappings of life, which created, sometimes, a deeply poignant counterpoint to the story of Sacher's life as it unfolded.

In *Extraordinary Lives,* a collection of articles by leading American biographers, Ronald Steel, biographer of the American political writer and journalist Walter Lippmann, discusses the difficulties incurred by biographers whose subjects are still alive. He describes his relationship with Lippmann as one in which both men were 'locked in a mutual endeavour and a mutual anxiety'. That was also my experience.

Behind the controlled demeanour that Paul Sacher used to hide himself from scrutiny, he was intensely sensitive. Some years ago, when I gave him an early draft of the first chapters, which dealt only with his family's history, he was troubled because the stories were more than 'just a listing of facts', and he later confessed that they had touched him more deeply than he wanted. It was then that he asked me if I would wait until after his death before publishing the book. After seeing his discomfort when he attended the screenings of the François Reichenbach documentary about his life (for which I wrote and recorded the English translation), I decided that I would try to honour his request.

Partly for this reason, in the year before he died we decided to leave the biography more or less 'on ice', though from time to time, when I visited him, I would ask a question which would help clarify an issue or story. In autumn 1998, he willingly agreed to let me use photos from his private collection which had never been lent or published before.

As for the direction the biography should take, Sacher offered only one suggestion: 'If you want to understand what I have done in Basle, you first need to study the history of Basle.' At first, that confused me. Did he mean that there was a parallel between Basle's story and his own? Did he mean that Basle's rich cultural history had somehow prepared his path? It was only as I researched his family back over ten generations that I understood what he meant. It wasn't the facts of Basle's history that were so important, but rather an appreciation of the character-developing power of the pervasive themes of freedom, independence, and rising above circumstance through the force of will that gave meaning to the history. It was how these elements of Basle's past impacted upon the shaping of his family that was so important to understanding who Paul Sacher was, and how he had done what he had done. So I decided to start with the history of Basle and the way in which it had motivated Sacher's ancestors as far back as they could be traced.

As I began the writing, however, I realized that a life so dedicated to, and immersed in, the arts would resist being told in a simple narrative or in an academic style. A life so steeped in dreams and ambition, so rich in the realization of personal, professional and artistic wealth, could not be told as a mere chronology of supposition and fact. The aesthetic with which Sacher's story was told not only had to reflect the depth and scope of his accomplishments but had to do so in a manner befitting the largely unsung story of this twentieth-century musical giant. Gradually, the material organized itself into the four major aspects that had shaped and expressed the whole of Sacher's life, like the movements of a symphony.

A symphony of dreams.

Prelude:
The Law of Stones

> *Wherever the stone falls, there it must lie.*
> *This is the law of stones.*

She never knew what made her turn; perhaps a sound or a trick of the light. She was a young dancer hurrying down Elisabethenstrasse, Basle, on her way to rehearsal. As she came level with the neo-Gothic Elisabethenkirche across the street, her attention was suddenly caught by a figure moving past the church's darkened sandstone façade. She had no time to spare, and yet this figure brought her to a standstill, etching itself so indelibly in her memory that she could still recall it in minute detail nearly seventy years later.

It was a young man, one she had never seen before. What fascinated her, however, was not simply the intense expression on his face, nor even the slight limp with which he walked. It was his appearance, dressed as he was, totally in black, not at all the fashion of Basle in the mid-1920s. He seemed to belong to a former age. 'He looked like Lord Byron,' the dancer remembered. 'He was different. Nobody looked like that then. All in black: his hat, his clothes, everything.'

If the young man noticed her – a beautiful girl with the finely chiselled features of a porcelain doll – he gave no sign. Instead, as she stared after him, intrigued by his appearance and wondering who he was, he continued to the top of the street, veered left into Freiestrasse and was gone.

The dancer's name was Els Havrlik. In a sense, her feeling that she had encountered something of another age was quite correct. She had seen a man still caught between the legacies of the past and his dreams for the future; a young man who was on his way to breaking the law of stones.

The black clothes were the remnants of another era. The black represented the seriousness of life, its toils and burdens. The clothes belonged to the legacy of his ancestry (a legacy he remembered in later years on grey days when he had succumbed, briefly and privately, to melancholy). Together, they spoke of hard-working farmers toiling in the Rhine Valley village of Pratteln, and in Zuzgen in the canton of Aargau. The lives and dreams of those men and women had been shaped for centuries by the law of stones.

For those born into serfdom, this meant staying where they were born, or paying dearly to leave. It meant life as tenant farmers within the feudal system. Their greatest ambition for the future was freedom, or perhaps becoming respected members of the communities in which they lived: a village elder, the village midwife, landlord of the village inn. Later, when the French Revolution brought an apparent end to feudalism, their aspirations expanded to include possessions of their own: their own lands, their own farms, their own lives. For some, their dreams were caught up in the mere struggle for survival: the survival of single mothers, illegitimate children and young widows at times and in places where charity was scarce.

It was the embodiment of the legacy of centuries in this young man that stopped Els Havrlik in her tracks. The young man's name was Paul Sacher.

He was nineteen when Els saw him. Even at that young age, he understood instinctively that every great work or achievement undergoes two stages of creation: a stage of visualizing or dreaming, and then a stage of concrete realization. A significant portion of the master plan for his life had been envisaged by then, and some of his goals reached. He had completed his formal education. He was a proficient violinist, and his studies in conducting and music theory were well under way. Within a few months, at the age of twenty, he would conduct the first performances of his first major creation, the Basle Chamber Orchestra.

He had already displayed his ancestors' tenacity and industry, but he would need more than that to break the law of stones. He had intelligence, and his mother's ambition, but the leap that would take him beyond the lesser shadow of his parent's means needed still more. First of all, it required the power to dream, and that power had already been awakened. His single-minded passion was to see each movement of his plan through to its climax, and beyond. The symphony of dreams had begun.

By itself, though, the power to dream would not be enough. Others before him had dreamt great dreams in Basle, had planned great acts or works, and had lived to see their plans realized. The Elisabethenkirche, commissioned in the late 1850s by Christoph Merian, bore testimony to that. Merian had envisioned and planned, and nurtured his dreams to fruition. He had dreamt and succeeded, but one essential ingredient of his success was not available to the nineteen-year-old Paul Sacher: money.

Merian was born rich. He had not had to break the law of stones to acquire the wealth that he increased. His father had matched his business acumen against the strength of Napoleon's continental blockade from 1806 to 1811, amassing a vast fortune by continuing to trade with Britain when most European ports were closed to British ships. His son, pious and determined to fulfil his social obligations, simply built on what was already there.

Sacher's dreams, however, exceeded the resources available to him, so for some time he would have to use his charm and his talent to woo the support of wealthy benefactors. But as long as others paid the piper, his power, his authority, could not be absolute. And absolute authority was the heart-blood of his dreams.

His goal was to become a conductor. He wanted to perform the music of his times, but contemporary music required an orchestra very different from the symphony orchestras commonly heard at that time. He needed a smaller group, a chamber orchestra; but none had been founded in the 1920s, so if Sacher wanted one he would have to create it. He also wanted to perform early music, the forgotten or unknown works of past masters, but to do so with authenticity he would need appropriate instruments. When he had acquired them, he would have to find and train specialist players who in time could train others. For that, he would need a centre, a school for early music – and none existed at the time. Also, of course, he would require a choir to sing the choral parts of both the contemporary and early compositions he wished to perform. He would have to found it and train it, and he did that, too.

One dream led to another, but the problem of money remained. Had the solution not come in the form in which it did, there would have been another solution, and a different story to tell.

The passion with which the young Sacher pursued his early vision would have seen to that. But then, unexpectedly, an answer presented itself – a stroke of fate – and Paul Sacher availed himself of it. To take what was offered, though, he had to break the law of stones. And for that there would be a price to pay.

I
The History

1

Dreams in the Passage of Time

In the canton of Basle, large stones had for centuries been used to mark the boundaries separating one village from another. In Pratteln, the stones were inscribed on the side towards the village with the eagle emblem of the Eptingers (the family who had once owned the village), and on the other side with a bishop's staff, the emblem of Basle. The stones were large, but not so large that they could not be moved, and in those days men could and did move the boundary stones to their advantage.

In Pratteln, a small farming community on the southern edge of the Rhine Valley, the *Gescheid*, a group of eight villagers, was responsible for the stones. Twice a year, in autumn and spring, its members inspected the stones for signs of tampering or decay.

At his initiation, each new member of the *Gescheid* was invested with secrets which he held fast throughout his lifetime and took unspoken to his grave. They concerned not only the stones themselves, but what lay under them. Any observant man could see the visible boundary stones, but what no one except a member of the *Gescheid* knew was the precise arrangement of the *Lohen*, the pattern of the bones and bricks or pottery shards buried beneath them. The *Lohen* acted as a safeguard against the stones being moved, because disorder in these hidden arrangements meant that the stone had been tampered with. If the stone were moved, the *Lohen* would have to be moved as well, and replaced in an identical pattern for the movement to go undetected. No offender, working at night as he would have to, could ensure that the *Lohen* remained unchanged.

Those who committed such a crime were answerable to the *Gescheid*, whose authority in border disputes or offences concerning the placement of the stones was absolute. It had the jurisdiction of a tribunal, and its rulings could not be questioned. To become a member of the *Gescheid* was the wish of Friedrich Dürr, Paul Sacher's great-great-great grandfather, and it was a wish that came true. On the day he was initiated, a single church bell began to toll. Dressed in the black coats that symbolized their office, the other members of the *Gescheid* escorted Dürr through the village and on to one of the large stones that marked its boundaries. Beside the stone a pole some forty feet high had been erected, and three bundles of rye were attached to its top. As the president of the *Gescheid* read the oath of initiation, the rye was set alight and Dürr was warned that the flames symbolized the hell fire in which his soul would burn if he ever misused his secret knowledge.

★★★

Dominated by a massive stone castle, Pratteln had once been the dominion of the Eptingers, one of the most important of Basle's noble families. In 1525, however, the village had been acquired by the city of Basle.

Pratteln was a God-fearing, conservative and superstitious community, still under the yoke of the feudal system. Its citizens were hard-working and resourceful tenant farmers, whose robust instinct for survival left its imprint on succeeding generations. Their lives were dominated by rules and rituals; their daily routine was dominated by the seasons.

The village was a single economic unit from which outsiders were often excluded on the basis of arbitrary decisions. It was a close-knit society, and those few strangers who were allowed to stay enjoyed even fewer privileges than the farmers themselves and, along with their permits, purchased only the right to be tolerated.

In spite of this, in 1662 a thirty-year-old baker, Hans Jacob Dürr, from the city of Aarau in central northern Switzerland, decided to make Pratteln his home.[1] He was a subject of Berne, and therefore under the Swiss feudal system he was not allowed to settle in Basle, just eight kilometres further west. Nor was he permitted to join its bakers' guild or to profit from the opportunities available in a larger city, where hard work, talent or connections could turn dreams into reality.

In Pratteln, there were no guilds. The village did not even possess its own mill. On the face of it, there was little to keep Hans Jacob Dürr in Pratteln, yet he chose to farm there. By 1663, when an official request for citizenship was made on his behalf, he had married Anna Bielser, the daughter of a respected local farmer, and sired his first son, Samuel. When citizenship was granted, the name Dürr was added for the first time to the list of family names in Pratteln's church register.[2]

As a farmer, Dürr had little time to dream, and in any case most paths to personal achievement were blocked by the endless demands of the land. Still, there were other possibilities for those who sought them. Men like Dürr, who had learnt a trade or additional skills, could expect that these would bring them something more. It was this promise of status and 'something more' which led Hans Jacob Dürr's second son, Jacob, to become a butcher. He established his premises in the village square, where his name and the dates of his business can still be read today on the stone façade of the house that was once his shop.

In a village where people ate meat only on Sundays, Jacob Dürr's prospects for profit seemed unlikely to fulfil his dream of having 'more'. But Pratteln also had two inns, where meat could be served daily to passing travellers and guests, and there he saw his opportunity. In 1702, one of the inns, the Weisses Kreuz, came up for auction, and Jacob bought it, intending to pass it on to his son, Johannes. Nine years later, however, he was bankrupt, and was forced to sell the inn to a rival landlord's son.

For some of Paul Sacher's ancestors, the sufficiency of land and crops may have been enough; but for others there was a further desire, perhaps unspoken, which remained unfulfilled. It was the dream of freedom. Neither Jacob Dürr, sometime landlord of the Weisses Kreuz, nor his son, Johannes, lived to see the end of feudalism. They had to content themselves with pursuing other dreams, such as that of improving their status in the community.

★★★

It was such a dream which had led Friedrich Dürr to join the *Gescheid*. After the oath had been read and sworn to, and the fire had burnt itself out, the stone concealing the *Lohen* was lifted and Friedrich Dürr could clearly see the configuration of the small shards and bones beneath. The secret was his. When the stone was replaced, the initiation was complete. Friedrich Dürr was now a *Gescheidsmann,* and he remained one until his death in 1804.*

---

* Paul Sacher's family tree is on p. 353.

2

On the Threshold of Freedom

Three major events in Basle's history influenced the lives of Paul Sacher's ancestors and forged the beginnings of the character he would possess. The first was the end of serfdom.

The harvest of 1788 had been poor, and as the new year began prices rose. Throughout Europe, the winter of 1788–9 was harsh with the bite of hunger. France, with the largest population in Europe, was affected worst, and hunger fuelled the French peasants' deep and growing resentment. The storming of the Bastille in Paris on 14 July 1789 was the beginning of a revolution which ultimately ended aristocratic privilege in France. It was a strident finale to the *ancien régime*, and in its wake the feudal system throughout Europe disappeared.

The ruling classes in the cantons of Switzerland could hardly ignore these changes. They condemned what had happened in France, but it was the condemnation of those who wished to avoid similar revolutionary violence within Swiss borders, out of fear for their own privileges. They were not yet ready to follow the example of the American reformers or the newly elected French National Assembly. On 20 January 1790, the Basle government declared an end to the feudal bondage of the peasants to their overlords, a token gesture designed to buy time and stave off strife. The country folk were now free to move and marry at will, without having to pay for the privilege of doing so.

This decree did not, however, bring about the end of feudal tithes and ground rents, and it ignored the issue of civil equality. The peasants still could not vote or stand for office, and the city's educational institutions were still closed to their children. They still could not own their own land, and the clocks of Basle city, which for centuries had been set an hour ahead of those in the countryside, remained an hour ahead as a reminder to the peasants of their status. When the villagers of Pratteln and the rest of the Basle countryside understood the decree, they realized that it represented only the abolition of a name. Little had changed. Disappointed, they turned their attention to local concerns, which in Pratteln meant what had been happening in the range of hills overlooking the village.

Before 1726, there had been only two private manor estates in Pratteln. Then, for more than forty years, the building of manors in the region had been prohibited by the Basle councils because just one sizeable estate could cost several farming families their livelihood. But in 1767 building recommenced. The new estate, with its breath-taking view of the countryside, was euphemistically called Schönenberg, 'Beautiful Mountain'. But the villagers called it by another name: the 'robber estate'. In 1769 Schönenberg was bought by a Basle trader, Johannes Zäslin. A few years later, a fourth estate sprang up on the hills, and then yet another in the valley below. By 1793, the new manor estates had gobbled up no less than one-quarter of the farmers' land.

The villagers complained to Basle city council, but their complaints were barely heard. In the early 1790s, the authorities in Basle were preoccupied with problems of a much more serious nature. The gulf between the politics of France and the rest of Europe had widened, and on 20 April 1792 France declared war on Austria and Russia. For five long years, this first Coalition War continued throughout Europe. Despite Switzerland's oath of neutrality, there were frequent border skirmishes, and Swiss soldiers were garrisoned in the border villages for four and a half years. In Pratteln, where resources were already stretched by the needs of a growing population and the loss of farming land to the robber estates, there were sometimes more than a hundred extra mouths to feed. Food was scarce, and by 1794 the Basle government was urging farmers throughout the countryside to use every available piece of land to produce extra food.

In November 1797 Napoleon, flushed with his victory over Austria in his Italian campaign, crossed Switzerland on his way north to the peace congress in Rastatt. Both his success and his timely appearance in Switzerland served as a catalyst to rekindle the peasants' demands for reform. Pressure from France, combined with that of the Swiss peasants, was sufficient to coerce Basle's Grosser Rat (one of the two councils comprising the city's government) to introduce a declaration of civil equality on 20 January 1798. The status of Basle's country folk was changed to that of full citizens. The bondage of serfdom was ended.

For a few days, both country folk and city-dwellers celebrated. In Pratteln, Friedrich Dürr's son, also called Friedrich, celebrated the fulfilment of the dream of freedom by marrying a local girl, Elisabeth Rebmann. He was the first member of the Dürr family in Pratteln to marry as a free man.

After the Swiss confederation had been transformed into a central government in April 1798, tithes and ground rents were abolished. Farmers could now purchase their land for a payment of twenty times their former annual tithes. But, in the excitement of reform, too little thought had been given to how to collect the payments; consequently, almost none were made. Hospitals, churches, schools, and welfare services, as well as the government, had been dependent on tithe revenue to fund their operations. Now, without either tithes or collected payments, they could no longer meet all their obligations. Basle – in fact, the entire country – was faced with a financial and social crisis, and in 1800 the Swiss Parliament could find no better solution than to reinstate the former feudal tithes.

The farmers, struggling in the aftermath of the European war and food shortages, rose in fury. In Pratteln, the village council prepared an open letter of complaint, to which *Gescheidsmann* Friedrich Dürr added his signature. Some farmers even joined a mass of their armed comrades and marched towards Liestal to meet the Basle government's delegate. The demonstration turned into a furious riot which was subdued only by the intervention of French soldiers. Humiliated and disillusioned, some of the country folk began to leave their villages. But Friedrich Dürr and his children stayed. They had seen the partial fulfilment of their dreams, and they hoped for more.

★★★

In May 1804, a law introduced by the Basle government once again gave the farmers the chance to buy their land. Once again, for a sum equalling twenty times their yearly feudal obligations, the farmers could buy the land on which their ancestors had laboured for centuries. By 1810, Friedrich Dürr the younger had bought seven sections of his family's land for his children. The sections were divided under the three-field system between the vineyards, the forests, and the tracts of farming land on the lush flats of the Rhine Valley. Four of the sections were small, but there were three larger parcels, each measuring over a thousand square metres. Two were forest land, but the third was a piece of choice farming land for which Friedrich paid a proud 448 Swiss francs.* The Dürrs, at last, were free.

---

* Monetary figures in this book indicate original values unless otherwise stated.

3

A House Divided

The second event in Basle's history which shaped the lives of Paul Sacher's ancestors was the division of the canton of Basle into two separate political entities: the cantons of Basle city and Basle countryside.

After the dissolution of Switzerland's central government in 1803, the cantons re-acquired their individual sovereignty. In Basle, a parliament was elected in which the country folk had more representatives than the city dwellers, while the government remained dominated by city men. In March 1814, however, political dominance in parliament was returned to the city through the adoption of a new constitution, voted in on a day when many of the country representatives were absent.

In defence of their actions, the men of the city argued that they were better educated and therefore better suited to assume the responsibility of re-establishing the sovereignty of the canton. Besides, the country men were told, it was only fair that those who carried the larger part of the canton's economic burden should dominate in affairs of state. In some ways, the city men's arguments were justified. When rain washed out the crops in 1816, and famine became widespread, it was the latter who came to the rescue, supplying the villages with *Dinkel* (an early form of wheat) and potato plants, often free of charge. The country folk survived, but their estrangement and mistrust grew.

The farmers' resentment was matched by the grievances of the country craftsmen. Even in the 1820s, they were still forbidden to work for city employers or to sell their work in the city, whereas city craftsmen could work in country villages, and were free to sell their wares as they pleased. By 1827, the country men had come to realize that, since they had lost their majority in parliament, the changes they wanted would never be made.

In 1831, a new cantonal constitution for Basle was adopted by a clear majority of both city and country populations. However, the political dominance of the city was retained, and agitation continued in the countryside. The opposing interests fixed themselves territorially, and there was talk of cantonal division; for over fifteen months, the country communities lived in uncertainty. Then, on 3 August 1833, Basle's government sent a troop of soldiers into the countryside, ostensibly to protect city sympathizers. Pratteln had been largely evacuated, and the soldiers planned to pass through it as quickly as possible. When they reached the village, they found just a handful of farmers, some of whom were city sympathizers, waiting in front of their houses.

One of them was Friedrich Dürr the younger (Paul Sacher's great-great grandfather); another was Friedrich's cousin Niklaus Dürr, fifty years old, father of five children, and a member of the village council. As the troops moved along the street, lined by the farmers' houses and hay-filled barns, shots suddenly rang out, and within seconds the village had become a battlefront. Ten farmhouses and several barns were burnt, and three of the farmers, including Niklaus Dürr, were killed. Friedrich survived, but the fire destroyed his entire property.

Sixty-five people were killed in Basle canton that day in skirmishes, and in Pratteln alone sixty were made homeless. These incidents turned the allegiance of the remaining city sympathizers towards the country and, by the end of the month, the defining event in the history of the canton of Basle had taken place: Basle's division into two separate cantons.

★★★

In the years that followed, two of the younger Friedrich Dürr's sons, Niklaus and his brother Friedrich (the third of that name), owned a half-share of a farm and a house in the centre of Pratteln. The half-share had been mortgaged by the brothers for a loan of a thousand francs in 1841, in order to cover other costs incurred in maintaining the property.

Some time between 1841 and 1844, a beautiful, raven-haired girl from Wangen in the canton of Solothurn came to the village. She was not yet twenty years old, and could neither read nor write. But she turned the head of Friedrich Dürr, and the couple married in 1844.

The young woman, Barbara Blauenstein, was not used to the thrifty ways of village farmers, and she is said to have driven her husband into increasing debt. When he died, there was no longer a farm in Pratteln for his two sons to inherit. His younger son, the fourth consecutive Friedrich in four generations, blamed his mother for the loss of his inheritance and remained bitter towards her for the rest of his life.

In 1853, Barbara Blauenstein and Friedrich Dürr the third were still living in Pratteln. But two years later the house was sold and the mortgage loan repaid, and the couple moved to a smaller home in the neighbouring village of Augst. There they remained for four years, and there the last of their five children, Elisabeth, was born. Little is known about the couple's movements after they left Augst in 1859. Friedrich Dürr, Paul Sacher's great-grandfather, is known to have died in 1864. Barbara Blauenstein spent the last three months of her life in a home run by the Swiss charitable society Grütliverein in Basle city. When she died in 1899, her belongings were listed as 'a cupboard, a bed, and her clothes'.[3]

4

City Bound

The lives of Friedrich and Barbara Dürr mirrored the changes that were occurring throughout the country areas of Switzerland in the second half of the nineteenth century. There was economic transformation and social rupture. The centuries-long cohesion of small farming communities had come unstuck, and the villagers had nothing with which to replace it. The consequences of this rupture, catalysed by the industrialization of Swiss cities, were the third formative influence on the lives of Paul Sacher's ancestors, and a defining influence on Sacher himself.

With nothing left for them in Pratteln, four of Friedrich and Barbara's children ultimately made their homes in Basle. The eldest son, Johannes, found employment there in the 1870s as a *Landjäger*, a border patrolman. His younger brother, the fourth Friedrich, married Anna Maria König, a farmer's daughter from the village of Bottenwil in the neighbouring canton of Aargau.

For six years Friedrich Dürr worked as the caretaker of a chemist's premises in Rheinfelden, a few kilometres from Pratteln, and for six years his enduring dream to work the land of his ancestors flickered and waned. After those six years, with a wife and four children to support, he chose to follow his elder brother to Basle, where he, too, donned the uniform of a policeman and tasted the authority that accompanied it.

In 1877, a year after Friedrich Dürr and Anna Maria König were married in Rheinfelden, another marriage took place ten kilometres away in the tiny, isolated farming village of Zuzgen in the Fricktal (Frick Valley). The groom was a twenty-four-year-old farmer, August Sacher. The bride was twenty-eight-year-old Adelheid Holer.

The two couples who were to become Paul Sacher's grandparents had much in common. They had grown up in small farming villages. They understood the importance of management of their land. They had faced and fought personal hardships and disappointments, learning from experience the value of tenacity. And they had learnt how to survive.

Friedrich Dürr had been raised during the disorientation that accompanied the breakdown of the country village units. He had witnessed the losses and restlessness of his own parents and other villagers as they grappled with changing realities. He had lost his family inheritance in Pratteln, and with it his chance of becoming the master of his own land. Anna Maria Dürr-König had been brought up in Bottenwil by her father's second wife, her own mother having died when Anna Maria was eight. She had grown up with a keen and stinging awareness of her step-mother's preference for her own children, a hurt she still spoke of when she was an old woman. As a young girl, she had rolled cigars with other women in a farmhouse on the outskirts of the village and had learnt that survival was equated with long hours of toil.

In spite of the hardships, Friedrich and Anna Maria were strong-willed and physically tough. These attributes had helped them survive, and enabled them to make the transition to city life successfully. For the other couple, August Sacher and Adelheid Holer of Zuzgen, the story was different.

★★★

The Fricktal belonged to Austria from the thirteenth century until 1802, when, after Napoleon defeated Austria in the First Coalition War, it was annexed to Switzerland and became part of the canton of Aargau. It was a triangle of fertile pastureland extending southwards from the Rhine to the ridge of the Jura mountains. Dotted with small farming communities, it had once been a farmer's paradise, but by the time August Sacher and Adelheid Holer married in 1877 the paradise had long since turned sour. For decades, the farmers in Basle and other Swiss cantons had dreamt of freedom. But in the Fricktal there was another dream – one which had endured for generations – and that was the dream of lasting peace.

August Sacher's grandfather, Fridolin Sacher, and his ancestors had been farmers born into serfdom. August's father, Oswald, born in 1817 after the Coalition wars, was the first of his Sacher family line in Zuzgen to be born Swiss, not Austrian, and to be born 'free'. But the Fricktal still bore the scars of Austria's rule. From the outbreak of the Thirty Years War in 1618 until the end of the First Coalition War in 1798, the valley and its inhabitants had suffered the effects of the repeated wars in which Austria had been involved. The wars had destroyed the integrity of village life, crushing the spirit of all but the most tenacious. Soldiers garrisoned in the villages of the Fricktal had stolen livestock, and destroyed the fields. Craftsmen were unemployed and, in many villages, fields had been left unattended for years as the farmers sought solace in alcohol. The villagers' strict Catholic morality had succumbed to a widespread loss of values, and the Fricktal had been branded a haven for beggars, deserters, and thieves. Depressed apathy of epidemic proportions had settled over the villages for decades, driving many to suicide.

Paul Sacher's paternal great-grandmother, Jenovefra Bourquard, was well into her first pregnancy when she married Oswald Sacher in summer 1853; on 9 September she gave birth to twin boys. Both infants were weak, and the younger, Anton, died when he was just a few months old. The elder, August, survived. When he was twenty-four, August Sacher married Adelheid Holer,* who had been born out of wedlock, and he continued to farm in Zuzgen for another five years. Shortly after his father's death in summer 1882, however, he decided to leave. Like tens of thousands of others, the Sachers headed for a city where they hoped to find a better life. They moved westwards, to Basle, the 'golden gate of the west', arriving within a year of the Dürrs.

For a year, August worked as a caretaker for a spice-importing business, and a year later he was employed as a warehouse labourer. But not for long. On 14 July 1884, as across the border the French were celebrating the ninety-fifth anniversary of the storming of the Bastille, August Sacher died of tuberculosis at the age of thirty-one. Adelheid, Paul Sacher's paternal grandmother, was left alone

---

* In the Zuzgen registers, Holer is spelt as here; in later Basle City records it is spelt Hohler.

with her young family and pregnant with a fourth child. This baby, Adolf, born three months after his father's death, did not survive.

★★★

The industrialization of Basle city had begun in the 1830s, its most important branches being related to the silk industry. In the eighteenth century, city manufacturers had provided the country folk with raw materials to spin or weave at home, but after the division of the canton in 1833, and with the increasing mechanization of production in the 1830s and 1840s, larger factories were constructed in the city.

There were eleven steam-powered silk factories in Basle in the 1880s. Raw silk thread was processed and woven into cloth, particularly into ribbons, and exported worldwide. Thousands of unskilled, untrained people went to work in the factories, and by 1885 Adelheid Sacher-Holer had joined them. As an unskilled country worker, with no rights in the city and a family to support, she had no other choice.

She was employed as a silk winder. The working hours were long – eleven hours on weekdays, and ten hours on Saturdays – and the winders' wages were low. If she worked fast and well, she might take home twenty to twenty-five francs at the end of the week. But in a bad week, when she could not wind so much silk thread on to the spools because her hands were tired or because the fragile threads kept breaking, her weekly wage might be as low as ten francs. It was a life of toil and sacrifice, and factory workers and their families often lived for weeks on potatoes, milk, and coffee substitute.

Most of the families lived in cramped workers' quarters. Some accommodation had no kitchens; and there was no plumbing at all, because in the very first referendum held in Basle, in 1875, the citizens had said 'no' to plans for installing a sewerage system. Waste was still dumped unceremoniously in deep ditches running behind or between the houses, a practice which continued until the outbreak of a typhus epidemic twenty years later forced Basle's citizens to think again.

After August Sacher died, his widow and children made a number of moves to apartments in the older streets of the city. Although the buildings were more dilapidated and the comforts fewer, the rents were lower. At one point, Adelheid rented premises in Imbergasse, a narrow alley near the market square, next door to the house in which Friedrich and Anna Maria Dürr had lived when they first arrived in Basle.

Adelheid fought a lonely battle for survival. Her tenacity helped, but her efforts won her only an existence. Somehow, though, she managed to ensure that her three children completed their schooling, and that each completed an apprenticeship, or learnt a skill. Then, in 1904, when she had turned fifty-five, her twenty-five-year-old son Oswald August informed her that he had met the young lady whom he wished to marry. She was a handsome young woman, who had spent some time in England. She spoke English and French as well as German and Swiss German, and she had also learnt a trade.

Anna Dürr, daughter of Friedrich and Anna Maria Dürr, formerly of Pratteln and Bottenwil, had indeed learnt a trade, like generations of Dürrs before her. She was a ladies' tailor with her own atelier.

Adelheid was delighted with the news of the match. Now that one of her children was engaged, she believed that her responsibilities had ended. 'Ach, ich bin so froh [Oh, I'm so glad],' she is reported to have said. 'Jetzt kann ich endlich gehen [Now at last I can go].' She died on 6 February 1905, six months before the couple's wedding.

II
The Dream

5

'That Which You Must Do'

Anna Dürr, Paul Sacher's mother, had been in no hurry to marry. There were other things she wanted to do first, other plans she wanted to fulfil. She was outgoing, interested in people and fascinated by life outside her home. She later told her daughter, Nelly, that she much preferred being out on the streets doing errands for her parents, or playing with her two younger brothers and their friends, to remaining indoors like her sister.

In her early teens, Anna had voiced a wish to become a shopkeeper, with a shop of her own, but this was immediately vetoed by her father. 'Shops are for whores,' he declared. 'If you want to do something more with your life, learn a trade.'

For generations, learning a trade had meant survival to the Dürrs. As a result of his parents' unsettled existence, Friedrich Dürr himself had never done so, but his belief in its importance was so pronounced that, when he joined the Basle police force in 1882, he entered one on the form he had to fill out. Because he had none of his own, he stole his wife's, and wrote 'cigar-maker' on his registration card. Now, with Anna, he was adamant. If she wanted more out of life, she had to learn a trade. Since Anna wanted a great deal more, she did just that. She acquired the skills of a ladies' tailor; but even that was not enough for her.

Situated at the doorway to both France and northern Europe, Basle was the hub of trade up and down the Rhine. Anna had observed that those who did well in business were able to communicate with their customers in the latter's own languages. Claiming that she would be nothing if she didn't speak languages, she set about learning French and English.

At the turn of the century, it was not common for a young Swiss woman from a modest working-class background to travel alone away from home. Undeterred, Anna journeyed to Fribourg in the francophone part of Switzerland, where she secured a position as a seamstress, and there she learnt French. Next, she travelled to England, where she cared for the two small children of a well-to-do family. There she learnt to love England and its people, as well as its language. According to the stories she later told her children, she was so happy there that she would probably never have returned to Basle had a temporary illness not compelled her to do so. When she did return, she set up her tailor's atelier in a room in her uncle Johannes's apartment. Later, she worked in a room of the apartment she shared with her parents and younger brothers.

By the time she met August Sacher, a friend of her younger brother Eugen, 'Anny' Dürr knew what she wanted. At twenty-eight, she was a proud, handsome young woman. It was important to find a partner who would not challenge her plans, someone who would be happy for her to organize their life together. In Oswald August Sacher – 'Gusti', as his family called him – she had found someone who seemed content to let her do just that. More importantly, she had found a man who pleased her. Dark-haired and dark-eyed, Gusti was an attractive, high-spirited, carefree young man who liked to sing. Most striking, though, was that when he moved he did so with an eye-catching ease and agility, so much so that his future father-in-law nicknamed him 'the gypsy'.

'My father had a phenomenal physical condition and agility, a real elegance,' Paul Sacher remembered. 'He always walked as if walking were a pleasure. And he had the most peculiar eyes I've ever seen. They weren't just one colour. They were like precious stones with different hues – brown, black, green, red, and yellow.'

Gusti may have been an engaging young man, but his fiancée's father was less than ecstatic at the news of the engagement. 'Silly cow!' Friedrich Dürr is reported to have shouted when he received the news. 'You're twenty-eight and you've chosen the poorest [of your suitors].'

The poorest, perhaps, but Gusti had a future. As a young man, he had been apprenticed to an international haulage firm, Schneider & Cie, which delivered exports of cheese, condensed

Paul Sacher's parents, Anna Dürr and Oswald August Sacher, on their wedding day

milk, chocolate and other Swiss products to continental Europe and Britain, and brought back imports of raw materials, especially sheet iron. The firm had been taken over in 1871 by Karl Erhard Schneider. Respected by customers and competitors alike for his high business ethics, hard work and correctness, he demanded the same qualities of his apprentices. Teenage boys like Gusti Sacher joined the business at its premises in a baroque mansion in the heart of Basle to learn book-keeping, correspondence, and the daily running of the haulage business. Many of them were the sons of lawyers and doctors, or had been born into well-known Basle families. Gusti Sacher had neither of those advantages, but the fact that Schneider's wife, Wilhelmine Sacher of Zuzgen, was his godmother certainly helped him secure his apprenticeship. He also had an exceptional talent for adding columns of figures accurately at high speed, a skill he used to advantage in preparing invoices and in book-keeping. By the time he met Anny Dürr, he had moved on to Danzas, another international haulage firm in Basle.

Danzas, which had been founded in 1815 just across the French border in Alsace, was a growing international company, and Anny was satisfied that opportunities for promotion would come Gusti's way. Until then, she had her atelier and could contribute to the family's income. Consequently, she could afford the luxury of choosing the suitor who pleased her the most, rather than the one who possessed the most. And the one who pleased her the most was Gusti Sacher. It didn't matter to her that he had little money. She knew she could make things work. They would thrive.

Her father, unconvinced, warned her, 'Once you're out of the house, you're out. Out is out.'

'Don't worry,' she replied. 'I shan't be coming back.'

★★★

Anny required that two conditions be met before she accepted Gusti's proposal. One was that she would manage all the money that came into the family purse. Another was that he would not interfere in their children's education.

Anny's role model was her own mother, Anna Maria, portrayed by family members as small, wiry, hard-working, stubborn and exceptionally efficient. 'My grandmother was the most remarkable woman,' Paul Sacher recalled. 'She not only took care of the housework but brought up the children, and she was incredibly competent. She was very smart.'

It was to be many years before women received the right to vote in the canton of Basle City,* but Anna Maria had her say much earlier. At voting time she would collect all the voting slips from her husband and her two adult sons, and fill them out. Then she called the men in and said, 'Now, boys, you can go and vote.'

Anny Dürr set about organizing her own family along similar lines and, according to her son, Paul, she succeeded. 'It was a matriarchy which operated in my grandmother's time, and it was the same for my mother. The men had nothing to say.'

The death of Adelheid Sacher-Holer had left Anny with a second family to care for, and she was determined to create a new home for her brother- and sister-in-law where they would have closer contact with Gusti. Even though she was working long hours in her atelier, and was pregnant within weeks of her wedding, she organized Fritz and Adele Sacher's move from their apartment on a workers' estate into attic rooms above the apartment she and Gusti had rented.

Adele Sacher, Gusti's older sister, had had an especially close relationship with her mother, helping her to care for her two small brothers after their father's death. With her mother suddenly gone, and her brother Gusti married to his new wife, she no longer felt needed, and was pitched into a deep depression. Anny later told her children that after Adelheid's death Adele often cried all night long.

Believing that a change of scenery might help her, Gusti and Anny encouraged Adele to go to America. There she would be able to support herself with her earnings from making and embroidering men's waistcoats, a trade she had learnt in Basle. But the journey failed to improve her condition. Two or three years after her return, she left the Sacher's apartment one stormy night, and never returned. She was presumed dead, but because her body was never found no Basle register officially recorded her death.

---

* Women in the canton of Basle City received cantonal voting rights in 1958.

Only Anny Sacher-Dürr's hushed announcement to her husband of Adele's disappearance, which was overheard and welded for life into the memory of Anny's young son, Paul Sacher, has preserved the story of Adele's fate.

★★★

Almost two months before Anny's first child was due, she went into labour. At 8.30 a.m. on the morning of 28 April 1906, she gave birth at home to a boy who showed all the frailty of a premature baby. Anny was over-tired from working so hard, and she found herself unable to breast-feed; to make matters worse, the baby showed an intolerance for cow's milk. His grandmother, Anna Maria Dürr-König, probably saved his life. As a farmer's daughter, she knew all about the healing properties of herbs and plants. She bathed the child in strengthening herbal infusions, and found replacements for milk with which to nourish him. With her help, he survived.

The baby was born on a Saturday, and Gusti Sacher made the fifteen-minute walk to the registry of births in the morning. From later conversations with his son, we know that as he headed down Nonnenweg his excitement was interrupted by a troubling thought. His wife had told him that the child was to be named Kurt, and normally he accepted all her rulings. Having Anny organize their lives left him free time in the evenings to join his friends at the gymnastics club, or to go bowling, or play cards, or attend the get-togethers of the men's singing club. Now, however, he began to doubt the wisdom of her choice.

Both Gusti and Anny had been raised in Swiss-German-speaking areas of Switzerland. At school they had learnt high German, and both had also learnt French. Anny spoke English as well, and loved England and its culture. Yet in Gusti's opinion she had selected a thoroughly German name for their son, one which did not lend itself well to pronunciation in French or English. How could their son move easily between the cultures and lands they appreciated with such a name? As Gusti approached the Spalentor, the most beautiful of the city's old gates, he realized that he would have to change it.

The gate, with its squat stone towers and brightly tiled central spire, was behind him as he made his way through the suburb of Spalen, veering left down a narrow cobbled alleyway to the huge central market square. As he headed up the hill to Münsterplatz, and the registry office near the cathedral, Gusti made up his mind: this was one of the very few times when he would openly oppose his wife's decision. He registered his son as Paul Oswald Sacher, and that was an end to the matter.

★★★

When Anny Sacher chose her family's first apartment, Nonnenweg 47, where her son was born, her choice was by no means random. First of all, it was in an attractive three-storey house, made of huge sandstone slabs taken from the old Basle wall when it was dismantled in sections after 1859. The large double windows in its front façade faced on to the street, which was a comparatively new one, laid down outside the boundary of the old city wall. Like many houses in Nonnenweg, Number 47 had a small garden at the back.

However, what was uppermost in Anny's mind was not the building's appearance, or its location in a quiet district, but rather its proximity to her parents. Despite her retort to her father that she wouldn't be coming back, Anny wanted to remain near her mother, who figured largely in her plans. Now her parents lived just five minutes' walk from her front door.

Anna Maria Dürr was the ideal grandmother for Paul. She had plenty of time to spare. Her husband still worked as a policeman and was away each day, and sometimes in the evenings. Her eldest daughter, Louise, had married a wealthy engineer and moved to Zurich; her two sons were independent adults who no longer required much of her attention.

The ensuing arrangement seems to have suited both women. Anny was free to devote long hours to the supervision of her atelier, and Anna Maria had no time to feel the absence of her own children. Paul was happy to play at his grandmother's, usually with his little wooden blocks, which he recalled were far better than expensive toys because he could use his imagination to build all sorts of things with them.

Paul, early in 1907

Although Nonnenweg was close to her mother, for Anny it was not close enough. In 1909, when Paul was three, the tenants of an apartment at Birmannsgasse 28, next door to her parents, moved out. Anny lost no time in moving her little family and her atelier in. Now her mother, with only one son still at home, was able to do even more for her daughter, a practice which increased in later years. Paul's sister, Nelly, recalled that her grandmother often did all the cleaning and cooking, and that, without her, Anny would never have been able to look after both family and atelier.

Pictures of the infant Paul Sacher show him at first in white and cream baby's gowns, and the occasional exotic hat. Anny, with her tailor's talent, dressed him well. There are photographs of the child at kindergarten and primary-school age dressed in dark wool jackets buttoning under large white Little Lord Fauntleroy collars. Some garments, like the frilled collars, spoke more of Anny's aspirations to status, and of her memories of the well-to-do doctor's children for whom she had cared in England, than of her own family's real position in life.

Whatever the apparel, one thing in particular emerges from the early photographs. It is the thinness and gauntness of the child's face, his eyes huge and underlined by dark shadows. Paul had survived his premature birth and early feeding difficulties, but the child in those pictures is far from robust.

Nor does he appear to have been a very happy child. 'My mother just probably had no time for me [when I was a young child],' he later commented. 'She told me when I was a grown man that I used to sit on my stool [in her atelier] and lay my head on her knee. "And imagine," she said, "the tears just ran down your cheeks." As an old woman she still didn't understand why. I had simply thought, "I have a mother. She should look after me." She didn't do that.'

When he was four, Paul began kindergarten. Anny or her mother would walk him to the corner of the next street, Eulerstrasse, and then on to the little schoolhouse further down the street. Kindergarten lasted for at least two years, and his outstanding memory of that time was of a little girl who impressed him deeply: Sarah Bornstein.

Paul during his early school years

Paul with his parents in 1915

Born in Lodz, in Poland, Sarah had just emigrated to Switzerland with her parents, Moritz and Tauba Bornstein-Laufer, in 1910. She met Paul at the kindergarten, or '*Häfelischule*' (potty school), as it was nicknamed, and took him literally under her wing. In the classroom, the children sat on wooden benches, each long enough to take five or six. Sarah, bossy and protective, insisted that Paul sit on the outside of the bench, with herself firmly entrenched between him and the other occupants. But Paul's frailty had not gone unnoticed, and their teacher was afraid he might fall off the end of the bench. 'Why,' she asked, 'does he have to sit on the outside?' 'Because,' Sarah replied, 'I don't want another girl sitting next to him.'

Sarah shared with Paul the matzo crackers she brought to school for her playtime snacks, instilling in him a life-long liking for them. It was Sarah whom the octogenarian Paul Sacher would describe laughingly as his 'first girlfriend'. The two had no further contact in later years, but Sarah remained in Basle. She married a man from her homeland, Adalbert Pulawski, and eventually owned her own business, trading in *Weisswaren*, bed- and table-linen. She died in 1983.

★★★

When Paul was not at kindergarten, he was sometimes allowed to perch on a footstool in Anny's atelier, watching his mother and the two or three young women she employed. The atelier was a hive of industry, for Anny saw to it that the seamstresses always had plenty to do. While Gusti was out with his friends in the evenings, she often worked late into the night preparing the next day's work.

In winter Paul's wooden stool was placed near the tiled oven, which was filled with glowing coals. One day, when he was about four, the oven suddenly exploded, spewing hot coals throughout the room. There was pandemonium as the women frantically brushed the coal fragments from their hair and clothes, searching anxiously for signs of damage to their customers' orders. Paul's screams were at first ignored – after all, small children were always crying. It wasn't until the screams became louder, and Anny went to investigate, that she found a red-hot coal lodged in the crook between his chin and throat. The resulting ugly red burn eventually faded to a circular scar the size of a quarter, a reminder of the incident for the rest of Paul Sacher's life.

Grandma Dürr remained his chief minder. She was a kindly woman, but not given to demonstrative affection. Displays of tenderness were luxuries that she had not known from her step-mother in Bottenwil, and she did not pass on a legacy of cuddling to her own children. Despite that, Paul much preferred playing in her apartment to the Sunday afternoon outings his parents took him on once he could walk.

He found those walks dull and dreary. 'My mother would stroll through the streets in St Alban, where there were big villas and gardens – because that was her dream. And she would say to my father, "Look, I'd like this garden" or "I like that house better." She lived in dreams.'

Gusti wasn't the only 'gypsy' living in the Sacher's neighbourhood. Their friend and neighbour, Karl Pellmont senior, was a Hungarian who had learnt a pastry chef's trade in Budapest and Vienna. In 1901, he arrived in Switzerland, married a Swiss girl, and secured a position as pastry chef at Basle's Confiserie Bandi (a pastry and coffee shop). 'He wasn't from here,' explained his son, Tibor, 'and because he was Hungarian, people often thought of him as a gypsy.'

Anny knew the Pellmonts from the years she had spent at Birmannsgasse before her marriage, and she and Karl Pellmont's wife, Elise, had struck up a good friendship. The two women had many things in common. Both were hard-working and had grown up in modest circumstances. Both were ambitious for their husbands, and determined to make ends meet. Elise's two eldest boys were in Paul's age group.

The Pellmonts' house was fronted by a long stretch of garden, and there Paul played with Karl junior and his younger brother, Géza, climbing trees or playing with their toys on the pebbled pathway. In later years, Paul's sister, Nelly, and the other Pellmont children, Ilia, Béla, and Tibor, would join in their games, but for the time being the three boys shared their adventures in their garden and on the quiet street.

★★★

Paul was five years old and still at kindergarten when, in the late summer of 1911, Anny became pregnant for the second time. Nelly Sacher was born on 13 May 1912. The age gap between the two children meant that, fascinated though he was by his little sister, Paul had no real sense of growing up with a sibling. 'I was an only child. You see, when you're six years old – and I was that old when Nelly was born – the age gap is too big. I was a lonely child. I was alone, and I mostly played on my own.'

With Grandma Dürr preoccupied with Nelly, and Anny busy with her atelier, Paul withdrew even further into his own world. But now he had a partner, an accomplice in his soliloquies and daydreams: his violin.

No one knows when or where Paul's first experience of music came from. During the first six years of his life there had been neither radio nor gramophone in his home; the only music he heard there came from his father's mouthorgan. His parents were not concert-goers, and the chamber-music soirées of well-to-do Basle families were not part of the Sachers' working-class existence. There was no 'congenital affliction', as Paul wryly put it. What he did remember was that, as a child, he had heard Bach's Passions in Basle Cathedral and that the music had made a deep and lasting impression. But that was after he had begun primary school, and his request for a violin on his sixth birthday preceded those concerts. It was, he claimed, simply a request deriving from his genuine and legitimate need for music.

The offer of his wealthy aunt Louise to pay for Paul to have his first violin lessons was accepted by Anny, and he was sent each week to Walter Krétlov, a violinist with Basle's symphony orchestra. For a time his lessons were shared with Géza Pellmont (who had also received a violin), which meant that the lessons for each boy cost less. 'You have to remember that the circumstances of our families were very modest,' Tibor Pellmont told me. 'A saving like that would have been important to both mothers.'

Paul practised daily, the length of his sessions depending on whether or not he was 'dreaming'. He would practise the études Herr Krétlov had asked him to prepare, and then simply try to

Paul with his sister, Nelly, in 1916

produce the most beautiful sounds he could. 'When I did that, I was improvising,' he explained to me, 'and I couldn't always separate practising and improvising. Sometimes, when I concentrated, the time I spent practising was shorter. But when I was dreaming, things were different... What fascinated me most about the violin was the sound, simply the sound of the instrument. I found it the most beautiful sound of all. I knew as a schoolboy that I'd never be a violin virtuoso, but that wasn't important. The fascination was the sound.'

In autumn 1912, Paul began primary school. A ten-minute walk from Birmannsgasse was the Spalenschulhaus, the boys' primary school, where students normally spent four years. For that time they had the same teacher, and were taught in classes of almost fifty students. Each year was divided into three classes, so the school had roughly six hundred students. Most boys, like Karl Pellmont who was in Paul's class, were seven when they began at the Spalenschulhaus, but Paul was only six.

Their teacher, Herr Gysler, taught them arithmetic, reading and writing. Once he had learnt to read, Paul recalled, his whole world changed. 'I was a passionate reader. From the time I could read, adults were just a nuisance.' Apart from Karl Pellmont, he remembered few friends. 'You mustn't forget that the violin played a very important role for me. I practised every day. I think it was an outlet for my soul. Something important. Something good.'

The violin, his reading and his daydreams were all-consuming, so much so that Sacher had few memories of his four years at primary school. One memory that did remain was a comment made by Herr Gysler to his mother: 'You see, he could be the best if he wanted to be. But he simply doesn't want to be.' Eighty-five years later the memory still provoked an indignant response. Paul conceded that he may have been caught up in his daydreams, or might have been thinking about other things. 'But it was certainly not the case that I deliberately didn't work. That was pure slander!'

In the long summer break between the second and third years of primary school, in July and August 1914, Paul spent his holidays in a children's home in Langenbruck in the Basle countryside. One day the children saw trains passing loaded with soldiers and equipment, with horses and gunners. In the days that followed, they watched as the army and its artillery passed by the village. The First World War had begun.

For an eight-year-old, the war meant little more than the constant sight and presence of soldiers; Paul Sacher had little recollection of change or hardship. But for the cantons of Basle, for Gusti and Anny Sacher, those war years were full of hardship and change.

Because of its geographical situation, Basle experienced the war quite differently from, and much more intensively than, any other major Swiss city. The thunder of cannon in Istein across the German border, and on the slopes of the Vogesen Hills, was heard throughout the city for years. From the Margarethenhügel, a hill to the south of the city, Basle's inhabitants were able to follow the war along the French border in Alsace as if they were in the gallery of a theatre. The city was transformed into a garrison, surrounded by military fortifications and manned by troops from all over Switzerland.

Before long, Basle became more or less conditioned to the sights and sounds of war, and people's concerns turned to more immediate problems. In the early months of the war there had been no rationing of basic groceries or fuel because it had been unclear how long the war would continue. Gradually, however, supplies ran short and the citizens could only look on helplessly as prices rose. Even when cantonal laws regulated distribution, the problems continued. The markets were no longer full of fresh vegetables from Alsace, so more than ten thousand small gardens were created throughout the city to compensate. But, with each passing year, want and poverty grew.

Of all this, Paul Sacher remembered little, except that the family moved again in 1915, this time across Missionsstrasse to 121 St Johanns-Ring. He had no recollection of carrying the pail his mother had given him to collect soup from the soup kitchen set up at St Johanns Platz, where rations of rice, oat or bean soup cost 15 Rappen a portion. It was his sister, Nelly, who trotted beside him on that errand, who remembered. Soup, she recalled, played an important role in family meals. 'Main meals nearly always began with soup. If you started with that, you weren't so hungry afterwards, and you didn't want to eat much more.'

Anny was determined that her family would thrive, even in wartime. Her thrift and organizational ability meant that her children suffered few of the war's effects. There was food to eat, and Anny's image of decent living was maintained right down to the linen or cotton serviettes, rolled neatly in their metal rings, that lay on the table at every meal.

A few months after the outbreak of war, Paul's grandfather Friedrich Dürr retired from the Police Corps of Basle City after more than thirty years' service. He had still been a member of the force in 1910 when the police were armed with Browning pistols, and in 1913 when the cars in Basle received their first numbered plates. But finally, in February 1915, as his younger colleagues were organized into military police squadrons, and were assigned wartime duties such as counter-espionage and control of the black market, Dürr retired on a yearly pension of SFr 2130.

6

'That Which You Want to Do'

One of Anny Sacher's dreams was to own her own house, a substantial dream for any girl from a working-class background. But this was Switzerland, where space was scarce and where, in 1915 as today, living in rented apartments in large houses divided into three apartments or more was the norm in the cities. Only the most affluent could afford to be a house's sole occupants. None of this, however, deterred Anny Sacher. She wanted her own house, and she was convinced that one day she would have it.

In the meantime, her family's new home in St Johanns-Ring was rented. The new apartment contained just three rooms, one fewer than in Birmannsgasse: a bedroom for Anny and Gusti, which Nelly also shared for more than three years, a bedroom for Paul, and a dining/living room. There were lavatories on the landings between the three floors of the house. The family bathed in the kitchen or with pitchers of water in the privacy of their bedrooms.

More importantly, there was no room for Anny's atelier. 'She did continue doing some tailoring in the house,' remembered Hedwig Frommlet, her neighbour at 123, 'but she had to work in her bedroom.' In spite of this, Anny remained registered as a ladies' tailor in the business pages of the Basle address registers for several years after the move.

Above all, moving to St Johanns-Ring meant losing the closeness to her mother, and at least part of her invaluable help. Although the two families lived within a fifteen-minute walk of each other, they were no longer neighbours. The main advantage of the move seems to have been the lower rent for the smaller, simpler apartment, which meant that there was more money available to fulfil Anny's long-term plans. By the time the family moved again nine years later, she had saved enough money to buy the new house. The apartment in St Johanns-Ring was only a step in her master plan.

Seventy years later, Paul Sacher admitted that he had hated living in rented apartments as a child because 'the stairways and passageways always smelt bad'. Nevertheless, he remembered the house at St Johanns-Ring, with its attractive sandstone façade, as being his favourite. There, as usual, he had his own room. 'As far back as I can remember, my mother always gave me my own room – usually the nicest of all. I could arrange it as I liked. The most important thing in it was my desk. Even when I was still very young, the desk was the most important thing.'

Their apartment occupied the second floor. At the bottom of the polished oak staircase, a short stairway led to the back door and out into a long, rectangular garden. The garden adjoined that of the neighbouring house, a two-storey home owned by an insurance salesman, Eugen Frommlet, and his wife. There Nelly and Paul played with the two Frommlet girls. The elder, Hedwig, who was just a month younger than Nelly, was an instant playmate. Her baby sister, Elisabeth ('Bethli'), was only a few months old when the two families moved to St Johanns-Ring within months of each other.

Two things about the Frommlets especially impressed Paul and Nelly. One was the fact that they were the sole owners and occupants of their house, complete with its own bathroom. The other lasting impression was made by ash-blonde, blue-eyed Bethli Frommlet, who grew into a delightful little girl. Sometimes, when Nelly and the Frommlets played hide and seek, Paul (whom the girls nicknamed 'Beppi') joined them. Given the difference in age between him and the girls, this was surprising. But for Hedwig Frommlet, who lived in the house until her death on 3 March 2000, Paul's participation was no surprise. 'My sister was an unusually happy child. She just bubbled over, and captivated everyone, and she swept us along with her. I think Paul only played with us because of her.'

Nelly characterized her brother's feelings more directly: 'Paul loved Bethli. I know because he had a picture of her in his "Ladies' Album".' (The photo album was so called by Nelly because it contained so many pictures of Paul's girlfriends.)

The friendship might well have endured, but in February 1925, a few months after Paul had graduated from secondary school, Bethli was suddenly taken ill. 'They believed it was appendicitis,' her sister recalled, 'but when they opened her up they saw that the stomach wall was totally infected. In those days they didn't have the penicillin that could have saved her.' Bethli died of peritonitis on 3 February, aged ten and a half. The death was a tragedy for the Frommlet family. Hedwig remembered clearly that she did not see her mother smile again for more than four years. Equally clearly she remembered that, the day before her sister died, 'a big bouquet of white roses arrived for her at the hospital. They were from Paul Sacher.'

★★★

Anny Sacher's dreams were not restricted to her own achievements. When she married Gusti, she had been bright with ambition for his future as well. But he simply had no interest in her plans for him.

'Why?' he is said to have asked when his wife urged him to seek promotion at Danzas. 'Haven't we got all we need? Why should I work more than I already do?'

Gusti had been apprenticed to Schneider & Cie as a young man, his son later claimed, only because he had realized that he would somehow have to earn a living. 'He wasn't really interested in the work, even though he could do it well. He simply had no ambition. And that was something my mother just had to accept.' On the Sunday strolls so disliked by their children, when Anny pointed out large houses with gardens she dreamt of buying, Gusti would respond, 'Anny, do what you want.' In time she was to do just that, but she had to accept that her husband did not share her dreams and ambitions. And that was not all she had to accept.

★★★

No family member can say exactly when, but some time between 1915 and 1920 Gusti Sacher's life changed dramatically. 'When he was a young man – maybe he was thirty-five, or in his late thirties – he had a religious experience, a primal religious experience,' his son recalled. 'Overnight he became pious in a naive and childlike way, and that became the content of his life: his belief in God. After that he was in touch with spiritualists and dealt with occult things.'

Gusti's 'epiphany' has been described by his daughter as a complete conversion, like St Paul's on the road to Damascus. Both children said that instantly the long evenings with his friends stopped, and there began a religiosity which could not but affect his family. 'This religious mania of my father's was rather embarassing for us, for the whole family,' Sacher later remarked. 'He would say prayers at the table for hours. Finally Mother would tug at his jacket, and say, "That's enough now," and then he would stop.'

Nobody knows just what the experience was that created this dramatic change in Gusti's life. His conversion may have been an escape from the monotony of his activity as a haulage contractor. However, in an interview in 1990, Paul made a connection between his father's 'experience' and the sombre legacy of the Sachers. Tracing his family history through to the disappearance of his aunt Adele, he spoke of his own and his sister's tendency to depression. Sitting in the half-light of Auf Burg, his townhouse overlooking the Rhine, while slanting grey rain swept across the water, the memory of his aunt's disappearance on another stormy night decades earlier became intertwined with his father's transformation.

'Even if we each have an individual fate,' he said quietly, 'one inherits something from one's ancestors. Just in the last generation, my father's sister took her own life. I think that this tendency to depression was common to all those people, to the Sachers. Fortunately there are only two of us in this generation. My father was probably also affected, and found an elegant way to deal with it. But my mother was not like that. She was positive and strong.'

Gusti Sacher's conversion may have been a means of escape from depression, or it may have been a genuine calling. Either way, the 'positive and strong' Anny Sacher-Dürr now assumed total control of family life. With her strong-willed tenacity and optimism, she was convinced that she could do that which she wanted to do, and she was to pass on that legacy to her children, as if instinctively realizing they would need these qualities to fight the shadows. 'She took responsibility for the whole family,' said her son, 'in every way – morally, financially, everything.' She even accompanied her husband as far as possible in his new calling, going with him to church and sometimes to seances with his spiritualist colleagues.

★★★

In summer 1916, with the First World War still raging, it was time for Anny to make some decisions concerning her children's education. Nelly had turned four and was old enough to attend kindergarten, but, with money and resources scarce, Anny decided to keep her at home until she reached obligatory school age. So Nelly waited until after the war and until, in 1919, she was old enough to start at the local St Johann's Primary School.

None of this mattered to Nelly, who was in no hurry to go to school. In fact, she said later that the lessons Anny taught her in those early years were so good that she needn't have bothered with school at all. 'I had thirteen years of schooling, but actually my mother taught me all I needed to know in four sentences: "That which you must do, you can do," and "That which you want to do, you can do." And then there were two other things. She said to me, "Girl, don't tell lies. You have to have a good brain to be able to lie because you have to be able to remember what you said." The fourth thing was "If someone says they don't have time to do something, they don't want to do it. People always have time to do what they want to do."'

With regard to Paul's education, there were more serious decisions to make. By the early spring of 1916, he had completed his primary schooling, and was ready to begin the long years of secondary school. Under the Swiss system, the decision as to which secondary school he would attend was important, because his selection would influence his later chances of further education. If he wanted to pass his *Matura*, the examination which serves in Switzerland as the university entrance requirement, more than eight years of secondary school stretched ahead. If he chose that option, there was then another decision to be made: which of the three types of secondary school he should attend. There was the 'classical' Gymnasium, where the curriculum included Latin and Greek. There was the 'modern language' Gymnasium where students could learn English and other modern languages. Or there was the Realschule (now called the Maths and Sciences Gymnasium) which specialized in mathematics and sciences. These were hard decisions for a ten-year-old, and Anny had no intention of leaving her son to make them alone.

Paul's growing obsession with his violin had not gone unnoticed, and it was misunderstood. For him, the instrument's magnetism was simply its sound, but Anny feared that he had ambitions to become a professional violinist. She did not want her son becoming a musician, a profession to which she disparagingly referred as '*brotlos*' (breadless). When he then made it clear that it was conducting which interested him, she had further concerns. 'She said there was no question of my becoming a conductor, because then I would have dealings with pretty singers, and that that wouldn't be good for me at all,' a grinning Sacher unrepentantly recalled.

Faced with Anny's opposition, Paul retreated into another of his early dreams. He announced that he would become a farmer instead, an alternative which came from a genuine interest. 'My daydreams at that time dwelt on my having my own farm, with lots of cows and horses. Those dreams were certainly inherited. I told myself that I would go to Canada, or Brazil, or Argentina. There I'd first manage a big hacienda, and then I'd buy myself one, and then I'd be a land-owning farmer.'

Of the three schools on offer, the Realschule lay furthest from Paul's talents and interests. Academically what was available there didn't interest him, but it was this school, attended by boys wishing to become engineers and scientists, that Anny selected. The decision could have been a formula for disaster, but Paul had learnt from childhood that 'That which you must do, you can do,' and he was determined to succeed at the Realschule.

'I understood immediately that I wanted to pass the *Matura* so that I could go to university. I only went to the Realschule so that I could go to the polytechnical college in Zurich afterwards, to study agronomy. And I told myself, "Well, you're not so stupid that you can't complete any school. ... I'd prefer Latin and Greek but it doesn't really matter.'"

Along with 339 other boys, Paul sat the admissions test for the lower Realschule in March 1916. A B+ in composition and a B in arithmetic,* added to his primary-school record, were good enough to secure him provisional admittance to the school, whose term began on 25 April, three days before Paul's tenth birthday. He was one of the youngest in his class of forty-eight boys.

Throughout the Realschule, the boys' marks were carefully monitored. Every quarter, each of the eleven or twelve subjects was graded with two marks, one for effort and one for test results. Six was the highest mark available, and represented excellence; one was the lowest mark possible. Paul's marks in languages and history, subjects which interested him, were consistently high (fives and sixes), but those in arithmetic and natural history were weaker (twos to fours). Halfway through the first year, he found himself in the bottom quarter of the class. For a boy who wanted to succeed, and who had no wish to lose valuable time by repeating a year, that was not good enough. By the end of the next quarter, he had risen to eleventh place in his class, even overtaking his clever classmate Otto Miescher. By the end of the year, he was third.

Asked if he had been praised at home when his efforts brought good results, Sacher slowly shook his head. 'My mother,' he said, 'didn't feel that praise was necessary. She took it for granted that you had to work for what you wanted, and that if you wanted to do something you would do it well. She didn't feel you needed praise for that.'

The strategy Paul used in his first year of the Realschule was so successful that he repeated it throughout the next three years. By working especially hard in the second half of the school year in the subjects in which he lacked talent or interest, and by gaining top marks in the subjects he liked, such as French, German, English, history and singing, he had acquired sixth place in his class by the end of his first four years at the Realschule. When it came to art – drawing was important for boys who were going to become engineers and architects – he described himself as having

---

* 'A' was the highest mark awarded.

been 'clumsy and awkward'. Nevertheless, it was his art teacher who awakened his lifelong interest in the visual arts.

'We had an art teacher who had an incredible imagination. His name was Niederer. He took us to the museum and showed us pictures. At that time I loved Hodler. I found his work fantastic. It portrayed my mental state and I understood a great deal of it. And we discussed it in our drawing classes. I had a real relationship to painting. It was a need.'

Despite his early fragility, Sacher also did well in physical education, and he believed he had inherited his father's physical agility. 'My father was an athlete, a gymnast, and I was good at those things at school. Running fast, and leaping over the vaulting horse. Wherever speed and daring were needed, that's what I could do best.'

Gusti Sacher – who for his eightieth birthday requested and received a Raleigh bicycle – took his superb physical condition for granted. He found it difficult, according to Nelly, to understand that not everyone was as well co-ordinated as he was. When she asked for swimming lessons, she said, he looked at her in utter amazement, and replied, 'You don't need lessons to learn to swim. You just swim.'

With her son making good progress at the Realschule, Anny was content, believing that he had given up his wish to become a musician. But even if that wish was partially eclipsed for a time by dreams of becoming a landowning farmer, the violin and his music were always close. Outside school, Sacher led, as he put it, 'a completely different life'. Sometimes he spent his free afternoons doing his homework with his classmate Otto Miescher. But usually he completed his after-school chores as quickly as possible, so that he could escape to his violin or to his books. He later claimed that, as a young man, he had read a book a day, the books being bought with his pocket money from the Brockenhaus, a shop which sold second-hand goods of all kinds. Still, intertwined with his music-making and his reading, his dreams of becoming a gentleman farmer persisted.

'I had a really close connection with nature. And while I was at school, I spent one holiday break with a farmer's family in the Jura, up on the hills overlooking Moutier.* No one would have

---

* A French-speaking Swiss town in the Jura mountains.

sent me there if I hadn't asked to go.' Memories of the farm remained with Sacher for the rest of his life. 'I remember the breakfasts. There was a huge Rösti [Swiss potato cake] with bacon and eggs. Everyone sat at the table together: the farmer, his wife, the grandmother, the farmhand, the children – everybody. With it they drank milk coffee. And afterwards, a strong schnapps: Enzian. The children drank it, too – less, of course, but they drank it. That was phenomenal!'

If this experience was wonderful, a year or two later, when the first phase of secondary school came to an end, an entirely new dimension was added to the fourteen-year-old's dreams. He found a place where fantasy and vision could be nurtured in a setting of such impressive natural beauty that his memories of it were a source of creative inspiration throughout his life, and he still recalled it in detail three-quarters of a century later.

It was the garden of Payerne.

7

The Garden of Payerne

When Friedrich Dürr, Paul Sacher's grandfather, moved to Basle, he traded his dream of reacquiring the Dürr family holding in Pratteln for the respect paid to a policeman. For Friedrich's older sister Maria, however, the desire to own her own land had not been extinguished. She had not followed her brothers and sisters to the city, where she would have no chance of buying land. Instead, in 1875 when she was twenty-six she had married a fifty-year-old photographer, Carl Baptist Estermann, from the canton of Lucerne.

The pair moved west into the French-speaking region of Switzerland, living at first in the township of Moudon. Later, with their two teenage children, Laura and Charles, they moved once more, and settled in an area where farming land was still available. There, displaying the same robust determination as her niece, Anny Dürr, later exhibited in the pursuit of her goals, Maria Dürr set about realizing her dream to own her own land. The place she chose was the village of Payerne.

When the Estermanns arrived in Payerne in 1902, Maria went to work at the Frossard cigar factory on the outskirts of town. Learning how to roll and box cigars, however, was not enough. For years she had saved and planned, and her dream was soon to become reality. In 1904 land became available on the slopes of the Invuardes, a hill to the south-east of Payerne. Since buying land was a man's business, she sent her husband to negotiate for it.

'My Aunt Laura always told me the story of how Grandfather returned stone-faced from the sale,' Maria's grandson Charles Estermann recalled. 'He told my grandmother that he'd been outbid, and that some other farmer had bought the section. Grandmother was so disappointed that she started to cry. It was only then that Aunt Laura, who knew that Grandfather was joking, took pity on her, and told her that the land – five thousand square metres of it – was really theirs.'

Within months, the Estermann's holding was extended to over eleven thousand square metres. Then, under the supervision of Maria and her children, a house was built on the lower portion of the incline, and named Chalet Fleurie. Although the land alone could have supported them, the family never depended upon it as their sole source of income. Instead, the Estermann children earned their living on weekdays canning condensed milk at the local Nestlé factory. During the weekends, they helped Maria with the endless chores in the immense orchard and garden.

The house had not long been completed when, in 1908, Carl Estermann died. Maria lived for another fourteen years and, before her death in 1922, her brother's grandson Paul Sacher paid his first visit to Payerne.

It was not only the tranquil beauty of the place which impressed him. The garden provided him with a refuge in which he could let his imagination run free. Time and time again in later years, he returned in his mind to the garden of Payerne and always found the same inspiration he had found there as a boy.

From the first floor of the house, where he slept in a corner of his Aunt Laura's huge room, he had an unbroken view of the surrounding countryside. He could see fields of wheat and potatoes, which unfolded for ever under his gaze into a vast patchwork of changing patterns and colours. There were no other houses to be seen, and no children of his own age to play with, but that didn't matter. He was used to playing alone, and anyway there was an endless selection of activities to choose from. There were eggs to collect, and ripe apricots to pick. In one corner of the garden, beehives were stacked along a wooden bench, and he could watch his mother's cousin Charles tending the bees and collecting the honey. Roaming the flower garden was Paul's favourite activity. Payerne was a paradise.

'I am convinced that the house and garden made a great impression on my imagination. The intimacy of the house, the wonderful flower garden.'

Chalet Fleurie

The garden of Payerne

★★★

In 1919, an event took place which changed the Sacher-Dürr family for ever. On 15 November, Anna Maria Dürr died of cancer. It was the only time that Anny ever let her children see her cry.

Friedrich Dürr was now alone, and Anny resolved to look after him. Her younger brother Fritz, a sales representative for an optical supplies firm, had recently bought a house five doors further down St Johanns-Ring from the Sachers' apartment. It was an imposing rust-red and cream brick building, with a terraced stone tower decorating its roof, and double French windows leading out on to stone balconies on the first and second of its four floors. More importantly, it contained four apartments, and Anny set about moving her father into the ground-floor apartment, below the one used by her brother and his family. Living there, he could take his meals with the Sachers, and Anny would be sufficiently close by to help him with his housekeeping.

One day, shortly after Grandfather Dürr had moved into his new apartment, Anny returned home from an errand to find seven-year-old Nelly packing her belongings into a suitcase. When Anny demanded an explanation, Nelly replied that she had promised her grandmother that she would take care of her grandfather. 'So as soon as Grandma died,' Nelly later explained, 'I moved into his apartment.'

Anny allowed the arrangement, and it seems to have suited everyone. After sharing their bedroom with Nelly for nearly four years, she and Gusti had it to themselves, and Friedrich Dürr was no longer alone in his apartment. Hedi Dürr, Nelly's cousin, suggested that Anny was also happy with the arrangement because, with Nelly as a companion, Grandfather Dürr was less likely to remarry.

With Anny's brother Fritz living so close, one might have expected there to have been regular contact between the two families but, according to Paul, Nelly, and Hedi Dürr, this was not so. Paul, absorbed in his music, his schoolwork and his dreams, remembered no formal contact at all with his uncle's family, but there were certainly get-togethers at Easter and Christmas. The festivities were held at the Sachers', and other family members recall that there was always lamb for lunch on Easter Sunday, and that at Christmas the Sachers' tree was covered with real red apples.

By the end of the First World War, Anny had saved enough to buy a piano for Nelly. From then on, the Christmas gatherings included performances of Christmas songs played by Paul on his violin, accompanied by his cousin Hedi at the piano. The piano stood in the sitting room, accessible to all, but except on these special occasions it was played only by Nelly. Paul, eternally fascinated with his violin, had no interest in the piano, an aversion which could have had serious repercussions.

'I never played or learnt the piano – I found it a dreadful instrument. It didn't have a noble sound, not a beautiful sound. The sound of the organ or the harpsichord was much more beautiful. But, of course, that's an extreme sin for a conductor. He should learn to play the piano, and should start learning early.'

That dislike of the piano's sound had consequences later in terms of his musical tastes and choices, but his inability to play the instrument never became a major disadvantage in his career because he did not let it. 'It never disturbed me that I wasn't a pianist, but it could have,' he later admitted. 'If I had chosen the normal path of a conductor, who begins in a theatre and has to accompany the choir or the ballet at the piano – well, I couldn't have done that. But I took a different path.'

In the early 1920s, the contours of that path were becoming increasingly clear. Though he still practised daily, Paul knew by his teens that he did not have the talent to become a solo violinist. He also knew that the life of an orchestral player did not interest him. What he wanted – and it was a wish he could articulate clearly by the time he was sixteen – was to become a conductor. If that wish was to become a reality, he knew he had a great deal to learn.

'I didn't hear a lot of music during my school years. It simply wasn't accessible in the way it is now. There were no records, no radio. If you wanted to hear music, you had either to play yourself or to go to a concert. But I didn't come from a musical family, and it wasn't until I was seventeen or eighteen that I really heard a lot of music. Before that, I mainly learnt about music through reading about it.'

In 1922, with little more than two years of secondary school remaining, and despite his mother's resistance, the sixteen-year-old set about finding someone who could provide him with the theoretical musical background essential for a conductor. He found his first mentor in Rudolf Moser, a composer and music theory teacher who lived in Basle. 'I went to see him and said, "Mr Moser, I want to be a conductor. I would like to study music theory with you." Moser said, "All right. We'll begin next Wednesday."'

For the next two years Paul took weekly private lessons with Moser, who trained his ear for music and taught him counterpoint and harmonic theory. 'He really worked hard with me,' Sacher recalled. 'He found that I had natural talent, and he felt that that talent should be encouraged and developed. I worked hard, too, because I knew I had to learn these things and, since at that time I wasn't a student at the conservatory, I had to do it privately.'

This phase of young Sacher's master plan was coupled with considerable expense. His pocket money may have been sufficient for buying second-hand books, but it certainly didn't stretch to expensive private lessons. Having learnt from his mother that he could do that which he wanted to do, however, Sacher soon found a solution.

'Already at home I had larger needs and the pocket money my mother gave me was simply not enough to meet them. My mother was not exactly tyrannical, but she was very domineering, and I didn't want to be financially dependent on her. I wanted to live the life I liked, the life to which I felt I was entitled. And I've always believed that one's income should match one's expenditure. So I began to coach students who were even dumber than I was – even in subjects like maths which I didn't understand very well. And their parents paid me well.'

The pressures on Paul and those of his classmates who had moved on in the spring of 1920 from their intermediate high school in the Lower Realschule to the Upper Realschule were considerable. Many of the students, including Paul, were again put on trial for their first year, and many had left by choice before that first year had ended. By July 1921, however, he had convinced his teachers that he could make it. *'Probe aufgehoben'* ('Probation ended') is written next to his name in that quarterly report.

At the end of the probation period, two reduced classes were combined into one, and from then until his matriculation in autumn 1924 this was Paul's class. He and his classmates began gradually to form a coterie which was to last far beyond their high-school days, and which – according to Rudolf Honegger, one of Paul's classmates – was not disturbed by the personal ambitions of any one boy. 'There was no one in our class who absolutely wanted to be the best. It was different in other classes.'

Sacher and seven of the eight of his classmates who were still alive in 1990 agreed that the class owed its special spirit and cohesion to two of their teachers: Dr Gustav Schneider, their form teacher, who also taught physics, and Dr Georg Steiner, who taught German and history. The two men made a deep impression on Paul, so much so that seventy years later his strongest memories from eight and a half years at the school were of them.

The Upper Realschule curriculum was exacting, and only eighteen of the twenty-eight students in Paul's class completed their high-school matriculation. He was one of them, despite a two-month absence from school shortly before his final examinations. Throughout his childhood, he had shown a recurrent tendency to respiratory illnesses, and in spring 1924 he was diagnosed with tuberculosis. He was sent to the Juventas convalescent home for adolescents in the alpine village of Arosa, where it was hoped that the mountain air would provide a cure.

The home was run by Reverend Fritz Streiff and his wife, and there Sacher promptly fell in love with Lili, one of Streiff's three daughters. According to her later account, he lost no time after his arrival in setting up court at the home. He even established a little orchestra, consisting of two violins, a guitar, an accordion and a kazoo.* According to Lili, Sacher virtually ran the home while he was there, replacing the after-supper games with his own readings from Oscar Wilde. During these evenings, it was Lili, and only Lili, who was allowed to hold the candle by which he read.

A short time after Sacher's arrival in Arosa, Lili left for Basle, where she studied painting (she later became a well-known book illustrator, and married the Swiss architect Emil Roth). From the letters Paul Sacher wrote to her during the remainder of his stay in Arosa and in the months that followed, it is apparent that his

---

* A simple pipe instrument.

Paul in the Juventas adolescents' home and sanatorium, Arosa, 1924

In Arosa, 1924

Paul with Nelly, 1922

convalescence was a period of both emotional turbulence and awakening. He was beginning to acknowledge and address the complex and often warring array of characters within him. In one letter he wrote, 'It often seems to me that all my fury, my hatred, the beast in me – that they lie just tamed, or only bound, at my feet. But they're still there. All these horrors. Oh, how I can hate! And then I get scared. If all that breaks out! How can one fight against one's own nature? What weapons do we have?'[4]

He also addressed such issues as destiny's intentions for him, his own tendency to tyranny, and his need for absolute control. 'It's only the orchestra I want to keep,' he wrote, 'which is really my achievement, where I possess unlimited power. ...I want to be free. And to rule over what is mine.'[5]

By the time he returned to Basle, his final exams were only a week or two away, but there was never any real likelihood that he would fail them. He had already proved himself, and, even though his final marks in algebra, geometry, and chemistry were barely passes, his record and his marks in the fine arts subjects were good enough to see him through. 'In the arts subjects he was outstanding,' confirmed Otto Miescher, later a railways engineer and a member of the Swiss parliament. 'But in algebra and geometry, we dragged him through, and we were happy to. He was such a wonderful classmate.'

★★★

While her children were growing up, Anny had made great efforts to provide them with every advantage she could, and she succeeded in meeting considerably more than their basic needs. There were, however, some things she couldn't provide, and one of these was 'a name'.

'I found out at high school that I didn't have a name that counted,' Nelly told me. 'I learnt that from our teacher's behaviour. The girls from well-known Basle families, who lived in their own one-family houses with gardens, were always bringing her things: the first roses in spring, the first strawberries in June, the first whatever. But I had nothing to bring. Through this I saw what it means when people judge people by what they have and not by what they are.'

Whether Paul was also aware that his family did not have a name which counted is unclear. What is absolutely clear, however, is that he was on his way to ensuring that his own name would matter. In 1922, shortly after he had begun his training with Rudolf Moser, and two years before his high school matriculation, he had caused a sensation at the Upper Realschule by creating an orchestra. As a result, the name Paul Sacher was already on the lips of his classmates, especially those who played a string instrument. Soon afterwards, his name became known to their families and friends when they attended the orchestra's concerts.

For Paul, the decision to start an orchestra was simple. Valuable as his theoretical music studies with Rudolf Moser were, he knew that he must also gain experience in his chosen field – immediate experience. He could not call himself a conductor if he had never conducted. For the many boys who played a string instrument proficiently, the orchestra provided a welcome break in the monotony of schoolwork. Rudolf Honegger, who played the violin, remembered the interest that Paul's plan generated. 'The orchestra gave us contact with each other outside classes, which everyone appreciated. People were keen to play.'

Rehearsals began on a weekly basis during autumn 1922. The 'rehearsal hall' was at the Post Restaurant, a few minutes' walk from the school, in an elegant banqueting hall with parquet flooring and stained-glass windows. It was there, on 10 April 1923, that the orchestra gave its first concert. Under the title 'Variatio delectat' ('Variety delights'), it performed a programme of twelve works from as many composers, including Beethoven, Verdi and Robert Volkmann, with Paul as both first violinist and conductor. Friends and family could attend for the grand sum of SFr 1.10 (at the time, double the price of a cinema ticket), and they did so in great numbers: the first concert sold out.

Rehearsals continued through the ensuing months. Six months later a second concert was given. It was attended by a local music critic, who was quick to notice the young conductor's interest in 'new' music: the programme included a composition by one of Paul's classmates, written at Paul's request.

Despite Anny Sacher's misgivings about her son's growing interest in conducting, she was, according to Hedi Dürr, immensely proud

Invitation to the first concert of Paul's high-school orchestra

of Paul's success with his orchestra. 'He was the centre of attention at home,' Hedi recalled.

On 27 September 1924, the students gave their last concert, to celebrate the end of secondary school and the completion of their matriculation exams. No tickets were sold; instead, Parisian-style, people were sent invitations to a musical 'Soirée', a pot pourri of different composers, styles, and tastes. Someone persuaded a critic from the widely read *Neue Basler Zeitung* newspaper to attend, and he gave the performance an excellent review, which focused largely on the conductor's talent. 'Sacher takes his task seriously, and has full control over his players. The discipline was good, the intonation clean, and one felt throughout the spirited, bright temperament of the conductor.'[6]

The 'control' noted by the critic was confirmed by Paul's players. Rudolf Honegger, too, spoke of Sacher's 'absolute authority' (a phrase repeated by dozens of musicians who worked with Sacher throughout his career) 'when it came to music. He could assert himself. We discussed the programmes together, but he knew much more, and his ideas or words were always decisive.'

The orchestra fulfilled many functions in Sacher's vision of ultimately creating his own professional ensemble. It was the conduit through which he experienced at first hand many of the musical works he had previously known only through reading, as well as an arena in which he had his first taste of power. It was also a constructive outlet for his frustration at being at 'the wrong school'. How wrong that school had been is highlighted by a list of his classmates' tertiary studies and careers. Of the seventeen boys who completed their final examinations with Paul, seven went on to study engineering, two became doctors, two studied commerce, two became architects, and four studied maths and chemistry. Paul was the only one to study an arts subject at university.

Although the orchestra provided Paul with the beginnings of a name that counted, the real driving force behind its creation was far simpler: he had to conduct. And, since no one was likely to provide an unknown teenager with an orchestra on which to practise, he created his own. While his growing reputation was a mere by-product of his work and achievement, his orchestra was the result of a deliberate strategy.

Paul (top row, third from right) with members of his high-school orchestra, 1923

There were other strategies as well. Some of them were the amusing devices of a clever boy.

Aged sixteen, Paul joined a number of other boys who were being prepared for their confirmation by the local priest. The lessons were held in the early mornings before school, and between lessons the boys had to learn large numbers of biblical verses by heart. Finding this an odious task, Paul quickly saw a way to avoid the worst of it. He noticed that the priest (whom he remembered as smelling of the flour-soup his wife had given him for breakfast) always asked the boys sitting in the front row to recite the first verses. 'So I always sat in the front row, and that way I only had to learn the first couple of verses. It always worked.'

Other strategies were not trivial. In fact, some were so far-reaching in their consequences that they would affect every area of his future life.

8

As Silent as Graves

At the age of seventeen, Paul Sacher made a decision which was to shape his character and affect his relationships for the rest of his life. He decided to hide his feelings.

'I didn't want people to see if I was happy or sad or anything else. I decided that I always wanted to appear like someone who is in control, and who always knows exactly what he wants and why he wants it. And I lived that way for decades.'

While he was ultimately to become a victim of this strategy, it provided a measure of protection for a spirit which Sacher in his ninetieth year still described as 'very sensitive and very vulnerable'. As he wrote to Lili Streiff in January 1925, 'Basically my nature is far too soft. But I would never show that part of myself to people. None of my friends know that I'm like that.'[7]

The only public expression of his inner darker side came in his choice of clothing. At a time when it was very unusual, Sacher dressed in dark colours, preferably black. This habit had begun early. At primary school, where he remembered being a sad and melancholic child, he was sometimes teased by the other boys for wearing his black 'confirmation suit'. But the taunts didn't stop him wearing dark clothes until he was well into his twenties. 'They corresponded to my mental state,' was his later explanation.

His fellow pupils at secondary school recalled little of his clothing, and knew nothing of the inner life it portrayed. They remembered Paul as a self-confident and friendly classmate. According to Otto Miescher, he was outgoing and popular enough to be elected class cashier, which meant that he collected weekly contributions from the boys towards their end-of-term excursions.

Some people did notice Sacher's sartorial habits. Els Havrlik, who first saw him passing the Elisabethenkirche dressed all in black, remembered feeling that he was different, almost from another age. Yet, despite their long friendship, even she was permitted only fleeting glimpses of what lay behind his sombre attire. As Sacher later explained, 'I never liked it when people tried to look into my soul. I always thought, "That only concerns me. It has nothing to do with others." So I trained myself to live in a very controlled manner.'

The mask of control may initially have been a protective mechanism, but it gradually assumed a chameleon-like character, becoming whatever he wanted it to be. It prevented others from sensing his vulnerability and over-sensitivity, but it could also be read as disdain, arrogance or coldness, and sometimes it was just that. It was also a device which helped him to elevate secrecy to an art form of extraordinary dimensions, and to hide his life-long loneliness and tendency to depression from all but his most intimate friends. Both in his private life and in his conducting, Sacher later paid a high price for his control, but he remained pleased with the results: 'I believe I have done well with this decision. It gave me the energy and the freedom to concentrate on the things for which I wanted to live.' As he said matter-of-factly to me one day, 'I can be as silent as graves.'

★★★

In autumn 1924, Sacher completed his final secondary school examinations, and enrolled at Basle University. His main subject for the next five years was musicology, but music was not all that he learnt. For him, university was not a place to gather specialized knowledge in just one subject, but rather a place where one could acquire a universal education. Consequently, he studied other subjects as well, attending lectures in history, national economy, and law.

In spite of his interest in musicology, Sacher never took his degree. The main reason was his lack of interest in the dissertation subject given to him by his musicology professor, Karl Nef: 'Some aspect or other of Beethoven's work,' he recalled dismissively.

There is no doubt that he profited from Nef's expertise in music history and analysis, and from his wide general knowledge of music, but when it came to the subject of his dissertation Sacher wasn't moved. 'It wouldn't have been an academic adventure. None at all. And I believe that every type of education should lead to adventure. Otherwise it's false. This dissertation on Beethoven simply didn't interest me. He could have given me another topic which fascinated me. Then, perhaps, I would have done my finals.'

The fact is that completing his degree wasn't important to Paul Sacher. If it had been, he later admitted, he would have requested another topic. But, by the time the matter of his dissertation arose, he was already a conductor. 'And I just wasn't prepared to spend time on something that didn't – in any way – get under my skin.'

In conjunction with his classes at the university, Sacher had also enrolled at Basle Conservatory. For a time he played viola with the Conservatory's string orchestra, and continued his music theory classes with Rudolf Moser. Having had his first practical taste of conducting with his Realschule orchestra, though, he was also interested in studying conducting technique in further detail, and the arrival of the conductor and composer Felix Weingartner provided the perfect opportunity.

★★★

Weingartner arrived in Basle late in his illustrious career. Born in Dalmatia in 1863, he was a protégé of Brahms, and had studied with Liszt at Weimar. He had been appointed court choir director of the Berlin Opera when he was only twenty-eight, and in 1907 succeeded Gustav Mahler as conductor of the Vienna Hofoper (Court Opera). As a composer he achieved no lasting distinction, but as a conductor he became internationally famous for his interpretations of Beethoven and Wagner, and for his pamphlet *Ueber das Dirigieren* (On Conducting), written in 1895.

In 1927 Weingartner was appointed artistic director of Basle's Allgemeine Musik-Gesellschaft, the association responsible for organizing the city's symphony concerts; the post of artistic director included planning and conducting a large number of the concerts. He was also elected director of the Basle Conservatory.

'He came to Basle as an old man, and when he conducted Beethoven or Schubert he received standing ovations,' Sacher recalled. 'People came from all over the world to attend his master classes. ... He was a first-rate teacher who taught elementary things well. He always said, "The upbeat is important. It has to be clearer. The orchestra has to be able to read it." And then he would say, "There are rests which the conductor needs to sustain, and others where he has to move on."'

Weingartner held conducting classes at the Conservatory during the school year, and in the summer his master classes were attended by young conductors from all over the world. The accounts of Sacher's participation in these courses vary.

Curt Paul Janz, a fellow student at the Conservatory and later a member of the Basle Chamber Orchestra, remembered that 'Sacher attended the courses in a strange way because he couldn't play the piano. It was normally a prerequisite for Weingartner's students that they be able to sight-read the scores. In the small hall of the Conservatory there were two grand pianos. The Conservatory orchestra consisted only of strings, so, while the orchestra played the string parts, one of the conducting students had to play the wind instruments on one piano, and another the brass instruments. Sacher could never do that. He was not a real participant. But Weingartner recognized his work with contemporary music, and invited him to come to his courses.'

Michaela von Herwarth, a violinist and viola player who played under both Weingartner and Sacher, also remembered that Sacher never played the piano, but did not remember this being a hindrance. 'One could see that, of all the young conductors, Weingartner held Sacher in the highest esteem. And Weingartner was one of the leading conductors, on the same level as Sir Thomas Beecham, or Furtwängler.'

Although Sacher denied that Weingartner was his role model, many of the latter's personal habits later became his own. 'His productivity was unbelievable,' Sacher later recalled. 'He was at his desk at 6 a.m., dealing with his correspondence, or writing. At 8 a.m. he was already at the Conservatory, and then at 9 or 10 he would have his rehearsal. His life was perfectly organized. And you know, he didn't allow any emotions to disturb him, but rather everything went its ordered way. That gives one an enormous capacity to deal with a huge workload.'

Weingartner's cool, professional demeanour confirmed Sacher in his belief that the cultivation of his own emotional control was a positive trait. He was also fascinated by Weingartner's spiritual beliefs, which led the latter to insist that a place be set at his table for his deceased first wife. Sacher was impressed, too, by Weingartner's appearance, and by the fact that he often had one of the pretty dancers from the theatre ballet corps escort him to his morning rehearsal. 'He was always very well and carefully dressed. And in some ways vain,' remembered Sacher.

As regards Weingartner's conducting, Sacher spoke with great respect of the maestro's 'majestic ability' to prepare and perform his chosen repertoire, especially the works of Beethoven. He was also impressed by the fact that Weingartner always conducted from memory (with the score lying closed in front of him). But good though Weingartner was, in Sacher's opinion his repertoire was limited to music that was widely and repeatedly performed. Such music was of no interest to Paul Sacher, who, although he learnt a great deal from Weingartner, had long since started down his own chosen path.

'When I was a young man,' he explained, 'eighteen or nineteen years old, I saw what was happening in the field of music. In our Swiss concert halls you always heard the same things being played as in concerts in any German city: Haydn, Mozart, Beethoven, or the Romantic composers of the last century, as well as music from the turn of the century. What was completely missing was contemporary music. No one was interested in that. No one thought that contemporary music was a task which they could make into their job. But it was exactly what I wanted.'

If he wanted to perform contemporary music, however, Sacher needed something very different from the symphony orchestras of the time. Those used by his teacher, Weingartner, for the performance of Beethoven, Brahms and Bruckner would simply not do. He needed a smaller and more intimate ensemble, of the size for which Paul Hindemith and Arnold Schoenberg had already begun to compose: a chamber orchestra. At that time, however, except for ad-hoc groups formed to give individual performances, there was no such thing as an established chamber orchestra.

'It's very simple,' Sacher explained. 'Today chamber orchestras are as common as red dogs, but at that time they didn't exist. The instrument one uses always matches the repertoire that one performs. There was the big symphony orchestra, and that orchestra covered the classical and Romantic repertoire. In theory, that began with Bach, Handel, late Haydn, late Mozart and went on to Brahms and Bruckner. But if I wanted to perform an early Mozart or Haydn symphony, or a Bach Brandenburg Concerto, I didn't need twenty first violins. I needed a small group, a chamber orchestra.'

There was, as he later put it, a hole in the market. 'Nobody played Bach's Brandenburg Concertos. No one played the early symphonies of Mozart or Haydn, or Concerti Grossi by Handel – not to mention the absence of contemporary music, the music of this [the twentieth] century.'

It never occurred to Sacher that the lack of an appropriate vehicle with which to carry out his plans should be an obstacle. If there was no established chamber orchestra, he would have to create one. He would form an ensemble whose performance goals would match his own. And in his search for musicians to play in the new ensemble, he did not have far to look.

His school orchestra had been disbanded in autumn 1924, but some of its members were interested in continuing with their young conductor. Sacher decided to create a new ensemble called the Orchester Junger Basler. He was looking for more players when he made the acquaintance of Annie Tschopp, a violin pupil at the Conservatory, and discovered that he had not been the only one to start a school orchestra. A few months younger than Paul, Annie had started a class orchestra in her final years at the Töchterschule (a Basle girls' secondary school). The ensemble had performed for fun, on prize-giving day and similar occasions, with Annie as its conductor. She, too, was interested in continuing with her ensemble in some form, and quickly agreed to Paul's suggestion that she and some of her players join his new ensemble.

On 29 August 1925, the Orchester Junger Basler was established as a society. A number of other students at the city's Conservatory also joined. The official Conservatory orchestra, an ensemble of string players, was forbidden to perform in concerts other than those organized by the school. Creating a new orchestra, however, allowed Sacher – and the students who joined his ensemble – to elegantly side-step this regulation: the string players in his ensemble could perform at will. 'He practically privatized the Conservatory orchestra,' confirmed Curt Paul Janz. 'In that way he was able to bring the ensemble to the public, and perform the programmes he wanted to perform. Even then, he had a sense of his mission.'

During the next year, the orchestra performed around ten mixed programmes, which always included works by Mozart, Haydn, or Handel. Sacher, meanwhile, nurtured his vision of his own chamber orchestra. Decades later, he told the French-Swiss film-maker François Reichenbach that he was 'always dreaming'. But throughout his life, even in his teens, he kept these dreams to himself until they were ready for realization. 'I never talk about my dreams,' he confided to Reichenbach, 'because I have found that, if I do, they disappear.'

This time, however, he did share his plans to some extent, and the recipient of his confidences was Annie Tschopp. The Tschopp family lived in the sort of home that the Sacher children had never had, but which both they and their mother aspired to. It was a spacious five-storey house built of concrete and grey stone, which stood on the incline of a forested hill known in Basle as Bruderholz, with a huge verandah looking out over their garden and the city below. The street-level entrance took visitors into a huge hall with tiled floors and a curious mixture of strong supporting columns decorated with *Jugendstil* design motifs, from which a massive staircase curved away to the floors above.

The Tschopp family's circle of contacts was extensive, and Annie used them to pursue the goals she shared with Paul Sacher. The Gothic-faced redhead shared his interest in performing early and contemporary music, and a close friendship evolved. There were long periods when no day passed without a call or a visit to the Tschopp home by Paul Sacher, which was facilitated by the fact that Annie had her own private parlour in the house. According to Annie's sister Else Schaub-Tschopp, 'Their friendship grew out of their work together. They had a common purpose. Annie was an excellent organizer, and was good at delegating. Just like Sacher.'

Annie Tschopp in the 1930s

The Orchester Junger Basler was simply an interim stage in Sacher's plan. In 1926, he achieved his first major ambition: on 4 November, his Basle Chamber Orchestra (Basler Kammerorchester – the BKO) was officially founded.

Articles setting out the new ensemble's aims and first programmes had been fed to the Basle press. They made it clear that Sacher's goal was the performance and cultivation of both contemporary and early music, and that it was his clear intention to eliminate from his programmes the nineteenth-century repertoire generally performed at that time. Just how serious that intention was became clear over the years: of the 181 composers whose works figured in the BKO's programmes during its first twenty-five years, only six were from the nineteenth century.

'As a conductor,' Sacher said later, 'I had a clear programme. In the early years when I played Mozart, or Haydn, Bach or Handel – well-known composers – I selected works which were unknown. Not *Messiah*, or other well-known pieces; everyone else was performing those. I always sought out forgotten works because, even in the field of early music, I wanted to perform unknown works, to make them familiar. Later that strategy changed somewhat, but the starting point was the unknown. I wanted to know these works for myself, and I wanted to introduce them to the public.

'Until the end of the eighteenth century, concert programmes consisted solely of contemporary music. No one would have thought of performing what we now call "early music". In the eighteenth century, music was under the control of clerical or secular gentlemen, and it was always their ambition to present the latest, the newest works. It was only at the end of the last century, and in our [twentieth] century, that people found out one could also perform older works.'

The BKO did not play only little-known works by past masters, however. Like the patrons of earlier times, Sacher also wanted to perform the music that was being newly written, but in his opinion, ignored. He wanted to hear the voices of his own time, and saw clearly that the emphasis on nineteenth-century music had all but eliminated these newer voices from Europe's concert halls.

The BKO's first performance took place on 21 January 1927, in the Martinskirche, Basle, and it reflected the mission behind the ensemble's creation. The first half consisted of works by Handel and J.S. Bach, in versions previously unplayed in the city, and Mozart's *Exultate, jubilate*. The second half was reserved for the world première of the Suite for Cello and Chamber Orchestra, Op. 35, by Sacher's teacher, Rudolf Moser.

'The Basle Chamber Orchestra presented itself…with notable success, which destroys any doubt about its right to exist,' wrote the critic from the *Schweizerische Musik Zeitung*,[8] while the *Basler Nachrichten* spoke of a 'total success', a performance which showed that 'quality work was being achieved'.[9] 'Mr Paul Sacher conducted with élan and elegance and apparent natural conducting talent' was the verdict in the *National Zeitung*.[10]

The harpsichord soloist in the first half of the concert was the Basle Cathedral organist, Adolf Hamm, whom Sacher often described as the finest organist he had ever heard. He was well known in the city's musical circles, and was a great supporter of Sacher's work. That support was practical as well as moral. According to Sacher, 'My mother told me later that he had gone to see her. He said, "You know, Frau Sacher, you can't forbid your son to become a musician. That simply isn't possible. It's clear that this is what he has to do. Give him your support instead of opposing him." And, ultimately, she did.'

With the organization and performances of his chamber orchestra, and his continuing studies at the university and the Conservatory, Sacher had little time to spend on anything he considered unnecessary. 'He was only open to his own universe,' Els Havrlik remembered, 'he was only looking to the heights.' Home became a place to sleep and eat and to receive the endless phone calls that seemed always to come at meal-times. Anny Sacher was not happy with Paul's absenteeism. While he had been fulfilling his first great dream, she had achieved a lifelong dream of her own. She had saved enough to pay the deposit on a new home at Thannerstrasse 47, and she didn't want him treating it like a hotel.

'I know it upset her that I gave nothing emotionally,' Sacher conceded. 'Part of the reason for distancing myself was that she was so domineering. If she'd shown some weakness, or clear needs, I would have talked to her more often.'

Each day in Paul's life was fully planned. Anny brought him his breakfast in his room. Shortly afterwards he went to his daily appointment at Herr Vonau's barber shop on Missionsstrasse, where a young woman shaved him for 30 Rappen, and also washed his hair. It was a habit he had begun towards the end of secondary school, and it remained a habit for his lifetime.

Asked later about this ritual, Sacher said at first that it was because he was manually inept, that he simply couldn't shave himself. On further questioning, however, he admitted that the quarter of an hour he spent at the barber's was a special time. 'No one could disturb me while I was there. No one wanted anything from me. I don't know where it came from, but I have always found it the most natural thing in the world that I should have people attend to me. And then I had time to dream, and time to plan.'

The BKO had emanated from years of dreaming and planning, and yet its continuation and development were to be riddled with obstacles. Ultimately, it survived only because Sacher would not have it any other way. 'I founded the BKO without money. With nothing. I was twenty years old. I knew what I wanted, but I had no money at all. It was a case of something that couldn't possibly work working because I absolutely wanted it.'

9

A Will and a Way

There were no guarantees that the Basle Chamber Orchestra's life would be a long one. Although there were musicians interested in performing early and modern music, plenty of works for them to perform, and a conductor to lead them, there was no money. For nearly ten years, the musicians who played in the orchestra's half-dozen or so concerts a year did so unpaid. Sacher, too, received no fee, but there were unavoidable expenses involved in the BKO's development and concerts. There was the rent of performance venues. There were printing costs for tickets and programmes. There were publicity and administrative costs, and fees for hiring outside soloists and additional musicians when a work required brass or woodwind. All these costs had to be met, and initially the returns were small.

The new orchestra and its performances of 'new music' did not have the support enjoyed by the city's symphony orchestra. Not only were the latter's concerts well attended, but they were subsidized by the machinery of the state-supported Basler Orchester Gesellschaft (Basle Orchestra Society). 'At that time,' explained Curt Paul Janz in 1995, 'the work of contemporary composers was regarded by the directors of the Basle music societies, their orchestras and many of the concert-going public with total hostility.'

Potential conflict, however, was no deterrent to Sacher. 'I see that I've begun a fight,' he had written to Lili Streiff – he was only nineteen, but already fully aware of his mission – 'a task which is threatened by countless obstacles. And I see that much of me is not equipped for this fight. But there is a will in me which is bigger than all energy, a great will to conquer.'[11]

It was with that will to conquer that Sacher set about modernizing Basle's musical life. 'He simply devoted himself to contemporary music,' said Janz. 'With Moser. With Hindemith. He moved Basle's musical life into a sector left untouched in many other larger cities. Right from the beginning, he saw that as his life's work, and he lived according to that. He regarded himself as a man in the service of his vision.'

Vision alone, however, could not ensure the orchestra's survival. Contemporary music was simply not good business, even though, according to Dr Albert Müry, a journalist and a member of the Basle Chamber Choir for fifty years, Sacher's early concerts in the 1500-seat hall of the Basle Casino were well attended. There were those who were eager for a change from the predictable diet dished up in the city's symphony concerts. Many people bought tickets to Sacher's concerts because they were curious and because he offered them something they couldn't find elsewhere.

Since the orchestra could not support itself fully, Sacher needed wealthy patrons. He found one in Otto Senn-Gruner, a retired Swiss army colonel whose family had made its fortune from the manufacture of silk ribbons (the factory still exists in the Basle countryside). The family was known for its love and patronage of classical music and musicians. In addition, the colonel had a collection of valuable musical instruments, and was greatly interested in the new direction being forged by the young Paul Sacher and his chamber orchestra.

Sacher had founded the BKO as a society, and he saw to it that Senn became the society's first president. It was public knowledge that during the two years between the orchestra's beginnings in 1926 and Senn's death in the autumn of 1928, it was he who covered the orchestra's deficits. 'Senn would say, "How much is needed? I'll send my cashier over in the morning,"' Sacher recalled. Additional funds were raised by selling society memberships; these ranged up to a life membership, which cost SFr 500, a very large sum at the time.

After Senn's death, the position of president was offered to Alfred Von der Mühll, the wealthy owner of a ceramics factory in Lausen in the canton of Basle, and a great music-lover. Marianne Majer, who played with the BKO for more than thirty-five years, remembered how the offer came about. 'He [Sacher] told me that he had met Von der Mühll at a social event. There was a buffet supper and Von der Mühll himself had served Paul very generously. Paul told me later, "I decided that, if he could serve me there in such a fatherly way, he could be president of the BKO!"' Von der Mühll accepted, and showed great initiative in fund-raising on the orchestra's behalf.

Sacher's choice of Von der Mühll as his orchestra's second president was not as arbitrary as the anecdote suggests. He had already shown acute perception in sizing up individuals, their talents and the role they might play in helping him reach his goals. With Von der Mühll and Senn, he had wooed individuals who could not only help him, but interested him as well. This ability to 'see' people, to assess their potential and to harness their talents to his own projects was criticized by some as a skill he abused for his own ends.

His friends saw the deliberate design behind his actions, but their assessments of it vary. Alfred Müry called it 'calculating', but Frau Majer saw it differently. 'He knew exactly what he could use people for. That's an art! In his masterplan, everyone had his place. And many people resented that,' she said. 'They said he used his ability to attract people in order to use them. But I don't agree. He did see people's talents, and what they were capable of, but I don't think he used them in a self-serving way.'

Whether it was mere coincidence or a case in point, shortly after Marianne Majer joined the BKO, Sacher suggested that she become the orchestra's librarian, which meant looking after the orchestra's music. The job also involved interacting with the staff of the Basle Casino concert venue, which for a shy young woman in her late teens was a horror. 'Sometimes, when I had to go to the Casino, I used to stand outside in the street for quarter of an hour before I found the courage to go in. But the job soon forced me to stop doing that.'

The lack of money that made the BKO's early existence so precarious was not, however, an obstacle to Sacher's early commissions. 'When I started, I was not as poor as a church mouse, but I was not rich; I didn't have money. However, when I asked a composer to write a piece for me for the chamber orchestra, I didn't have to offer him money. I offered him a performance of the work by the Basle Chamber Orchestra. No money, but a good performance. There were composers who thought it was wonderful to know that "I'm composing a work for him, and he will perform it with his orchestra."'

Even if more money had been available, Sacher pointed out that in the 1920s it was not usual to pay for commissions. 'In 1926, giving commissions was no longer as commonplace as it had been in the eighteenth century, when a composer wrote in the service of a great gentleman or a ruler – like Monteverdi at the court in Mantua. It was no longer usual for someone to say, "Write a work for me. And here are five hundred francs. That's your fee for the work." It wasn't usual last [the nineteenth] century, and as far as I know it wasn't usual at the beginning of this century. I know of no examples.'

Sacher's early unpaid commissions were from Swiss composers like Rudolf Moser, who, although originally from St Gallen in eastern Switzerland, had lived and taught in Basle for many years. His first commissioned work had been performed in the BKO's first concert in 1927. At the end of 1928, a second composition of Moser's was introduced to the Basle public: the Concerto in D minor for Violin and Orchestra, Op. 39, followed by the première of a work by Ernst Kunz, a Swiss composer who did not live in Basle.

Looking back at these early commissions, one is struck by an apparently systematic progression. With each new one, Sacher seemed to move further away from his base in Basle. The next commission, for instance, was for a work by Conrad Beck, a young Swiss composer who lived in France, where he had made an international reputation. Beck's Symphony No. 5, dedicated to Sacher and the BKO, was performed in 1930. Three years later, Sacher had moved beyond Switzerland's borders: his first commission for a non-Swiss composer was to the German Wolfgang Fortner, whose Concerto for String Orchestra was given its première by the BKO in December 1933. However, Sacher later contended that what looked like a carefully planned strategy was simply a case of one thing leading to another.

'I never gave my commissions in a systematic way. I never considered, "Who lives in this century? Who is important or interesting? With which works could one perhaps become famous oneself?" I never thought like that. I limited myself to those composers whose music I knew well, whose music touched me. That was really my criterion: my personal taste.'

In addition to his commissions, Sacher introduced the Basle public to many existing works which had not previously been performed in the city. These included, in the BKO's second concert on 3 June 1927, Paul Hindemith's *Das Marienleben* (The Life of Mary) Op. 27, for soprano and piano, and on 10 March 1928 three further works by Hindemith. On the latter occasion, Hindemith himself was the soloist in his Sonata for Unaccompanied Viola, Op. 31 No. 4.

'At that time,' Sacher recalled, 'Hindemith was just starting out. He was the bad boy of contemporary music. His early music was really impudent, without consideration for his listeners, outside the tradition. ... He was fairly small, and had a big skull, and then this huge viola. ... I liked him very much, and naturally his music as well. In contrast to that of the Second Viennese School, his music – like Stravinsky's – had a strong rhythmic element, and that appealed to me greatly. And he could be merry and humorous. I got to know him when he first came to the BKO as a soloist, and that was the beginning of our friendship.'

The words 'rhythmic element' appeared repeatedly in conversations with Sacher about his favourite composers. It was one of the main criteria that attracted him to, or turned him away from, a composer's work. It was also a yardstick for judging the ability of the musicians who performed in his orchestras, as the story of Marianne Majer's audition for the BKO illustrates.

Majer had left school early to study music. She auditioned for the BKO shortly after its first concert in 1927, even though she had not yet begun her studies at the Basle Conservatory. 'I played Vivaldi's G minor concerto. Then Paul said, "You're at the lower limit of what I can accept. But you played the syncopations so well!" It was rhythmical, and he liked that.'

Michaela von Herwarth, who played with the BKO from 1936 to 1938, recalled that the 'rhythmic element' was not only a leading aspect of Sacher's aesthetic taste in music, but also one of his hallmarks as a conductor. 'His two great musical strengths were his rhythmic ability and his ability to elicit a good sound. He had to work very hard on the orchestra's intonation, but then he's someone who always worked hard.' She also remembered his severity in early rehearsals. 'He was extremely firm and not very cheerful. We weren't actually allowed to laugh.'

Musically, Sacher's severity and cultivated control prompted frequent criticism of his manner of conducting early classical works. For instance, when he performed Mozart, many of his peers felt that he was too reserved to show how beautiful he found the music, and that reserve led to the comments that he was 'ice-cold', and 'just an organizer'. Some of Sacher's professional colleagues also found that he lacked the elegance and intimacy necessary for conducting the smaller, early works of Mozart or Haydn that he loved to perform. Judging by archive films of Sacher's early rehearsals and performances, such complaints were justified, but at the time Sacher did not care about elegance when he was conducting. For him the commitment of energy was important, and in his early years he conducted with excessively robust physical gestures. Nor was he physically disposed to elegance. His short, strong, stocky form was better suited to the farmlands of his ancestors than to the drawing rooms of the nobility. In his later years, elegance of person and form in his conducting took on greater meaning, and the contours of his physical performance became smoother, but there were still complaints that the way Paul Sacher conducted classical music did not do justice to the influence of his teacher, Weingartner.

On the other hand, confirmed his associates, when he conducted contemporary music he was supreme. The inhibitions that stilted his performances of the classical repertoire vanished when he conducted new works, some of which were made up of many different elements requiring sure coordination and control. 'That was, in my opinion,' Majer said, 'Paul's greatest strength. To control a huge apparatus like that, to keep it together. It was unbelievable how he did it. Then, he really made music from his soul.' The critics agreed.

On 4 June 1929, Sacher performed Arthur Honegger's 'symphonic psalm', *Le Roi David* (King David), for the first time in Basle. The forces required were considerable: his own orchestra strengthened by wind, brass and percussion players; a large choir and solo actors and singers. But Sacher was equal to the work's formidable demands, and seemed completely at ease.

The *Basler Anzeiger*'s critic wrote that 'His conducting ability... allows him to hold the many branching threads in sure hands like an experienced commander. His calm and decisive signals are particularly striking. Such conductors are internally and externally controlled, and are able to transfer this state to all their performers.'[12]

Conducting the BKO was not the only activity in which Sacher was preoccupied with the problems of performing modern music. On 24 June 1927, he and four colleagues founded a group called Gruppe der Fünf (Group of Five), whose name was probably inspired by Les Six, a group of six French composers who were disciples of Erik Satie in the 1920s.

Of his four associates, Hans Ehinger was a music journalist and critic; Max Adam was an oboist and a teacher at the Basle Conservatory, as was Ernst Mohr. The fourth, August Wenzinger, was the solo cellist with the BKO for its first season, and later a founding member of the Schola Cantorum Basiliensis.

As Sacher explained, the point of the group was 'to examine and tackle the problems of unknown music'. The group organized and performed a series of 'study performances', either in the Conservatory hall or in the homes of wealthy patrons like Otto Senn's son, Willy. These performances did not aim to be concerts. 'The material was indigestible – new. Unknown things which most people thought were terrible. We wanted to really tackle these new works, and usually in the course of the "performance" we spoke about them because the public, too, had to tackle them.'

Innovative as these informal performances were in terms of the musicians' direct interaction with their audiences, the concept was by no means new. It had been introduced four years earlier in the Swiss city of Winterthur by Dr Hermann Scherchen – then conductor of the Winterthur City Orchestra – as part of his own lifelong mission to promote contemporary music. Sacher had simply borrowed the idea, and over the next two years fifteen 'study performances' were given in Basle. Then, in 1929, the Gruppe der Fünf was offered an opportunity to put its work with contemporary music on a formal footing. The International Society for

Contemporary Music (ISCM) had one Swiss branch, in Zurich. The branch's work had, however, stagnated, and on the initiative of one of its founding members, the Winterthur businessman and arts patron Werner Reinhart, the Gruppe der Fünf in Basle agreed to take over as the Swiss branch of the ISCM.

Like the BKO before it, the new organization survived initially thanks to the generosity of wealthy patrons, but the problem of Sacher's own finances was slowly becoming acute. Although he still lived at home with his parents, his private financial needs were growing, and many of his conducting jobs were still unpaid. Then, in 1929, he found a solution.

There were a number of choirs of differing types and standards in Basle in the 1920s. One of them was the Basle Bach Choir, founded and conducted by Adolf Hamm. There was also a madrigal choir, and the Basle Men's Choir, whose members had a predilection for singing folk songs. In November 1929, when the Men's Choir sought a new conductor and artistic director, Sacher was offered a trial rehearsal by the choir's board. Apparently he satisfied their requirements because he was offered the job, which he accepted even though it lay far from his musical interests. The real reason for his acceptance was financial: the position carried with it a generous wage, and his decision was a pragmatic one, based on his needs at the time.

'Imagine. That was sixty years ago. They paid me five hundred francs a month, for a rehearsal every Monday evening from eight to ten. Oh la la! That was a lot of money then! I found that princely.'

The payment may have been princely, but Sacher later described the job as agony. 'I like conducting concerts with choir and orchestra,' he explained, 'but I find it boring to study a work with an amateur choir. I'm not a patient teacher. ... It takes so long, and they still sing out of tune. And a men's choir is much worse than a mixed choir, where there are at least a few pretty women to look at. But I was twenty-three years old, and they were offering five hundred francs a month!'

During the first three years of Sacher's work with the BKO, he performed two works which required a choir, Purcell's *Dido and Aeneas* and Carissimi's *Jephte*, and for these performances Adolf Hamm's Bach Choir was an obvious choice. In return, the orchestra accompanied the choir in a number of Hamm's own choral concerts. The Basle Bach Choir, however, was not Sacher's ensemble. Relying on someone else's choir meant relinquishing control to outside circumstances, something Sacher was reluctant to do. He also wanted the choir with which he worked to be trained to sing both contemporary and early music, a requirement which posed problems for an outside group.

As he had done with his chamber orchestra when a need arose which others could not meet, Sacher set about meeting it himself. 'I had incredible luck,' he remembered. 'The madrigal choir directed by Dr Alfred Wasserman had just been disbanded because he had been called away from Basle for professional reasons. I was able to take over practically the whole ensemble. They were not professionals but selected amateur singers. They formed the basis of the Basle Chamber Choir, and they were very good.'

It was important to Sacher that the ensemble's high standards be maintained. Many of those who auditioned later were told that their acceptance would depend on their willingness to take singing lessons. Alfred Müry remembered that Sacher, despite his severity in rehearsals, could 'really excite people, sweep them along with him. It was exciting to be working towards the première of a famous composer, and later the possibility of travelling abroad with the choir was an additional attraction for new members.'

★★★

During the 1920s, if he could not have financial control of the institutions blossoming from his dreams, Sacher ensured that he at least had total artistic control. At home, too, his authority was unquestioned. After 1927, home was a three-storey house at Burgfelderstrasse 23, which Anny had bought after selling the property in Thannerstrasse. As for many years previously, Paul shared an apartment on the second floor with his parents, while Nelly remained with her grandfather on the ground floor. And, again as always, the best room was given to Paul. 'It was on the left, as one entered,' Nelly remembered. 'On the right was a dining room which was never used, with *Jugendstil* furniture: a sideboard, a lovely table and chairs – all for occasions which never took place.'

Els Havrlik remembered Paul's room at Burgfelderstrasse 23 as being somewhat dark, with a chaise longue on which they sometimes lay to talk. 'And there was his desk at the window. I couldn't ever imagine him at the table with his family because he seemed to be something extraordinary. He had breakfast in his room. He told me that his mother brought him rolls and coffee at seven thirty.'

By this time, Anny was no longer listed in the business pages of the Basle address book as a seamstress. Now she made her extra money by helping her friends and former neighbours, the Pellmonts, in the pastry and coffee shop that they had taken over in Basle's inner-city shopping area. Sometimes there were large parties, or holiday crowds, and then she was called in to work the till, or to help serve. But her sewing machine still stood on the lounge room table and it was never idle for long.

'She was very hard-working and practical,' Marianne Majer said. 'I had kept my mother's wedding dress, a lovely black gown, and out of that Frau Sacher made me my first concert dress for the BKO concerts. And she was always giving me helpful hints about how I could make small improvements to my clothes: a row of braid here, or new buttons there.'

For a time, Marianne went each Sunday morning to help Nelly knot a huge carpet she was making. She was then often invited upstairs to join the Sachers for lunch. 'There was a sofa and a few chairs. When Paul was there, he sat on the sofa and all the others sat around on ordinary chairs. I was allowed to sit next to him on the sofa because there was always a chair too few.'

★★★

As their reputations grew, Paul Sacher and his orchestra performed not only in the BKO's official concerts but at other functions as well. His growing network of contacts, supplemented by those of Annie Tschopp, led to invitations to perform at weddings, funerals, and social events of all kinds. Sometimes the entire ensemble performed; sometimes just selected individuals.

One such event remained clear in Sacher's memory throughout his life. It was the occasion of Felix Weingartner's birthday on

2 June 1930. Weingartner's wife asked Sacher and his orchestra to perform one of Weingartner's works, his Serenade in F major for String Orchestra, Op. 6, at the party she had arranged in the Summer Casino. After the performance, Frau Weingartner led Sacher to the table where he was to sit for supper. On his left was Mrs Dora Von der Mühll, the wife of Hans Von der Mühll. On his right was the wife of Dr Emanuel Hoffmann, Maja Hoffmann-Stehlin.

10

More than a Name

Maja Hoffmann-Stehlin had been born in Basle on 7 February 1896. Her mother, Helene von Bavier, was from the Swiss canton of Graubünden, and had grown up in Rome. Maja's father, Fritz Stehlin, and her great uncle J. J. Stehlin were important architects, who had helped shape the face of Basle in the second half of the nineteenth century and the first half of the twentieth.

'Maja had an extremely talented father,' recalled Paul Sacher, 'a really talented man. He built half the city. Big villas, all in classical style. There aren't many left now, but for instance, he built the main building of the Musikschule [Basle city music school], and the De Wette school. ... He was the fourth generation of the Stehlin family in Basle. The first Stehlin came to Basle – a masterbuilder. The next was an architect. Then there was a politician, and then Maja's father, another architect. Then there were just four girls, and the family line died out.'

The bond between Maja, the third of those four girls, and her father, was very strong. As a child she often accompanied him on his inspections of the construction sites of his building projects, and her early and serious dream was to follow in his footsteps and become an architect as well. A generation later she might have realized her dream, but at the beginning of the twentieth century it was considered impossible for a woman to become an architect.

However, there were branches of the fine arts in which she could still interact with the relationships of material to space and which were more accessible to women. Maja chose the closest alternative and became a sculptress.

When her private schooling was completed, she began her apprenticeship with the German sculptress Baroness Wildenstein in Münich, but the outbreak of the First World War forced her prematurely back to Basle. As soon as the war ended, she left again, this time for Paris. There, she continued her studies with Antoine Bourdelle, and formed her first contacts with other artists such as Amedeo Modigliani and Max Ernst.

In 1921, Maja married Emanuel Hoffmann, the eldest son of Fritz and Adèle Hoffmann and heir to the pharmaceutical company F. Hoffmann-La Roche & Co., which Fritz Hoffmann had founded in 1896. The young couple moved briefly to Paris in 1925, and then in 1926 to Brussels, where Emanuel Hoffmann took over the direction of the Brussels branch of the firm. The couple had returned to Basle with their three small children just weeks before Maja's meeting with Paul Sacher on 2 June 1930.

Like most of the guests that evening, Maja was a member of the upper echelon of Basle society, known in Basle as the *Basler 'Daig'* ('pastry' or 'upper crust'). Most of the families who belonged to the *Daig* were extremely wealthy, and, as Marianne Majer explained, 'They could be recognized by their special dialect of Basle Swiss German, even if you didn't know which family they belonged to.'

Like the Hoffmanns and the Stehlins, these families had names that counted. They resided in Basle's great old mansions, many of them in the exclusive suburb of St Alban, where residents are still referred to as '*D'albaneese*',* and the upper-class families as '*DDs – Daig D'albaneese*'.** Lilienhof, the Hoffmann-Stehlin home in Gellertstrasse built by Maja's great-uncle – and described later by Sacher as a palace – was a focal point for social gatherings and was frequented by important guests.

Paul Sacher, on the other hand, was not of that echelon. The name Sacher was of itself not enough to open doors for him, or to provide him with special privileges. It did not mean the same in Basle as names like Vischer, Sarasin, Burckhardt or Imhof. Paul Sacher and his sister, like their parents, had not been born with a pedigree. Still, they had learned from their mother that they could reach out for – and attain – the things they wanted, and Sacher had reached. By the evening of his meeting with Maja, he was

---

* 'Those from St Alban'.
** 'Upper crust of St Alban'.

known as a young conductor of considerable achievement. It was his talent, effort, and personal achievement which had provided him with an entrée to Weingartner's party.

At supper, Frau Hoffmann-Stehlin made an enduring impression on twenty-four-year-old Sacher. 'I understood immediately that this woman interested me. I understood that immediately.' For her part, Maja soon found that she and her husband shared a special passion with the young conductor: a passion to experience, to live with, to foster and to cultivate the voices of their time.

Sacher had chosen contemporary music as the medium through which he could fulfil his need to hear those voices. He had brought the young Hindemith to Basle to perform his compositions, and Stravinsky, Honegger and Bartók would soon follow. In everything he did, his quest to know the new music, and the men and women who spoke through it, remained a driving force.

For the Hoffmanns, the most fascinating voices were those which spoke the language of form. During their years in Brussels, a centre for contemporary art in the 1920s, they had begun to build a private collection of modern paintings and sculpture, which included works by Marc Chagall, Max Ernst, and Pablo Picasso. They bought numerous works from the artists of the school of Belgian Expressionism, many of whom – like Gustav de Smet, and Floris and Oscar Jespers – became their friends. In 1924 they added aquarels of Joan Miró to the collection. When they returned to Basle, however, they were confronted with a very different landscape for the fine arts, one which had been described in 1923 by a former director of the Basle Kunsthalle, Wilhelm Barth, as 'a desert'.[13] In Basle, in the fine arts as in music, it was the works of the past which bore the stamp of validity.

The Hoffmanns' choices in art were not determined by any particular strategies or considerations. Their wealth meant that they could build their collection undeterred by private or public opinion. Their acquisitions were guided by their personal taste and by Maja's sense of the spirit of the times. In 1927, that spirit had already led her to buy one of Picasso's early cubist works, *Mademoiselle Léonie*, a portrait from 1910. Her friends shook their heads at this 'crazy art', and her husband called her a dreamer. But for Maja the picture was 'just right'.

Weingartner's birthday party marked the beginning of a friendship between the Hoffmanns and Paul Sacher based on mutual admiration and a shared vision. Sacher soon became a regular guest at Lilienhof, moving with ease in the Hoffmanns' circle despite the huge differences between their life style and his own. The Hoffmanns and many of their friends were hugely wealthy, and well-travelled. Sacher at twenty-four was neither. He depended on his position with the Basle Men's Choir for a substantial part of his income, and on the generosity of wealthy patrons to cover the deficits in his orchestra's budget. Unlike his parents, or his Aunt Laura, he had never lived away from home for anything more than a holiday break or the two months of his convalescence in Arosa. It was still Anny Sacher who cooked most of his meals, and it was she who laid out his concert attire. Within a very few weeks of Weingartner's party, however, it became apparent that Sacher was giving consideration to leaving Basle.

★★★

At that time, the German pianist Edwin Fischer was also the conductor of a choir in Berlin. 'He was a famous pianist and he had a very good choir,' recalled Sacher. 'He told me that he was looking for a successor for the choir, and asked me if that would interest me.'

Although Fischer's inquiry never materialized into a concrete offer, it served as a catalyst for Sacher's decision to make Basle the centre of his artistic ventures. 'I wouldn't have gone to Berlin just for a choir, but if I had been offered an orchestra I would certainly have tried to get the job. Berlin was a tremendous city at the end of the 1920s. A phenomenal city. Theatre, music – all that you could want. Think about it. Furtwängler, Bruno Walter, Klemperer, and more. There were at least seven important conductors in Berlin. [Erich] Kleiber was there, too. At that time you could see all those people conduct during a weekend.'

But Sacher didn't go to Berlin. Instead, he chose to stay in Basle, a decision which would alter the city's musical profile for ever. 'And I made something special out of staying here. I decided that if I stayed here I would really stay here. I wanted to make something special of this situation.'

By the late 1920s, Sacher had already begun to 'make something special' out of being in Basle. In 1929, he and his orchestra and choir had had a triumph with the first German-language performance of Honegger's *Le Roi David* (King David). The work required exactly the type of co-ordination and organization of large forces at which Sacher excelled. The Swiss-born, Parisian-bred Honegger had written the work for actors, solo singers, choir, orchestra and organ and, according to Curt Paul Janz, Sacher's performances of the work in June and September 1929 directed a spotlight not only on him and his orchestra, but also on Basle.

'His concert at that time with Honegger, with *King David*, was a sensation. It resonated throughout the whole world. And for that – that it took place in Basle, and not in Leipzig, or Berlin, or Paris – for that, one must honour him.'

Sacher remained faithful to his decision to make Basle the centre of his activities for the rest of his life. Several later offers of prestigious positions in other Swiss cities were unable to tempt him away. For example, in 1944 he was offered the directorship of Zurich Conservatory, which included conducting Zurich's symphony orchestra on a regular basis. He declined, and also turned down the post of lecturer in music at Zurich's Eidgenössischen Technischen Hochschule when it was offered to him in 1958 and again in 1968. 'To my regret, I had to turn down these interesting and attractive offers because I wanted to continue my work in Basel,' he wrote in 1982.[14] However, his claim that, out of love for Basle, he also turned down the position of conductor of the Beromünster Radio Orchestra in Zurich in 1957 was simply untrue. That decision had far more to do with his losing a battle with the Swiss radio and television union over the planned size of the radio orchestra.[15]

★★★

On 2 October 1930, Sacher's first commissioned work from the Swiss composer Conrad Beck, the latter's Symphony No. 5, was given its première in Basle by the Basle Chamber Orchestra. Beck, who enjoyed international fame as a young composer, became a life-long friend of Sacher's, introducing him in the early 1930s to his fellow composers at the Ecole de Paris (which he had helped to establish), among them Bohuslav Martinů and Marcel Mihalovici. 'When Beck was young and lived in Paris,' recalled Sacher, 'he was fashionable, and his works were performed by all the people there then. Koussevitzky, Ansermet – by everyone. All of them performed Conrad Beck. His new works sold like warm *Semmeln* [bread rolls], and he became famous at a young age. Later he didn't have the same success he had had at the beginning. And that was very sad.'

Conrad Beck was one of the growing list of contemporary composers whose works were performed by the BKO in its early years. By the orchestra's fifth anniversary in 1931, that list also included Honegger, Satie, Stravinsky, Milhaud and Bartók. But the expansion of Sacher's network did not mean that composers whose works had appeared in earlier concerts were suddenly put aside. Paul Hindemith's work continued to appear regularly, as did Rudolf Moser's. 'Once he had made up his mind about a composer,' explained Marianne Majer, 'Paul stood by his belief for his lifetime. For instance, there were some composers whose works he performed time and time again. It just didn't matter to him whether people grumbled about their music or not, or whether they were successful or not.'

Sacher's support for music which interested him was part of his strategy of cultivating the new, and the new in the old. A vital element in this strategy was the planning of his concerts, in which he strove to combine works which carried inner relationships to one another. These inner relationships were based on creative and historical associations, such as the key in which they were written, the subject of the texts if the works had vocal parts, and the period and style in which each work was written. Marianne Majer, who was the orchestra's representative at the planning sessions of the BKO Society, recalled, 'We met every fortnight for about two hours. It was there that I was able to see how Sacher made his programmes. Sometimes he waited years until he found the right spot in a programme for a certain work. He waited until it could be shown to advantage. In that respect he showed great patience – impatient as he could sometimes be. In small things he was terrible. But in these big things he was fabulous.'

Sacher, who spoke in later years of the necessity for 'a long breath' (*'einen langen Atem'*) to do what he had done, was prepared to wait. His vision was unfolding in a series of successful projects supported by a large and expanding network of friends and admirers. There were new friends to help in the organization of his concerts and with fund-raising. There were growing numbers of composers and musicians who were happy to participate in his quest to perform contemporary music. And the large majority of those who participated in Sacher's projects seemed to have an interest in him personally as well as in his mission, an interest which Sacher understood perfectly and used to his advantage. He had learnt about the power of belief in one's mission at the age of seventeen, when he joined a young men's group known as the Ring.

The group was led by a small group of Basle academics, of whom Professor Alfred 'Fred' Schmid remained outstanding in Sacher's memory. Schmid was about ten years older than Sacher, and at that time a lecturer in the mathematics and sciences department of Basle University. 'He had considerable experience in working with young people,' Sacher recalled, 'and he had a huge following. He freed people from their parochial Basle attitudes, and introduced them to the worlds of their imagination. He was capable and smart and talented.'

The members of the Ring met regularly for lectures, discussions and outings, and it was from Schmid that Sacher learnt about the importance of charisma and leadership. 'In my youth, there were a number of personalities like this Alfred Schmid, from whom I learnt how they influenced their environment and why they influenced their environment. I understood at a very young age that when you are fulfilled by something, and when you believe in what you want, others are convinced by it. One's own belief in a thing convinces others that it is so.'

Through his example, Schmid influenced Sacher's own style of leadership. 'I always had people around me who helped me. For instance, it was like that with the chamber orchestra. I said, "You do this. You do that." Someone was always saying, "Sacher doesn't do anything himself. It's always other people who do things for him." And there's some truth in that, because I've always had a group of people around me who shared my ideas and helped.

'People wondered why these supporters were so committed to me. Of course there were a few girls among them who were in love with me. That was easy. But it wasn't only that! When one creates something new, then there are always people who are attracted to it, and who help you.'

Several of those who joined Sacher's network of friends and helpers arrived with considerable talents, which they placed at his disposal. Some, who shared his vision and his goals, remained his life-long associates. One such was Ina Lohr, a Dutch musician whose vast experience of early music complemented Sacher's more limited knowledge, and he came to rely heavily on her advice. By 1931 she had become his official assistant, aiding him particularly in the painstaking choices of works for his concerts.

'Ina Lohr played a big role. She was very knowledgable about early music. She made many suggestions, and I really discussed all the programmes with her, all my life, until she died. It didn't all come from me – neither the ideas for the programmes, nor the works themselves – it was all mixed. Lohr wasn't the only one who helped me, but she was the most important.' Sacher's lasting tribute to the woman whom he described as a pedagogic genius was made decades later, when a room of the Sacher Foundation was given over to Lohr's library of scores and books and memorabilia.

Another early example of Sacher's ability to find people who could help him was Anita Mascioni, a beautiful young woman of Italian descent. Sacher had been searching for a secretary for the newly founded BKO, and persuaded Mascioni in 1927 to take the job. For seven years she worked unpaid, sometimes dipping into her own pocket to cover secretarial expenses when the cash kitty was low. Even after her formal resignation in 1935, she worked periodically over the following decade to help with the BKO's growing administrative load.

The most significant long-term contribution to the day-to-day running of the BKO, however, was made by August Vortisch, who had been a fellow student at the Upper Realschule. Three years younger than Sacher, he was enormously impressed by his colleague's sense of mission and strength of personality. Two of his five younger sisters, Sybille and Madeleine, remembered that August announced, while still at school, that he wanted to work for Sacher and his new orchestra. 'Our father said he had to study something else as well, in case this new group disbanded after a year or two.' So Vortisch studied law, and then became Secretary of the BKO Society, a position he held for nearly forty years.

Vortisch was, according to those who worked under him, precise, methodical, well-organized, full of ideas, and ambitious to do his job well. That ambition grew to be an obsession, and the management of the BKO became his entire life. 'He made all his friends there,' his sister Elisabeth told me. 'The musicians, the other co-workers. He did everything with them. When he took his holidays, it was with members of the BKO Society. It was everything. Even after he retired, and moved to a retirement home, he still couldn't leave it. He regarded Paul Sacher as his best friend, and was happy to know that his work was helping him.'

Like Anita Mascioni, Vortisch was responsible for creating the rehearsal plans of the orchestra and choir, for correspondence with soloists and composers, and a hundred other things. He was also largely responsible for the launching of the BKO subscription plan in 1930, which meant increased financial security and facilitated planning. In 1934, Anita Mascioni and August Vortisch were made the first honorary members of the BKO.

★★★

By the early 1930s, the face of Sacher's chamber orchestra was changing. 'At the beginning,' Marianne Majer explained, 'it was a real chamber orchestra – six to eight violins, four violas, two or three cellos. We played a lot of works which were specifically written for strings, because we could only afford a work which needed lots of wind players [who had to be hired] once a year.'

Not only was the original ensemble small, but a number of the founding members were good amateur musicians who earned their living elsewhere and could only attend evening rehearsals. However, as the concerts of the early 1930s became filled with more ambitious works, which presented the players with rhythmical and technical difficulties they had not previously encountered, extra rehearsal time became necessary. For some of the original players, this meant giving up their seats in the chamber orchestra.

As the faces changed, the size of the group began to wax and wane according to the needs of each programme. But the core remained, and would always remain, an ensemble of strings.

Sacher's love for the sound of the strings was already beginning to influence the artistic output of others, as the artistic vision of those composers from whom he commissioned became interlinked with his own. Although his commissions were accompanied by certain freedoms – for instance, there were rarely deadlines – the composer knew he was writing for a string ensemble. In a discussion of his commissioning procedure, Sacher recalled, 'Usually I said, "What are you working on now? Could that be something for me?" or "What are your plans?" Or I asked, "Would you like to write this or that?" It's not good when you force someone. He has to have the feeling that he is free. But I did sometimes say, "I would like a piece to begin a programme, or a solo work. Do you want to compose something for voice with orchestra, or piano, or violin?" I gave the composer as much freedom as possible, but he had to know something about my orchestra.'

From the late 1920s onwards, Sacher's work with his orchestra and choir was no longer confined to Basle. Guest performances were scheduled in other Swiss cities and, in 1930, across the French border in Strasbourg. In February 1931, accompanied by the Orchestre de la Société d'Etudes Mozartiennes, Sacher and the Basle Chamber Choir made an acclaimed guest appearance in Paris with a concert performance of Mozart's *Idomeneo*, then all but forgotten. Three months later, in Basle, the BKO gave what is thought to be the opera's first complete performance in modern times. 'At that time, the work was totally unknown, and wasn't performed in any opera house,' explained Sacher in a newspaper interview in 1993. 'At any rate, only arrangements of it were known. I wanted to perform *Idomeneo* in concert in the original version. We only had the complete work, and we had to write out the parts ourselves.'[16]

In addition, Sacher's performances were no longer limited to conducting his own orchestra. In 1930, he began to work as a guest conductor with other orchestras, in Switzerland initially with the Lausanne Chamber Orchestra, and in Sweden with the Göteborg Symphony. But the focus of his work remained the

BKO, with which he celebrated a further triumph on 20 January 1932, when he conducted Honegger's epic oratorio *Cries du monde* (Cries of the World). The work's Basle première was also the world première of its German setting. The oratorio was performed to a capacity audience in the concert hall of the Basle Casino, and was so successful that it was repeated a fortnight later.

★★★

Late on the evening of 3 October 1932, Emanuel Hoffmann was returning home from visiting a close friend. It was a wet, stormy evening and as his car was passing over a railway crossing it appears to have stalled. The approaching train had no time to stop. Sacher recalled that, 'The next day I was invited to lunch at the Von der Mühlls'. When I arrived, Mrs Von der Mühll said to me, "Have you heard? Dr Hoffmann has been killed in an accident." I went to Maja straight away. I knew immediately, "That is now my way. That is now my path."'

In the short time between their return from Brussels in 1930, and Emanuel Hoffmann's death at the age of thirty-six, the Hoffmanns had moved their patronage of contemporary art from a private to a public sphere. In 1931, Hoffmann had been elected president of the Basler Kunstverein (Basle Art Society). The society gave him a platform from which to direct the city's cultural attention towards the present and the future, rather than so predictably towards the past.

Now, in the aftermath of Emanuel's death, Paul Sacher was at his widow's side, offering his support. According to the Hoffmann's younger son, Lukas, Sacher was not the only one. 'There were quite a number of men who tried to come close to my mother in the two years following my father's death. Among them were some old friends of my father who gave my mother support, but there were also those whose motives were less altruistic. Paul was one of the people I did not know before. There were two or three other men who tried to come close to her whom we decidedly disliked, but that was not at all the case with Paul.'

When the Basle Art Society held a memorial service for Emanuel Hoffmann in October 1932, it was Paul Sacher and his chamber orchestra who provided the music. It was Paul Sacher with whom Maja began to discuss her plans for a foundation to be established in her late husband's name. It was Paul Sacher, too, to whom she turned when her thirteen-year-old son, Andreas, fell ill with leukemia just months after his father's death.

'She was not only an attractive woman, she also had a heart-rending fate,' said Sacher. 'In 1932 she lost her husband in a car accident. Within a year her eldest son died from leukemia. That's a bit much. A bit much.'

For many months, Paul's attentions to the wealthy widow were the attentions of a close and caring friend. It was his friendship and support, said many of their acquaintances, which helped Maja survive the gruelling months of her son's illness, and her desperate grief at his death. And then, employing the discretion and reserve which he had begun to cultivate as a teenager, Sacher began to court Maja Hoffmann-Stehlin.

'One day,' recalled Sacher decades later at a Hoffmann family party, 'Maja and I were travelling in the car with the children. Vera was sitting with us in the back, and Lukas was in front with the chauffeur. Suddenly Vera screeched out at the top of her lungs, "Luuukas, Herr Sacher just called Mims Sweetheart!"'

The courtship progressed slowly, and in secret. Nelly Sacher, who was away from Basle studying nursing in a private clinic across the French border in Belfort, knew nothing about it until she received a letter from her brother in the late spring of 1934 telling her he was going to get married.

Tibor Pellmont, the younger brother of Paul's boyhood friend Karl Pellmont, remembered Anny Sacher voicing her concerns to his mother. Anny had always wanted a secure financial existence for her children, but suddenly the scale of what was on offer had leapt far beyond anything she could have envisaged. 'If only this marriage works out,' she is reported to have said to Elise Pellmont. 'There's so much money, far beyond normal conditions.'

For Sacher himself, Maja's wealth and the difference between their social backgrounds was hardly a concern. 'That never put pressure on me. And the change from my background to this new situation, that didn't worry me for a moment. I was actually born [to live this way]. I had absolutely no trouble with it.'

Far from Sacher's having trouble with the gigantic change in his private circumstances, there was an element in the situation which was a perfect opportunity for the part of him that loved a challenge, loved a risk, and loved a dare. 'You know,' he said in the early 1990s, 'I have done many bold things in my life. Imagine. Maja: a grand lady in her mid-thirties, Frau Hoffmann-Stehlin, married to Dr Emanuel Hoffmann, the sole heir to Hoffmann-La Roche. She lives in Lilienhof, a great palace in Gellertstrasse. She belongs to high society. Well, when a young boy musician comes along, ten years younger, and finally marries her, there's danger in that. This lady can say to every suitor, "There's the door." There is an element in this scenario which makes it highly improbable that it will succeed.'

Improbable as the relationship may have appeared to outsiders, however, Sacher had been raised with the belief that he could do that which he wanted to do. He wanted to marry Maja Hoffmann, and he was convinced that he, too, had a lot to offer. 'I had a great deal to bring [to this marriage]. I was an interesting figure. I was someone of whom people were almost afraid. They had respect, and a certain admiration, a certain amazement – "How does he do that?" and so on. And in any case I was accepted as the wunderkind who comes as a nothing and then has great success.'

In June 1934, Paul Sacher married Maja Hoffmann-Stehlin. He was twenty-eight; she was thirty-eight. Friends of the couple received notice of the marriage shortly before it took place, printed on each of the inner sides of a folded cream notecard. 'Maja Hoffmann-Stehlin is honoured to inform you of her coming marriage to Mr Paul Sacher. Paul Sacher is honoured to inform you of his coming marriage to Mrs Maja Hoffmann.'

Sacher's compassion and life-long admiration for Maja were genuine. Nevertheless, his marriage was also an example of his colossal opportunism. Since his youth, he had wanted and envisaged a different life to the one he led with his parents, a life in which he would be able to realize his dreams on a grand scale. He had even told his schoolfriends that someday he would marry a wealthy woman. When the opportunity presented itself, he lost no time in seizing it.

The ease and eloquence with which Sacher moved in the circle of the wealthy woman he married have been commented on by

Paul and Maja's official wedding photograph, June 1934

more than one astute observer. 'People were very surprised at the marriage because the Basle milieu [of the *Basler Daig*] was socially very closed,' recalled Maja's second cousin, the Swiss historian Professor Jean Rudolf von Salis. 'And then Maja married this Paul Sacher who was totally outside this Basle patrician strata. But he was so intelligent and well-mannered, and sociable, that he was able to mix easily in these circles.'

In retrospect, however, the ease with which Sacher took on his new wealth and its responsibilities was no surprise at all. He had been planning for it for more than a decade.

★★★

Despite Von Salis's comment, there were those in the Hoffmanns' circle who received the news of the marriage with something less than elation. 'After I married Maja, there were perhaps those established families where I was no longer so welcome because, for instance, they had wanted a male relative to marry Maja, and I got in their way,' admitted Sacher. 'I was suddenly a grand and powerful man, and they would perhaps have preferred a Burckhardt or an Iselin. But it doesn't matter.'

For those who might have wished to oppose the marriage, there was simply no time. 'By the time they looked around, I had married Maja. It was all too late. It took their breath away. And there were certainly people who said, "What's this? This Sacher? This little conductor who's married his way in?" There was certainly some of that, but I ignored it. It didn't disturb me.'

The surprise of Sacher's marriage after a secret courtship may well have taken some people's breath away, but there were still many people in Basle who had enough breath left to gossip. The marriage opened the door to the realization of Sacher's dreams on a grand scale, but it also earned him additional names. Suddenly there were nicknames like 'parvenu' or 'social climber', nicknames that would be used by some throughout their lifetimes. It didn't matter to them that Sacher had proven his artistic ability long before the summer of 1934, and that his marriage simply meant that the scale of his achievements would change. He had broken the law of stones, moved away from his appropriate place in the grand scheme of things, and for that there were those who never forgave him.

Among his friends and associates, the news of his intended marriage had caused not only a sensation but also some grave disappointments. 'The Basle Chamber Choir was full of the daughters of wealthy Basle families,' claimed Michaela von Herwarth. 'Each of them had thought, "Paul Sacher will be my husband." People said at that time, "Well, he chose the wealthiest."'

Nor were the disappointments confined to choir members. Within a few months of Sacher's marriage, there were resignations from both the secretarial office and the board of the BKO. Anita Mascioni, who had also been Sacher's mistress for a time, found it difficult to remain in the secretarial office after Sacher's marriage, as did Margrit Staehelin, whose father 'would have had nothing against Paul Sacher as a son-in-law'. Her father, Dr Max Staehelin, president of the Swiss Banking Corporation in Basle from 1928 to 1944, also resigned from his position on the BKO board, which he had joined in 1931. Three other women left in the same period for reasons which cannot now be ascertained.

Former BKO members claim that Annie Tschopp was also greatly shocked by the news of Sacher's marriage, but family members say she defended his decision. According to her sister Else, 'She said that Maja had had to deal with such hard things, and that if Paul could help her it was worth all the trouble.'

Sacher himself remained adamant that any disappointments experienced by other women came from their unfounded expectations. 'I never – really never – told one of those girls that I would marry them. I certainly said many times that I didn't want to get married. I spoke of marriage only once in my life,' he stated categorically, 'and that was with Maja.'

Despite his adamance, there was one woman, virtually unknown to his Basle circle, for whom the news of Sacher's intended marriage was an unbearable shock. She had been his secret love for almost ten years, and had believed that their relationship would last through both their lifetimes. And, in a way, she was right.

Her name was Romana Segantini.

III
The Reality

11

The Price of the Dream

Basle, 19 November 1925

Fräulein Segantini

In front of me lies a card. It shows the stern, lucid picture of your famous ancestor. On the border of the card in small letters, written in your hand, is your lovely name: Romana Segantini. And I say these words out loud to myself, 'Romana Segantini'. And with these words the vivid picture of your beautiful home suddenly appears before me. Perhaps you remember the grey figures who were at work in Maloja this past summer. And perhaps you remember a short visit. If you can see the younger of your two visitors before your eyes, then you know who is writing to you. His name is Paul Sacher …

Paul met Romana Segantini for the first time in the summer of 1925 when he was on holiday with friends in the Swiss region of the Engadine.* He was nineteen; she was two years younger. Their meeting marked the beginning of a relationship which ended only with Romana's death in 1992, and which was remarkable both for its duration and for its secrecy. Its most important ground rule, laid down in Sacher's first letter, was silence.

> No one knows about this letter, and I beg you not to disturb the magic of the unspoken with words! Please also forgive me when what I do appears to cut across all convention. There are things which are greater and more important than [adhering to custom]. Finally, accept the greetings of a person you hardly know, and don't be angry with him.
> Yours, Paul Sacher [17]

* Upper portion of the Inn Valley in the Swiss canton of Graubünden.

Romana Segantini was the granddaughter of the painter Giovanni Segantini, the 'famous ancestor' Sacher referred to. Born in Italy, Segantini had lived most of his short adult life in the isolated Swiss mountain villages of Savognin in Oberhalbstein, and Maloja in the Engadine, where he painted two of the three works comprising his famous *Triptychon*. While both Italy and Switzerland later claimed him as their own, Segantini had never taken official citizenship of either country. Described by Romana's half-sister, Gioconda Leykauf-Segantini, as 'not a comfortable man', he had died aged only forty-one, leaving a young widow and four children.

Giovanni Segantini's son, Gottardo, also became a painter. After he married, he moved for a time to Rome because the harsh winters of the Engadine were too taxing for his wife's health. There, one of his daughters was born, and she was named after her birthplace: Romana. A few years later the family returned to Switzerland and settled in ruggedly beautiful Maloja. When Gottardo's first wife died in 1938, he married Charlotte Portner, who was more than thirty years his junior. According to their daughter, Gioconda, Charlotte was a city girl from a well-to-do German-Jewish family who disliked the isolation and hardship of life in a Swiss mountain village, and who escaped from it regularly into illness.

Romana grew up in an environment of contradictions which combined a laissez-faire permissiveness with domestic formality, and a struggle for financial survival with the more abstract concerns of the artist. Her father, Gottardo, an open-minded and tolerant man who encouraged his children to be likewise, was seldom seen without his jacket and tie, even while painting. Romana, who displayed the same traits of generosity and tolerance as her father, grew up observing at close hand, as she later put it, 'the slavery of art as a breadwinner'. As she told me a year before her death, she had always known that her friend Paul Sacher would need money to fulfil his life's ambition, money she didn't have.

Sacher was clearly captivated by the grey-eyed, slender and serene young woman; she was described by Nelly Sacher as 'very beautiful and very elegant'. Early photographs in Paul's 'Ladies Album' show Romana to be beautiful indeed. In 1925, however, there was no chance for the two teenagers to meet with any frequency. Romana was away at school in Fribourg in the French-speaking region of Switzerland, and Sacher's plans for his chamber orchestra were just approaching fruition. There was neither the time nor the money to cover the distance that separated them. For two years after their first meeting, their friendship continued largely through an intermittent, formal correspondence. Then, in the autumn of 1927, their relationship changed. They met again, and became lovers.

For long periods in 1928 and 1929, they wrote to each other almost daily. By this time, '*Liebes Fräulein Segantini*' ('Dear Miss Segantini'), had become '*Geliebte Romana*' ('Beloved Romana'), and '*Sie*', the formal 'you' in German, had changed to the more intimate '*Du*'. The affair remained a secret, which meant that meetings had to be carefully planned. 'Let us meet!' wrote the twenty-three-year-old Sacher in 1929. 'I, too, can get away on 5 July. But where?'

Always aware of the importance of Sacher's mission, Romana accepted the distance, the secrecy and the irregularity of their meetings. She did not, and could not, know that one of the reasons for Sacher's insistence on secrecy was that he had a number of other discreet relationships in Basle, and wanted to avoid gossip and jealousy among his other admirers. When he once invited Romana to a BKO concert in Basle, it was Nelly who was assigned to look after her for the evening.

Romana never figured in the group snapshots of Sacher's young friends, taken during the summer breaks when they holidayed together. Marianne Majer, 'Gusti' Vortisch, Annie Tschopp, Sacher's high-school friend Eduard Preiswerk, who died young of tuberculosis, and others can be seen with Paul and Nelly, smiling out at the photographer. But not Romana. She was, as Sacher later put it, '*à prendre à part*'. Perhaps it was the very fact that she was 'set apart' and unknown to Sacher's friends that made it possible for the friendship to survive as it did for decades. There was little threat from a friendship which was known to no one.

Because Romana was distanced from Sacher's life in Basle and his other friendships, she was caught unawares when he told her of his plans to marry Maja Hoffmann. For him, the situation was clear: his relationship with Romana would compromise his marriage, and it had to end. What he had not counted on was the depth of feeling that had grown up between them.

Romana Segantini, 1932

'A woman whom I believe I loved greatly,' he admitted to me in a 1989 interview, 'was Romana Segantini. She lies heavily on my heart somewhere. It wasn't good that I left her as I did; I don't know how she coped with it. She was phenomenal, phenomenal. She never complained. She never made any sort of reproaches.'

Far from making reproaches, Romana showed enormous understanding of Sacher's decision to marry, and to marry well. She did not condone the 'ugly and mean gossip' in Basle that accompanied his decision. In fact, she remained an endless source of support. In 1944, ten years after the marriage, she wrote to him:

> You said to me at that time, 'And, most unluckily, she is rich.' I didn't find it unlucky then, and today even less so. On the contrary, it was a great comfort and blessing, and the fulfilment of my request to Destiny on your behalf. You see, it was always clear to me that you would absolutely need the freedom that money can bring to develop your being and the harmonious ordering of your life. My reverence for your mission as an artist always stood above my love, and I realized early how dangerous it would be for your art if you had to harness it into a daily fight for existence …
>
> Money brings responsibility and obligations, power and temptations. Only the fewest wealthy people are capable of dealing with all these challenges. … You, however, belong to the chosen ones in whose hands wealth blossoms and bears fruit. … You are also strong enough to resist its temptations, and to go your way calmly as an artist. I knew all this exactly, and never doubted you for a moment, and now you have proven it to the whole world.[18]

'Dearest Romana,' Sacher replied, 'do you feel how I love you?'[19]

★★★

The bond between Romana Segantini and Paul Sacher was impaired by Sacher's marriage, but not severed. A year before Romana's death, Sacher willingly admitted that they had met again more than once. 'Romana was a romantic woman. No matter what else was happening in my life, from time to time I saw her.'

Later in her life Romana married briefly, but after her divorce in 1946 she never remarried. She was an educated and highly intelligent woman, a trained librarian who had worked in municipal libraries in the Swiss cities of Lausanne and Biel. She was employed for a time as secretary to Carl Jakob Burckhardt, the Swiss historian, writer and statesman, accompanying him to Danzig for the difficult years of his appointment as high commissioner of the League of Nations from 1937 to 1939, and assisting him with his multi-volume biography of Richelieu. She had a life, but it was a life deeply intertwined with her enduring love for Paul Sacher.

'I must live so long that I tire of loving you,' she wrote to him in 1975, half a century after their first meeting.[20] And for more than half a century she honoured the request made by Paul Sacher in his very first letter: she told no one.

To those around her, Romana always seemed carefree. 'She never spoke about herself, but she was always there for others,' recalled Gioconda Leykauf-Segantini. 'There were so many shadows on our life, but Romana was the mediator. She was always serene.'

Behind the serene exterior, however, was a deeply sensitive woman, whose sense of loss at the end of her relationship with Sacher was most poignantly realized by her family after her death. It was not until then that, among the bundles of neatly tied letters from Paul Sacher, they found a copy of a fairy tale she had written years earlier. The tale, entitled '*Versiegelt und eingeschlossen*' (Sealed and Locked In), was an allegory of the young couple's love and Sacher's departure. In it, a young man, in order to fulfil tasks of a higher order, is forced by Destiny to forsake his mistress. She sends her soul to bring him back, but it happens upon the young man as he is locking away his mistress's love letters in a secret place, and is inadvertently locked away as well. The young woman therefore has to live on empty and soulless, 'as if she were already dead, without a soul, without sorrow, without tears [*als wäre sie schon gestorben, ohne Seele, ohne Leid und ohne Tränen*]'.

Romana Segantini died on 23 February 1992.

The extent to which she had honoured Sacher's request and remained a mistress of silence and secrecy became apparent at her funeral. Shortly before the service, a huge spray of pale-pink roses, large enough to cover her entire coffin, arrived at the church in

Maloja. The attached card was signed 'Paul Sacher'. No friend or family member, not even her half-sister, who had spent a large amount of time with her, had ever heard the name 'Sacher' from her lips, or had any inkling of the long love that had just ended.

★★★

Not everyone in Basle was as understanding as Romana of Sacher's new wealth and the power that accompanied it. 'There was a whole clique of opponents,' recalled Michaela von Herwarth, 'people who begrudged Sacher the money. They said, "Well, no wonder he can do that. With so much money."'

The people who made such claims failed to realize that Sacher's professional success was not merely a product of the wealth into which he married. 'You see,' he told me on many occasions, 'people always say it's all just a question of money. But that simply isn't true. Many people composed works for me for nothing, nothing at all. Just to have the work performed. It's also true that certain fees which I paid in the first years of my career were so modest that anyone could have offered them. For instance, Béla Bartók received very modest fees.'*

The demands on Sacher's new wealth did not end with larger commission fees. After his marriage, members of his chamber orchestra felt that their services should be changed from honorary to salaried. 'The [BKO] had been founded with young, ambitious musicians who all wanted the same thing: to play contemporary music,' remembered Michaela von Herwarth. 'But those same musicians also had to build up a financial existence in the meantime. Gradually they had the feeling, "We should be paid." They had never been paid fees. They were honorary members, and played in maybe six concerts a year. Apart from that, they gave lessons. It was hard to find places in other orchestras. There was the economic crisis, and then the war. So there was quite a bit of tension. After Sacher married, some said, "Now Paul Sacher is rich. Now he can pay."'

The first who dared voice this idea was Annie Tschopp. Her open confrontation with Sacher over salaries ended their working

---

* Bartók's fees of SFr 500 for *Music for Strings* and SFr 1000 for the *Divertimento* appear considerably less meagre in the light of historical perspective.

relationship, and inflicted a wound on their friendship from which it never fully recovered.

'Annie felt that, now that Sacher had money, the musicians in the chamber orchestra should also be paid,' explained Else Schaub-Tschopp. 'Sacher didn't like that at all – he found that absolutely wrong. Annie left the orchestra with a bang.'

Paul Sacher may not have liked the suggestion that the musicians be paid, but ultimately he acted on it. Michaela von Herwarth remembered that, not long after the conflict between Annie and Sacher arose in 1936, 'every individual player was invited to an interview. There were twenty of us or more. And each of us was asked to say what was not to our liking. I said, "Why don't you found another society from which we can all be paid? It can be a proper salary, because all the players are now professionals."'

While Sacher's new access to wealth had raised the problem of payment for his players, it ultimately offered a solution. Soon after the interviews and discussions, recalled Marianne Majer, the players were offered a certain sum for the six-concert season (to be financed out of their conductor's own pocket). 'He promised me that I would be paid a hundred francs for the six concerts, but in the end it was only eighty francs.'

Annie Tschopp never worked with Paul Sacher again. In 1937, she married a Hungarian musicologist and later settled with him in America, where she continued her work as a teacher of the viola and viola d'amore and as a performer of early music. Many of her activities there paralleled the path she had started upon in Basle with Paul Sacher. She founded and directed the Camerata of the Boston Museum of Fine Arts, and in 1959 she became the director of a community music school in Boston which flourished and grew to many times its original size and importance during her fifteen-year stewardship.

In later years, she returned to Switzerland in retirement. She and Sacher had been reconciled to some extent, and there was intermittent social contact between them for some years before her death in 1978. Paul and Maja Sacher attended her funeral.

Although she was made an honorary member of the BKO in 1951, Annie Tschopp's family has always believed that she never received the public recognition to which she was entitled for her assistance in its foundation and for her supporting role in the founding of the Schola Cantorum Basiliensis. This point of view was later validated by a comment made by Sacher in an interview about his early work with her. 'If it is possible for me to have a bad conscience at all, I have one about Annie Tschopp. She gave so much and received so little.'

★★★

In autumn 1933, a new phase of Sacher's pioneering work reached fruition with the founding of the Schola Cantorum Basiliensis. Initially established as a private teaching and research institute for early music, the Schola was the natural consequence of Sacher's interest in early music.

'The lectures and seminar exercises given [at Basle University] by my honoured teacher, Karl Nef,' wrote Sacher in a publication celebrating the Schola's golden jubilee in 1983, 'helped me realize how inadequate and helpless our attempts to bring early music to life really were. I believe that it was then that the vision emerged which later led to the founding of the Schola Cantorum Basiliensis.'[21]

Sacher's initial vision in the late 1920s of a centre for the study of early music gradually materialized into concrete plans for an institution which was then unique in all Europe, and which was to be the blueprint for similar institutions worldwide in the decades to follow. Its purpose was 'the research and practical examination of all questions which are related to the revival of early music, with the aim of establishing a lively interaction between theory and practice'.[22]

As the BKO's early-music repertoire had grown, so had the debates concerning performance practice. There were questions to which Sacher simply had no answers, and those questions ultimately led to the founding of the Schola Cantorum. There, answers could be researched and found and then made public in both performances and articles. 'One can even say', Sacher's assistant Ina Lohr wrote in an article commemorating the Schola's twentieth anniversary, 'that the problems that arose in the BKO's concerts of early music contributed to the creation of this institution.'[23]

Detailed plans for the Schola had been drawn up by late summer 1932 and Sacher managed to woo financial backing for the Schola's first three years from a number of influential and well-to-do Swiss, including the Winterthur arts patron Werner Reinhart, who had been largely responsible for the mutation of Sacher's Gruppe der Fünf into the Swiss branch of the International Society for Contemporary Music four years earlier. When the Schola's doors opened in 1933, it offered an impressive curriculum taught by a number of early-music specialists, including Ina Lohr, the musicologist Walter Nef, the tenor Max Meili, and August Wenzinger, a leading cellist in Basle in the 1930s and 1940s and a viola da gamba specialist.

However, a few weeks before the first semester began, Sacher was facing a serious problem. The Schola urgently needed students. 'At the beginning,' recalled Marianne Majer, 'there were very few students, perhaps ten or fifteen. Several of them were not musicians. There were actually very few musicians studying at the beginning, because – although today it seems unthinkable – it was something unusual, almost abnormal, to play early music. It was as if you had joined the Salvation Army.'

Majer, who later became a teacher at the Schola, was still a student at the Conservatory in 1933 when she received a phone call from Paul. 'He said, "The Schola is opening now, and we have too few students. If you like, you can take two courses for nothing." He simply wanted students there. I said that I'd like to study Gregorian Chant, because I couldn't take that at the Conservatory, and then church modes. I studied those subjects with Ina Lohr, and the next semester I took another course and paid for it myself.'

The Schola eventually grew to fulfil a variety of functions in connection with early music, but at first the emphasis was on teaching and public performance. The recognition of its performance group in concert and its course-attendance statistics were the criteria on which its legitimacy was initially judged.

In June 1934, four months after the Schola had been introduced to the press, its performance group, drawn from its teaching faculty, faced the public for the first time in programmes featuring instrumental and vocal music from the twelfth century to the seventeenth. The concert's success resounded even in the German and Austrian press, and signalled the beginning of the Schola performance group's national and international concert activity.

'No one could think after such performances that early music was just dead theory,' wrote Heinrich Strobel in the *Berliner Tagblatt* in 1935 after attending two of the Schola's concerts. 'Monteverdi, when it's properly played, is a hundred times livelier than much of that which pompously suggests itself to us as lively today. It simply depends on the spirit with which one performs such early music. The right spirit reigns over the Schola Cantorum Basiliensis. May it do what it can to plant this spirit in young musicians.'[24]

In the Schola's brochure for its first school year, 1933–4, Sacher was listed among the teaching staff. Teaching was an occupation which had always intrigued him. 'I could have studied music history, aesthetics, science, and become a professor. That's something which fascinates me – lecturing, explaining something to people, narrating – and I think I would have been a very good teacher. But that would have been the only other profession apart from conducting which would have really interested me.'

Despite this professed interest in teaching, however, Sacher never taught at the institution he directed for over thirty years. Instead, he used his immense administrative and organizational talents to create and solidify its structure. This meant not only carefully formulating its curriculum, but also selecting those who would implement it. For more than thirty years, he monitored its work in detail, discreetly steering his staff while at the same time allowing them great scope to develop their individual gifts. There is no better example of Sacher's ability to collect the talents he needed to ensure a project's success, and then to co-ordinate them into a functioning whole, than the success of the Schola Cantorum.

★★★

Sacher's musicology professor at Basle University, Karl Nef, was the cousin of Otto Lobeck, who in the 1930s owned the largest private collection of early musical instruments in Switzerland. Lobeck had played many of them, and had kept the collection in excellent condition. When Nef introduced him to Sacher, the meeting proved a blessed union. Lobeck wanted his instruments brought to life by musicians who could play them, and the Schola had a circle of musicians who needed instruments. Within a year of the Schola's opening, and probably at Sacher's suggestion, four of the Schola's young teachers visited Lobeck at his home in the canton of Appenzell, where they performed on his instruments. Excited that his instruments would be used again by musicians of such virtuosity, Lobeck lent his entire collection of more than three hundred instruments to the Schola in 1935 for ten years. At the end of that period, the loan was extended for a further decade.

Sacher's interest in many early instruments, especially the harpsichord, later influenced a number of the compositions he commissioned. There were occasions on which a composer wrote for an early instrument solely because Sacher had suggested he do so. 'If I remember correctly, Frank Martin told me, "I'm writing a work at the moment for piano and harp." And I said, "Why not for harpsichord as well?" I had a strong relationship to the harpsichord, and I thought, if he's going to do something with a plucked string instrument and a keyboard instrument, he can write for the harpsichord as well. And he took up the idea and said yes, he would do that.' The result was Martin's *Petite symphonie concertante*.

With the assistance of the experts he had selected to teach, research, and perform at the Schola, the answers Sacher had sought during the 1920s to questions of early music performance were being found. In fact, the Schola's work was so proficient that it led Sacher to alter his programming strategy for the BKO.

'At first I performed the works of many early composers, not just Bach and Handel but others,' he later explained. 'But after the foundation of the Schola Cantorum I moved away from that repertoire again, because the Schola had more adequate means of performing the music of the fifteenth, sixteenth and seventeenth centuries. I found that with the resources at their disposal they could simply do it better.'

With the Schola setting out to win interest in, and understanding of, early music, Sacher was able to concentrate more fully on winning a public for contemporary music. 'If you think back – 1926, 1930, 1935, the years before the war – when you wanted to perform Stravinsky, Hindemith, Webern, Berg, Schoenberg, the contemporary music of that time, people weren't prepared for it.

It didn't appeal to them, and they weren't interested in it. You had to lead them to it. It was an education. Of course, the concert-goer must never feel that a programme is intended to educate. The concert-goer simply wants to hear music, and doesn't want to be educated. But it was an education, and it took a great deal of time before it was successful.'

The patience that accompanied Sacher's mission over decades was fed not only by his interest in the musical voices of his time, but also by his interest in the people whose messages he presented so painstakingly to the public. 'In my whole life, nothing fascinated me more than man and his secrets,' he wrote in 1975.[25] The personalities of the composers were reflected in the pages of their completed scores. Both curious and secretive by nature himself, Sacher could read in their work their idiosyncrasies, their circumstances – in short, their secrets.

'I think Conrad Beck is a true Swiss composer,' he explained to me in 1993 while searching for examples. 'Beck is Swiss music because the character of the man comes out through his music. You can't avoid it. All these little difficulties in the voices. These little shifts and complications. It's the man who is so complicated, and you find the same thing in his music. I'm telling you this story because in the written score you find the character of the man who wrote it.'

Sacher's preoccupation with his contemporaries' musical language, and what it had to say about them as people, was certainly not shared by all. During those early years, he recalled, 'I made a really strange discovery. There are really very few people who have a need to know the language of their contemporaries. I think it's the most natural thing in the world that I want to get to know the works of a member of my generation who creates musical works in my time. But unfortunately that's not at all normal. People don't want to hear that in concerts.

'I have a good friend, a professor at the university, who said to me, "I think it's wonderful when a concert lasts a long time." Then I said to him, "Professor, that is an error. After a time you're no longer capable of taking it in." Then he said, "No. But I can think about other things so well." He was simply using this background music to hang up his thoughts. But when you really want to take in music, and to confront its content, then your ability to do so is limited. You don't hear what extends past sixty minutes.'

★★★

In the same year in which Sacher's dream of the Schola was realized, his wife-to-be was moving her interest in contemporary art into the public domain. Still grieving the loss of both her young husband and her eldest son, Maja Hoffmann-Stehlin set about establishing a memorial to her late husband's efforts to win public acceptance for contemporary art. In 1933 she set up the Emanuel Hoffmann Foundation, whose aim was to buy works from artists 'who use new means of expression which point the way towards the future, and which are not yet generally understood'.[26]

Maja's double loss, however, had taken its toll. Friends remember that she seemed 'ill with grief', and she had not had time to recover before her marriage to Paul in June 1934. Sacher himself was well aware of his new wife's fragile state of health. Leaving the activities of his orchestra and the Schola in competent hands, he and Maja left Switzerland within a few weeks of their marriage for a period of travel which was to last an entire year. They travelled in Eastern Europe, in Italy, throughout the Mediterranean, to South America and the United States. And wherever they went, Maja drew. 'We travelled for a whole year,' recalled Sacher, 'and she was always drawing on square paper.' What she was 'drawing' was in fact the plans for the home that was to be built for the new couple and Maja's children, of which Maja was the sole architect.

When their journey was over in the autumn of 1935, the family moved into the *Jugendstil* villa that stood near the site of their new home overlooking Pratteln. When construction began, Maja oversaw the building just as she had watched her father do decades earlier. 'It was absolutely unheard of for a woman to be on the site like that, wearing overalls and giving orders,' remembered Alice Bielser, who lived in Pratteln. 'There was a lot of talk about it, but the men learnt to respect her because they saw that she knew what she was doing.'

It was not the first time there had been a lot of talk in Pratteln about what was going on on the hill above. More than a hundred and sixty years earlier, the Basle trader Johannes Zäslin had built his 'robber estate' on that very site. This time, however, the owner was not an outsider but one of their own. For this time, Paul Sacher, the great-great-great grandson of Friedrich Dürr, *Gescheidsmann* of Pratteln, was the lord of the manor.

12

The Lord of the Manor

In late summer 1935, Paul and Maja Sacher returned to Basle where Sacher took on his new roles as the husband of a wealthy heiress, step-father to two children, and the master of the Schönenberg estate on which his new home was being built.

Within weeks of his marriage, he had arranged for his parents to move out of their apartment into an elegant home in the outer Basle suburb of Riehen. It was a two-storey stone house with a generous garden, the purchase of which was financed by his wife. 'I could only do that after I married Maja. I couldn't have done that before,' he later admitted. Anny Sacher, whom Paul had hated to see doing household chores, now had a great deal of help. 'There were four of us,' remembered Susi Bächtold, who was housekeeper and cook for Sacher's parents for more than five years. 'There was a gardener, a girl to do the ironing, someone for the laundry, and myself.'

His parents' new home represented an important step in Sacher's attempt to blot out his life-long dread of poverty. 'I hated poverty in every form,' he confessed to me in 1991. For him, poverty meant things like the smell of too many people in an apartment, the bad smells on the stairways, and his mother's drudgery. Any reminder of his paternal grandmother's impoverished existence as she laboured in a Basle silk factory to support herself and three children was almost unbearable for him. A life of want was not one he was prepared to endure, and his fear of having to do so was a major force behind his successes and his disciplined work ethic.

There was little on the Schönenberg estate to remind Paul of poverty. When the house was completed in 1936, the family moved from the rather dark, high-ceilinged rooms of their temporary home into the more functional luxury of the one Maja had designed for them.

There were large studies, one each for Maja and Paul, on the first floor of the L-shaped house, each fronted with large window panels and situated so that the couple could see each other at work. Below, on the ground floor, there was a small entry foyer with a mirrored niche where guests could check their appearance on arrival or before departure, and make use of silver-backed brushes and combs and embroidered linen handtowels. The foyer led into a hallway from which doors opened into three large rooms. One was the dining room, in which some of Maja's sculptures were displayed. The other two, when divided by a discreetly placed folding door, were a lounge and sitting room. When the dividing door was left open, they joined to become a reception room large enough for soirées and large parties.

All three rooms looked out across the Rhine Valley below Schönenberg, and on to the dark shape of the Black Forest beyond. The windows in the lounge were wall-length glass panels which could be lowered by remote control into the floor, allowing guests easy access to the garden or the patio with its wrought-iron tables and chairs.

The gardens, as carefully cultivated as any public park, contained pines, blue cedars, ginkos and silver birches, which would be interspersed over the following decades with sculptures, including a number by Hans Arp and Sophie Täuber, and an electrically powered fountain and mobile sculpture created by Jean Tinguely. There were rosebeds and, beyond the swimming pool with its adjoining changing pavilion, a vegetable garden. The driveway was lined with rows of rhododendrons which became a mass of pinks and apricots in the summer.

Inside the house, the family rooms were filled largely with modern furniture, some of it bought from the Belgian designer Joe Bourgeois, whom the Hoffmanns had known in Brussels. There were square-based black leather and chrome chairs, and multi-sided, glass-topped tables. On the walls of the downstairs rooms and the stairways hung paintings by Braque, Klee, Picasso, Chagall and others, many bought by Maja on instinct long before their creators became famous.

'Lord of the Manor'

Maja Sacher-Hoffmann, 1934

Asked about his early memories of life at Schönenberg, Dr Georg Martz, a schoolfriend of Maja's son Lukas, remembered with amusement the discrepancy between the white-gloved servants who served dinner, the mirrored bathrooms, the paintings, the luxury, and Lukas himself, whom Martz described as being 'so undemanding'. Maja, on the other hand, who habitually wore heavy gold necklaces, he remembered as being like an empress. The necklaces were heavy waist-length chains of interlinked yellow gold, some ending in large gold pendants. One favourite pendant was flat, and formed in the shape of a bird, reminiscent of an Aztec motif; another took the form of a frog.

It was to Maja – helped by her mother and the faithful family butler, Werner Kocher – that the responsibility of parenting her two children fell. Martz remembered that Paul was more like an elder brother or friend to his stepchildren, and that they sometimes played cards together. There seemed to be no real attempt on Sacher's part to fill the role of a father-figure and the children, particularly Lukas, appear to have been happy about his lack of intervention.

'I don't think he ever tried to assume the role of father,' confirmed Lukas, who was twelve when the family moved to Schönenberg, 'and I certainly never expected it from him. I had quite an independent mind.' As a boy, Lukas's independent mind was preoccupied by things far removed from music. On hearing of his mother's plans to wed a conductor, he had asked anxiously, 'Do I have to take music lessons now?' He had been relieved when the answer was 'No.'

Lukas had showed some early interest in the visual arts, but his passion was nature, a passion which led him in the late 1950s to become one of the initiators of the World Wildlife Foundation, and its vice-president. By the age of twelve he was already following in the footsteps of his great-uncle Hans Georg Stehlin, a zoologist and commission president of the Basle Museum for Natural History for twenty-one years. With a group of schoolfriends, Lukas spent most of his free time out of doors, roaming the forests and fields around Schönenberg or making field trips across the French border into Alsace where there was great diversity of bird and plant life. Occasionally, some of these creatures found their way into the family home.

'I had fish and reptiles and amphibians in aquariums, animals I caught in nature, but I generally didn't keep them inside for very long,' recalled Lukas. Amongst these visitors was a crow which Lukas rescued and named Strauss, which lived with the family for quite a while. 'He was very tame, and used to spend a lot of time in the bathroom, pecking holes in the soap,' Sacher remembered. Another visitor was an ailing duck Lukas found during a cold spell. When it arrived at the house, he filled the tub in his parents' bathroom with water, and built a small hill of stones rising from the water on which the duck could rest. 'In the middle of the night,' said Sacher, 'there was a terrible noise and we all went to see what had happened. The hill of stones had collapsed into the bath and all over the floor, and the duck was very excited.'

Lukas may have enjoyed his early freedom and independence, but some in the Hoffmann family suggest that Sacher's lack of interest in, or ambivalence towards, adopting a parental role was far less ideal for Lukas's younger sister, Vera. 'Paul didn't devote a lot of time to Maja's children – or, rather, his attention was negative,' said a family member who preferred to remain unnamed. 'He criticized a lot, but he never played a real father role. ... After Emanuel Hoffmann's death, Vera didn't receive a lot from her parents, but she bore that.'

In retrospect, Vera Oeri-Hoffmann saw the situation differently. While not denying a lack of parental attention, she suggested that her mother may even have told Paul from the outset that the children were her responsibility, not unlike Anny Sacher's clear-cut message to Gusti Sacher.

'My mother was a very strong woman and – although I don't know this definitely – I am convinced that she said to him at the beginning of their marriage, "They are my children and they will be brought up by me",' Vera wrote to me in 1995. 'And he kept strictly to that, just as he never interfered in the domain of the visual arts which my mother claimed for herself.

'In any case, we had virtually no family life. Lukas and I went to school in Basle and had to leave early in the morning before our parents had got up. We didn't get back home until towards evening, and by then our parents were no longer at home. Often we didn't see each other for weeks, and when problems came up they were solved in writing. But I am quite sure that Paul was happy to have us in the house. [Later, after school and a year in Geneva] I was Paul's private secretary for four years before my marriage. Paul was strict and demanded a lot, but he was also very understanding. He actually had more trust in my ability than my mother ever had, and gave me a lot of encouragement.'[27]

★★★

Despite Sacher's year-long absence, it had been business as usual for the BKO and the Schola Cantorum Basiliensis. Sacher had left the administration of the BKO in the capable hands of Gusti Vortisch, and had elected the musicologist Walter Nef as his deputy at the Schola. He had also entrusted members of his growing network of musician friends with the musical preparation of the BKO's six-concert series during his absence, matching his talent for attracting and selecting the right co-workers with his ability to delegate.

'You see,' he explained in an interview in 1993, 'it's a great art to be able to delegate. It's very important for all collaborators, very important. They have to feel that they are an important part of your life, and they only have proof of that if you give them projects in their areas of competence, if they are allowed to do something themselves in your business, or in your life. It's true that I like to delegate, and I delegate a lot. I had a tremendous workload, and I had many collaborators.'

During the last decade of Sacher's life, he was asked more than once how he had managed his gigantic workload, and he replied, 'I do nothing. Others do the work for me.' While it is true that Sacher delegated a great deal, his intrinsic need for total authority meant that he rarely, if ever, genuinely relinquished control. 'There are many things you can't delegate,' he responded when questioned about the issue. 'You have to do them yourself.'

It has been suggested by one of Sacher's former colleagues from the Schola, the viola da gamba player Hannelore Mueller, that there was another aspect to his delegation. 'At the Schola, Sacher had to delegate. Not necessarily because he wanted to, but because he simply didn't know a lot about early music. Ina Lohr was the expert. Whenever he was preparing a concert of early music, it was she who prepared the scores, and she was present at every rehearsal. If there were a query from the orchestra, a query about anything, he would stop the rehearsal, and say, "Ina, what do you think?" He delegated huge responsibility to her. He needed her.'

Mueller's opinion that Sacher was not at home with early music was shared by others at the Schola, among them August Wenzinger, one of the Schola's co-founders, who later initiated and led the internationally renowned Consort of Viols. 'His conducting technique was clear enough,' Wenzinger conceded, 'but he didn't understand the spirit of early music.'

Whether Sacher agreed with these opinions is questionable. If he was aware of them, the man who had decided as a teenager that he would not display his feelings showed no sign of being affected. And in autumn 1935, as he resumed his conducting activities, he had little time to dwell on what others might consider his weaknesses.

★★★

Sacher's first BKO concert after his return to Basle took place on 2 October 1935, and consisted of four world premières. Three were by composers whose music was already familiar to Basle audiences: the German Wolfgang Fortner, and the Swiss composers Alfred Moeschinger and Conrad Beck. The fourth was a newcomer to the BKO audiences, the Swiss Robert Blum. Since all four works had been completed in 1935, it was truly an evening where the public could hear the voices of their time.

Of the remaining five concerts in the 1935-6 season, one was comprised solely of contemporary works, another was devoted exclusively to early music, and three were a combination of both. But in 1985, Sacher – who had performed mixed programmes of contemporary and early music for decades – voiced his doubts as to the wisdom of this mixture.

'I'm also not sure now whether it's right to make mixed programmes – that is, to mix contemporary music, music which people find modern and foreign, with earlier music. If one is good at it, and makes intelligent programmes, it can be successful from time to time, but not necessarily every time, because each kind of music has its basis in the cultural, spiritual and economic circumstances under which it was written.'

Despite such doubts, Sacher's control of the programming of the BKO concerts, with Ina Lohr's assistance, was absolute. 'He had the reins in his hands,' commented Professor Edgar Bonjour in 1986. Bonjour was vice-president of the BKO Society's board from 1939 to 1969, president from 1969 until 1978, and honorary president from 1978 until his death in 1989. 'Paul', he elaborated, 'put together the programmes and presented them to us. We were allowed to discuss them.'

These discussions, though, rarely led to changes. Sacher did not take kindly to counter-suggestions. 'Of course I knew [how to put together a concert programme] better than the members of the BKO Society board did. That was my job,' Sacher responded irritably when asked about his dislike of having his plans questioned. 'When they made a suggestion, I had a reason why that suggestion wasn't so good, and why we should do it differently. [With the notable exception of the organist Adolf Hamm] the presidents and vice-presidents of the BKO were not musicians but music-lovers. They were the real old Baslers who attended the Gymnasium at Münster Platz and who did their *Matura* there. Afterwards most of them went into business.'

'Every person has their shadow side,' observed Curt Paul Janz, who was a member of the Basle Orchestra Society's music commission board for several years. 'Sacher had his shadow side as well. He was dictatorial when he was standing up for his opinion. One could discuss things with him objectively. But when he had made his decision, that was it.'

In 1935, Sacher's activity as a guest conductor included a highlight in Basle itself. On 26 November he led the Basle Symphony Orchestra (BSO) in a three-work programme of Haydn's Symphony No. 48 in C major, *'Maria Theresia'*; Mozart's Piano Concerto No. 24 in C minor, K491, and Beethoven's Seventh Symphony. The pianist was Rudolf Serkin.

This was not the first time Sacher had been invited to conduct the work of a nineteenth-century master, nor was it the last. He had already conducted Beethoven's Seventh Symphony three times with the Göteborg Symphony Orchestra in Sweden, so he was well-prepared for his début as a Beethoven conductor in Basle. And yet, successful though the concert is reported to have been, it was a full seven years before Sacher was again invited to conduct the BSO. At least part of the reason for this was conflict between Sacher and the orchestra's new conductor, Hans Münch, a former cellist and organist who had been selected as Weingartner's successor after the latter's retirement in 1935.

'We could have had Fritz Busch as Weingartner's successor,' said Curt Paul Janz, who played in the BSO under both Weingartner and Münch, 'but the president of the Allgemeine Musikgesellschaft [General Music Society] at that time was a close friend of Münch's. He secured that position for him.'

'There was a battle,' according to Michaela von Herwarth, who also played under Münch and Weingartner, 'between Sacher and Münch. Sacher went to Münch's concerts, but Münch never went to Sacher's concerts.' This, Janz claimed, was because Münch didn't feel he needed to learn anything from anybody.

Sacher conducted three concerts with the BSO during the Second World War, and was also invited to conduct in its jubilee concert in 1946, but later guest appearances with the orchestra were rare. Although he continued to conduct and record Beethoven symphonies elsewhere, he did not conduct another Beethoven work with Basle's symphony orchestra until 1972.

Throughout continental Europe and in Britain, however, Sacher was in increasing demand as a guest conductor. From the early 1950s onwards, in addition to rehearsals and performances with his own orchestras, it was not unusual for him to conduct ten or more concerts with major orchestras throughout Europe in a year, and increasingly those concerts contained works he had commissioned. Not only did he love to conduct such works, which he could perform with the authority of the composer behind him, but conducting this contemporary repertoire also meant that his conducting ability was less likely to be compared unfavourably to that of predecessors like Weingartner or peers like Herbert von Karajan or Sergiu Celibidache.

In the 1930s, however, the ultimate shape of his conducting career was of far less importance to Sacher than his growing interaction with contemporary composers and the interlinking of his plans with theirs. As early as 1930, his reputation was such that composers of international repute were ready to entrust him with the premières of their new works. One of those composers was Igor Stravinsky.

★★★

Sacher had met Stravinsky on 19 March 1930 at a concert in Winterthur conducted by Ernest Ansermet, which included the Swiss première of Stravinsky's *Capriccio* for piano and orchestra.

Stravinsky was no stranger to Winterthur. Werner Reinhart, who had given Sacher material support for the foundation of the Schola Cantorum Basiliensis, had started his own patronage activity by sponsoring the world première of Stravinsky's and Ramuz's *L'Histoire du soldat* in Lausanne in 1918. He and Stravinsky had become good friends, and a number of the composer's works had already been performed in Zurich and Winterthur on Reinhart's initiative.

Since Sacher planned to give *Capriccio* its Basle première the following October, he used the March meeting to ask Stravinsky whether he would play the solo piano part himself as he had done in Winterthur. He also asked him if he would conduct his *Apollon Musagète* in the same programme, and Stravinsky liked the plan: 'As regards *Apollon Musagète*', Stravinsky wrote, 'I would happily conduct this piece although I have forbidden myself to conduct on the same evening when I'm playing because conducting always tires my hands. Having your promise that you will conduct the rehearsals so that I am spared from tiring my hands in the days before I play my *Capriccio*, I am making this exception.'[28] *

Shortly before going on stage to play his *Capriccio* in the Basle concert, Sacher recalled, 'Stravinsky took me by the shoulders and asked, *"Sacher, croyez vous en Dieu?* [Sacher, do you believe in God]?" I replied, *"Maestro, c'est l'heure* [Maestro, it's time]"*, because we had to go on stage, and that just wasn't the moment to be discussing the existence of God.'

---

* Archive film of Stravinsky rehearsing *Apollon Musagète* in Basle reveals just why conducting tired his hands: he conducted throughout with clenched fists!

Paul with Igor Stravinsky (middle) and Conrad Beck (left) in Basle, October 1930

Another composer of international stature who collaborated with Sacher in the 1930s was the Hungarian Béla Bartók. 'I saw Bartók for the first time in Basle on 30 January 1929, in a concert with Stefi Geyer and the singer Ilona Durigo,' he recalled. 'The concert was composed entirely of his chamber-music works. I was twenty-two years old at the time, and the music made a deep impression on me.'

A year later, Sacher gave Bartók's *Rumanian Folk-dances for String Orchestra* their Basle première (in the same concert in which he introduced the Basle public to Stravinsky's *Suites* Nos. 1 and 2). In 1935, during Sacher's absence, Bartók's Piano Concerto No. 2 was performed by the BKO with Bartók himself as soloist.

In 1936, Bartók spent his summer holidays in Switzerland as he had often done, that year in the alpine terrace of Braunwald overlooking the valley of Glarus. A letter from Sacher reached him there at the end of June, asking if he would be interested in accepting a commission for an orchestral work for strings alone or for strings with a few extra instruments. The BKO's tenth anniversary would be the next year, and Sacher hoped that the anniversary concert could include a new work by Bartók. Within days Bartók replied, saying that he would accept the commission and that he was thinking of writing a work for strings and percussion instruments.

The concert took place on 21 January 1937. It consisted of the world premières of three works, all commissioned by Sacher. The first two were compositions by two of his favourite Swiss composers, Conrad Beck and Willy Burkhard. The third was Bartók's *Music for Strings, Percussion, and Celesta*. All three were dedicated to Paul Sacher, or to Paul Sacher and his Basle Chamber Orchestra.

'The world première in Basle was very good, and had great success, the last movement was repeated', Bartók wrote a week later from Amsterdam to his English publishers, Boosey & Hawkes.[29] For Sacher, Bartók's *Music for Strings, Percussion, and Celesta* was one of the highlights of his conducting career. He described rehearsing the composition as 'exploring a new landscape'.

This success led Sacher and his colleagues from the Basle branch of the International Society of Contemporary Music (of which Sacher had been elected president in 1935) to commission a further work from Bartók for the following year. The resulting Sonata for

Two Pianos and Percussion was given its world première in Basle on 16 January 1938, and was again a triumph; Bartók and his wife, Ditta, performed the piano parts.

In the same year, Sacher commissioned a second work from Bartók for the BKO, asking, 'This time, if possible, could it be a work for strings only?' Bartók agreed, and accepted a further invitation to come and work on the composition in Switzerland as the Sachers' guest. For several years, Maja Sacher had rented Chalet Aellen in the alpine countryside of Saanen for her family's summer holidays. Bartók stayed in the chalet from 2 to 19 August 1939, and he wrote to one of his sons, Béla junior, about his life as the Sachers' guest.

> Somehow I feel like a musician of olden times – the invited guest of a patron of the arts. For here I am, as you know, entirely the guest of the Sachers. They see to everything, from a distance. In a word, I am living alone in an ethnographic object, a genuine peasant cottage. The furnishings are not in character, but so much the better, because they are the last word in comfort. They even had a piano brought from Berne for me. I had been notified that it would arrive on 2 August at 10 o'clock, and, just imagine, it did not arrive at noon or sometime in the afternoon (as usually happens at home) but was actually here at 9.45…
>
> However, I wasn't able to take advantage of the weather to make excursions. I had to work. And for Sacher himself – on a commission (something for a string orchestra); in this respect my position is also like that of a musician of former times. Luckily the work went well, and I finished it in 15 days.[30]

Later in the letter, the composer informed his son that 'the Sachers are coming to see me for a few hours'.[31] When they arrived, recalled Paul Sacher, they found him composing at the piano dressed in his bathing suit, an incongruous counterpoint to the news they had brought him, filled with the threat of war. Although Bartók had seen the Swiss military forces preparing roadblocks in their alpine passes, he had been fairly isolated in Saanen and was unaware of the growing gravity of the political situation. Shortly after the Sachers' visit, he was forced to end his summer retreat and return to Budapest. The work he completed in Saanen was his *Divertimento for Strings*, which was premièred in Basle on 11 June 1940.

★★★

The dividing line between the Sachers' professional relationships with musicians and composers and their private interactions, was almost always an elastic one. Friends like Conrad Beck, Arthur Honegger, and the pianist Dinu Lipatti accompanied the Sachers on family holidays. Others were guests at Schönenberg for visits of varying lengths.

'There were very, very often guests,' recalled Lukas Hoffmann. 'It was quite rare that we were just the family together. The guests were mainly the musicians who came to Basle for concerts. Often they stayed at Schönenberg for the night, or they just came to lunch.'

Some, like the cellist Mstislav Rostropovich and his family, or Bohuslav Martinů, spent far more time at Schönenberg than just the occasional night. Arthur Honegger and his family lived there for almost an entire year. Martinů spent the last weeks of his terminal illness in Maja Sacher's care, and was initially buried on the estate grounds. For years, one of the rooms in the main house was known as 'Pierre's room' because Pierre Boulez stayed there so often. A guest apartment in a renovated farmhouse on the estate was christened by the Sachers' staff as 'Slava's apartment' because of the frequent visits by Rostropovich and his family.

Sacher's musician friends quickly became Maja's friends, too, and as his world slowly encompassed hers she became its new centre. 'She certainly had a very passionate love for him, all her life,' her son confirmed in 1993. 'From the beginning, she subordinated her interests to Paul's interests. She had disappointments later, but they didn't affect her deep passion.'

All who experienced Maja Sacher's hospitality at Schönenberg second the description of her by Arthur Honegger's daughter Pascale as a 'sublime hostess'. Her guests' problems often became her problems, and the smaller ones were usually solved by delving into her 'Magic Cupboard'.

'She had a cupboard which she kept locked, full of little things she bought when they took her fancy,' recalled Pascale. 'Then, when one of the guests would say, "Oh, I've forgotten my cuff links," or "Darn, I've broken a nail," she would disappear and come back with some incredible cufflinks, or a beautiful manicure set in a leather case, and give them as a present.'

'She functioned everywhere as a good spirit, also for the people from the Schola,' remembered Marianne Majer. 'Wherever she found something she could do to help, she did it. For instance, once she was at the final rehearsal for a Schola concert where there was just a small group of musicians performing. She felt that the stage looked too bare, so she bought beautiful flower arrangements to put on either side of the group to close the visual frame. That was typical of Maja.'

Maja's combination of generosity and modesty endeared her to many. 'One time,' said Friedl Beck, Conrad Beck's second wife, 'I invited them both to dinner. Paul was sick and had to cancel. I said to her, "You come, though." She said, "Is it really all right? May I come alone?" Then she came – with a Dali as a gift. She brought me an original Dali painting! This modesty: "May I come alone?"'

Since his early years, Sacher had shown the same generosity. Now, with a like-minded partner and an accessible fortune, he could make the lavish gestures of the olden-time patron of whom Bartók was reminded. By the late 1930s, his life had an international focus, and he had begun to build an ever-widening sphere of influence and patronage throughout the musical world.

But on 1 September 1939, all that changed. The Second World War and the changes it brought presented Sacher with an opportunity to consolidate and enlarge the wealth he had married into, but at the cost of having to restrict his attention and efforts to within Switzerland's borders. As so often in his life, Sacher turned the situation to his advantage.

13

The Share Majority

In May 1938, Paul Sacher was elected to the board of directors of the pharmaceutical company F. Hoffmann-La Roche. The vote by the company's shareholders at their annual general meeting in 1938 to initiate a mere musician into the inside workings of the firm was based on the recommendation of some, but not all, of the company's board members.

For Sacher, the world into which he was catapulted by his marriage to Maja was one of immediate interest. 'For me,' he later explained, 'Hoffmann-La Roche always had a fascination. And I was also somehow inspired because it was so different. I liked moving from one world to another, from here to there, and it did me good. My work in that world taught me a lot, and through it I met people who enriched my existence; amongst business people you can find important people with creative natures, who are really artists themselves.'

Although they never met, an obvious source of Sacher's fascination was the company's founder, Fritz Hoffmann, in whom Sacher recognized many traits of his own. Hoffmann, a businessman with remarkable entrepreneurial vision and flair, had taken over a small pharmaceutical manufacturing plant in 1894 with the German pharmacist, Max Carl Traub, calling it Hoffmann, Traub & Co. When the partnership was dissolved two and a half years later, largely because Traub's business vision and integrity did not match Hoffmann's, the operation was transformed into F. Hoffmann-La Roche & Co, its new name being derived from Hoffmann's surname and the maiden name of his wife, Adèle La Roche.

Both of Hoffmann's parents had belonged to well-established, affluent families of the Basle '*Daig*'. His father, like generations of

Hoffmanns before him, was active in the textile industry, first in silk-ribbon production, and later in the raw-silk trade. Hoffmann's mother, Anna Elisabeth, was a Merian, and it was her uncle, Christoph Merian, who had sponsored the building of the Elisabethenkirche where Els Havrlik first saw Paul Sacher.

Fritz Hoffmann himself was neither a chemist nor a pharmacologist, but his training as a business man had included working for Swiss and German companies which produced and traded in pharmaceutical products. He was fascinated by the emerging pharmaceutical industry and convinced of its economic future and social importance, especially after witnessing at first hand the 1892 cholera epidemic in Hamburg. He recognized a growing need for packaged prescription drugs whose quality and uniformity were guaranteed by a reputable manufacturer. Foreseeing that the market for pharmaceuticals would develop worldwide, he also saw the importance of orienting the company's research and production to consumers' needs, and he used advertising to launch excellently designed, consumer-oriented marketing campaigns of a scale and breadth then unusual for small companies.

Hoffmann's concepts were sound, but their realization was initially difficult. The new company's first year ended with it barely afloat. Hoffmann was faced with the cancellation of his credit by the Basler Handelsbank, and his father's plea to liquidate and try cement instead. Only his tenacity, plus financial support from his mother, his father-in-law and his new financial partner, Carl Meerwein, ensured the survival of Hoffmann-La Roche.

Like Paul Sacher, Fritz Hoffmann had great vision and great style. He understood that his firm would survive only if it could sell its products worldwide, and he set about building the international network which he knew would be vital to worldwide distribution. Like Sacher, he understood the importance of delegation, and he, too, had the ability to read the talents of others. Within a few years, he had used his connections and talent to build up an impressive network of overseas agencies and branches, from Italy to France and Britain, and from the USA to Russia and Japan.

Both Fritz Hoffmann and Paul Sacher were imposing pioneers in their chosen fields, with great talent for feeling out potential opportunities in unknown or unexplored areas. Both could be chivalrous and handsomely generous, but there were great differences in temperament. Whereas Hoffmann was impulsive and tempestuous, often given to public displays of rage, Sacher was deliberately reserved. Whereas Hoffmann's speculative and creative fantasy was said at times to 'verge on rashness', there was nothing rash or reckless about Paul Sacher. His risk-taking and daring were largely premeditated, planned down to the last detail.

Like Sacher, Fritz Hoffmann loved luxury. In the years before the outbreak of the First World War he was increasingly able to indulge that love, because by the turn of the century Hoffmann-La Roche's fortunes had improved dramatically. Its profits were secured by large sales of products like the orange-flavoured cough syrup Sirolin, which was supposed to prevent colds and more severe respiratory illnesses (but which was later proven to be largely ineffective); Pantopon, a painkiller which contained all the natural alkaloids of opium and which is still sold today; or the drug Sedobrol, which provided the basis of epilepsy treatment for decades to come.

Growing sales, supported by a well-organized distribution network, meant that by 1907 Hoffmann was able to move his young family into the Lilienhof mansion in Basle's Gellertstrasse. Built in 1866 by Maja Sacher's great-uncle J.J. Stehlin, one of Basle's foremost nineteenth-century architects, it contained several spacious salons and a dining room which easily seated thirty.

Hoffmann continued to carve out a worldwide empire of outlets for his company's products, and by the outbreak of the war in 1914, Hoffmann-La Roche was active on four continents. But its fortunes were to change dramatically.

Before the war, the company had entrusted its production increasingly to its factory across the Swiss border in German Grenzach. In summer 1915, a German court commission arrived unannounced at the factory and confiscated its accounts. A former employee of the factory's shipping department had shown German customs authorities copies of documents which indicated that small amounts of the Roche product Pantopon had been taken from Grenzach into Switzerland by the Swiss manager of the factory, Dr Emil Barell, without being declared. Believing that the product was destined for France, with which Germany was at war, the

German authorities immediately arrested Barell and took him to Berlin, where he was detained for two and a half years. Hoffmann-La Roche was accused of smuggling its products to Germany's enemies, and was placed on the Germans' blacklist. Only by changing the factory's name to Chemische Werke Grenzach AG, and creating a predominantly German-staffed and -financed enterprise for the duration of the war, was Hoffmann able to ensure that production continued.

This strategy, however, nurtured suspicions in France and Britain that Hoffmann-La Roche was really a German firm. Hoffmann had to prove to the French authorities that he and his wife belonged to long-standing Basle families, and in Britain he fought a battle of negotiations when his company was blacklisted owing to a rumour that it was producing poison gas for the German army. For the rest of the war, Hoffmann's survival strategy was to replace his company's name wherever possible with the names of other people or firms, in order to avoid being placed on French, English, Italian or American blacklists.

A further huge blow to the company was the nationalization of Hoffmann-La Roche's branch in St Petersburg in 1919 – a consequence of the Russian Revolution. This meant that the entire Russian market, representing one-fifth of Roche's global business, was lost, and more than a million francs in accounts receivable had to be written off. Forced by these losses and his own failing health to listen to the suggestion of his associates, Hoffmann allowed the company to be transformed into a joint-stock company in April 1919 with a paid-in capital of SFr 4 million (at the time, around US$ 760,000).

Of the other intriguing and talented individuals who left their mark on the company's fortunes between its founding and the Second World War, the most important was Hoffmann's associate and right-hand-man Emil C. Barell.

Barell had joined Hoffmann's new team in February 1896 at the age of twenty-two, having already completed his doctorate in chemistry. Hoffmann quickly recognized the young man's exceptional talent,* and involved him in the running of the business

---

* As a school-boy, for instance, Barell had single-handedly salvaged his step-father's failing business, and turned it into a profitable enterprise.

to such an extent that, within three years, Barell was no longer working in the laboratories as a chemist, but had been made manager of the company's factory across the German border.

There, Barell set the tone for management which would become Roche's model for nearly half a century. He was brilliant, extraordinarily disciplined, hard and exacting with the company's employees, but generous towards those who fitted in with his wishes or proved their own brilliance and capacity. He extracted the fullest commitment from his co-workers, himself checking in his early years that every employee arrived punctually at work. Under his management, the atmosphere of the Grenzach factory, where he even tried to forbid singing or whistling during work, has been described as 'almost cloister-like seclusion'.[32]

Barell took responsibility for turning Hoffmann's vision into practical, workable forms. He accompanied him on many journeys, or travelled himself as Hoffmann's emissary. When the firm was made a joint stock-holding company in 1919, he was elected one of the three executive directors, while Hoffmann himself became company vice-president and delegate of the company's new board. When illness forced Hoffmann to retire, Barell was elected managing director and, after Hoffmann's death from kidney disease in 1920, he was appointed general director, a position which at that time carried even more power than that wielded by a chief executive today.

The late Swiss historian Hans Conrad Peyer, author of a detailed chronicle of the history of F. Hoffmann-La Roche which was published as part of the company's centenary celebrations in 1996, claimed that Barell showed considerable reserve towards the involvement of Hoffmann family members in the company. Whether he feared a challenge to his control, or whether he felt that Hoffmann's heirs or their representatives could make no real contribution, is uncertain, but there is plenty of evidence that control was important to Barell.

After Fritz Hoffmann's death, a number of changes took place in the company's personnel, only some of which were voluntary. The others were the 'theatrically staged dismissals'[33] of employees who had not toed the line or who, in some cases, posed a threat to Barell's autocratic leadership. The dismissals and the form they took have become part of the Hoffmann-La Roche legend.

A worker might arrive at his office, only to find the door locked and the notice of his immediate dismissal attached to it. Or he might simply be told, '*Prenez votre chapeau, quittez la maison, mais tout de suite. La porte est grande ouverte*' ('Take your hat and leave the building immediately. The door is wide open').[34] On the most dramatic occasions, Barell would take the dismissed employee's hat and stick and throw them out the window, requesting that their unfortunate owner follow his belongings.

Despite Barell's resistance to the Hoffmann's involvement, both Fritz Hoffmann's sons entered the company. Alfred, the younger, was with the company for only a short time after his father's death, and left again in 1921. That year, his elder brother, Emanuel, entered the firm after studying law. Barell himself supervised Hoffmann's training, which began with packing boxes for shipment. Hoffmann, with his talent, ambition and charm, dealt well with Barell's harshness, and in 1925 was appointed director of the Hoffmann-La Roche branch in Brussels, where he enjoyed considerable success. He returned with his wife and young children in 1930 and, as the company's vice-director in Basle, took charge of its overseas branches until his early death in 1932.

Emil Barell's accomplishments on behalf of the company in the inter-war years were considerable. When Hoffmann-La Roche was faced with an economic crisis in the aftermath of the First World War, it was Barell who pulled it through with a discipline and thrift which have been described as 'grim'.[35] It was Barell who reorganized the firm's working structure in the early 1920s to improve its efficiency (and ensure that he made the final decisions in all departments), and who led the firm to a financial highpoint in 1929. It was Barell, too, who led the company through the difficult period of the early 1930s; because of the worldwide depression, between 1929 and 1934 the company's profits fell by 50 per cent. In 1933 he was elected to the company's board of directors, and F. Hoffmann-La Roche became increasingly his, so much so that people said, '*Roche, c'est Barell*' ('Roche, that's Barell').

By the time Paul Sacher joined the company's board in 1938, its fortunes had greatly recovered. From 1933 to 1938, Roche had risen from 'almost nothing' to become one of the biggest vitamin manufacturers in the world, and had continued to profit from sales of sleep-inducing drugs and pain-killers which had been introduced into the market in the 1920s and early 1930s. By 1938, the firm had almost managed to return to its 1929 highpoint of over SFr 50 million in total sales, and it considerably exceeded that figure the following year. The company's future looked bright, but once Paul Sacher saw clearly the circumstances regarding the standing of his wife and her heirs in the company, he was less than delighted.

★★★

When Hoffmann-La Roche was converted into a joint stockholding company in 1919, its share capital had been set at SFr 4 million, divided into 4000 shares of the nominal value of SFr 1000 each. Of these, Fritz Hoffmann himself took 3790, but had to surrender the larger part of them as collateral to the Basler Handelsbank, then presided over by his brother-in-law Albert Koechlin-Hoffmann, who was also the first president of the Hoffmann-La Roche board. The remaining 210 initial shares had been divided between the three newly appointed company directors, one of whom was Barell, and the members of the board.

Six months after Fritz Hoffmann's death, in the midst of the company's fight for existence, the share capital was doubled from SFr 4 million to SFr 8 million through the creation of a further 4000 shares. Since the Hoffmann family were not in a position to buy these new shares themselves, the majority were taken by leading employees of the Basler Handelsbank, the remainder being bought by private individuals and leading company employees.

In 1924, Hoffmann's younger son, Alfred, sold to Barell the shares he had inherited from his father. Barell passed on a small number of them to the Basler Handelsbank, while retaining the majority for the syndicate of Hoffmann-La Roche directors and branch managers he had established after the First World War. Emanuel Hoffmann, however, retained all the shares he had inherited from Fritz Hoffmann's estate. The result was that after 1924 the company's capital was divided three ways, with the Basler Handelsbank functioning as a strong neutral party between Emanuel Hoffmann and the Barell syndicate.

Further changes in the company's capital structure in 1928 and 1931 meant that by 1938, when Sacher took his seat on the board, 16,000 company shares with voting rights had been created, plus 48,000 *Genussscheine* (dividend-right certificates); the latter offered their owners the same dividend as the shares, but carried no voting rights. According to Sacher, at that time Emanuel Hoffmann's heirs owned 'relatively few' of the 16,000 voting-rights shares but a great many dividend-right certificates.

'That was during the war,' said Sacher. 'I was still very young, a greenhorn, totally inexperienced, but I said to myself, "This is nonsense. The family has all its money in an undertaking, and can't even give the orders. If I have all my money in an organization, I want to be in command. I want to be able to say, 'I want him as president. I no longer want him as president.'"'

The Hoffmann family's inability to affect decision-making suited Barell, whose obsession with control had grown to the point that, when a new industrial and administrative complex was built in the mid-1930s, he had a small hidden stairway built next to the director's office, enabling him to enter the plant unobserved before anyone could give the alarm. But, as the Second World War loomed, circumstances within the company changed.

On 10 May 1940, the Germans began their advance westwards, and Switzerland feared it would be attacked. Barell, chief executive (and president of the company's board since 1939), was urged by the management of Hoffmann-La Roche's American operation based in Nutley, New Jersey, to move the company's base to America, thereby putting it under American protection. Ten days later, when the fall of France and Belgium seemed inevitable, he reluctantly agreed. On 21 May 1940, after creating a three-member committee to oversee Swiss operations, he left for New York.

For the next six years, Barell made intensive use of letters, cables and the phone to maintain considerable influence over the company's activities in Switzerland, while ensuring its expansion and development in Nutley. But his absence meant that Paul Sacher was in a better position to seize the advantage when the opportunity arose.

For years, the Basler Handelsbank's large holding of Hoffmann-La Roche shares had meant that no one else could gain a majority share of the company. However, the bank had made large investments in Germany and had incurred huge losses. By the end of the war it was facing liquidation, and was taken over by the Schweizerische Bankverein (Swiss Banking Corporation). While the Hoffmann-La Roche board debated possible courses of action, such as buying back the shares and dividing them amongst the company's shareholders, Paul Sacher had other ideas.

'I am a very curious person. Even though I knew nothing about that world, it interested me. I learnt a lot quickly. I had to. And that included the acquisition of the share majority of Roche for the Hoffmann family. I understood quickly that that was of supreme importance to the value of this family's fortune. No one told me that I needed to do it. My gut knew that it had to be done, and my head.'

Sacher's plan was to purchase the voting shares by exchanging them for larger numbers of the dividend-right certificates, of which the Hoffmann family had a great many. It would be, he told the family, a very expensive operation. 'I said, "The money you have inherited from your father is all lying with Hoffmann-La Roche, but not in such a way that you have the share majority, and so can rule. You have relatively few shares with voting rights, but you have a ton of dividend-right certificates. I want to buy the majority of the shares, and I'll pay for them with dividend-right certificates."'

After the family had agreed to the plan, Sacher recalled, 'I went my way, and turned myself into a clever businessman, and bought shares everywhere, some in large portions. And people were astounded by this musician who arrives, understands nothing, and wants to buy shares. And I continued until I had exactly the majority – 8001.'

In the 1980s and 1990s, Sacher spoke breezily of his feat in regaining what he claimed amounted to the share majority of Hoffmann-La Roche for the Hoffmann family. But at the time he used his tactical skills to the full in pulling off a swift and silent coup.

'Imagine. You have a director sitting there, who's experienced everything, who knows everything. He's experienced fraud – the lot. He sits there in his chair, an important, powerful man, and a young man comes to see him, who's a conductor! And this young man says to the director, "You have two thousand (or I don't know how many) Roche shares, and I'd like to buy them from you." It's a situation which wouldn't work because the director would first say, "How do you know that? I have no intention of selling them. Why should I?" If you approach him like that, really anything can happen to you. He can kick you out and say, "There's the door. You're wasting my time. You don't know if I have the shares, much less if I want to sell them." You can't do it like that. You have to pack it in flowers. You have to package it in such a way that the bank director is amazed. You mustn't let him get angry. I believe that I understood that, in every area, when I was very young.

'I went to the President of the [Schweizerische] Bankverein in Basle, and said, "When the Handelsbank was liquidated, you acquired a couple of thousand Roche shares. I'd like to buy them." He laughed out loud, and then he said, "Well good, and how do you wish to pay for them?" And I said, "With dividend-right certificates. You give me two thousand shares, and I'll give you two thousand five hundred, or three thousand, dividend-right certificates." And so it went. I continued to buy – also small portions, only a hundred, or five hundred. It happened fast because if it had been talked about it wouldn't have gone well. It was my job. I did it quickly. After that, though, I had a certain notoriety among business people, because they said, "My word, this conductor who knows nothing has bought the share majority of Hoffmann-La Roche!"'

Sacher's coup took place largely in 1945. The president of the Schweizerische Bankverein to whom Sacher referred was Dr Rudolf Speich, who held his post from 1944 to 1961. Sacher's claim, however, that he gained the share majority at that time, 8001 shares in all, cannot be confirmed. Copies of the correspondence relevant to his purchases of Hoffmann-La Roche shares from the Bankverein in 1945, for instance, are today held in the archives of UBS AG, a Swiss banking multinational which merged with the Bankverein in 1998. Although the director of the UBS archives confirmed that correspondence between Sacher and Speich existed, he was unwilling to pass on any information about the number of shares Sacher acquired, because the correspondence was deemed confidential. When in the early 1990s I asked Hoffmann-La Roche's former head of finance, Dr Henri B. Meier, for confirmation of

Sacher's claims, he told me I would have to ask Sacher. Sacher, when questioned again, repeated his original story. Further information provided in November 1995 by a long-standing Roche board member suggests, however, that Sacher's version was inaccurate. According to this source, who wished to remain unnamed, Sacher had gained almost 45 per cent of the shares by the end of 1945, but it was not until 1971, in connection with capital changes made at an extraordinary general meeting of the company, that the Hoffmann family's true share majority was reached.

Nevertheless, Sacher's early coup was of such significance that it appears to have overcome Barell's reluctance. Just a few weeks later, at the latter's suggestion, Paul Sacher was voted on to the board's policy-steering committee. From that time on, he was initiated into all the company's internal business by Barell, who made a habit in later years of visiting Sacher on Sunday mornings to discuss his plans and concerns for the company's future.*

Through his actions, Sacher had earned the respect of the business community and his fellow board members. If his appointment to the board in 1938 had been considered in any way a pro-forma gesture to the new husband of the Hoffmann heiress, it was not to remain so.

'It would be a misunderstanding,' Professor Jean Rudolf von Salis told me in 1988, 'for anyone to think Paul simply had an honorary position on the board of Hofmann-La Roche. I know he had a great influence on the company's policies. I have been told by people working in the relevant circles that all these financial people were very surprised by this musician, who trained himself completely in this field, and who displayed great understanding and authority.

'It wasn't a case of someone's husband just sitting there. He was a man with an enormous will, and I was told that he often displayed more understanding than the others, especially in questions of personnel. And that his word counted for a lot in the Hoffmann-La Roche board of directors.'

---

* The written correspondence between the two men was largely destroyed after Barell's death, ostensibly at the request of the latter's family.

14

The Lemonade Years

The wisdom of capitalizing on circumstances was well expressed by Dale Carnegie in *How To Stop Worrying and Start Living*:

> While writing this book, I dropped in one day at the University of Chicago and asked the Chancellor, Robert Maynard Hutchins, how he kept from worrying. He replied, 'I have always tried to follow a bit of advice given to me by the late Julius Rosenwald, President of Sears, Roebuck and Company, "When you have a lemon, make a lemonade."' [36]

Sacher's achievements during the Second World War can be best appreciated from this perspective. Switzerland's isolation – political, geographical and cultural – was his lemon. 'We were totally cut off. Foreign countries were unreachable. There was no possibility of going to Germany, or France, or anywhere. And during this period, when I was concentrated completely on Switzerland, I certainly did more here than usual, because I had no alternative.'

★★★

Under the influence of National Socialism, music in continental Europe had begun to change before the outbreak of war. The works of a number of leading European composers had been banned in Germany, either because the composers were Jewish or because their music and political sympathies were seen as conflicting with Nazism. America, far from the threat of war in Europe, acquired the image of a refuge where creative development could continue, and became the new home of a number of European composers.

In 1933, for example, Arnold Schoenberg was dismissed from his position as director of master classes in composition at the Prussian Academy of Arts in Berlin because he was a Jew. He left Europe that year for the United States, where he lectured at the University of California in Los Angeles; he became an American citizen in 1940, and remained there until he died in 1951. Sacher's friend Paul Hindemith was ousted from his teaching post at the Berlin Musikhochschule in 1938, having been denounced as a 'cultural communist'. Fearing for the safety of his Jewish wife, he moved to Switzerland and then in 1940 emigrated to the USA. He taught at Yale University for several years, and became an American citizen in 1946. He did not return to Europe permanently until 1953.

Béla Bartók is said to have emigrated to the United States because he found the political situation in Europe intolerable. Sacher himself believed that Bartók's departure was permanent, largely because of a letter sent to him by Bartók on 14 October 1940, as he and his wife passed through Geneva on their way to New York.

> We've arrived here safely from disaster-struck lands having received all that is necessary from Mrs Stefi Geyer, and will travel on ... early tomorrow. Maybe we are travelling into the unknown, but we cannot do otherwise. For how long? God knows. I thank you and your wife for your friendship and all the beautiful things that you have given us. For the future I wish you – well, what should I wish you? That your country be protected from being trampled down![37]

Bartók's son Peter, however, claimed that his parents' departure was never foreseen as permanent. It was the course of the war, he said, which meant that their planned return to Europe had to be postponed several times.

The outbreak of war in 1939 put an end to the international activities of many other composers and musicians who remained in Europe. Honegger, who had celebrated a major triumph in Basle with Sacher in May 1938 with the world première of his oratorio *Jeanne d'Arc au bûcher* (Joan of Arc at the Stake), was trapped in Paris under its German occupation. There was no further direct collaboration between the two until after the war. Notwithstanding, the resourceful Sacher gave the première of Honegger's Symphony No. 2 for strings and trumpet in Zurich in May 1942. While on an official trip to Vienna, ostensibly to research an article on Mozart for the French newspaper *Le Figaro*, Honegger had managed to pass the score to a colleague who then took it to Switzerland.

Sacher's own successes as a guest conductor, like that in Paris in 1937 with Bartók's *Music for Strings, Percussion and Celesta* and works by Swiss composers, or his triumphs at the festivals of the International Society for Contemporary Music in Venice and London in 1938, became distant memories as the Swiss borders tightened.

★★★

In Switzerland, other changes occurred in the circle of Sacher's musician friends. One was the death of his great friend and mentor, the organist Adolf Hamm, on 15 October 1938. Hamm had been well known in Basle's musical life, and had accompanied the BKO as organist, pianist and harpsichordist in ten of its first seventeen concerts. Later, as the orchestra moved more towards contemporary music, his collaboration had become less regular, but he still performed with the ensemble in a dozen more concerts before his death. Sacher and the BKO played at his funeral.

In the same period, an event took place in the life of Sacher's friend Conrad Beck which changed the shape of his career and his relationship with Sacher forever. A devoted alpinist, Beck was climbing with a friend in the French Alps when soldiers on a military exercise in the Mont Blanc region triggered a landslide, catching the two men unawares. Falling rocks smashed Beck's thigh and left him unable to walk. Setting his alarm clock at quarter-hour intervals so that he wouldn't fall asleep and freeze to death, he survived a wait of several hours in sub-zero temperatures while his friend went for help; the latter was wearing only his underpants and mountain boots because he had left the rest of his clothes behind for Beck as extra protection.

The accident meant more than a year in hospital for Beck. Paul and Maja Sacher visited him regularly, and during one of those visits Beck told Sacher of his interest in two disasters which had befallen Basle in the fourteenth century: the plague of 1349 and the earthquake of 1356. Both had decimated the city's population, shifting the balance of power and prosperity to the few wealthy families that survived. Sacher saw to it that books on the subject were sent to Beck, and the plans and text of a major oratorio, *Der Tod zu Basel* (Death to Basle), resulted. (When Beck was released from hospital, it was the Sachers who paid for him to undergo further rehabilitation at a Swiss thermal spa.)

Beck's career was affected not only by the accident but also by the war. 'My husband was with Schott publishing house [a German music publisher]. He was one of the few composers who received a monthly wage from Schott at that time,' recalled Friedl Beck. 'He received two letters from Goebbels saying that all he had to do to retain his current status was to prove his Aryan identity, but he wouldn't. As a result his music wasn't allowed to be performed during the war, and he no longer received financial support. Then, while he was still in hospital, the former director of Basle radio came and asked [unbeknown to Beck, at Sacher's suggestion] if he would perhaps take over the musical direction of Radio Basle, which at that time was really small. My husband knew that because of the war he had to stay in Basle – he couldn't return to Paris – so he gave them a conditional yes.'

★★★

Sacher's tuberculosis in his final year of high school meant that he was ineligible for compulsory Swiss military service. However, for at least part of the war he was relegated to the Hilfsdienst (HD), the emergency relief service. Half a century later, the Paul Sacher who had become accustomed to getting his own way spoke of his duties with clear contempt. 'It was idiotic! I was placed in an automobile detachment. We had to collect people's cars, put military numbers on them with stencils, and assign them to the army. Totally ridiculous, to take me [away from my other tasks] for that.'

The war also brought changes to the lifestyle at Schönenberg. With most cars requisitioned by the army, and petrol strictly rationed, the Sacher-Hoffmann family had to organize its trips between Schönenberg and the city with great care. 'Paul had an electric car during the war,' recalled Vera Oeri-Hoffmann. 'It had to be charged overnight, and that was sufficient for one return trip to the city. So he organized himself in such a way that he drove into the city to work and then stayed on for his rehearsal in the afternoon or evening. My mother had to organize herself to do the things she had to do in town at the same time, and then she visited friends, or watched his rehearsal.'

★★★

For the BKO, it was business as usual. Despite the separation from many of his composer friends, in his 1939-40 concert series Sacher was able to present to the Swiss public a number of new commissions which had been completed before the outbreak of war, including Martinů's Double Concerto for two string orchestras, piano and timpani. Martinů had been in the midst of composing the work when he stayed at Schönenberg as the Sachers' guest in 1938. Sacher was not only greatly impressed by Martinů's compositions and the speed with which he composed, but was also greatly moved by the man himself, claiming that he had never met a man 'who was less affected or more sincere'.

Not long afterwards, the outbreak of war forced Martinů to return to Paris, and he could not attend the première of his Double Concerto in Basle in February 1940. According to Sacher, it created a sensation. 'It was a great event. I remember that Honegger was present, and that after the performance he wept, and said, "That is what one would like to have written."'

Parallel to Sacher's work with his Basle orchestra during the war years, plans were being laid for what was to become the second of Sacher's three ensembles.

In 1940, Sacher was approached by Walter Schulthess, composer, pianist, and founder of the concert agency Konzertgesellschaft Zurich, who wanted to set up in Zurich an ensemble similar to the BKO. The idea had arisen largely in connection with the needs of Zurich musicians who could not perform outside Switzerland during the war.

'Walter Schulthess wrote to me one day,' recalled Sacher, 'saying that there were a number of excellent young musicians in Zurich, including some of his wife's students, who would be delighted to play in a high-calibre chamber orchestra, and that his wife would even be prepared to play herself, as first violinist. He asked if I would be prepared to take over as director.'

Schulthess's wife was the beautiful Hungarian violinist Stefi Geyer, whom Sacher had first seen in 1931 performing in a concert of Bartók's music. Bartók had been deeply in love with her and, although she had rejected him as a suitor, the couple remained close friends until Bartók's death. It was for her that he wrote his Violin Concerto No. 1, an outpouring of his feelings. Geyer never performed the concerto in public, but kept it to herself until shortly before her death, in 1956, she sold it to Sacher with clear instructions for its first performance.

'So in this way the Collegium Musicum Zurich was founded and Stefi Geyer was its leader for a long time,' recalled Sacher. 'She was a superb violinist, a major soloist, and an excellent musician, and she brought the fame of her name to the ensemble.' The new orchestra was to cover the same deficit in the musical life of Zurich that Sacher had encountered as a teenager in Basle.

'With the Collegium Musicum Zurich I performed programmes similar to those I performed with the BKO, with one particular difference,' Sacher elaborated. 'In Basle, I also performed a great many works for larger orchestra, and for choir and orchestra. In Zurich, we really limited ourselves to the true chamber-music repertoire, including symphonies by Haydn and Mozart and works by Bach and Handel as well as contemporary music, works of this century which were written for an ensemble like ours.'

The Collegium's first concert took place on 3 December 1941, and its early programmes indicated that Sacher had quickly recognized the synergy that the creation of this sister ensemble could bring to his work with the BKO. New contemporary works, which sometimes needed up to a dozen rehearsals, could now be repeated in Zurich within weeks or months of their Basle performance, or vice versa. Martinů's *Double Concerto* was an early example of this strategy, being performed in Zurich by the Collegium three months after its world première in Basle. On the other hand, several commissioned works were premièred in Zurich rather than Basle. One, Honegger's Symphony No. 2 for strings, had been commissioned for the BKO, and completed in 1941. Honegger managed to get the main score to Sacher soon after its completion, but the orchestral parts were not available for the planned BKO performance in January 1942, so the work was premièred by the Collegium four months later.

Just as the BKO had initially been financed by Otto Senn-Gruner, so a wealthy patron was found in Zurich to support the new orchestra. Shortly after the Collegium's foundation, a society of the same name was created, and Dr Hans Conrad Bodmer became its first president. Dr Bodmer, a member of a famous Zurich family, was a music patron and collector. 'He had the most wonderful collection of Beethoven autographs. He had all that one could buy in the way of original Beethoven manuscripts, and had certainly invested enormous sums in that passion. Dr Bodmer was the first president of the Collegium, and as long as he lived he paid the orchestra's deficit each year.'

Sacher's claim that he never supported the Collegium financially in later years is not borne out by statements made by other Collegium supporters. Dr Bodmer's niece, Mrs Andrea Bodmer, said in 1996, 'It's true that while my uncle was alive Paul Sacher didn't pay anything, though from the very beginning he never accepted a fee for conducting the orchestra. In later years, however, he did pay. The fees for the soloists increased and, despite a subsidy from the city of Zurich in later years, there was mostly a deficit. But he didn't like people to know, so we never talked about it.'

Dr Christoph Krayenbühl, a member of the Collegium's board from 1982–1992, was quick to confirm this. 'Paul's support for Zurich's music life was also material. He didn't accept a conducting fee. And mysteriously, somehow, the Collegium's yearly deficit in the last few years was always covered.' Sacher, however, remained adamant in his claims: 'After Dr Bodmer's death we found no one who would have done what he did. But we collected money from time to time, and always found it. Not from me, but from sources in Zurich.'

Those 'sources' included a handful of wealthy music-lovers who were each prepared to pay SFr 10,000–15,000 a year to support the orchestra and for the privilege of sitting on its board. Among them were the Swiss musicologist Dr Willi Schuh, Dr Martin Hürlimann (who became president of the Collegium's board in 1956) and Heny Winterstein-Bosshard, who later married the pianist Géza Anda.

Dr Christoph Krayenbühl, whose father Hugo Krayenbühl was a pioneer in neurosurgery and also a member of the Collegium's board from 1956–1982, remembered that after Collegium concerts his parents sometimes held receptions for Sacher and his friends at their lakeside home. 'When I was a child,' he recalled, 'Paul Sacher fascinated me. It was his person – enigmatic and fascinating. I was taken to concerts when I was very young – five or six years old – concerts where Sacher was performing new works, and they were terribly exciting. I learnt to understand and enjoy contemporary music, but it was difficult at first. It was Paul Sacher who brought this music into the musical life of Zurich.'

★★★

In 1944, as if his workload were not already heavy enough, the Swiss government appointed Sacher a member of the Swiss arts council, Pro Helvetia.

Pro Helvetia had been created in December 1938 as an autonomous, permanent Swiss institution, whose mission was to preserve and promote Swiss culture both at home and abroad. Its members were expected to participate in a minimum of two of the council's working groups. Although the professional interests of each individual member were considered when appointments to the working groups were made, there were always individuals whose professional interests had little or nothing to do with the subjects at hand.

This was policy on Pro Helvetia's part, and has been defended by Luc Boissonnas, general secretary of Pro Helvetia from 1959 to 1992, as a means of providing an 'important non-professional element'. Important, he said, because Pro Helvetia had not been meant to be an insider affair. This policy, however, was a source of immediate and ongoing concern for Sacher, and one with which he was never able to make friends.

'So I was appointed to Pro Helvetia, and joined Group 4 [radio, film, education, family] and Group 2 [literature, media, theatre, music, visual arts]. There were three musicians [including me]. ... But there were also a lot of other people who didn't understand anything about music. I was horrified at the amateurism. ... Everyone said what they liked, what they thought was nice – really total amateurism! And they always said such stupid things! [After a time] I said, "This is no good. The money we want to distribute is taxpayers' money, given by the Swiss federal government. It has to be done professionally. We can't just decide [according to our personal preferences]. The whole thing has to be thought through and planned on the basis of professional criteria."'

During his fifteen years with Pro Helvetia, Sacher's influence on the organization was enormous. No matter what business was being discussed, the minutes of the working groups' meetings show that he was always prepared and well-informed. In fact, his preparation was so complete that, even when non-musical projects were being discussed, his detailed input and arguments for or against a scheme could turn an initially favourable view into a rejection, or vice versa. When it came to music, of course, his influence was even greater.

From 1938 to 1945 there was little opportunity for Pro Helvetia to promote Swiss cultural activities abroad. Its mandate during that period was reduced to protecting the Swiss cultural heritage and promoting cultural exchange within Switzerland, which included appropriate support for Swiss artists. The council's music group began to discuss the idea of giving limited financial support to composers, and Sacher was asked to prepare a report on the feasibility of Pro Helvetia giving commissions. The report, outlining the advantages and disadvantages of commissioning, was to provide the early guidelines for the council's decisions, and afforded Sacher a new source of power in his role as the commissioning expert. At his suggestion, Honegger received the first Pro Helvetia music commission in 1946 to complete his Symphony No. 3 *(Sinfonie liturgique)* for a fee of SFr 7000.

Since his proposals for the Pro Helvetia commission recipients were researched and presented with characteristic thoroughness, and since he simply believed he knew better, Sacher did not take kindly to his suggestions being questioned. It happened only once. According to Sacher, 'I simply said, "If you refuse this proposal, then thank you very much but you won't see me here again. I will have resigned." I did a really professional job at Pro Helvetia. I spent a lot of time working out how things could best be done. Finally they understood. There was never another proposal of mine which was rejected. You can't ask a professional to work on a problem, and then reject his solution, saying you'd rather have pale blue! That doesn't work.'

Between 1946, when Sacher's choice for the second Pro Helvetia commission was Willy Burkhard, and resulted in the opera, *Die Schwarze Spinne* (The Black Spider), and 1959, when his term of office ended, Sacher's proposals led to the selection of every commission recipient. Officially, decisions were made in co-operation with others, but in practice they were largely his own. And, since those decisions had all the force of his experience and will behind them, no one was likely to question them.

Professor Jean Rudolf von Salis, president of Pro Helvetia from 1952 to 1964, confirmed that 'In practice, he was the most competent man on the Foundation Council. Of course, the proposals of the working groups had to be confirmed by the executive committee – that was a question of organization. But of course we always accepted what he proposed. What else could we do? We couldn't say, "We don't want Paul Müller. We don't want Regamey." There was no question of that. One can really say that Paul Sacher formulated this section of the Pro Helvetia commissions himself.'

Sacher's use of Pro Helvetia as a tool to serve his own ends was not limited to the support of his composer friends. For instance, in autumn 1947 Pro Helvetia received a request from Radio France (Radiodiffusion Française), which was interested in organizing and recording a performance of Willy Burkhard's oratorio *Das Gesicht Jesajas* (The Vision of Isiah) in Paris with the French radio orchestra. The organizers were seeking a suitable conductor, a choir and additional financial support for the concert. Sacher had already commissioned a handful of works from Burkhard and, although it remains unclear whether he had instigated Radio France's initial request, he certainly turned it to his advantage. He provided a plan, a budget and suggestions for the venue. Once his proposals had been accepted, it seemed obvious that only a conductor who had already performed the piece would be sufficiently well acquainted with its demands to ensure a quality performance. From there it was only a small step to accepting the idea that the choir to perform the work in Paris should be Sacher's own Basle Chamber Choir, with Sacher as conductor.

In anticipation of objections to this apparently self-serving proposal, Sacher wrote to Dr Karl Naef, then general secretary of Pro Helvetia, 'I am worried about conducting a concert supported by Pro Helvetia with my choir, and I would like my colleagues to voice their opinions on the matter freely.'[38] Not surprisingly, none of his colleagues felt inclined to dispute the plan publicly, and in February 1948 the executive committee approved an allocation of SFr 15,000 for the project.

A month later, however, there were undercurrents of dissent when Sacher opposed a request from another Swiss conductor, Walter Reinhard, for Pro Helvetia's support for a concert which Reinhard had been invited to conduct with his choir and the Winterthur City Orchestra at La Scala, Milan. That dissent was captured for posterity by an anonymous hand which wrote politely in the margin of the official executive committee protocol of October 1948, 'People were of the opinion, certainly unfairly, that [Sacher] begrudged his colleague the journey to Milan, which was doubly curious since he himself is going to Paris with his choir with Pro Helvetia's support.'[39]

Pro Helvetia later subsidized other ventures for Sacher and his orchestras, including Collegium Musicum's participation in the 1954 Edinburgh Festival, and in 1955 a performance of *Das Gesicht Jesajas* under Sacher's direction at Carnegie Hall, New York.

Another example of Sacher's skilful use of his power at Pro Helvetia involved Conrad Beck. By 1950, a full twelve years after his climbing accident and his initial discussions with Sacher about his plans for *Der Tod zu Basel*, Beck was seeking a way to subsidize the oratorio's completion. Sacher wrote to Karl Naef, informing him that Beck had been planning to write an oratorio for several years, and asking him whether Beck could be the recipient of the 1951 Pro Helvetia commission. In his reply, Naef reminded Sacher that it had already been decided that the 1951 commission should be offered to Othmar Schoeck. According to existing guidelines, the commission could be offered to someone else only if Schoeck refused it.

But Sacher, described by so many as a master tactician, was not to be thwarted. By the time Pro Helvetia's bi-annual report was published that summer, a new variation in the commissioning procedure had been introduced. Two composers, Conrad Beck and Othmar Schoeck, would be commissioned simultaneously, the fees being paid out in two portions over two years. In November 1951, Sacher could write to Beck, '…and then we will talk about the *Totentanz* [the oratorio]. I think I have good news for you!'[40]

It may be argued that Sacher used his position with Pro Helvetia to ensure support for both his own music ventures and those of his composer colleagues. The facts support this view. His domination of the council's commissioning process meant that the composers he favoured, or whose work fitted his music preferences, were given priority. However, it is also clear that he led Pro Helvetia towards greater professionalism; and that he helped channel the resources apportioned to music into sensible support of Swiss composers during the war.

★★★

To the outside observer, the increase in the workload that Sacher carried during the war – his involvement with Hoffmann-La Roche, the Collegium Musicum Zurich, his activities with Pro Helvetia and other music societies, when added to his commitments with the Schola Cantorum and the BKO – seemed too much for any one individual. When asked, however, how he had managed to combine all these diverse interests, Sacher replied that he recovered by moving from one activity into the next, and in the fascination of working with the composers from whom he commissioned. His new family's fortune gave him the freedom to support not only those composers' creativity but also – sometimes – their whims. During the war, one of those whose 'whims' he supported was Richard Strauss.

'In 1944, Dr Willy Schuh [a musicologist and music journalist] rang me up and said, "Strauss has arrived in Switzerland, and is

Paul with Richard Strauss in Zurich, January 1946

very depressed. He's staying in Baden near Zurich, and no longer has any means of support. Couldn't you give him a commission?" I said, "That's not exactly my music, but if he'd like that, yes…" So I went to Baden, and there was Strauss already standing by the door. That was impressive. He was one of the last great German composers. And he told me that he had just read Goethe's complete works for the second time. For the second time! I've never read them…

'Then he said, "My wife would like to meet you, but she's not very well." So we went to her. She was lying in a big bed, this small woman. I had to sit on the edge of the bed. We exchanged a few words, and then Strauss said, "She agrees [to my composing a work for you]." They had probably arranged a sign. Then he asked what strings I had in my orchestra. I told him… Then I asked Schuh, "How much will it be?" And he answered, "Very modest. Five thousand francs." Think about it. It was 1945!'

Shortly before the world première of Strauss's new work, *Metamorphosen*, given by the Collegium on 25 January 1946, Schuh contacted Sacher once more. '"The maestro would like to come to the final rehearsal. He doesn't want to come to the performance." So he came, and on the way he said, "Herr Kollege, could I perhaps conduct the work once myself?" I said, "Of course. Naturally." It was all ready, you see. Everything was already prepared. He sat himself down. He made almost no movement – that is the secret of a great conductor like Strauss. When he makes a movement which is just a tiny bit bigger, it's already almost an event! He played it through from A to Z. He never stopped. Never said a word. At the end he said, "Thank you," and left. In that way the work went through his body again.

'Then Schuh rang again, and asked if I would like to have the score. I said yes, although I hadn't begun to think of the foundation at that time. I asked, "How much is it?" He replied, "The same again."

'Three months later, Schuh rang again and said, "Strauss says that the score you received is one which he wrote, but it is not the original. Wouldn't you like the original?" Then I said, "Very much. Of course." Five thousand. There the story ends. I paid a total of fifteen thousand francs for Richard Strauss.

'I paid much more for Stravinsky.'

15

Uncle Paul

After the end of the Second World War, the borders slowly reopened. Vera Oeri-Hoffmann, who worked as her step-father's secretary from 1943 to 1948, recalled that 'Paul would sometimes leave to conduct a concert. I can remember endless visa applications that I had to fill out for him in quintuplicate, and such things.' From the beginning of 1946, Sacher was able to resume his activities as a guest conductor abroad; in addition, the threads of friendships with musicians living in other parts of war-torn Europe, and those who had emigrated to America, were gradually woven back into the far-reaching net of his contacts. But, by 1946, one musician whose commissioned works had been milestones in Sacher's own career was no longer able to resume his working relationship with the forty-year-old conductor.

★★★

Bartók and his wife had left Europe in October 1940. Their plan had been to remain in the USA for a one-year concert tour but their longed-for return home had to be postponed repeatedly until the end of the war. Letters in Peter Bartók's possession show that, as late as 1945, his father was still considering an eventual return to Hungary, despite the post-war economic and political chaos.

Eighteen months after their arrival in the USA, Béla Bartók suffered an attack of what appeared to be 'flu. The attack passed, but his temperature remained high. A doctor prescribed aspirin. 'Looking back,' reported Peter Bartók, 'it appears that this episode was the beginning of his slowly advancing leukemia.'

While in the United States, Bartók had continued composing. He also participated in a research project on Serbo-Croatian folksongs, sponsored by Columbia University. Milman Parry, from Harvard University, had recorded the songs during several journeys in the Balkans, and Bartók's task was to transcribe the songs from recordings to paper for publication.

In 1943, Bartók was invited by Harvard University to give a series of lectures on New Hungarian art music, but his illness meant that he was unable to complete the series. 'Whether it was two lectures or three, I don't know exactly,' recalled Peter Bartók. 'He wrote more than he delivered – I think there are texts of three lectures, and they have been published. And the outlines of the direction he was going to take with the rest also exist. That was in 1943, and I remember that I had to write a letter in which he told Harvard that he wouldn't be able to continue. He wasn't even able to write the letter – he dictated it. Then we had to leave the place where we were living because it was outside the city limits of downtown New York, and it was hard for a doctor to come and visit us. So we had to move elsewhere, and we never had a proper home of our own after that.'

In summer 1943, the American Society of Composers, Authors and Publishers (ASCAP) became involved in the family's precarious situation, and sponsored a summer sojourn for Bartók at a nursing home by Lake Saranac in the Adirondack mountains in New York State. It was there that Bartók composed his *Concerto for Orchestra*, a commission from the Serge Koussevitzky Foundation for the Boston Symphony Orchestra. Bartók had at first refused the commission, feeling that he was too ill to complete a new work. However, Koussevitzky told him that the foundation board's decision was binding, and that the money would be paid whether the work was completed or not. His vigour temporarily renewed, Bartók completed the concerto in 1943.

'I remember in a letter, some time in the summer, my father wrote to me and said that the big news was that he was working on the commission,' recalled Peter Bartók. 'I had rented a room in New York that summer, for about $8 a month, and had found a job, so we all lived at separate places. My mother rented a small room on 57th street, and that's where she gave her piano lessons. In the autumn, my father was put up in a hotel, and then for the winter he was sent to the south, to another nursing home in North Carolina, and that's where he wrote the Sonata for Unaccompanied Violin, a commission from Yehudi Menuhin.'

According to Peter, the Koussevitzky commission enabled his father to start composing again in what proved to be the last two years of his life. More than a year earlier, in May 1942, Bartók had responded thus to the query of his English friend and publisher, Ralph Hawkes, as to why he wasn't composing:

> My health is, I am sorry to say, in a rather bad state. Since the first days of April I have an elevated temperature. Even after a rather costly 6-days examination in a hospital, doctors are unable to find out the cause. I feel now as if [I am] on a deserted island where no doctors, no drugs are available! Some general remedies which everybody knows are recommended – good food, rest, no worrying, change of climate – most of which cannot be done because of lack of money. All my reserves have dwindled away, and we three are living now on my $245 a month salary at Columbia University. This makes me rather low spirited, very weak, and hampers me in my work. Therefore, I really don't know if and when I will be able to do some composing work. Artistic creative work generally is the result of an outflow of strength, high spiritedness, joy of life, etc. All these conditions are sadly missing with me at present. Maybe it is a breakdown. Until 60, I could marvellously bear all annoyances and mishaps. But lately, I have often wondered how long I will be able to endure all those sad experiences I continually was exposed to. Maybe I have reached the limit.[41]

Some of Paul Sacher's critics have suggested that he should have helped Bartók in his plight in America, because his own career had benefited so much from the works commissioned from Bartók. However, the claim that he ignored Bartók's plight is unfounded. Although there was a postal service between Britain and the USA during the war, continental Europe was sealed off from both those countries. Neither Sacher nor Stefi Geyer had any inkling of

Bartók's predicament; moreover, said Peter Bartók, even if Sacher had known, he would have been powerless to help.

'No one outside our immediate circle in New York, especially no one my father knew in [continental] Europe, could have had any idea what his circumstances were in the USA. Paul Sacher could not have known, nor would he have been able to do much to help, since the problem was mainly my father's incurable illness.'

Not only that, but Bartók was a proud man who accepted money only for work completed. He was unwilling to accept help even from his own son. For part of the duration of his father's illness, Peter Bartók was conscripted into the US Navy after applying for US citizenship. When he was released the summer before his father's death, he found the money he had sent home from his wages each month lying almost untouched in a bank account.

Shortly before Bartók's death, he and his family were served an eviction notice by their landlord because Peter was sleeping temporarily on the floor of what was stipulated as a two-person apartment. By this time Bartók was so ill that his doctors finally insisted that he be hospitalized.

'The doctor came,' recalled Peter Bartók, 'and said that my father had to go to hospital right away because there they could help him. My father asked, "Can I go tomorrow, and not today, because there is something I want to finish, there is some work I want to do." But the doctor said, "It's very important that you go now because by tomorrow it may be too late." To me this sounded like they had a way to help his illness, so I told my father he should go if the doctor could help him, and he said, "All right."

'An hour or two later the ambulance came and took him away, and [while waiting for the ambulance] I found out what the work was that he wanted to do. He was orchestrating the Third Piano Concerto, and he was two pages from the end. In one more day he would have finished. But it was my mother's next birthday present, and he didn't want to mention it to the doctor in front of her. He couldn't tell him what it was he wanted to do. That's why the last two pages are not orchestrated by him. ... To him the experience of being in a hospital was very distasteful, and he couldn't do the work. He had me draw the seventeen barlines on the manuscript paper, so that if someone else finished the orchestration he would know how many [measures] there were left to fill – where it had to fit. And then he wrote, "This is the ending."

Béla Bartók died five days later, on 26 September 1945.

A month afterwards, Sacher returned to the chalet in Saanen where Bartók had composed his *Divertimento for String Orchestra* and wrote an eulogy which he entitled *In Memory of Béla Bartók*. His enormous respect for what he described in that eulogy as the composer's 'crystal-clear mind, pure heart and Promethean spirit'[42] was evident on many later occasions when he spoke about their work together. It was evident, too, more than half a century later at Sacher's own funeral: the music included two movements from Bartók's *Music for Strings, Percussion and Celesta*.

***

In January 1947, the BKO celebrated its twentieth anniversary. Its concert to mark the occasion was a celebration not only of the orchestra and its conductor but also of the restoration of international communication. It consisted of the world premières of Sacher's first post-war commissions: Martinů's *Toccata e due Canzoni*, Stravinsky's Concerto in D minor for string orchestra, and Honegger's Symphony No.4 (*Deliciae basilienses*). The celebratory mood was articulated by Martinů in an article about his new work. 'After several years I am returning to Europe with a new work and a world première. That has almost symbolic importance for me. During my sojourn in America, I composed five orchestral symphonies. Now I am returning with pleasure to my favourite [musical] form, the *concerto grosso*.'[43]

And then, in the midst of Sacher's return to international activity, a meeting took place which was to show once more the extent of his ability to remain silent, to keep secrets, and, against any and all odds, to do that which he wanted to do. The meeting, which took place in Switzerland on an unknown date in the late 1940s, was between Sacher and his wife's younger cousin, the Countess Nina von Faber-Castell.

***

By the end of the war, Paul and Maja Sacher had been married for over a decade. Despite the synergy that emanated from their shared support of the visual and performing arts, and the deep mutual respect that was the basis of their friendship, certain of Paul's traits were becoming a source of concern for Maja. Having spent so much of his young life solving his own needs in silence, he appeared to have great difficulty sharing them with others.

'He never showed his needs,' explained Pascale Honegger, 'and that was perhaps also one of the problems with Maja … She would have liked him to say more. It was Maja who mentioned to me that Paul was a Pisces and that he didn't talk.'

Born on 28 April, Sacher was actually not a Pisces but a Taurus. Maja's comments to Pascale suggest that she had read the horoscope drawn up for Paul nearly two decades earlier in 1928 by his friend Max Luginbühl. It was a double horoscope, because Luginbühl claimed that the effect of Pisces was so strong that Sacher displayed not only the traits of a Taurus but also those of a Pisces. When Paul showed me that horoscope in the late 1980s, its tremendous influence on his perception of himself was clear: I recognized dozens of phrases or sentences I had heard him use to describe himself during the fifteen years I had known him.

Among many accurate forecasts of Sacher's personality, talents and achievements to be found in the horoscope is his preference for the sound of strings, explained as a characteristic of the Pisces man. The Pisces subject's tendency to dream, and his need to harness his intellect to those dreams to create order in them, is discussed repeatedly. But, although mention is made of his need for privacy to develop his creative spirituality, Maja's idea that a Pisces man would probably have difficulty in communicating is not mentioned. Rather than a fault 'lying in the stars', it seems far more likely that, given the strength of his teenage resolve to communicate and share his feelings only on his own terms, Sacher's unwillingness to talk about his needs was selective and deliberate.

From their earliest meeting, however, Countess Nina von Faber-Castell was a woman with whom Sacher seemed able to communicate with the greatest of ease. Nina was Swiss, a descendant of the Von Sprecher family from Maienfeld in Graubünden. The family was a well-established one, with an illustrious history of members who had been high-ranking military officers in the Swiss and Austrian armies. Nina, a beautiful, vivacious and talented young woman, who had studied the piano in Berlin in her late teens, had married young, and well. In 1938, aged twenty-one, she had joined Germany's aristocracy by becoming the second wife of Count Roland von Faber-Castell, heir to the fortunes of the pencil company Faber-Castell.

Nina's life after her marriage must at first have seemed like that of a fairy tale princess. During their courtship, the Count is said to have sent her a hundred roses a day. After their marriage, they lived in the Faber-Castells' *Jugendstil* castle in Stein near Nurenberg. One section of the castle had been built in the 1840s by the 'Pencil Baron', Lothar von Faber, while the later neo-Romanesque building called the 'New Castle' had been added in 1906. An entire traincar-load of coal was needed each day to heat the festive halls and salons of the two buildings.

The immense sum of DM 3 million had been splurged in 1906 on furnishings for the castle, so that its interiors took on fairy-tale elegance and opulence. The main entrance hall, with its solid marble pillars and vases, the costly *Jugendstil* mosaic inlays of mother-of-pearl and precious foreign woods in intricate designs, and the ceilings decorated with gold and silver stucco, remain unequalled in the late Art Nouveau architecture of the early twentieth century. Nina had three reception rooms, a library, a study, a private cloak-room, dressing room and bathroom for herself and, when these rooms no longer sufficed, there was the winter garden, renowned for its winding paths and streams, its exotic Far Eastern trees, plants and birds, its grotto and oriental pergola.

At the outbreak of the Second World War, the family – Nina, the Count, and the four children from his first marriage – were spending the summer as usual at the Count's hunting lodge on his estate in Dürrenhembach, sixty kilometres from Nurenberg. During their absence, German soldiers occupied the castle and remained there until shortly before the end of the war, so the family was obliged to remain on the estate.

'I think Germany and the Second World War were a kind of nightmare for her,' explained Nina's eldest son, now Count Anton von Faber-Castell. 'She had wanted to return to Switzerland when the war broke out, but she couldn't go because she was caring for the children from my father's first marriage.' Then in 1941 Anton, the first of her own children, was born, after which she was tied to the hunting lodge and its surrounding woodlands for the remainder of the war.

Count Roland von Faber-Castell had studied forestry and agriculture, and was greatly at home in his vast woodlands, which stretched for more than three thousand hectares from the artificial oasis of blossoming gardens in which his hunting lodge had been built. He was a kind, generous, gentle, principled man, who apparently shied away from conflict to the extent of asking one of his business associates to reprimand his younger son, Andreas, for a bad school report.

'He knew every plant, every tree,' Sacher said of him. 'He was a good hunter, and knew every animal. He was a real country nobleman, and had a huge estate and many assets. He understood about that. He managed his estate very well.'

The isolation of Dürrenhembach, however, was not easy for a young woman who preferred the excitement of the cultured city life of Berlin in the mid-1930s, and who did not share her husband's affinity with, or interest in, nature. And then, to make matters worse, early in the war, the Count – an officer with the German Wehrmacht (armed forces) – was ordered by his superiors to Stalingrad.

A superb horseman, the Count had been an officer in the cavalry of the Reichswehr (German army) when he was a young man. With the outbreak of the Second World War, he became a tank driver in the Wehrmacht, although he never officially became a member of 'the Party'.

'My father always made a very big distinction between the Wehrmacht and the Party. He was never in the Nazi Party,' explained Count Anton von Faber-Castell. 'But he [still] felt a duty to the oath he had made as a very young man in joining the Reichswehr.'

Fortunately for both himself and his wife, the Count went down with typhus en route to Stalingrad and had to return to the west. Of the hundreds of men who had served with him and who went on to Stalingrad, only a handful returned. After he had

The future Countess von Faber-Castell, Nina von Sprecher

Count Roland and Countess Nina von Faber-Castell in 1938

recovered, he saw active service in France and in Poland until his wife determined upon a strategy to have him recalled. Knowing that no one would want to risk the collapse of an important German company because its director was absent at war, she claimed that the Count was needed at home to supervise Faber-Castell's activities, and he was duly recalled. While he involved himself once more with the pencil business he had inherited, Nina's plans for a return to Switzerland were hatched in secret.

The factors that ultimately led to her departure from Germany are given variously by different family members, and the reasons were obviously complex. Nina's daughter Katharina, who was born later in Switzerland, believed that the war and the Count's frustration with the political and social situation led to growing differences between the couple. Her brother Andreas saw it differently. 'Mother was an adventurer. She was always a woman who looked for other things, and for action. I think my mother was a woman who was never satisfied – with herself, or with life.'

Whatever the real reasons, at the end of the war Nina returned to Switzerland. There she made the acquaintance of Paul Sacher, who was greatly taken with her, and an affair began which was to last for more than three decades. It became a saga of intertwined relationships which was to be kept secret from family and friends for years; in the case of Count von Faber-Castell, possibly for a lifetime. Sacher was adamant, however, that the relationship did not grow out of any weakness in his marriage. It was simply a case of his and Nina's mutual fascination with each other.

'She was a fascinating wench,' he said. 'She was beautiful, vivacious, slender, bright, educated, musical, talented. She was a remarkable woman.'

Nina established her new base with the Count's children in the wealthy town of Küsnacht, on the shores of Lake Zurich, eight kilometres from Zurich city centre. The three children spent their primary-school years in Küsnacht, and then their high-school years largely at Swiss boarding schools. The Count continued to pay regular visits to his family, and the children spent most of their school holidays roaming the woods around the hunting lodge in Dürrenhembach, living carefree, privileged lives. It was years before either of the Count's sons with Nina had any inkling of the true nature of the relationship between their mother and the man they came to know as 'Uncle Paul'.

Because of the Collegium's rehearsals and concerts and Pro Helvetia's meetings, there were many reasons for Sacher to make the sixty-kilometre journey to Zurich. With time, he organized his life in such a way that he could spend regular weekends there, often staying at the Countess's house where his relationship with her children became firmly established. Count Anton von Faber-Castell recalled having made Sacher's acquaintance in the mid-1950s. 'He was like a nice uncle.'

'I have to say that all my memories of Sacher are very positive,' added Andreas von Faber-Castell. 'He was really like a father-figure. He was virtually the only uncle I ever had.'

In 1952 Nina von Faber-Castell had a daughter, Katharina. The child was adored by Count von Faber-Castell, who indulged her every whim. 'I was very spoilt,' Katharina admitted in 1987. 'The Count visited us at weekends, and we went to Hembach on holidays. When I wanted to ride, I rode. And when it rained too much, he had an indoor riding hall built. Can you imagine that? The riding hall was built for me! And I sat next to him at the table and I could eat whatever I liked.'

The riding hall, larger than a school gymnasium, was not the only gift the Count showered upon Katharina. There was a merry-go-round, big enough for two children actually to ride on. And a photo in Count Anton von Faber-Castell's possession shows an infant Katharina 'driving' on the lawns of the hunting lodge in a child-size, custom-built red Mercedes.

Katharina's early memories of Sacher, like those of her elder brothers, are of a kind uncle. 'For me he was a totally minor person, my godfather. As a child, I saw him occasionally. My mother always smiled a lot when he was there, and I found that silly. He was always close by and would ask, "Can you already read? Can you read books?" and so on. And I thought, "What does he want?" I found him kind, but exaggeratedly so. He busied himself with me, sat on the chair and looked at me...' Eventually Sacher's attentions made sense. 'I knew when I was eleven. ... One day I asked my mother whether he was my father, and she said, "Yes." I thought, "Good. That's OK," but it didn't move me greatly.'

For Sacher himself, the births of Katharina and, nine years later, his second daughter, Cornelia, were associated with considerable conflict because he knew that he could not live with them and their mother. 'Nina asked no one. She never asked me if I wanted a child,' he said. 'I told her [from the beginning] that I didn't want children, but then, when I was away on holiday [with Maja], and she knew that she was rid of me for four weeks, she rang me and said, "Maybe you don't know yet, but I'm expecting a child." She always [gave me such news] like that.'

Sacher's reasons for not wanting children were, he claimed, 'honourable'. 'I didn't want to have children if I couldn't show myself to be the father.' For both Katharina and Cornelia, it was Count von Faber-Castell who fulfilled the role of father-figure in their early lives. Sacher continued to be the kind, strangely interested uncle who visited them on weekends, and it was not until her mother divorced the Count in 1969 that Cornelia at last learnt who her real father was.

'I was eight or nine years old, and my mother probably wanted to comfort me because the divorce didn't suit me. Although Papi [the Count] was seldom with us ... I always went to Hembach in the holidays ... And so I thought, "Now everything is ruined. No more Hembach, etc." I wanted order in the family, and I wanted a father. Then my mother said, "But you still have a father" – and she told me that Paul was my father ... Then I asked him if I could call him Father, or Papi or something like that, and somehow it pleased him that I did that.'

The complex and clandestine nature of the couple's relationship meant that it was also successfully kept from Maja Sacher for several years. When she learnt about it, said her daughter, Vera, it was by coincidence. The realization of her husband's betrayal was terrible for Maja. It was also considerable for her children on her behalf. When asked about his feelings on learning of the affair, seventy-year-old Lukas Hoffmann's eyes still filled with tears at the memory. 'It was not an easy matter. My mother only rarely talked about it. Her position was always, "He will come back. You will see. He will come back."'

Although Sacher remained in the marriage, continuing to love and admire his wife, he never did 'come back' in the way in which

Maja Sacher hoped. Instead, she slowly learnt of, and assimilated, the events of his 'other life', often years after the particular incidents had occurred. Nelly Sacher recalled conversations during a holiday with Paul and Maja in the 1960s after both daughters had been born, which illustrate the complexity and secrecy of the whole affair.

'During a walk one day with Maja, she told me that Paul had had a daughter with Nina. The next day I went for a walk with Paul. He told me that he had two daughters with Nina! Within a day it went from one daughter to two. And there was a nine-year difference between them. Probably all Basle knew, but I didn't.'

The knowledge of their true father's identity did nothing to impair the close relationship that both girls had with the Count. Nor does it appear to have affected the admiration the Count's sons felt for their 'uncle'. Andreas von Faber-Castell, for example, didn't become aware of Paul's real relationship to the girls until he was in his late twenties. And then, he explained, he couldn't possibly have been angry with him. 'It was because I liked Uncle Paul too much. I mean, it didn't faze me at all. On the contrary, I had to smile to myself. Uncle Paul did it so well. … He was just too important a part of my life. Maybe for him it wasn't so important, but he played a bigger role than he actually realized with us children. He was there. Looking back at it, as far as I'm concerned he was a gentleman and a scholar. He was almost a role model for me.'

A major unanswered question in the complex array of relationships is whether the Count himself ever knew that his beloved Katharina and Cornelia were not his daughters. Although Sacher never spoke directly to the Count about the situation, he believed the Count knew the truth and had once indirectly tried to show his acceptance.

'There was an occasion when the wife of a German duke was expecting the child of another man. "That stupid so-and-so," Roland said of the Duke, "doesn't understand that it's good when better blood comes into the family." And I believe he thought, in the case of these two girls, that it was good for the von Faber-Castell family to have two bright and pretty girls joining it. And it simply didn't bother him that [they were mine].'

Other family members did not agree. 'I don't think he knew,' Andreas von Faber-Castell told me in 1993. 'My mother was quite a woman ... The conversation I had with my father around the time of his divorce led me to think he didn't know.'

Sacher's public recognition of his daughters took place only gradually through the 1980s, with many of his closer friends learning of his true relationship to the girls or even of their existence only after they were grown women. Before that time, to the world at large Sacher was only 'Uncle Paul'.

16

The Catalyst

'Few other countries have done so much for the development of contemporary music as Switzerland. ... For example, consider what a man like the Basler Paul Sacher has done. ... Paul Sacher – quite apart from his capacity as an interpreter of music – is probably the most important collector of music and one of the most important catalysts that the world of music has ever had.'[44]

Alexander Pereira's statement to a Zurich newspaper in 1992 during his reign as director of the Zurich Opera House is typical of assessments made by observers of Sacher's overall achievement. Sacher's interactions with hundreds of musicians and artists did indeed have a catalytic quality, with his material and moral support often leading to the realization of others' plans or dreams. The Swiss artist Jean Tinguely described Sacher in this regard as 'a medium through which the creativity of countless artists was able to blossom'.

Sacher himself saw the situation less dramatically. 'I didn't want to be a catalyst. It's just the result of certain activities. It was not my intention, it just happened. All I have done as a conductor, and in giving commissions – I haven't done any of it out of theoretical reflections. There was no theory. It was simply life.'

Though he contended that there had been no theoretical reflections, there were no random choices. If he was convinced of an artist's talent, or if the artist interested him as a person, he gave unstinting support. This was nowhere more evident than with Arthur Honegger.

Sacher had first met Honegger in Basle when the latter attended the Basle première of his oratorio *Le Roi David*, performed by Sacher and the BKO in 1929. 'He was very impressed by our performance,' recalled Sacher proudly. 'He not only told me that, there's also a letter to Vaura [Honegger's wife, Andrée Vaurabourg], in which he talks about it. Then we got to know each other better, and he began to write works for me. ... We developed a very close relationship, which had to do with the fact that Maja got on so well with him, and that I got on well with Vaura.

'He had the handwriting of an architect, an engineer, and I would say that he always thought like a masterbuilder. His music always had a perfect form. Composing was the most important thing for him, but he certainly suffered for his profession. Whoever composes has to come up with something wonderful every time. That's no fun. But he had a very sensible approach to it. He said, "When I write a symphonic work or a cantata, that's like when a writer writes a poem. When I compose film music, that's like a writer when he writes [for] a *feuilleton* [the review/ lifestyle section of a newspaper]. That's part of the business." And he told me that he had learnt a great deal from writing film music, that when one had only three minutes and twelve seconds for a piece, one learnt a lot.'

The close friendship that developed between Sacher and Honegger led to their families spending a great deal of time together. Honegger's daughter, Pascale, had vivid memories of the holidays she and her parents spent with the Sachers, particularly one at the end of the war in Sils Maria in the Engadine.

'There are photos of Paul, my father and the pianist Dinu Lipatti,' she recalled. 'Everyone played *boules*, and they ate a ton of chocolate – poor Maja just didn't know how to get [them] enough of it! It was just after the war and these gentlemen wanted to eat chocolate every day, even though chocolate was still rationed. ... They were happy men who lived and played with great passion.'

Sacher's interest in Honegger extended beyond his music to his private life, which in some aspects was as complex as Sacher's own. He was particularly intrigued by the circumstances of Honegger's marriage. After their wedding, Honegger's wife had said to him, '*Alors, à demain. Je rentre maintenant chez Maman* [Well, see you tomorrow. I'm going back to mother now].' Although they had apartments near each other, they never actually lived together. 'Pascale lived with her mother,' Sacher said. 'Honegger lived alone in his apartment, but he went to have lunch with them every day.'

Paul with Arthur Honegger (middle) and Dinu Lipatti (right) in Gstaad, 1946

But it was Honegger's music and Sacher's total understanding of it which really cemented their friendship. 'I had a special affinity for his music. The *lapidare* element appealed to me, and also his rhythms. The harmonies, too. They all appealed to me. His music was for me, in the good sense, without mystery. I understood it immediately. Then we had an enormous success together with *Jeanne d'Arc au bûcher*, the world première in Basle, and then in Zurich, and then at La Scala in Milan, and so on. He had great trust in me, and we experienced a great deal together.'

Pascale said of their relationship, 'I think that they understood each other very well at two levels: at the level of music, and at the level of work. My father understood Paul's personality very well, and one even sees that in the works he wrote for him. They always have a quality of precision. He knew that with Paul he could make music almost like Mozart – like the Fourth Symphony, which is the most difficult. With Paul he could do that. When he composed for others he didn't write in exactly the same manner. If he was writing for [Charles] Münch he didn't write as he did for Sacher, because Münch wouldn't have been able to do things as impeccably, as precisely. ... Paul and my father understood each other very, very well.'

Between 1939 and 1953, Sacher commissioned four works from Honegger: the oratorio *La Danse des morts* (1939), Symphony No. 2 for string orchestra (1941), Symphony No. 4 '*Deliciae basilienses*' (1946), and the *Cantate de Noël* (Christmas Cantata) for solo baritone, choir, children's choir, orchestra and organ (1953). In addition, Sacher was also involved in the world or Swiss premières of other works by Honegger, such as *Jeanne d'Arc au bûcher*.

Their synergistic relationship meant that Sacher had many opportunities to influence Honegger's work. When, for instance, the composer wanted to pay hommage to Basle in his Fourth Symphony, Sacher suggested that he use the folksong '*z'Basel a mim Rhy*' (In Basle on my Rhine). Honegger took up the idea, and incorporated the song into the slow movement, where a horn plays the whole melody.

Paul Sacher richly rewarded those he favoured, and for Honegger, whose life and music touched him deeply, his support and generosity were unlimited. Honegger's sixtieth birthday in 1952 was celebrated in Basle with a BKO concert dedicated entirely to his compositions (*Cries du Monde* and Symphony No. 5, '*Di tre re*'). There was support of other kinds as well when, during a sojourn in the USA in 1947, Honegger had a heart attack. Although he recovered sufficiently to continue composing, his general health was impaired. 'He composed a number of pieces [after the attack],' recalled Sacher, 'including his Fifth Symphony and the *Christmas Cantata*. And he spent the second last year of his life [1954] here at Schönenberg with his wife and daughter. A whole year! Maja had to make him his special diet – he was only allowed to eat '*Rüebli mit Wasser*' [carrots and water, i.e. boiled vegetables]. Then he wanted to go home to Paris to die.

'At the end, we went to his funeral. The French government gave him a state funeral, although he was Swiss and never became a French national. He was a true, dear friend, an intimate friend, with whom everything was natural.'

★★★

Sacher's personal taste, the depth of his interest in individual composers, and his ability to understand their music were the primary criteria which influenced his commissions and the inclusion of works in his concerts; the importance of a composer's output from a musical-historical perspective was secondary to these criteria. This is demonstrated particularly clearly by the fact that not one of the three proponents of the so-called Second Viennese School was included in his impressive list of commission recipients. Despite the impact of their compositions on the development of twentieth-century music, Arnold Schoenberg, Alban Berg and Anton Webern never received commissions from Paul Sacher.

In answer to the inevitable question 'Why not?' Sacher often responded: 'Apart from the reality of my strong affinity for Stravinsky's music, the reasons lie not in the music, but in life. I never met Schoenberg – that's very important. Anton Webern spent a few days in Basle as my guest. I spent time with him. I found his music the most accessible. I have performed some of his works, and I would conduct his works again any time. But this music simply wasn't the *Erlebnis* [experience] for me that Stravinsky was. Stravinsky's works jumped out at me. There I didn't have to search. But the most decisive fact was certainly that I didn't know these people at all, or [knew them] too little.'

In the same context, Sacher often explained that he had not made the acquaintance of Alban Berg until shortly before the latter died in 1935, and too briefly to develop a relationship which might have led to collaboration.

These plausible-sounding explanations were classic examples of Sacher's life-long tendency to provide interviewers with good reasons for his transactions and decisions, rather than with the real reasons. It is true that Sacher never met Schoenberg. It is also true that his contact with Alban Berg was brief – had it been longer it is possible that he would have commissioned from Berg, who of the three composers had maintained the closest links with tonal music.

On the other hand, Sacher's limited contact with Anton Webern was by design. He had not been drawn to Webern on their first meeting, describing him later to Pierre Boulez as 'a bourgeois little professor'. Most significantly, however, he neither particularly liked nor understood Webern's music at that time. Its severe serial construction and its melodic, harmonic and rhythmic disintegration were the antithesis of Sacher's aesthetic taste, which had at its heart linear melody and a strong rhythmic element.

In June 1941, Anton Webern – keen to build a relationship with a patron of Sacher's growing stature – had sent Sacher the score of his *Variations for Orchestra*, Op. 30, offering him its world première. Sacher responded to the offer by first writing to Werner Reinhart, who was well acquainted with the compositions of Schoenberg and Webern through his patronage of both men's work.

'Webern has sent me his *Variations for Orchestra*, Op. 30, and has offered me its first performance. However, I have decided not to include this work in my programme because I am too unfamiliar with this style. I am sending the work to [Ernest] Ansermet on behalf of Universal Editions, with the request that he forward it to you after he has had a look at it.'[45]

The music of the Second Viennese School proponents simply did not touch Sacher personally. Although he embraced atonal music more closely after the 1960s, in 1984 he admitted that his relationship to cerebral, serial music had never been close.

Paul and Frank Martin at the Schola Cantorum Basle, 1942

'I never had such an intimate relationship to twelve-tone music as I did to the music of Stravinsky, Bartók, Honegger, Martin, etc. Today's young composers will see that as a failure, but I can't change it. The list of "my" compositions is a lovely collection, but not a complete structure. There's a lot missing, and that has come about because everything went out from me. ... I am not an institution like the radio, which has to try to be fair. As an individual, I am only responsible to myself, and I have to do what I think will give me something and what's important to me and my orchestra.'

The fact that Sacher could afford to give commissions on the basis of his personal taste was well matched to his profound need for control. As a conductor he saw control as an inherent part of the task: 'The conductor is by definition the boss. He directs the rehearsals and the performances. In the ideal case, however, there's a mutual service to music ... a community brought together in the creation of a work of art. The conductor stimulates the performers who, in turn, can stimulate the conductor.'

Sacher, however, did a good deal more than just direct the rehearsals and performances. He selected his players, and selected the works they performed. His personal tastes and interests channelled the musical education of his audiences, and affected the lives of his musicians, some of whom were not always happy about the 'works of art' they were asked to help create.

One example was Marianne Majer, who performed with the BKO from 1928 to 1963. 'Unfortunately, I don't like some modern music ... We often played pieces which we knew we would only play once, and then never again. But they still needed a lot of practice time, because they were either difficult or badly written. Finally I went to Paul and said, "I'd rather spend the little time I have outside my other activities practising other things than these awful, terrible pieces." Then he looked at me and said, "I understand that, but you must realize that you will then prematurely become quite one-dimensional." I agreed that that might well be, and I stayed on for a couple more years. Two or three years later, I went back to him and said, "Do you remember our conversation? Well, now it's come to the point where I prefer to be one-dimensional." He accepted that graciously, and it didn't disturb our relationship.'

Sacher's wealth and growing international status meant that he could afford to choose whom to support, and pursue his choices even in the face of opposition. And opposition there was, especially when he began to support the work of a young French composer called Pierre Boulez.

'After the war,' Sacher remembered, 'I asked Honegger, "Are there any good composers in France whom no one has heard of?" Then he said, "In Vaura's classes there is a certain Boulez." Boulez studied counterpoint with Vaura for three years. That's where I heard his name for the first time.

'Then I conducted a series of performances of *Jeanne d'Arc* at the Basle theatre. One evening the orchestra manager said to me, "The woman who plays the ondes martenot [an electronic keyboard instrument] hasn't come, but she's sent a young man as her replacement." You know what it's like in the theatre. Someone says, "Today someone else is singing. The tenor is ill. The one who is here hasn't had any rehearsals" … so it didn't disturb me further. I thought, "We'll see." And this young man played perfectly, as if he'd been at the rehearsals. After the performance I asked to see him, and I was shown into a small room where there was a young man. He introduced himself as "Boulez".'

Sacher met Boulez again in 1958 at the sixtieth birthday party of Heinrich Strobel, musicologist, music critic and director of Südwestfunk (South-West Radio) in Baden-Baden in Germany. 'Boulez had gone to Baden-Baden after the war – Strobel had invited him there. And then Strobel said to me, "Couldn't you do something in Basle for Pierre? He earns very little with us [Südwestfunk was in its beginnings] and it would be good if he could earn more."

'I was director of the Music Academy in Basle at the time, and I said, "We'll hold a composition course. Master class with Pierre Boulez." A lot of students came. And then he very quickly grew more famous. Already by the second year he had to have Stockhausen replace him as teacher of the master class. A couple of years later, Boulez held a conducting and interpretation course in modern music. At these times he always stayed with us, in his room. He sometimes stayed with us for weeks, and was looked after by Maja.'

Sacher's position, combined with Boulez's talent, ensured the young composer a warm reception in Basle. He and Sacher became good friends, and the friendship continued for the rest of Sacher's life. 'He's a marvellous friend,' Boulez told me. 'He's not only marvellous, he's unique. He's unique because he's very generous. I don't mean just money-wise – that he is anyway. But I mean he's generous in his way of approaching the universe. He's open-minded, and he's a very safe friend. Faithful. You can trust him absolutely.'

In the 1960s, however, not everyone shared Sacher's belief that Boulez was a voice worth listening to. For example, the conductor Ernest Ansermet, a protégé of both Stravinsky and Werner Reinhart, was 'deeply shocked' to hear of Boulez's employment in Basle, and wrote indignantly to Sacher: '*Sacher, vous avez perdu le nord*' ('Sacher, you have lost your direction'). Others, including Conrad Beck, shared Ansermet's reservations but wisely kept their feelings to themselves. 'Boulez is foreign to me', Beck admitted privately in 1987. 'He thinks he has brought order to music, but he has brought disorder. It would have come anyway, but with him it has come more quickly.'

Sacher, however, was unperturbed. Claiming that a music patron could neither afford to make absolute value judgements, nor think in historical categories, he did not allow the opinions of private individuals or those of the public to deflect him from his path. His attitude was demonstrated perfectly when he simply shrugged his shoulders after members of a capacity audience in Zurich booed the 1987 première of *'Machine's Party'*, his third of four commissions to the German composer Patricia Jünger.

Just as he had been convinced that Stravinsky would remain 'the peak of the twentieth century', he was also convinced of Boulez's ability and significance. 'Of this generation, the compositions of Boulez and the works of Stockhausen made the most important impression on me.'*

Sacher was always fascinated by the creative process, and by the musical secrets of successive generations, but he eschewed the practice of collecting as many world premières or new composers

---

* Sacher's sole commission to Boulez in 1996 (*sur Incises*, 1996–98) was later declined by the composer, who preferred to offer the work to Sacher as a testimony to their friendship.

as possible. Instead, he took continuing responsibility for works he had commissioned, including them at strategic intervals in concerts by the BKO or the Collegium and, in many cases, in concerts overseas. This was particularly true of the works of Stravinsky, Bartók and Martinů, as well as those of his compatriots Honegger, Beck, and Burkhard, and was part of his intentional education of the public.

At the same time, as Boulez has pointed out, Sacher followed every new development in the musical world. 'There are sometimes arts or music patrons who begin in their youth, and then they get tired with time. Let's say in this case they support Bartók and Honegger, and then nothing more. What I find exceptional with Paul is that he continued all this time to be interested by young people, also people younger than me, like Heinz Holliger, for instance. That I find extraordinary. It was the same with Maja with painters. They both constantly kept following what was happening, giving their support. Well, they could – that wasn't a problem. But the main problem for a patron is to keep following what is going on. Paul and Maja were really interested in the new things that were happening, not just, let's say, in supporting pseudo-Bartóks or such.'

Sacher's curiosity meant that he moved on with each succeeding generation, learning the voices of each new era and its proponents. He therefore never got bored. 'I think that I get bored quite quickly when the profits are small,' he told me. 'When I reach the boundaries quickly, and see that something doesn't go further, I get bored quickly. As long as someone stimulates me through his presence, or his questions, or his answers, or through his knowledge, or at least through his curiosity, then I'm not quickly bored.'

★★★

As Sacher's musical empire grew, observant colleagues noticed how well he used his wealth and the slyest of diplomatic strategies to people his network with trusted friends or colleagues. 'He was an unbelievable tactician and initiator,' Conrad Beck said in 1987. 'He could just as well have been Bundespräsident [president of the Swiss Federal Council].'

However, there were those, Beck among them, who wished to retain their independence, and therefore resisted Sacher's charm. 'Once Sacher asked my husband if he would like to become director of the Conservatory,' recalled Friedl Beck, 'but my husband didn't want that.' Similarly, when Sacher asked Pascale Honegger to replace his step-daughter Vera when she gave up her duties as his secretary, Pascale declined. 'I knew my life would become too confined if I took the position. And I always needed my independence. He asked me two or three times – very seriously. But he understood that it wouldn't work with my independent side, and he accepted that very well.'

Margrit Staehelin was another friend who preferred to remain independent. Disappointed by Sacher's marriage, she had left the BKO secretariat, but later re-established her friendship with the couple. 'I got on very well with Maja. They asked me to go and live with them – perhaps because I could have helped more with the BKO – but I wanted to remain free, and to live on my own.' Nevertheless, Sacher still found a way to involve Staehelin in his plans. When he heard her reports of a trip to New York in the late 1940s, he suggested that on her next trip she take some records of music by Swiss composers, so that Americans could learn that Switzerland had more to offer than cheese and chocolate. She agreed, and the consequences of that suggestion were all that Sacher could have hoped. For the rest of her life, Staehelin was involved in promoting cultural activities between the USA and Switzerland. A wealthy woman, she used her contacts to help ensure that Sacher's American début at Carnegie Hall in April 1955, and his later appearances as a guest conductor in the USA, were well publicized and attended. She was an important part of Sacher's growing support network.

'Paul Sacher had something like a community,' Michaela von Herwarth confirmed. 'They always went to Zurich, or to Basle for his concerts. That's how it was with Paul Sacher. It was absolutely not objective. Either people were enthusiastic, or they didn't want to have anything to do with him.'

★★★

Sacher's organizational talent meant that, once he set his sights on a certain project, he would realize it. The maxim he had learnt from his mother Anny Sacher in his childhood – 'That which you want to do, you can do' – was firmly intact. Armed with authority, ability, power, and wealth, he could now get what he wanted simply because he would not have it any other way. This can be seen in his handling of the transition of his Schola Cantorum Basiliensis from a private to a state institution.

By 1953, the Schola had survived for twenty years without a penny of city or cantonal support. What Ina Lohr had once called 'the Schola family' now had a teaching staff of sixteen, and its initial handful of students had grown to an enrollment of 250. Its dual mission of teaching and performing early music had been fulfilled so successfully that it had grown into an institution of international reputation, with Sacher still at its head and still planning its future.

By the early 1950s, Sacher could see that the initial situation, in which the appointment of teachers was based on personal friendships and contacts, and in which formal employment contracts had been considered unnecessary, could not continue. He could also see that his original teaching staff was growing older and that provision needed to be made for them. Looking around for a solution to these problems, he began to think about the other major music schools in Basle.

In 1867, the Gemeinnützige Gesellschaft Basel, a city society which supported community projects, had founded the Basle Music School, which was expanded in 1905 to Basle Music School and Basle Conservatory. Sacher believed that the Schola's future should also be a state responsibility, and conceived a masterplan to join the Schola, the Conservatory and the Music School into a single umbrella organization, the Basle Music Academy.

'The idea of merging the Schola with the other music schools,' believed Hannelore Mueller, who taught at the Schola for over twenty years, 'had to do partly with the fact that Sacher didn't want to get involved in organizing and paying his teachers' retirement pensions.' Clearly, the merger would bring the Schola all the benefits of the other two state-supported institutions. Its teaching staff would enjoy the social benefits and financial security of other state employees, and Sacher would not have to deal with the bureaucracy and expense of pension schemes and other necessities. But for this to happen, he had to ensure that the merger took place, and he faced some strong opposition, including that of the director of the Conservatory and Music School, Walter Müller von Kulm.

'Müller von Kulm fought against early music,' recalled Hannelore Mueller. 'He regarded it as a sort of curiosity. He said in 1952, "It's all right to play the viola da gamba as dessert, but not as a main course." Still, Sacher got the idea past him. He was a fantastic diplomat.'

Discussions between the two men about a merger began in 1951. Claims that the idea was originally Müller von Kulm's cannot be substantiated, and are unlikely to be true, particularly in the light of his documented lack of enthusiasm for early music. In any case, whoever the actual initiator was, Sacher was prepared to underline his interest with expansive gestures. One of his friends, the Swiss artist Theo Meier, had often described the skill of packing one's strategies attractively as *'verblüemele'*,* and Sacher sometimes used this expression to explain his own successes. The size and quality of the flowers he used to wrap round his plans for the merger were considerable. While Müller von Kulm remained largely unmoved by arguments in favour of the value of early music, he was susceptible to Sacher's plan for enhancing prestige and practicality.

As the steps towards unifying the three organizations were progressing, the sizeable Lotzsche estate at 4 Leonardstrasse in Basle came up for sale. The property opened on to the same cobbled inner courtyard as the Conservatory and Music School, in effect completing a quadrangle. There were many would-be buyers for the beautiful estate, on which a three-storey stone house stood. When the deed of sale was signed, however, the names of the purchasers were Paul and Maja Sacher.

Now, after three previous homes, a permanent location for the Schola was ensured, close to the other two institutions. The purchase of 4 Leonardstrasse provided a practical basis for the merger, and this helped strengthen the arguments for implementing Sacher's plan. Sacher had other levers at his disposal, too.

---

* Swiss-German for 'to make something look like flowers'.

Otto Lobeck's collection of early instruments was still on loan to the Schola. After Lobeck's death on 18 April 1951, Sacher asked the heirs if they would be prepared to sell him the collection, on the understanding that he would then donate it to the Basle Museum of History. In this way, the museum's own instrument collection would be joined by Lobeck's to form the largest public collection of early instruments in Switzerland. The family agreed, and the sale took place in 1953.

It is highly likely that Sacher knew from the outset that the Basle Museum of History had a serious storage problem, and that his generous donation would mean the museum could no longer house its enlarged instrument collection on its own premises. It 'just so happened' that two floors at the Music Academy could be made available to house the instruments – if the municipal government would undertake the necessary renovations. In 1955, the government of the canton of Basle City accepted Sacher's gift on behalf of the museum, and ordered the work to be done.

Sacher and Müller von Kulm became joint directors of the Music Academy in 1954. All the threads of Sacher's plan were brought together in May 1957, when the joint opening of the new museum of musical instruments and the house-warming of the Music Academy took place.

★★★

Sacher's resolution of the Schola's situation was a masterly example of planning, politics and meticulous attention to detail. With the blueprint of his goal clear, he could afford to take advantage of the fortuitous and timely 'coincidences' that presented themselves along the way, offering solutions and further openings to each of his projects. It was then just a matter of bringing the component parts of the strategy together, a skill he had demonstrated on countless occasions in his conducting of large oratorios. Sometimes, though, his efforts led to creations which even he had not initially envisaged.

'The Max Planck Society,'* recalled Sacher, 'wanted to found an institute for music, a Max Planck Institute for Music. Some of

---

* The Max Planck Society supports a number of institutes which carry out research in the arts and sciences.

their professors got together and asked a number of musicians to discuss their plans with them. I was asked to attend a number of meetings. At a certain moment, I said, "This would interest Boulez. We should invite him to come as well." On the basis of these discussions, the group wrote an outline for the founding of a Max Planck Institute for Music. But the society rejected the plan in the end. They said, "It doesn't suit our society. We only want to do something purely scientific." The blueprint, however, remained.

'One day,' Sacher continued, 'Pierre rang me and said, "Have you still got a copy of the outline we made? I've lost mine, but I've been asked to found an institute in Paris, and it would be a great help to me." So he used the original plans that were made for the Max Planck Institute of Music to found IRCAM* [an organization in Paris for research into, and performance of, contemporary music].'

---

* Institut de recherche et coordination acoustique/musique.

17

Everything Flows

'You know my horoscope ... Through the role played by Taurus and Jupiter in my life, I am destined for success, seamless success, when all that you want happens.'

Sacher's belief in the influence of the stars and planets on his life's achievements was genuine, and yet he also believed in luck – not the luck of happenstance to which envious onlookers sometimes referred when they tried to cheapen his accomplishments, but the 'luck' of perseverance whereby a person uses his will to influence and fashion his own destiny. 'I always say that luck is a personal trait, but it's not something that just falls upon you,' he explained. 'One attracts it. One sees to it that it comes.'

The mechanism Sacher employed to attract luck throughout his lifetime was the combination of his preparedness, and his ability to recognize – and exploit – opportunity. It was this combination which had led to his regaining of the Hoffmann-La Roche share majority, to his fruitful reign at Pro Helvetia, and to successes with dozens of other projects, including his orchestras.

His success, however, came at a price. Elsa Cavelti, a Swiss singer of international repute who performed with Sacher and the BKO in many Swiss and world premières of contemporary and early works, told me in 1996, 'There were many people who were jealous of Paul Sacher, particularly because of his money. I'm afraid it's a Swiss thing, this jealousy. It comes because Switzerland is so small and we're so close together that we can observe what everyone is doing. Personally I thought it was wonderful that Sacher used his wealth so creatively. Most don't.'

Whatever its roots or form, jealousy did not deflect Sacher from his mission to promote the voices of his time, and by the end of the 1940s those voices also included a number of contemporary English composers.

On 6 February 1948, the BKO introduced the Basle public to Michael Tippett's *Concerto for Double String Orchestra* and Benjamin Britten's *Serenade for Tenor, Horn and Strings*, Op. 31, in which Britten's partner, Peter Pears, sang the tenor solo. A week earlier, Britten himself had conducted the Collegium in a concert of English music which included his *Prelude and Fugue for String Orchestra* and *Les Illuminations.* These concerts marked the beginning of a close and regular working relationship between Sacher, Pears, and Britten, of which the world première of Britten's *Cantata academica,* performed by the BKO for Basle University's 500th anniversary on 1 July 1960, was a highlight.

Another postwar highlight was the Basle première, in 1949, of Hindemith's *When Lilacs Last in the Dooryard Bloom'd (Requiem for those we love),* written after the war while the composer was still in the USA. Hindemith himself had translated Walt Whitman's poems into German for the work's European performances.

Despite the friendship between Sacher and Hindemith in the 1920s and early 1930s, and Sacher's real interest in Hindemith's music, the latter did not compose for Sacher until he returned from the USA in 1952. One of the main reasons was Hindemith's relationship with Werner Reinhart in Winterthur, in whom he had found a mentor, patron and friend long before he began to work with Sacher.

Hindemith had made Reinhart's acquaintance in 1923 through Dr Hermann Scherchen, conductor of the Winterthur City Orchestra from 1923 to 1950. Scherchen had conducted the world premières of Hindemith's *Die junge Magd,* Op. 23 No. 2 and *Kammermusik,* Op. 24 No. 1 in Germany in 1922; with Reinhart's support, he began in 1923 to perform the composer's early works in Winterthur.

Reinhart himself was greatly taken with Hindemith, and equally convinced of his talent. The former's role as registrar of the Winterthur Musikcollegium (which administered the Winterthur City Orchestra), and the fact that he personally covered a considerable portion of the orchestra's deficits, meant that his influence on the musical life of Winterthur was enormous. Hindemith became

Paul with Paul Hindemith and Maja Sacher in New Haven, USA, 1949

a regular feature of that musical life, and Scherchen conducted more than half a dozen of his orchestral works with the Winterthur orchestra between 1928 and 1934.

Nor was Reinhart's support of Hindemith limited to paving the way for an acceptance of the composer's 'new music' in Winterthur. It included financial assistance in the form of generous 'holiday money' and the purchase of a number of the composer's scores, as well as considerable emotional support when Hindemith was forced to resign from the Berlin Musikhochschule before the war. Reinhart even became Hindemith's financial advisor, and was instrumental in obtaining his US visa when the composer made his decision to emigrate to the USA early in 1940.

Reinhart had also given Paul Sacher help of various kinds, and their correspondence suggests a cordial friendship. Nevertheless, Sacher's early attempts to conduct in Winterthur were seldom successful. Reinhart had found the conductor he wanted in Scherchen, and Hindemith was closely tied to both men; he wished to avoid offending either of them by composing for a 'rival' patron and conductor. By the early 1950s, however, the tide had changed. Scherchen was ousted from his conducting posts with the Winterthur City Orchestra and the Beromünster Radio Orchestra in Zurich in 1950, due to conflict arising from his political views.* Werner Reinhart died in 1951.

Sacher's first Hindemith commission resulted in the symphony *Die Harmonie der Welt*, completed in time for the BKO's twenty-fifth anniversary concert in January 1952. The second, an orchestral march for the 500th birthday celebrations of Basle University, was composed in 1960.

'I don't know if you can imagine this, because you were born at another time,' Sacher explained to me. 'At the end of the twenties, and in the early thirties, there was no one else like Hindemith. He represented something new, something carefree, and he appealed to us greatly – we were still young. Then came a scandal in Berlin. He was accused of being a *Kulturbolshevist* [a cultural communist] and – also because he feared for his Jewish wife – he emigrated to America.

---

* Sacher's role in the 'Scherchen Affair' remains controversial, but in the late 1940s he clearly belonged to the anti- Scherchen lobby.

'Then his style changed greatly, and there wasn't a lot left of the carefree musician. It was more the continuation of the style of Brahms and Bruckner. After the war he returned to Europe, and thought that he would be received like the Messiah. But that was not the case. A lot had changed in Europe in the meantime, with the influence of the Second Viennese School. But he still had considerable success in some parts of Europe, particularly in Vienna where the public was very faithful to him.'

Sacher's eagerness to commission and perform works by non-Swiss composers did not mean he neglected his Swiss friends. A notable example was Conrad Beck, who in 1952, with the help of the Pro Helvetia commission secured for him by Sacher, finally completed his oratorio *Der Tod zu Basel* (Death to Basle), begun more than twenty years earlier. Sacher and the BKO gave the work its world première in May 1953.

★★★

All who knew Sacher well have attested to his huge capacity for work. According to Pascale Honegger, for him holidays simply meant getting up half an hour later than on working days. Sundays, Vera Oeri remembered, he often spent at his desk.

'I am passionately fond of working. Work for me is a joy,' Sacher told a journalist in 1984. 'To accomplish my work I need a lot of discipline. I get up at six thirty, always. I breakfast alone – a cup of tea. It's a ritual. And this discipline is important.'[46] The austerity of Sacher's breakfast ritual was lessened somewhat by the soft dark-blue velvet dressing gown he wore, and the little red woollen egg-warmer in the shape of a rooster's head which covered the boiled egg he sometimes ate with his cup of tea.

Some aspects of Sacher's disciplined daily routine were not easy for his associates and assistants to deal with. 'He knew exactly what he wanted,' said Flandrina von Salis, his private secretary from 1962 to 1987. 'He displayed unbelievable self-control and discipline. When he worked, he was absolutely impersonal, as short and precise as possible. At the beginning it was difficult. Sometimes I felt like a machine. After a year I said so, and afterwards he was different.'

That discipline was nowhere more evident than in his conducting. 'The conducting ability Sacher brought with him when he founded the Basle Chamber Orchestra was rather modest, even though he had studied with Weingartner,' wrote his associate Dr Willi Schuh in 1961, in a publication celebrating the twentieth anniversary of the Collegium Musicum Zurich. 'But one has to be born to conduct. The ensemble would not have been destined to exist for long if Sacher had not had the inner calling. He grew ... in his work and through the tasks he set for himself to what he is today.'[47]

To reach the standard he had attained as a conductor by the end of the Second World War, Sacher had worked with a degree of effort which Schuh described as 'impetus bordering on obsession'. The demands he made on his musicians were severe, if not ruthless. Ten or more rehearsals for a contemporary work were not unusual in the BKO's early days, because both Sacher and his musicians had to feel their way into an idiom with which no one was familiar.

A characteristic of Sacher's conducting which appealed to the composers who wrote for him was that he was not interested in upstaging their works and that he had no need to charm his orchestra – or, for that matter, his audience. On the contrary, he claimed that for the first decade of his career he had little, if any, relationship to his audience. Speaking to me in 1985, when he still conducted both the BKO and the Collegium Musicum Zurich, he claimed that earlier in his career he had had no relationship with the public at all.

'That has only begun to change a little bit in the very last few years,' he conceded. 'Earlier I would have said to you that I don't do it at all for these people; that I do it for me, for my orchestra, for my singers. We do it for ourselves in the first instance. Then with time I thought, "No, of course I also do it for the people who are listening." But that is relatively new ... only perhaps in the last ten years.'

Instead of wishing to become a star conductor with stylized gestures selected for aesthetic rather than practical reasons, Sacher aimed to enable the spirit of the work to dominate. He saw his task as realizing the score itself, and he was not interested in stamping his personality or 'interpretation' on the work.

'I never wanted to do that. That would be like a rape. I think that's really bad. But I know such people. Ansermet was like that. He always knew better than the composer. Why it had to be played a certain way, and couldn't be another way. ... But doing that is an overestimation on the part of the person who does it. It's nonsense. Because whether the conductor's name is Ansermet, or Toscanini or Sacher, he always has the score of Beethoven. Every note is from Beethoven. One shouldn't delude oneself ... Of course, he performs "his" Beethoven, but he has to stick to the score.'

Some of the more astute observations about Sacher's ability and limitations as a conductor were made by Brenton Langbein, the Australian violinist and conductor who succeeded Stefi Geyer as first violinist of the Collegium Musicum Zurich in 1956.

'Basically, he's not a performer as a conductor,' Langbein told me in 1991. 'He's not a showman. He's not a "Genius Of The Baton", let's say. ... But all the backstage work he does! The way he used to rehearse! Now of course he's older, but it's still amazing at times how he works with us. And even with a lot of second-rate players in the earlier days, the results he got were quite extraordinary because of the way he rehearsed. All that groundwork and, of course, his excellent taste and his fabulous choice of programmes. But it was the basic spadework for which one can respect him most.

'And at times, when there was a sort of relaxation of all his barriers, he came up with some of the most beautiful moments in music I have experienced in my whole life. And I'm grateful to him and I love him for that. The difficult sides that one has had to put up with from him have been overridden by some of these flashes that have come through.'

Langbein also recognized Sacher's reluctance to show emotion, even if he was not aware of its source. 'He seemed afraid of being sentimental, afraid of showing too much emotion or being extrovert with his passions. But sometimes he did. And I got to love him from a musical point of view when he worked with the choir. He was able to open up all his passion and all that emotional side, especially in Honegger. Everything just came together. ... Paul could express himself best in that kind of music.

'He also adores Haydn, but I never feel that he expresses Haydn the way he wants to, for the public. But with Honegger he does.

Honegger, Martinů, these sort of things – that's his world. There have been a couple of performances with him like that which have been absolute revelations. You know, you don't often see an orchestra in tears after their concert.'

Elsa Cavelti largely agreed. She described Sacher as 'a victim of his emotions' and as a conductor 'who couldn't show his heart'. But she also said that working with him was very fulfilling. 'He gave us [the soloists] terrific freedom to express ourselves. He accompanied us wonderfully. There were other conductors such as Ansermet with whom things were very different. And difficult.'

★★★

In the 1950s, as recordings and radio transmissions left their infancy, Sacher's agenda included performances for these media as well. In 1952, for instance, he recorded works by Honegger, Haydn, Mozart, Hindemith, Martin, Burkhard and Mihalovici in Rome, Zurich, Paris, and Baden-Baden. In the following decade, London, Vienna, Hamburg, and Cologne joined the extensive list of European cities in which he made recordings for the radio or for records. In the late 1950s, his appearances as guest conductor also included international festivals such as Aix-en-Provence, where in 1959 he conducted the Dutch Chamber Orchestra in works ranging from Handel to Stravinsky; and in 1961 Aldeburgh, where he conducted the English Chamber Orchestra in music by Martinů, Martin and Honegger.

Sacher's career also included opera and staged versions of oratorios. He conducted Honegger's *Jeanne d'Arc au bûcher* (in Italian, as *Giovanna d'Arco al rogo*) at La Scala in 1947; Burkhard's *Die Schwarze Spinne* in Zurich in 1949; and in 1951, this time at the Basle Stadttheater, Honegger's *Jeanne d'Arc*, which was followed by Stravinsky's *Oedipus Rex* in 1952.

For several years in the 1950s and early 1960s, Sacher spent part of each summer as a guest conductor at the Glyndebourne Festival in Great Britain, where he conducted Stravinsky's *The Rake's Progress* and Mozart's *Die Entführung aus dem Serail* and *Die Zauberflöte*. He returned briefly to conducting opera in 1978, with performances of Mozart's *Idomeneo* at the Basle Stadttheater.

An aspect of opera which particularly appealed to Sacher was that there were normally several performances of a work which had been rehearsed for weeks. 'You know, it always seemed absurd to me that one has five, or three, or seven or ten rehearsals for a concert work which is then performed only once. The best thing for me about conducting opera was that one rehearsed the work for a long period, and then performed it ten or twelve times. Then every performance had a special colour, its own colour. Something works particularly well, or one hears something new – something one should have known ages before and one suddenly discovers it. That happens much more rarely in concerts, because you experience the concert two or three times at the most.'

An important part of Sacher's preparation was his habit of continuing to study the score between performances. Not being a pianist, he used the same method for this revision process as he did when studying a new score. He simply read the score as he had trained himself to do as a teenager and, in reading it, he heard it. Sometimes his reading was punctuated by his humming or half-whistling the lines as he read. His revision of the scores between performances was a crucial part of his preparation for both opera and orchestral scores. 'I don't do what some conductors do, who leave the score lying in the theatre, and open it again the evening of the next performance. I work with it again and again before the remaining performances, so that I can get into the world of the piece directly, to penetrate it immediately. To be in the work from the first note on. But apparently other people don't need that.'

★★★

The success and luck that continued to mark Paul Sacher's public life after the war appeared to be matched in his private life. But in the late 1950s and on into the 1960s, Sacher's marriage was heavy with the burden of his other lives.

In numerous discussions about the changes and developments of those years, Sacher often returned to the subject of his horoscope. It was his belief that while the influences of Taurus and Jupiter on his life and work were positive and success-oriented, other influences from the stars had a dampening effect.

'*Der Hüter der Schwelle* [the guardian of the threshhold] is Uranus,' he explained. 'It's he who prevents you from becoming arrogant. It's he who stops you from thinking, "I can do everything. I can accomplish everything. I only have to want it." Suddenly this dampening arrives – Uranus arrives – and everything changes. Throughout my entire life, when everything looked as if the sun would shine for ever, Uranus arrived. And then for me there was only the possibility of escape into Pisces.

'A genuine Pisces lives in dreams, daydreams, in his imagination, and doesn't need success – no success at all. He needs only water, and that played a huge role for me as a child. I wouldn't have asked for a violin if I hadn't been a Pisces. The sound of string instruments is the sound of Pisces. That is what speaks to my soul.'

Up on Schönenberg, the 'dampening' effect that had settled over Sacher's marriage appeared to be caused more by the births of his daughters with Nina von Faber-Castell than by Uranus. The births were bitter for Maja Sacher, who had hoped to have children with Paul and who, for reasons apparently known only to herself, never did.

'She became extremely depressed,' recalled Pascale Honegger, 'and her depression led to severe anaemia. It was a psychological anaemia from which she ultimately recovered, but the years that followed were difficult ones. At that time I was there a lot.'

Despite the cloud over the couple's relationship, Maja continued to play her roles of wife, hostess, and patron of the visual arts impeccably. Perhaps she played them too well for a man who may have needed to feel more keenly her need for him. Having recovered from the personal tragedies she had suffered in the early 1930s, her determination to carry on seemed boundless. 'She was astonishingly independent,' said Sacher in a tone akin to awe. 'She found her strength in herself, and no one could deflect her from her path.'

Since their marriage in 1934, the couple had separated their interests into clear domains: music was Paul's, and the visual arts were Maja's. 'She was content to go to his concerts,' said Pascale Honegger, 'and tell him they were good.' Perhaps this is why Professor Edgar Bonjour once referred to Maja affectionately as 'the second violin'. Judged from the point of view of her involvement in and knowledge of music, compared to Paul's, this was true.

But in her own domain, the visual arts, Maja's role was in no way secondary.

'I assure you,' said Pascale Honegger, 'that there she was the first violin. She did an enormous amount. The museums alone! The Hoffmann Foundation, and the Museum of Modern Art she created are very important.'

Despite Pascale Honegger's characterization in 1990 to François Reichenbach, in his documentary film *Paul Sacher*, that the couple 'complemented each other perfectly with this common foundation in their love of art', there was little real sharing of their domains – at least, not according to Sacher himself, who felt he was not integrated in Maja's world as he would have wished to be. 'In the sphere of the fine arts, she did not treat me well. I would have been an excellent student. She could have shared more, taken me with her more. But she probably thought, "What does he understand about all this?"'

On being asked whether he had ever spoken to Maja about his resentment, he replied, 'She was very sensitive in this area. It was better not to. She had her domain, and probably thought I had mine. But she shared in mine...'

Few of the Sachers' large circle of friends and associates were aware of the cloud that had descended over the couple's relationship, or of Sacher's feelings that the sharing of their domains was not equitable. For most people, they were a couple to admire and envy. Friends or colleagues who visited them at Schönenberg continued to be received and cared for by Maja. The house was constantly full of people, often leading figures from the worlds of music and fine arts. On any day, guests could find themselves sitting at the Sachers' table next to artists like Mstislav Rostropovich, Jean Tinguely, Pierre Boulez, Witold Lutoslawski, Peter Pears or Luciano Berio.

It was Maja who welcomed such guests and saw to their travelling arrangements and other immediate needs, supported by her loyal household staff. It was Maja, too, who solved more unexpected problems. For instance, one evening she discovered that Rostropovich was about to be driven to perform in a concert with Paul with paperclips holding his shirt-sleeves together because he had forgotton to bring his cufflinks. It was from Maja's Magic

Cupboard that the gold cufflinks he wore in the performance appeared. There was an extraordinary ambience at Schönenberg, and that ambiance was created by Maja Sacher.

Not only did Maja see to Paul's needs, and to those of their guests, but she also busied herself with Paul's parents, visiting Anny Sacher almost daily in the years following Gusti Sacher's death. Anny, despite her genuine pride in her son's achievements, had never quite accepted his decision to become a conductor. In later years, she was fond of telling him just how, if she were given the chance, she would rule at Hoffmann-La Roche.

Anny Sacher-Dürr died on 13 May 1970, aged 93.

★★★

There is no doubt that Sacher was enormously appreciative of how Maja ran their home for him and their guests, and that this was an essential aspect of his development as an artist. He referred countless times to the role of Schönenberg and all that his life there symbolized for him.

'This house played a dominant role, and it was identical with Maja. It's like when a warrior goes to war, and then he comes home. The battlefields were always women, or the concerts or such, and then I found my peace here, and protection.' Nevertheless, echoing Anny Sacher's complaint half a century earlier that her son treated their home like a hotel, Maja Sacher's companion and housekeeper Hedwig Baldegger once commented: 'You know, I always thought, "Paul is not the master of this house. He behaves more like a guest. He comes and goes."'

Sacher may have felt that he was not sufficiently involved in his wife's world, but she certainly included him in her friendships with her artist friends. The painter Georges Braque, who was 'a very good friend', often spent Easter at Schönenberg, and the Sachers – whose home was adorned for years with more paintings by Braque than by any other painter – made frequent trips to Paris where they visited not only Braque, but also many other artists as well. On one occasion, despite Maja's misgivings, they visited Picasso's atelier.

'We were with Braque,' recalled Sacher, 'and he said, *"On va voir Picasso* [Let's go and see Picasso]." So we went with him. Maja wasn't very happy to go. She was afraid of Picasso; she found him sinister. It was for that reason we hadn't seen him previously, and we never visited him again. She didn't want to. She always visited Braque and Arp and many others, but she always left out Picasso.'

In the late 1950s, the recognition of his responsibility for Maja's depression, and the strain of having a secret family in another city, began to show in Sacher's normally robust health. In 1963, with his father's failing health adding to the stress, Sacher himself fell ill. In June he had to abandon his final rehearsals of Frank Martin's opera *Monsieur de Pourceaugnac* with the Netherlands Opera for the Holland Festival, and the performances were conducted by Martin himself. Further cancellations of concerts and recordings in several major European cities followed over the next four months.

The symptoms of Sacher's illness – stomach-ache, headache, general weakness and fatigue – were all common to stress and likely due to it. But in 1964 a formal and different diagnosis was made.

'I was in Berlin, and I felt terrible again. I felt ill and didn't know what was wrong with me. A doctor came and examined me, and said, "There's nothing the matter. You're absolutely healthy." And then came words I had never heard before: "Do you know if your adrenal glands are in order?" He had a suspicion that it might be connected with that.'

In 1966, Sacher was hospitalized in Zurich to have his tonsils removed. Because an abcess behind his tonsils had not been detected, the surgery led to a dangerous infection – at one point, Sacher, then aged sixty, was close to death. He was fond of telling the story of how, ostensibly unconscious and expected to die, the words of the hospital director filtered through to him: 'We've got to get him out of here. We can't have Paul Sacher dying in our hospital.' That, he claimed, was enough to pull him back from the edge.

The exhaustive examinations made at that time revealed that Sacher had Addison's disease, a condition of deficient functioning of the adrenal cortex. Although there are various causes for this condition, the possibility that it was a secondary sequela to his earlier tuberculosis cannot be ruled out. However, once the diagnosis was made, his symptoms of fatigue and increasing emotional distress in later years became easier to understand. For the rest of his life, he was required to take medication.

How far Sacher's ill-health and the disease itself resulted from the enormous and understated stress under which he had lived for years cannot be determined with accuracy. But the death of his father, Gusti Sacher, on 18 June 1965, was not only a further burden on his health but a great personal loss.

Oswald August Sacher had remained in the employment of the international transport firm *DANZAS* until his retirement. He had risen to the position of a departmental manager, responsible for the transport of goods between Switzerland and France. A younger colleague, August Döbelin, who joined the company six years before Gusti's retirement, remembered him as 'a calm, kindly man with white hair and glasses, who was very religious'.

The religious fervour that had taken precedence over all else in Gusti Sacher's life in his late thirties had not abated. He had remained deeply and naively religious, obstinate in his belief that God would protect him. When he developed diabetes in his old age, he was told by his doctor to stop eating the large meringues and other sweet things he liked, but his answer, according to his son, was, 'God will look after me.' Two years before his death, as a complication of his worsening diabetes, one of his legs had to be amputated.

Although no evidence has been found to support his claim, and research refutes it, Sacher believed that somewhere in Gusti's ancestry there had been nobility. The belief had sprung partly from his own rather naive faith in comments made about his father by Nina von Faber-Castell. 'Nina said something very strange,' he said in 1992. 'She said, "Somewhere in your ancestry there has to have been a very great nobleman, a prince or a general, because your father has the allure of a nobleman. He moves like one, and he's physically built like one. And he doesn't concern himself with reality. The realities of this life don't touch him. He's above them."

'I don't know where it comes from but, looking back, I often think that maybe she was right. You know, Nina knew German nobility through her marriage. All these counts and princes. ... She could distinguish between what was laughable and what somehow had a certain *grandezza* ... It's a pity. I would like to know him now. Now I could really talk with him.'

IV
The Legacy

18

Sunshine and Shadows

By the 1960s, Paul Sacher had become a national figure in Switzerland, so much so that he was able to tell a young admirer who lived overseas, 'Oh, you can just address your letter to "Paul Sacher, Switzerland" and it will get to me.' But by the end of the 1970s, he was well on his way to becoming a living legend.

The legend was enhanced in April 1976 by the publication of a book entitled *Dank an Paul Sacher* (Thanks to Paul Sacher). Initiated by the cellist Mstislav Rostropovich, the book celebrated both Sacher's seventieth birthday and the half-century of his musical achievements. It contained messages of gratitude and recognition from twenty-one famous musicians, including Boulez, Britten, Ernst Křenek, Hans Werner Henze and Rudolf Serkin. Rostropovich's own description of Sacher was characteristically dramatic:

> The Milky Way is in constant motion: at one moment the stars approach each other; the next they move away from one another. But when one celestial body moves too close to a larger gravitational field and comes under its influence, it will change its course and the smaller body may even become the satellite of the larger.
>
> It is almost the same with people. ... a person who thinks a great deal, who works intensively, thereby enlarging the sphere of his influence, and attracting increasing numbers of people to him, suddenly becomes a type of sun himself with his own system of satellites, which circle him at varying heights, who approach him and move away again, without ever losing contact with their sun. ... There are also such stars on Earth. There's one not far from Basle.[48]

Not all the accolades written that year were so theatrical. Those by musicologists and music journalists were more scholarly appreciations of what Sacher had accomplished. The seventy-year-old maestro was hailed as 'the most important private patron of contemporary music', and his achievements were listed and analysed from musical-historical perspectives. One comment made in many of the articles was still valid a decade later; namely, that from 1926 to the mid-1970s – a period described as 'the Sacher era' – the history of music in Basle was determined largely by the personality and initiatives of Paul Sacher. In turn, the works performed in Basle as a result of those initiatives influenced the history of music in the world.

One of the sources of Sacher's influence was sheer volume. By 1976, he had commissioned no fewer than ninety-seven works and had conducted the world premières of ninety-five of them. By his death in 1999, another fifty commissions had been added to the list, raising his private patronage of contemporary classical music to a level unrivalled in the twentieth century. The nearest to a competitor in this regard was Serge Koussevitzky, the renowned music patron and conductor of the Boston Symphony Orchestra, whose commissions included Bartók's *Concerto for Orchestra* in 1943. However, while it is true that by 1994 the Koussevitzky Music Foundation had commissioned 255 works, well in excess of Sacher's total, fewer than fifty of those works had been commissioned by Koussevitzky himself before his death in 1951.

As Sacher's long list of accomplishments was highlighted for his seventieth-birthday celebrations, one question asked was why such an important patron should be Swiss. Hans Oesch, former professor of musicology at Basle University and a former staff and board member of the Paul Sacher Foundation, linked Sacher's success to the relatively late development of radio and state support for the arts in Switzerland.

> It's an undisputed fact that in our century in the field of music there has not been, and there will not be again, another private patron of Paul Sacher's importance. ... The fact that this role was allocated to a Swiss ... becomes easier to understand when we remember that, from the very beginning, the support of

The conductor Paul Sacher, 1986

creative musicians by the state and radio was far less intensively pursued in Switzerland than in a number of comparable countries in the western world.⁴⁹

In the absence of a well-developed system of state support with its attendant bureaucracies, Sacher's single-minded vision was free to flourish – so much so, in fact, that commentators in the 1980s and 1990s expressed concern that he might have imposed too much of his personal aesthetic on the contemporary repertoire. But in the 1970s, it seemed, Sacher could do no wrong.

Part of the legend derived from the sheer number of significant and enduring works he commissioned, from composers whose names speak for themselves. It is with awe that one realizes just how many of those works have retained their places in the international repertoire. His commissions include so many 'masterpieces' that the German newspaper *Die Welt*'s music critic, reviewing the 1974 world première of Wolfgang Fortner's *Prismen* (Prisms),* commented drily, 'As the world knows, [when composing] for Sacher, it's best if one writes masterpieces right from the beginning.'⁵⁰

The secret of Sacher's success in selecting commissions of quality remains controversial in the literature. None of the commentators produces convincing reasons for the high percentage of Sacher's successes and, in the absence of more reasonable explanations, some writers have again attributed at least part of that success to luck. Even the sensitive and well-connected Oesch, for instance, claimed that, though the quality of the works commissioned betokened a sure feeling for artistic quality, Sacher was also lucky, because he could not have known what the fate of his commissions would be.

In fact, there is a clear and simple explanation for Sacher's success. The commentators have failed to find it only because they have failed to search back far enough. That explanation is not luck but the power created by the synergy of the two most important forces in Sacher's life: his immense curiosity and desire to uncover secrets, and his mission to play the music of his time.

Since early youth, Sacher had exercised his passion for discovering other people's secrets, while keeping his own. It was but a small

---

* The fifth of six Sacher commissions given to Fortner.

step from learning a private person's secrets to deciphering those that a composer had coded into a score. For Sacher, there was less joy in decoding the obvious than in penetrating the depths of these subtle yet powerful statements of the composer's life and beliefs. Compositions which maintained an internal integrity of structure and theme, while expressing the artist's deepest thoughts and emotions, were the compositions (and composers) to which Sacher was unerringly attracted.

'There is no form of expression', he wrote in the introduction to a catalogue for an exhibition of original handwritten musical scores in the Basle Kunstmuseum in 1975, 'which betrays more than writing. It is unique and has a symbolic meaning, even a magical power. A document in the hand of the observer can bring the writer so close that he's almost tangible.'[51]

While his passion for discovering secrets provided the drive for Sacher's efforts, his mission to perform contemporary music functioned as a screen for significance. He was not seduced into selecting music of moods or whims, but made choices consistent with his vision and, of course, with his own aesthetic. His desire to speak with the voices of his own time was so genuine and strong that he found it impossible to understand artists who did not share his need. In 1972, when he was awarded the Kunstpreis der Stadt Basel (the Basle City Arts Prize), he closed his acceptance speech as follows:

> He who only looks backwards [in the arts] lives outside his epoch. I will never understand any artistically sensitive person who doesn't want to embrace the message of his own time, even if it announces chaos and disorder. Therefore all my love goes to those who journey to new shores on the current which has carried the rest of us along as well.[52]

In 1976, the oldest vehicle for Sacher's journey to new shores, the Basle Chamber Orchestra, celebrated its golden jubilee. With its chamber choir, it had caused a long series of sensations in Basle since its foundation in 1926. The BKO's performances had a special legitimacy because the composers usually attended not only their works' premières but often rehearsals as well, discussing questions of interpretation with Sacher and his players. Those who attended the BKO performances did so in the certain knowledge that what they were hearing was new, and that they were the first witnesses of creative processes which were changing the face of modern music.

Such close contact between orchestra, composer and conductor is normal today, but at that time it was highly unusual. The German author Thomas Mann, in his novel *Dr Faustus*, immortalized the practice by describing a concert to which 'the conductor Herr Paul Sacher had invited [the fictional composer] Adrian Leverkühn under very attractive conditions, expressing the wish that the composer lend a special importance to the concert by his attendance'.[53]

The BKO's jubilee concert in January 1977 consisted of Bartók's *Cantata Profana: A kilenc csodaszarvas* (The Nine Enchanted Stags), Stravinsky's *Symphony of Psalms*, and a new commission from Luciano Berio for orchestra and solo cello. Those who attended remember an atmosphere of virtual euphoria – and relief.

Concern about the orchestra's future had arisen at the end of 1975 when Sacher wrote in the BKO's *Mitteilungen*,* 'It is my intention to end my activities with the Basle Chamber Orchestra in 1977. Fifty years in a person's life is a long time, and I have set myself some tasks whose fulfilment will require time and leisure. I hope to experience a few more lovely concerts with you before my resignation.'[54]

There was an uproar. The extent to which Sacher's work with his orchestra and the public was both appreciated and wanted became clearer than ever. Musicians, friends, composers, the press and the public at large – all sent the same message to Schönenberg: Sacher would have to seek his leisure some other way.

A main argument used by those who wanted Sacher to change his mind was that he had not allowed sufficient time to re-organize the BKO, particularly from a financial standpoint. This argument, Hans Oesch claimed, was the most effective one. 'Since it's not possible to create a new foundation for the Basle Chamber Orchestra overnight,' Oesch wrote in the jubilee publication of the BKO in 1976, 'Paul Sacher has fortunately been persuaded to stay at the helm for a few more years.'[55]

Sacher allowed himself to be coerced with flattery and pressure of many types. He was persuaded that his robust health, youthful

---

* An information pamphlet for BKO subscribers.

appearance and seemingly endless energy reserves would stand him in good stead for some years to come. Whatever his final reasons for bowing to the opinions of others, the Basle Chamber Orchestra, albeit increasingly under the baton of guest conductors, survived for another ten years.

★★★

As Sacher's fame grew, certain traits he had felt the need to curb in his younger years began to push through his carefully controlled exterior. Those who knew him well noticed a growing self-importance which sometimes bordered on pomposity and arrogance. Increasingly, his impatience and his need to impose his will turned to rudeness.

Throughout his professional life, Sacher had attended dozens of meetings each month, and this practice continued until he was in his late eighties. Never known for his patience in discussing minor matters at such meetings, he now employed a bulldozing technique. If he did not agree with what someone was saying, or felt that they had gone on long enough, he simply began to speak again as if they were not there.

Sacher had continued to attend yearly (later half-yearly) reunions with his classmates from the Upper Realschule. By the late 1980s the group had been reduced to eight, and for years it was Sacher who set the date and venue, and who insisted on paying the bill. His colleagues were forbidden to thank him. Most of them accepted his lordly demeanour because, as one reported, Sacher was 'the richest and most interesting of the group'; but former classmate Dr Sigismund Remy ultimately stopped attending the reunions because 'he would rather play golf than listen to Sacher talk about himself'.

On holiday in 1991 in the Parkhotel Flims-Waldhaus in Graubünden, Sacher appeared at an outdoor lunch with family and close friends with an upset stomach and ordered a plate of grated apple. The apple duly arrived, and Sacher was convinced that it was canned instead of fresh. 'I want fresh apple,' he demanded. 'You can give that to Müller or Meier, but not to Sacher.'

Sacher had demonstrated his ruthlessness in his early years. When he could not get what he wanted, or if he felt someone posed a threat to his interests, he could be as sharp as steel. 'I can be a terrible enemy,' he once told me with a grim half-smile. This side of him became clear to a number of those who crossed his path over the years, but virtually none of them was willing to speak openly of it. Associates who had witnessed at first or even second hand the crushing edge of Sacher's displeasure were prepared to speak privately, but, given Sacher's capacity for reprisals, they usually asked me to treat such comments as 'off the record', or not to mention their names. Many of them were fully aware of Sacher's difficulty in dealing with criticism, and of the steps he or his protective colleagues were capable of taking in retribution.

For instance, Rosmarin Jäggi, the daughter of Stefi Geyer and Walter Schulthess, told me in an informal conversation that Sacher's behaviour while negotiating his purchase of Bartók's Sonata for Solo Violin from her gravely ill mother had been 'atrocious'. When I later asked her for verification of her comments, she refused to provide the necessary details, saying that Sacher's heirs would sue her if she criticized him, and that re-telling the story would create a storm in her family.

The Zurich pianist Daniel Fueter had been asked to review one of Sacher's Collegium concerts in January 1972 for the Basle newspaper *National Zeitung*. The concert comprised two contemporary works, plus a work by Salieri and Mozart's Symphony No. 28 in C major, K 200. Fueter was not the *National Zeitung*'s regular critic, but was covering for a colleague. He did not know that there was an understanding among critics that, unless one could say something good about Sacher's Mozart or Haydn, one simply said nothing. Fueter made the mistake of writing a less-than-flattering review of the Mozart: 'Further weaknesses include rhythmic imprecision, unfounded variations in the tempo of transition passages, hasty execution of the ornamentation.'[56] Sacher is reported to have been livid. At the time, Fueter's father was the director of the Zurich-based Condor Films, which was under contract to Hoffmann-La Roche for making advertising and documentary films. Sacher's colleagues at Roche only just managed to stop him withdrawing from the Condor contract because of his anger over the review. Years later, however, when I discussed this incident with Fueter, by then director of the music department of the Hochschule für Musik und Theater in Zurich, he hastened to point out that Sacher and he had enjoyed cordial relations in later years.

People were afraid of Sacher's power, and remained so. In 1983, the Basle radio station DRS2 decided to celebrate his seventy-seventh birthday with a sixteen-hour programme of music he had commissioned or performed, interlaced with interviews with Sacher and other commentators. The station also asked three music journalists to prepare critical articles to counterbalance what might otherwise have bordered on hagiography. One of the articles, by the pianist and music journalist Christoph Keller, was turned down as being 'too disrespectful for a birthday celebration'.

'The article went first to Andreas Wernli, head of the music department, and then all the way to the director of the station, Andreas Blum,' Keller told me in 1993. 'Blum said he was sorry, but it just wasn't possible to broadcast the article. Later he told me at a party that he thought the article was very good. I had already written twice about Paul Sacher. The first time was for the *National Zeitung*, a concert review. It was critical, and the editor Jürg Erni [who had worked as a writer for Sacher in the past] wouldn't print it. Sacher has a lot of power and it's not surprising that people are afraid to print something like this, especially in Basle. But I would have expected the radio to broadcast my text. They wouldn't have risked losing anything by that. It wasn't dangerous.' (Keller's article was published shortly afterwards by the Zurich-based magazine *Magma*.)

Despite his famed 'fidelity' to friends like Honegger, Martin, Beck, or Boulez, Sacher was quite capable of betrayal. As a Hoffmann family member said, 'Paul expected absolute loyalty from his friends, but he did not always return it.' During our long friendship, and dozens of lengthy discussions, there were many occasions – even in formal, taped interviews – when Sacher made cutting, biting, or cruelly unfair and unsolicited comments about people he knew, including close associates or people for whom he ostensibly cared.

He was also capable of turning suddenly on a true friend. A case in point is his relationship with the Australian violinist Brenton Langbein, who had been a staunch Sacher supporter for decades. Their relationship highlighted all the elements of Sacher's contrariness, and Langbein's sensitivity and perception allowed him better than most to see behind the barriers that alternately appeared and faded.

At first, all went well. Langbein was selected to lead the Collegium Musicum after Stefi Geyer's death, and in 1967 he became the BKO's leader. In the early days, he said, 'I didn't feel strong affection for Sacher, but I admired him, and I enjoyed the work I was doing with the Collegium. He kept his distance, but was friendly. For instance, he commissioned a work for me from Henze, the Second Violin Concerto. We were having lunch together, and he asked Henze, "Hans, what are you going to write for me next?" And Hans said, "Well, I thought I would like to write a piece for Brenton, because he's the only friend I have who's never asked me for anything. A concerto." And I thought, "Oh God, not another concerto. I want a sextet!" But I couldn't say that, of course. And so Paul immediately said, "What a wonderful idea." There, he was so generous. He agreed immediately to that. But still he kept his distance.'

It was Langbein's initiative which led to the Collegium Musicum attending the Adelaide Festival in Australia in 1974, and to a closer bond between the two men. 'When we got to the point with the Collegium Musicum where I was the one who was more or less responsible for getting the tour to Australia, he suddenly became quite a different person towards me. He really took me into his inner circle. I think he was so grateful for that wonderful time. I think it was one of the best times of his life.'

At the end of the 1980s, however, Langbein experienced the limits of Sacher's friendship with sharp disappointment when he put forward a plan to build up the Collegium Musicum. 'I wanted to keep the younger players together [instead of just playing in six to eight concerts a year]. To have a core of twelve or so, with lots of work for them – and then add players where necessary for the bigger works.' The plan meant that some of the musicians would be working together more frequently than they had been with the orchestra in its original form, and it would require an additional administrator. 'Paul encouraged me to put the plan on paper. We made copies, and we organized a board meeting to discuss it,' recalled Langbein.

The night before that meeting, a conversation between Sacher and a member of the Collegium board took place in my presence. The board member attacked the plan for personal reasons and illogically suggested that it could pose a threat to the existing ensemble. Sacher was persuaded to 'drop it', and the next day, when the plan was announced, he targeted it with cold contempt.

'He suddenly looked on it as a rival group,' Langbein recalled three years later, disbelief still audible in his voice. The plan went no further, and Langbein felt betrayed. 'He could have had a St Martin-in-the-Fields group, but perhaps he was worried about his own ability' was the violinist's last comment to me on the subject, a year before his death.

What Langbein and many others didn't recognize was Sacher's extreme reluctance to share (which was in no way a contradiction to his legendary generosity), and the plan for the new ensemble would have entailed his sharing the Collegium. His adversity to sharing began, he told me, when his parents' friends sometimes brought a gift to the house – sweets or nuts, or even a toy. 'If they said it was for both of us [Paul and Nelly] to share, then I wouldn't touch it,' he stated categorically.

Aged seventeen, he had decided not to show or share his feelings. He refused to share such friends as Romana Segantini with the rest of his circle, and later admitted that he found it difficult to share his daughters with their boyfriends. He claimed, too, that he would prefer to own one painting he could view in privacy than to visit a gallery full of pictures that he had to share with the general public. Later, it became quite clear that he did not want to share his orchestras permanently with any other conductor.

Langbein's trust in Sacher was never fully reinstated. Nevertheless, when Langbein died of cancer in 1993, it was Paul Sacher who delegated to a friend in Zurich the task of getting a good lawyer to handle Langbein's estate. The bill, which ran into many thousands of francs, was 'taken care of' by Sacher.

Disarmingly, alongside the whims and coldness, Sacher could and often did display great sensitivity, generosity and caring, which won him lifelong friends. Such displays, which in my opinion were wholly genuine, sometimes made his critics revise their opinions. Despite the growth of his legend, Sacher remembered his origins:

he had long since left the place where his stone had fallen, but the memory of that place could never be erased. He remained capable of showing respect for and great empathy with others, both on a large scale and over small details. One instance of the latter remains indelible in my mind.

It occurred during the first two weeks of my new life in Switzerland, when I was staying on Schönenberg for the first time as the Sachers' guest. Lunch and dinner at the house were always served formally by the white-gloved butler, and female guests were always served first, then came female staff members like Paul's secretary, the housekeeper, then Maja, then male guests, and Paul last. And I noticed that there was a clear hierarchy of serving among the guests. The most important were served first. I was twenty-one at the time, and usually the youngest at the table, so older female guests were served before me, and after me came the staff and Maja. But one day there were no other female guests, so I was served first.

That day, beside the main plate there were extra glass sideplates, which I'd never seen before, and I wasn't sure what they were for. The meal was *Siedfleisch*, boiled beef, which was served with a number of accompaniments, including, in the Sacher household, *Senffrüchte,* fruit marinated in mustard and sugar. Well, I put my *Senffrüchte* next to the beef on my main plate, and then saw to my discomfort that all the others put theirs on the glass sideplates. But when Paul was served, he put his on his main plate, as I had. Over the years, I often ate *Siedfleisch* again at Schönenberg, and Paul never again put his *Senffrüchte* on his main plate. I know he did so that first day simply to prevent my being embarrassed.

19

The Crown of Dreams

> The Foundation should provide the means through which the research of today and tomorrow can extend our knowledge of modern art. This aim seems appropriate to me as an extension and development of my efforts on behalf of contemporary music for over seventy years.[57]

Such was Sacher's definition of the aims of his foundation, which opened its doors to the public on 28 April 1986. Since its opening, the Paul Sacher Foundation – an international archive and centre for research into twentieth-century music – has offered musicians, musicologists and the public at large a unique wealth of resources. To Paul Sacher, though, it was a final project which would ensure the sustaining of his influence upon the music of his times. It was the crown of all his dreams.

★★★

The creation of the Paul Sacher Foundation was, like the creation of the BKO and the Schola Cantorum, the result of long years of planning and preparing. 'Let's put it this way,' Sacher told me in 1993, 'I already knew twenty years ago that I wanted to have a foundation. I had an important library. I had a lot of important manuscripts. I had a lot of documents about the music of this century, correspondence with the composers, and so on. And I always knew that I wanted to preserve these documents. This finally took shape in the form of the Paul Sacher Foundation, and funnily enough it took shape only after I had the opportunity to buy the right house. I always knew that I would need a house for my foundation.'

Not only did Sacher know he would need a house, but in the early 1970s he already knew which one. It was at 4 Münsterplatz, in Basle's Cathedral Square, and had been built between 1844 and 1846. It was an example of unpretentious classicist architecture with its simple three-storeyed front façade looking towards the cathedral. The side of the building hidden from the square faced on to the Rhine, and had a festively structured, six-storeyed façade. The rooms were of classic proportions, and had decorative panelling, stucco ceilings and tiled stoves.

In 1908, its former owner, Maria Margaretha Steffensen-Burckhardt, had bequeathed the house to the Voluntary Academic Society of Basle for use as accommodation for university professors or their widows. The last such occupant, the Swiss historian Werner Kaegi, lived in the house for more than forty years, during which time he wrote his biography of Jacob Burckhardt, Basle's great nineteenth-century historian of art and civilization. Sacher probably met Kaegi, who was five years his senior, through Edgar Bonjour.

'I had already known Kaegi for a long time,' Sacher said. 'When I was at the university, I often ran into him. He usually had his violin with him. Later from time to time he invited me to tea.

'One day this Kaegi rang me and said, "I can't finish my biography. I've been given notice to quit my apartment. I have twenty thousand books in this apartment which I need for my work. I'll never find another place where I can store all these books, and I'm much too old to move. I would have liked to finish my biography." Then I thought, "Okay, I'll buy the house. Kaegi can stay, and later I can have the foundation there." When I reconstruct the sequence of events today, I think that's how it was.'

Whatever the exact sequence of events, Kaegi's call to Sacher was made in 1973, and that year the Paul Sacher Foundation was established. The purchase of the house, however, was not completed until 1974 and provided another example of the trouble that awaited anyone who got in Sacher's way.

'The Voluntary Academic Society of Basle had decided to sell the house because it was expensive to maintain, and the rent they got from the professors was modest,' recalled Sacher. 'The society's president, the lawyer Lukas Sarasin, whom I know well, sold it to a building society [the Basler Baugesellschaft] of which his brother, Alfred Sarasin, was president.'

Unfortunately for the Sarasin brothers, Sacher wanted the house, and not only because of Kaegi's predicament. He had, he claimed, indicated his interest to Sarasin on an earlier occasion, and he was not about to be thwarted.

'I said to Lukas Sarasin, "You remember I told you once before that I was interested in buying this house? Now you apparently want to sell it to your brother, but you can't do that because no matter what price he offers I'm going to offer a higher price. No matter what the price is, I'll pay a hundred thousand francs more. And it would be disloyal management [of the Voluntary Academic Society] if you sold it for a cheaper price instead of giving it to me for a higher price." Sarasin answered that it was too late: the sale had already taken place and there was nothing more he could do. Then I told this story to a lawyer and said to him, "Please ensure that I can buy this house." He was pleased with this task and, despite considerable difficulties, managed to buy the building two days later.'

In a brief discussion with Lukas Sarasin in 1999, I heard the same story from a very different perspective. Sacher, claimed Sarasin, had never confirmed his interest in the property in writing, and the sale to the Basler Baugesellschaft had been honourable, irrespective of whether Sarasin's brother was its president. The incident had humiliated Sarasin professionally to the extent that he described it as having 'banged some nails into his coffin' and, even a quarter of a century later and months after Sacher's death, he was reluctant to discuss it. 'Don't go writing anything stupid,' he admonished me after telling his side of the story.

As a result of the purchase, Werner Kaegi was able to remain in the house until his death in 1979. The affair illustrated Sacher's remarkable ability to turn problems into opportunities, as Professor Jean Rudolf von Salis confirmed: 'One day Paul Sacher wrote to me, "I have bought the house, Professor Kaegi can stay." Of course, at the same time he's very cunning. He knew that Kaegi was already an old man. He knew that this house would be valuable to him. The professor then, in fact, died one day of a stroke. He wasn't so terribly old, he was seventy-nine when he died. Then Sacher was able to set up the foundation in the house. From 1979 he could use the house as he pleased.'

When he bought it, the house was 'very cheap', according to Sacher. 'It was a little more than a million Swiss francs. But it was a lousy house. No central heating, and everything a hundred years old. Restoring the house cost ten times more than the house itself.'

The restoration, which took from 1982 to 1985, was entrusted to the architects Katharina and Wilfrid Steib. Their team had the demanding task of rearranging the house's interior in such a way as to meet the Sacher Foundation's requirements, while preserving its exterior and the original fixtures and adornments of its rooms. Though virtually no change was noticeable from the outside, the building underwent drastic interior alterations, with the expansion of the top floor and the cellar, and the construction of a two-storey atrium that replaced the backyard and coach-house. In spring 1985 the foundation moved in, and its staff had just a year to prepare before its official opening on 28 April 1986 – Paul Sacher's eightieth birthday.

In his original vision, Sacher saw the foundation as 'actually only for my own legacy, for everything that I own in the way of books and music. And also for my correspondence, everything which has come together during my long life as a conductor.'

His collection contained many treasures. In the years after Stravinsky's death in 1971, for instance, he had acquired eight of the composer's music autographs, including full scores of *Le Sacre du printemps* and *Symphonies of Wind Instruments*, as well as sketches for *Renard*, *Pulcinella* and *Apollon Musagète*. Yet Sacher's collection of original scores, as it stood in the late 1970s, was limited by international standards and was unlikely to have brought the foundation international recognition.

'I am absolutely not a collector,' he often told me (a curious claim considering the number of items he had already amassed). 'At no level. If I had been, I would have asked the composers for their original manuscripts. I simply said, "I want to perform this work, I want the right of first performance." I could very well have said, "And the manuscript." But I didn't. At that time I didn't know I would have the foundation. That was very stupid of me. If I had known about the foundation then, I would probably have made possession of the original score a condition, but I didn't. I just have those few scores which were given to me.'

Then, in 1983 there arose an opportunity for which the establishment of his foundation had prepared him. Across the Atlantic, Stravinsky's own musical collection became available for sale. If Sacher could acquire it, he would be able to provide the foundation with immediate international standing through a single purchase.

★★★

Throughout his life, Stravinsky frequently gave away or sold individual manuscripts, or left them with his publishers. Nevertheless, when an inventory of his manuscripts and papers was drawn up after his death in 1971, the musical autographs totalled 225. Some scores and documents were sold individually during the following decade, but the rest – about two-thirds of the total – were to be included in a single sale in New York in 1982.

'Then Mr Albi Rosenthal, with whom I was already acquainted, came to see me,' remembered Sacher. 'He said, "The Stravinsky *Nachlass* [musical estate] is up for sale in New York. It costs such and such ... That would be something for your foundation."'

Albi Rosenthal was a fourth-generation member of the Rosenthal family, who were international dealers in original manuscripts and music autographs. Described by Sacher as 'a highly educated connoisseur of music', he had known Stravinsky well, and had continued his friendship with Stravinsky's second wife, Vera, after the composer's death.

'As early as 1976,' Rosenthal wrote, 'Paul Sacher ... [wrote and] asked Vera Stravinsky and Robert Craft whether there were any sketches in the Stravinsky archive for the cantata *A Sermon, a Narrative and a Prayer*, which Stravinsky had composed for him. This query arrived just as I was eating lunch with Vera Stravinsky and Robert Craft in their apartment on Fifth Avenue. Robert Craft brought out the sketches, and I took them to Basle.'[58]

Rosenthal also negotiated the acquisition of other Stravinsky works for Sacher, including the original score of *Le Sacre du printemps*. The purchase of that score, which had been given to Vera Stravinsky by her husband before his death, embroiled Rosenthal briefly in a legal battle between Vera and her step-children.

'Paul asked if there was any possibility of buying something else from Vera,' he recalled. 'She wanted to sell *Le Sacre du printemps*, to make some money [for her legal fees], because Stravinsky's children were always suing her for this and that ... When she sold [*Sacre*] her step-children sued her, saying that she didn't have the right to sell it, and that if she did they should have part of the sale price. There was a hearing in England. Three lawyers came over from New York, and I was invited to attend – to be grilled – because I had negotiated the sale. One of the lawyers said, "So, Mr Rosenthal, you bought this *Sacre du printemps* very cheaply and then sold it for a large price to Paul Sacher." I said, "Nothing of the kind. I never bought the manuscript. I was only the agent. Here are all my papers. The price was established. I received a commission fee of less than five per cent." Next question: "Why didn't you offer this manuscript for two or three times the price to a Texas oil millionaire?" I replied, 'There are two reasons. First of all, once a price is established, it doesn't matter who buys it – whether it's a millionaire or a poor institution, the price remains the same. Secondly, if I had talked to a Texas oil millionaire about Stravinsky, he would have asked me, "Is that a racehorse?" There was general laughter, and that was the end of that.'

Rosenthal's capable handling of this and other negotiations on Sacher's behalf meant that Sacher had great trust in his recommendations and ability to represent him.

'It was Rosenthal who told me in 1983, "Now you could buy Stravinsky." I said, "Go ahead." It was very difficult because he had to deal with the whole family: the sons, the daughter, and Robert Craft, the sole heir of Stravinsky's widow ... I neither wanted nor was able to deal with that, so he did it. It was long and difficult, full of obstacles because there were also other people who wanted the estate. Rosenthal and I had to speak money. I told him, "Listen, I can't pay that [amount]. It's impossible. But let me say..." and I said a certain sum. And Rosenthal answered, "I will try. I can give you an answer later."

'And one night – I remember it very well: I had rehearsals in Zurich and I slept at the Hotel Baur au Lac – in the middle of the night, the phone rang. It was Albi, who said, "Listen. Now you have to decide immediately because there is another man offering a high price, and I think offering the sum I am now proposing to you will get it for you." So I said, "Okay. I will pay that. You can offer it."'

While the New York Public Library searched in vain for a benefactor to exercise its first option on what represented the most significant body of musical manuscripts and memorabilia of the twentieth century, Rosenthal acquired the collection for the Sacher Foundation in June 1983 for US$ 5.25 million. *'Valium vincit omnium'*,[59]* a jubilant Rosenthal is said to have cabled Sacher when the deal was done. A decade later, Sacher laughingly described the purchase as 'a very good start for the foundation'.

'I don't know if you can understand,' Sacher continued, 'You want to set up a foundation – for music of the twentieth century. I think you have to have a good start, and the legacy of Stravinsky was the best start possible. So I thought I not only paid the Stravinsky family but gave the foundation a brilliant debut.'

Besides original scores of Stravinsky's works, the collection contained the composer's carefully preserved correspondence. There were personal albums kept from 1912 to 1939, as well as numerous other documents ranging from Stravinsky's Russian passport to the diaries which he kept in his last years – the collection filled 116 large boxes. There was also a photographic archive, containing numerous albums with family photographs, hundreds of pictures showing contacts and encounters, and many documents from concert tours and performances.

Although Sacher 'never paid the same for anybody else afterwards', within a few years several more collections – including the comprehensive Moldenhauer collection of Webern manuscripts** – had been added to the foundation's resources, the latter purchase showing clearly that Sacher recognized the importance of Webern's music, even if it did not touch him personally. Other composers whose collections were purchased during the following decade included Elliot Carter, Luciano Berio, Witold Lutowslaski, Pierre

---

* 'Valium conquers all' (referring to a source of Sacher's wealth).
** The larger part of the foundation's Anton Webern collection was acquired from the Moldenhauer Archives in Spokane, Washington, in 1984.

Boulez, and the German composer Wolfgang Rihm. These acquisitions cemented the foundation's reputation as an international archive and one of the world's foremost collections of contemporary classical music.

★★★

The foundation was the culmination of Sacher's personal ambitions and dreams. It brought together the threads of his rich and complex artistic life. It was also a huge financial investment.

'I had to pay a great deal of money for the foundation,' he told me in 1985, shortly before its official opening, and before the later additions had been made. 'The purchase of the house, the renovations [almost as much again as the purchase of the Stravinsky collection]. And the foundation needs a fortune from which it can live, because it has a staff and many running costs. A sufficiently large fortune so that it never gets into trouble, and can continue. I gave that fortune. Since then, I am not exactly poor, but poorer.'

In 1984, just months after the Stravinsky collection had reached Basle, part of it was displayed in an exhibition at the Basle Art Museum. At the opening, Sacher made a speech in which he referred to the Prussian entomologist Carl August Dohrn. 'An inner voice had told him that all personal wealth must be justified, and that it was only on loan. I think exactly like this man.'[60]

A year later, I asked Sacher if the establishment of the foundation was his way of justifying the wealth brought to him by his marriage. His reply was: 'Listen, from the beginning until now I have spent a tremendous fortune for the foundation. It is not my private hobby. It's an institution serving music and musicologists. It's not mine. It's given away. It belongs to everybody … I gave it a large fortune because I wanted it to remain independent. I wanted it to be autonomous – not to have to depend on money from Basle, or Berne, or from rich people. And now the foundation lives on the interest from that fortune. Of course there can be a revolution, or something I can't know now, and we might lose all the money, but then we will have to see how we can go on. As far as a man can think in the future, I did what I thought necessary, and what was possible for me.'

★★★

While the foundation represented the crowning of his dreams, Sacher's private life in the early 1970s was beginning to resemble a crown of thorns.

Nina von Faber-Castell's health had begun to deteriorate in the late 1960s. 'In the Von Sprecher family there was a real susceptibility to migraine,' said Count Anton von Faber-Castell in 1993. 'My great-grandfather suffered from it, and apparently also my grandfather. My mother had the same tendency, already as a young woman, and she also had a certain vascular weakness. Something unusual.'

Bad though the migraines were, Nina was to undergo a far worse trial. When she was still a young woman, she began to suffer episodes of the torturously painful trigeminal neuralgia, a condition so excruciating it has been known to lead to suicide. She later described the pain of these episodes to Sacher as 'a feeling as if the point of a knife is being twisted around in your face'.

Around the time of the Second World War, the medication normally prescribed for trigeminal neuralgia was morphine, a drug which not only was addictive but could initiate huge mood swings. With time, the drug began to take its toll. Nina's son Andreas confirmed that her behaviour towards Sacher began to change during the 1970s. Whether it was the result of her growing drug-dependence, or delayed guilt following the death of her ex-husband, or because – as Andreas claimed – she was 'self-destructive', her interactions with Sacher took on a darker tone, and conflict between the couple grew.

At the same time, Maja Sacher, already in her early eighties, was beginning to experience loss of memory and symptoms of physical decline. Sacher, on the other hand, with his sleek, well-cared-for good looks and robustness, looked considerably younger than his seventy years. With both the women in his life entering phases of mental and physical crisis, he had become vulnerable and – at some level – 'available' to others once more.

★★★

In 1974, a young doctor from northern Germany joined the Basle Chamber Choir. Green-eyed, chestnut-haired, vibrant, sensitive and academically brilliant, thirty-one-year-old Irmtraut Schmid attracted Sacher's attention. She caught him almost unawares.

'She had studied medicine. Then she had worked in a hospital as an intern ... and then she came to Basle. She was bright, clever. She had a first-class brain, and she was very good at science ... She would have preferred to be a musician, but she didn't have the necessary musical training. I think she had a lot of talent. She sang tunefully. She had a good ear for music. She played the transverse flute very nicely and she played the piano a little. If she had had time to study music...'

The affair between Paul and Irmtraut progressed in secret. It was not until nearly six years later, according to Cornelia von Faber-Castell, that Sacher informed Nina of his 'new' love. Her reaction was to end their relationship.

Maja Sacher, too, very likely knew of her husband's involvement with Irma, but chose to ignore it. In 1976, she once referred obliquely to his outside relationships by saying to me, 'Life has not always been easy with Paul.'

As with Romana and Nina, Sacher's relationship with Irma remained a secret from the outside world for several years. And it might have remained so, except that Irma then informed Sacher that she wanted a child. His response, he told me, was 'There's no question of my having another child. Find someone else. I'm covered as far as children are concerned. I already have two daughters who have another name. If I ever have another child in my life, I want to live with that child. I don't want things to be the same way as they were with the girls.'

Sacher's feeling of loss at not having been closer to his daughters when they were growing up was one they shared. When asked by the film-maker François Reichenbach about Paul's role as a father, Katharina von Faber-Castell replied, 'He has been a good father. But he wasn't around to be a dad.'

Irma was not about to give up her dream, however. When her wish to have a child was continually refused, she eventually threatened to leave. 'I told her, "You may have to bring the child up alone. ... I don't know how long I will have to be with you both."'

Irmtraut Schmid, 1985

But she still persisted.' In the end Paul relented, and in 1981 his son, Georg Schmid, was born. Irma was thirty-eight. Paul was seventy-five.

During Georg's infancy, he lived alone with his mother, out of sight of Paul's family and closest friends. Sacher paid his new family daily visits, and spent his weekends and holidays largely with them, but they were set apart from his other lives. Few people knew initially of the existence of this third family; Sacher's own daughters were not told about their half-brother until several weeks after his birth. It seems likely that Sacher would have waited even longer to tell them, had not his boyish pride in a son overcome his customary reticence.

'I was studying at a language school in England,' recalled Cornelia von Faber-Castell. 'Paul and Kätheli [Katharina] came to visit me, and we met in London. Kätheli and I shared a room in the hotel, he had his own room … He came in his pyjamas and dressing gown into our room, took out some Polaroid photos and threw them on to the bed – photos of an infant. We looked at each other, and said, "No – are you crazy?" He was very proud.'

Paul's wish to live with any other child he sired seemed unlikely to be fulfilled at the time of Georg's birth. He was married to Maja and, as he stated categorically, he never had any intention of ending the marriage. 'I told Nina, and I told Irma, "I am married to Maja. I will not leave her."'

As so often with Sacher's visions, dreams and desires, his wish to live with his son was to be realized – but this time, cruelly, by an uncanny twist of fate.

20

Solitude

In 1984, when their son was three years old, Irma was diagnosed as having breast cancer.

'I still remember,' said Ernst Würmli, Sacher's long-standing chauffeur, assistant and friend. 'I picked him up at 11 p.m. In a heavy voice he said, "Now Frau Schmid has cancer." That's when it actually began. That was dreadful.'

Despite immediate surgery and brief remissions, Irma's cancer spread unabated, a catalyst for changes of unprecedented size in Sacher's life. He was prepared to do anything that would help her, and when it was suggested that public acknowledgement of her and Georg might have a positive effect, he acquiesced. In September 1984, Sacher boarded the luxurious ocean liner *Mermoz* for a Mediterranean cruise, with Irma and Georg in tow. It was no ordinary cruise, but the 26th Festival of Music at Sea (26. *Festival de Musique en Mer*), for which Sacher and the Collegium Musicum Zurich had been engaged to perform a series of concerts for an elite audience, both on board and at venues of note along the way.

The task of accompanying soloists with the star allure of Jean-Pierre Rampal, 'Slava' Rostropovich, James Galway, Maurice André and Shlomo Mintz, most of whom planned to perform works outside Sacher's usual repertoire, would have been a challenge for any conductor. But at seventy-eight Sacher – preoccupied with Irma and their son – was, according to an orchestra member who wished to remain unnamed, 'quite clearly overloaded'. Why he had chosen this awkward occasion on which to acknowledge his new family is unclear.

He certainly wished to help Irma, and believed that the sea air would benefit her and the child. Perhaps he also believed that his public acknowledgement of his new family would be easier with the support of his friend Slava and those in the orchestra with whom he was on closer terms. The presence of Irma and 'Beppi' (Georg's nickname as a young child), however, created conflict for some of Sacher's older friends, who felt that they were being forced to compromise the integrity of their relationships with Maja Sacher. Others, both those who wanted to please Paul and those who were genuinely interested in his new family, made such a fuss of Georg that the three-year-old had to be taught a new phrase which, according to all accounts, he repeated constantly: '*Ne touchez pas!*' ('Don't touch!'). Whatever the reasons for Sacher's choice, the hoped-for therapeutic effect did not appear.

During the course of Irma's and Maja's illnesses, Sacher began to question himself deeply, wondering whether his very contact with Irma and his two other partners had led to their illnesses. 'Sometimes I wonder whether I have brought bad luck to these women,' he once speculated. 'They have all had to suffer so much.'

The concern that he himself might be the source of their suffering emerged from the superstitious side of Sacher's nature, which was carefully hidden behind his public mask. It was both endearing and frustrating for those who knew him well. For instance, a few weeks after his eightieth birthday, the loss of his diary symbolized for him the approaching end of his life, causing him to cancel professional commitments in order to make his will. 'When you no longer have tasks to do, your life is over' was his comment at the time. When the diary was found at Schönenberg two days later, his relief was huge.

Only those few of Sacher's friends who really knew him well had any sense of the mental anguish he faced in the mid-1980s. The mask he had developed over six decades was still firmly in place, but gradually he was obliged to set it aside and share his burdens with a few trusted friends. In autumn 1987, with Maja bed-ridden and sometimes unable to recognize him, his relationship with Nina von Faber-Castell in shreds, and Irma's chances of survival increasingly unlikely, he railed, 'We're locked in a cage. I always thought I'd be looked after in my old age. And here I am: two ill women and a small son. One can adapt oneself, of course. But it is not what I expected.'

During the opening of his foundation, and the celebrations for his eightieth birthday, Sacher could escape to some extent by immersing himself in his work. Once the blaze of publicity surrounding the foundation's opening had subsided, however, he had to face his domestic situation more clearly than ever before. A year later, shortly after his eighty-first birthday in 1987, he admitted in private, 'Until about a year ago, life was a series of successes. I always did too much, always said yes, and enjoyed having all these jobs. But there was never stress like this – with Maja, Irma, and Nina.'

With the strain of this situation, Sacher began to question his own health. On 2 June 1987, he telephoned me and said, 'Lesley, you might be the last person I speak to. I'm finished. I've been so tired since the beginning of the year. And it's not that I haven't had enough sleep. Now I feel so heavy. I'm having trouble breathing. And I know it's the end. Last night I had such a dream. There were two huge fires blazing with great intensity.'

At the time of this conversation, another metastasis of Irma's cancer had been discovered. As a doctor, she was now convinced that she could not survive. She was no longer fighting for life, but fighting against a world that allowed this to happen, and for time to spend with her young son.

Her illness, and Sacher's real love for her, caused further changes in his lifestyle. By the middle of 1987, he had pared down his social life to those few social occasions required in connection with his professional activities. Leaving Maja in the care of her devoted nurses, Sacher visited Irma and their son almost daily.

'You see,' he said at the time, 'at the moment I see my son and his mother on every possible evening. I have the impression that they need that, that it's a question of existence for them. I should have dinner, for example, with the Becks – visit them, or invite them. But I don't do any of that any more because I live exclusively for this child and his mother. I just know that this way they will perhaps remain alive. And that's important for the child. That's the building up of his life.

'He must be certain that he has a father, and that he's there. That he owns [his father]. I have to stick to what is absolutely necessary. And that's perhaps an important part of my character. I know when

I have to do something. And then I do it completely. I am capable of giving everything. And that is important in all that one does.'

Sacher's single-minded devotion to Irma and their child was fuelled by both his pride in having a son and Irma's ability to express her needs so openly. His other partners had been strong, independent women but, as Ernst Würmli has pointed out, they showed perhaps too much understanding for Paul's foibles, which Irma did not. She openly challenged who and what he had become.

'He just loved the woman incredibly,' explained Würmli shortly after Irma's death, 'perhaps because she was the way she was. Maja had done everything for him. She had idolized him, relieved him of almost every job – there wasn't so much he could do. But Irma piled more and more jobs on to him. He wasn't used to that. She didn't see him in the light of "He's Mr Sacher – one has to be nice" and so on. On the contrary, she treated him rather brutally.'

The reduction of his social life was not the only change in Sacher's life. In November 1986, he wrote to the members of the Basle Chamber Orchestra, informing them that the ensemble was to end its activities for ever. Ten years earlier, he had succumbed to outside pressure to remain with the orchestra until a suitable replacement for himself, and secure financial backing, had been found. Now, with no replacement to his liking in sight, the orchestra would simply cease to exist.

'Now it's time to put my earlier decision into action', he said in his letter. 'At the close of the current season the BKO will end its activities. I would like to thank our members, our public, the artists who have participated in our concerts, the authorities for their support, especially our board of directors and my associates. I am very happy that I have been able to realize my vision…'[61]

The final decade of the BKO's activity had seen Sacher remain true to his initial goals for the orchestra. The programmes of those years included over sixty works which were given their world premières, their Swiss premières or their Basle premières. Among the composers represented were two generations of Swiss composers (Heinz Holliger, Josef Haselbach, Rudolf Kelterborn and Norbert Moret), as well as new names from other parts of the world, such as Marek Kopelent, Edison Denissow, Isang Yun, Cristóbal Halffter and György Ligeti.

Sacher had also used his BKO concerts in the late 1970s and early 1980s to test potential replacements for himself. Of the eighty-seven concerts performed by the BKO during that period, forty-seven were conducted by other people. A number of these other conductors were overseas guests, composers like Boulez, Henze, Lutoslawski and Krzysztof Penderecki, who were invited to conduct programmes which included their own works. But a considerable number were Swiss musicians and composers who had more or less conducting experience, such as Brenton Langbein, Karl Scheuber, Jürg Wyttenbach, and the world-renowned oboist Heinz Holliger, who conducted twelve concerts and who was tipped by insiders to be Sacher's likely choice for his successor. But the orchestra's end came without Sacher designating a replacement.

The Swiss press snatched up the news of Sacher's decision, describing it as the 'apparently solitary and quick decision of Paul Sacher, founder, director, and financial supporter of the orchestra'.[62]

Sacher did not agree. 'The decision wasn't quick at all. I said ten years ago that I wanted to stop with the chamber orchestra. At that time there was strong pressure from outside. People said, "You're young. You're healthy. You can continue." Now people can still say, "You're healthy," but they can't really say, "You're young."

'You know, I founded the chamber orchestra on my own. Of course, friends helped, but I'm speaking about the initiative. I think it's reasonable that I also decide, on my own, that I want to stop. Of course it's possible that I could go on for a couple of years. Maybe ten. No one knows. But I'd rather stop at a time at which people are sorry that it's ending. I don't want to wait until people are thinking, "Now it's getting to be high time he left." And I think it's a good moment, because by the next concert in January [1987] it will be exactly sixty years since our first concert.'

Another reason why Sacher believed he was entitled to decide the orchestra's fate was that he had carried the orchestra's entire deficits for almost half a century. It was only from 1982 to 1986 that the canton of Basle City subsidized the BKO's work, with payments totalling SFr 800,000.[63] The size of this sum gives a clue to just how much Sacher himself probably invested in the orchestra between 1934 and the early 1980s, a figure that can no longer be established with any certainty.

The end of the BKO by no means signalled an end to Sacher's conducting activities in Basle. Since 1968, he had repeatedly collaborated with solo percussionists from the Basle Orchestra Society (Basler Orchestergesellschaft), who were known collectively at that time in Basle as the Schlagzeug Register der BOG. These musicians had joined the BKO for a performance of Stravinsky's *Les Noces* in May 1968 in the framework of a Stravinsky festival in Basle, and for its first Basle performance of Carlos Chávez's *Toccata for Percussion Instruments* in January 1972. Sacher was greatly impressed by the players' virtuosity, and gradually established a close working relationship with the group's three leaders – Jean-Claude Forrestier, Markus Ernst and Sigfried Schmid – including them increasingly in his programme planning meetings. In 1971, following changes in the Basle Orchestra Society, the six leading members of the group were reconstituted as the Basle Percussion Ensemble (Basler Schlagzeug Ensemble: BSE), with Paul Sacher as conductor.

The creation of the BSE was the creation of Paul Sacher's third and last ensemble, and it mirrored both his life-long interest in music with strong rhythmic elements and also his ongoing interest in accessing and performing new repertoire. Like his two previous ensembles, the BSE had its own unique influence on the shape of the compositions of Sacher's composer friends in the 1980s and early 1990s. Two late works by Conrad Beck were clearly influenced by Sacher's growing interest in percussion, as was Henri Dutilleux's *Mystère de l'instant* (1989) and Wolfgang Rihm's *'Gebild'* for string orchestra, high trumpet, and two percussionists (1982).

Sacher also commissioned a number of works for the BSE, which again influenced the output of the commission recipients. Sven-Erik Bäck's *'Signos'* for six percussionists, 1980; Patricia Jünger's *'Oh You My Sweet Evening Star'* for six percussionists (1982); Rudolf Kelterborn's *'Resonant Visions'* for six percussionists and six obbligato instruments (1979), and Norbert Moret's *'Visitations'* for soprano, mezzo-soprano, tenor, organ, piano et percussion (1981-2) were among these commissions, and were shaped directly by the ensemble's formation and capabilities. The works were composed either exclusively for percussion instruments or for percussion instruments with the addition of other solo instruments.

Sacher regularly conducted the BSE in concerts in Basle and other major Swiss cities, and integrated soloists from the group in his BKO and Collegium concerts as the need arose. His last performance with the group took place in January 1999, just four months before his death, in a concert in Basle for Greenpeace.

★★★

The vacuum created in the contemporary music scene in Basle after Sacher's single-handed dissolution of the BKO did not remain for long. On the initiative of Rudolf Kelterborn, Jürg Wyttenbach, and Heinz Holliger, who had all appeared as guest conductors of the BKO, a new ensemble under the name of Musik Forum was created to carry on where Sacher had stopped. As Jürg Wyttenbach later explained, 'We didn't want to lose the interest and support of the BKO subscribers.'

Like the BKO, the Forum planned to perform both contemporary and early music, and it was able to draw some eighty per cent of the audience for its first concert series from the ranks of earlier BKO subscribers. It also managed to obtain financial support from the Basle city government. When the concert series began, however, there was no word of recognition in its programme of the advantages gained from the BKO's past, and no mention of the fact that the way to filling the new series had been paved by Sacher's 'education' of the Basle public for sixty years. Asked in 1998 about this omission (which had hurt Sacher), the Forum's administrator said that Sacher's contribution had been recognized in so many other ways that 'it had been considered unnecessary' to mention him in the programme.

★★★

By summer 1988, Irma Schmid's cancer had spread widely. Although she accompanied Sacher to Oxford in June, when he was awarded an honorary doctorate for his services to music from Oxford University, that was her last public appearance with him. As the summer drew to a close, her condition had begun to deteriorate rapidly. Four months later, the fight was nearly over.

For the last weeks of her life, until she was taken to hospital, Irma was moved from her apartment above the Sacher Foundation at Münsterplatz to the Schönenberg estate, where she was cared for in the old 'Ferme', a renovated seventeenth-century farmhouse which had housed many of the Sachers' famous guests. Then, for a short time, both she and Maja lay within five hundred metres of each other. Sacher, fighting for his own emotional survival, was imprisoned between them.

'Irma's nothing but skin and bones,' he reported in October. 'I've never watched someone die before. This is the first time. I always wanted to live. But now I have to watch. My next task will be her funeral.'

Irmtraut Schmid died at midnight on 9 November 1988.

The funeral took place in the Niklauskapelle (St Nicholas Chapel) of Basle Cathedral, where Rostropovich played for Paul and Georg and their friends during the service. Sacher performed his role as host of the proceedings impeccably, displaying great affection and concern for his young son. His own grief over Irma's death had been spent largely while she was still alive.

'It's something very strange. I believe I've always cried before the event has happened. I know very exactly that I mourned Irma's death while she was still alive, once I understood how it would end. There have been a number of things which I have mourned, but always before the event. Irma's death hit me unbelievably hard.'

Sacher saw clearly that his relationship with Irma had made changes in him, as had his relationships with Maja and Nina. 'I believe that women have developed me. They made a different person out of me. I have learnt a huge amount from women, and my person, my being, my character has changed through them. For instance, I've learnt to be more considerate, to be gentle... My relationship with Nina, for instance, certainly changed me greatly at that time, and the relationship with Irma changed me greatly once again. I can show you that with a silly example.

'Irma was playing with Georg. I arrived and, as I'm used to doing, I drew attention to myself. And then she was very angry and disappointed, and said, 'Can't you learn to behave in a way that doesn't disturb us? You can come in, and see what we're doing, and watch. But it is not necessary for you to talk every time you enter the room, and it is certainly not necessary for you to talk about yourself...'

'One has to learn that. No one told me that. But I've learnt it. Now I can come in and be very quiet and watch and listen.'

After Irma's death, these personal changes did not end, but now they were shaped by the needs of a seven-year-old boy.

'In reality, I live for him,' Sacher explained in 1989. 'I organize my life around him. He knows that. He sees it. He experiences it. And he knows that those are not just words but reality. That's important for him. A child has to know that it's loved. He has to know that even when he makes the biggest mess of things, he can come home and he will still be loved. That's very important. And I say that to him. And I believe that that is an explanation for his getting over his mother's death. He's a happy child. He's not a sad being.'

In late June 1989, Georg accompanied Sacher's friend and director of the former Roche-funded Institute of Immunology, Fritz Melchers, and his wife Ursula, on a week's trip to Philadelphia. Without his son, the eighty-three-year-old Sacher felt his loneliness and his mortality. 'I suddenly realize what it feels like to be alone,' he told me. Not surprisingly, with his son away, Sacher sought the solace of Schönenberg, where ninety-three-year-old Maja Sacher was living out the last weeks of her life. 'I've known Maja since 1930,' he told me that week. 'When she dies, my support will be gone. Then I could go, too.'

Maja Sacher-Hoffman died on 8 August 1989.

A couple of hours before the official funeral service held in Basle Cathedral, a private family ceremony took place at the Basle cemetery Friedhof am Hörnli. It was attended by Maja's two surviving children and members of their families, Paul, Ernst Würmli and his wife, and members of the household staff, including Maja's devoted nurses. Here, Sacher comforted those who showed their grief openly as they cast red roses down onto Maja's coffin, which lay in the place prepared for it next to the graves of Emanuel and Andreas Hoffmann. In the cathedral, however, it was Sacher who could no longer restrain his grief.

★★★

Not long afterwards, on a day when he was feeling particularly vulnerable and alone, Paul told another story which showed the sensitive reality beneath his carefully cultivated façade:

'In the year before Irma died, she was desperate. One night she lay awake and scolded me. Who else could she vent her anger on? I was the only one who was reachable. I told her that she shouldn't talk so loudly, because Beppi was asleep between us. Then she started yelling even more loudly. And Beppi woke up.

'This is a true story – as true as I'm sitting here. He woke up. It was about 2 a.m. This five-year-old child sits up in bed with his eyes very wide, and looks at his mother and his father, and says, "Daddy is so kingly and Mummy is so lonely." Ploom. He lies down and goes back to sleep.

'Those words weren't in his vocabulary – "kingly" and "lonely". I get gooseflesh just thinking about it. "Daddy is so kingly, and Mummy is so lonely." But don't you see, it's the same thing. It's always the king who is lonely.'

21

The Grand Old Man of Roche

Sacher's covert acquisition of the share majority of Hoffmann-La Roche in 1945 was his first assault on the control of the company's boardroom, but not his last. Although the Hoffmann family and the company itself ultimately profited hugely from his intervention, Sacher saw clearly that the realization of his own life's goals on the grand scale he had long envisaged was dependent on Maja Hoffmann-Stehlin's wealth, and that her wealth was closely aligned with the success of Hoffmann-La Roche. Through his representation of the Hoffmann family on the company's board, he could influence policy at Roche, but in order to protect his financial power base, he had to gain control – and he already knew how.

'I saw that I could do business well, that no one could fool me,' he stated breezily in the 1980s. Having learnt to discern the subtle secrets of composers from only their notations, and armed with his ability to read people quickly and accurately, Sacher found it relatively straightforward to decode the personalities and intentions of some of those with whom he had business dealings.

'I know these sharks. I know what they are like. I get on well with them. I know them well, and they also amuse me. They are not at all complicated.'

His ability to respond to the demands of his 'business' life as if he had undergone long years of formal business education was inexplicable to many of those who knew him only as a musician. Yet the relationship between the worlds of music and business was far closer than many perceived it to be, as Fritz Gerber, a former president of Hoffmann-La Roche, pointed out in his tribute speech to Sacher during a Roche international managers' meeting shortly before Sacher's eightieth birthday.

'An artist, in particular a musician, can only be successful if he is creative and innovative. Creativity and innovation are only possible if the artist is not afraid of taking risks or breaking new, unfamiliar ground. ... He needs courage and determination. He must not be afraid of criticism and, at times, not even of shocking the public. ... Every modern manager should also be an artist, guided in his daily work by the artist's creativity and courage. In the final analysis, there is probably not such a big difference between Paul Sacher the musician and Paul Sacher the businessman.'[64]

In the business world, Sacher applied the same thinking and the same principles as he applied in his life as a conductor. Working to principle allowed him to change direction when necessary and to see problems as opportunities which he could exploit to the full. Speaking in the 1990s about his need to respond to the demands of his differing activities, he underlined the importance of being able to change direction.

'I think that intellectually, and in my feelings, I am flexible,' he explained. 'It was easy for me to prepare a rehearsal and then to deal with a business matter, and to be as concentrated as I am now, speaking to you, as I am when I have to study my score.'

Whether this flexibility was really a 'gift from God', as Sacher once put it, or the acquired result of working to principle, it was already evident early in his career. 'He once told me,' recalled Els Havrlik, 'that he not only had a plan for his projects, but that his success came from being prepared to let in something new, from being prepared for the unexpected and remaining open enough to adapt to it. He let himself be taught by the unexpected. He had a feeling for it.'

During the fifty-eight years of Sacher's active participation in the affairs of Hoffmann-La Roche, his ability to remain open to change was severely tested, as in the late 1970s in the aftermath of the Seveso incident (an accident at a Roche-owned chemical plant in northern Italy resulted in the release of toxic chemicals into the atmosphere, leading to an environmental scandal), and a decade later when the company underwent a huge process of financial restructuring. Astoundingly, until 1987 Hoffmann-La Roche had never had recourse to the capital market, a fact of which Sacher was hugely proud. The closest the company ever came to capital market debt had been in 1920, when its original shareholders were asked to double their subscriptions, a debt later repaid in full.

But in 1986, the company's head of finance, Dr Henri Meier, began the challenging task of persuading Sacher and other board members that incurring capital market debt was an important step in the financial restructuring process he needed to implement, and that it would profit the company in the long term. Sacher initially resisted, but finally agreed, exhibiting his willingness to change an opinion when he was convinced of the advantages of doing so. In 1987, Hoffmann-La Roche raised SFr 250 million on the capital market through the issue of bonds with attached gold warrants.

Sacher's pioneering spirit, so clearly evident in his commissions, also found expression in his business dealings. He was future-oriented, an aspect of his personality that helped him to do good business. The most tangible expression of his pioneering spirit in business was his active interest in the research carried out by Roche, particularly through the Roche-funded Institute of Immunology in Basle.

Other important traits which helped Sacher succeed in business were his meticulous preparation and his tremendous discipline. Preparation was done largely behind closed doors at Schönenberg, and he rarely wasted time talking about it. When meals were over, he seldom lingered with his guests after coffee, but returned to his study where the preparation of his meetings and rehearsals continued.

Because his preparation was so quiet and methodical, others were often led to think he had no need to prepare, a misconception which Sacher cultivated. Fritz Gerber, in his eulogy at Sacher's funeral in Basle Cathedral on 2 June 1999, said he had noticed in business meetings that Sacher 'hardly read the reports, but always asked the right questions'. The ability to ask the right questions was, however, due to the fact that, besides being extremely well prepared, Sacher could tease out the essentials of a discussion with remarkable rapidity.

Another example of Sacher's careful preparation was his speech-making. During his lifetime, he made hundreds of speeches in both business and artistic circles. Many were made in German, but a large number were made in English. Comments by his listeners often indicated that they thought his ease in making good speeches – often without notes or barely referring to the notes he had – meant he had a natural speaking talent. Having worked from 1976 to 1998 as a ghost-writer and translator for dozens of Sacher's English speeches, I see things very differently.

Sacher's speeches were well-planned, fine-tuned, and polished for days; he often reworked a finished speech completely when a new idea came to him. At other times, he would summon me to Basle to check his pronunciation, often ringing me up within hours of an event to check a word he was suddenly unsure of. Nor was this just at the end of his life; it had been the case for at least twenty years.

Preparedness, flexibility, fascination and ruthless discipline – all of these traits enabled Sacher to translate his success in music and administration into business success. But there was something else, another trait which destined Sacher for success in the special climate of Hoffmann-La Roche, and that was his discretion.

★★★

Right up to the late 1970s the discretion and downright secrecy that attended Hoffmann-La Roche's dealings were frankly amazing. After the Second World War, the company had grown to become a worldwide leader in vitamin production, and by the late 1960s it had climbed to the top of the pharmaceutical ladder. Increasingly, it prided itself on being a 'family', answerable to no one, and it resisted – usually successfully – public scrutiny wherever possible.

The Swiss historian Conrad Peyer has suggested that this inscrutability was the legacy of the low profile adopted by Fritz Hoffmann and his associates during the First World War to avoid the company being blacklisted by the Allies as a German company. But that silence was created in vastly different circumstances, which by no means applied in the following four decades. It is far more likely that the containment of the firm within the firm had been perpetuated by Emil Barell to maintain total control, and continued by Sacher and former Roche president, Dr Adolf Jann, for the same reasons. The fact is that all the personalities who dominated the company from Fritz Hoffmann's death to the end of the Gerber era in 2001 were men who believed in the tactical strength of silence.

Between the end of the Second World War and 1960, Hoffmann-La Roche's yearly total revenue had risen from SFr 200 million to SFr 833 million. After 1960 that figure continued to grow until, according to figures published by the company, it had reached almost SFr 4 billion by 1970. Between 1967 and 1977, Hoffmann-La Roche was unquestionably the top pharmaceutical company in the world.

During those golden years, the company's leadership behaved as if the frequently heard cynical description of Roche – *'Reden ist Silber, Schweigen ist Roche'* ('Speaking is silver, silence is Roche')[65] – had become its official motto. Dr Jakob Oeri, the husband of Sacher's step-daughter Vera Oeri-Hoffmann and himself a member of the board from 1966 to 1996, recalled clearly the pride taken by the company in keeping public information to a minimum, thereby avoiding public scrutiny. The dominant philosophy during Oeri's early years on the board was simply: 'We have no capital market debts. We don't have to tell anyone anything. We're doing well. We don't ask anyone for money, and so we have to open ourselves to scrutiny only as far as the law dictates.' Sacher, Oeri confirmed, 'was definitely also of this opinion'.

A large part of the reason why Roche became the centre of international focus in the early 1960s was linked to the discoveries of the Polish-Jewish chemist Dr Leo Sternbach, who had joined Roche in Basle in 1940 before being transferred a year later to Roche's research team in Nutley, New Jersey. During a period when the pharmaceutical industry worldwide was seeking to produce a tranquillizer which could calm without inducing sleep, Sternbach isolated the active ingredient of Librium while working on benzodiazepine derivatives.

Librium was introduced on to the market in 1960, and a chemically related form was introduced three years later in the form of Valium. Described by a stock analyst as 'the most profitable products ever produced by the pharmaceutical industry',[66] these two tranquillizers alone had earned Roche over SFr 4 billion by 1974. But while public interest in this 'lucky company'[67] grew, Roche continued its policy of reticence, helped by the fact that Switzerland at the time had relatively permissive securities laws.

The lack of transparency, for instance, in Roche's financial reporting at that time was illustrated in 1973 when for the first time the company published consolidated yearly accounts of its two holding companies SAPAC (SA Pour l'Application du Celluloid, originally planned as a small trading company for ready-made celluloid products) and Roche. The 'Balance Statistics' consisted of just one page, with exactly twenty-five figures on it.

By the mid-1960s, curiosity was growing in the media and elsewhere about this family company. Not only did the price of its shares rise astronomically high in the years after the phenomenal success of Librium and Valium (in 1971, a single share cost US$ 45,000, then worth about SFr 200,000), but the company's shares and dividend certificates, when they changed hands at all, were traded on the so-called *Vorbörse*, or 'over the counter', not on the central stock exchange. Questions were treated with disdain, as a small shareholder who dared to pose a question at an annual general meeting of the company in the 1970s recalled.

An indication of Roche's reluctance to divulge information, a 1971 article in *Fortune* magazine bore the title 'The Secret Life of Hoffmann-La Roche'. The author, Robert Ball, had attended the 1971 annual shareholders' meeting in Basle, and his description gives a powerful picture of the clan-like dynamic that pervaded the company at the time.

> 'It could be the annual meeting of a medium-sized family enterprise. Most of the few dozen soberly dressed shareholders live nearby, and before and after the transaction of business there is the cozy conversational buzz of a gathering of the clan. ... The seven points of the agenda are approved unanimously by a simple show of hands. Nobody asks for the floor, nobody puts a question. It is all over in an hour. Viewing the proceedings, an uninformed observer would hardly suspect that this modest gathering in Basle was the annual meeting of the world's biggest ethical-drug manufacturer, undisputed world market leader in vitamins and psychopharmaceuticals, and a company that is currently one of the most profitable enterprises on earth, thanks to the tranquilizers Librium and Valium. ... The company's policy of secrecy about its affairs is also in accord

with the wishes of its effective owners – that small group of wealthy and tradition-minded Patricians of Basle ... renowned even in Switzerland for its conservative ways, dislike of ostentation, and congenital tendency towards understatement.'[68]

For Sacher, the policy of discretion and understatement simply mirrored the trait that had moulded his character and marked his transactions for decades. At Hoffmann-La Roche, he continued to use his discretion to advantage.

'I never showed how good I was, you see,' he confided proudly in the 1980s. 'I was very restrained and extremely discreet. I did my job softly and silently, the way one should if one isn't born really stupid. So I never got myself into a situation in which I felt unsure or uncomfortable. I found it all quite normal and natural.'

The extent of Sacher's restraint and discretion meant that even his step-son, Lukas Hoffmann, while aware that Sacher had in effect single-handedly chosen the company's presidents after Barell, seemed unaware of the real influence his step-father had had on the company's decision-making for more than half a century.

'His intervention was very important at the beginning, due to the fact that he could regain the majority,' Hoffmann told me in 1992. 'Later on, I don't think he interfered with the way the successive managers of Roche did their work, but he had a very important influence on the choice of the new executive officers. It was really his decision who was appointed.'

In some cases, Sacher's back-seat driving was so subtle that the presidents or other executives did not realize just how far his wishes were directing company policy. 'I don't tell him how to play his music; he doesn't tell me how to run the company,'[69] Dr Adolf Jann, president from 1965 to 1978, is said to have responded when asked about Sacher's influence. However, there were others who saw the scope of Sacher's impact on the company more realistically.

'Of course he did a great, great deal,' commented Dr Jakob Oeri in 1994. 'One has to say that, without his involvement, Roche would otherwise be in a completely different position. In the best-case scenario perhaps something like Sandoz, or it would have merged with Sandoz, like Ciba and Geigy.'

Sacher himself was always reluctant to discuss the real extent of his influence. On the rare occasions when he was prepared to do so, he preferred to talk about his activities in terms of workload rather than in terms of decision-making. Any mention of real intervention was made carefully, and with characteristic understatement.

'I did a great deal of work at Roche. Of course the interest there is about money – not for me – but the undertaking has the goal of making money. Still, I was fascinated by the people I met there, by their behaviour, by the way they did their work. There are a few people who have good ideas. They chase something that they really want to realize. Sometimes they're not able to, or sometimes they've been wrong, and it's like being at the cinema. They can become vicious. I didn't have to participate in this malicious film, but I was allowed to watch. And sometimes I said, "No, no, we're not doing that." Sometimes I did intervene.'

One of the reasons for Sacher's reluctance was that he did not wish to compromise the power of the company's presidents, or to cloud his relationships with them. His presidents had to be strong, front-line men with the easy confidence necessary to take the fire when and as it came. Sacher's deliberate low public profile in his dealings at Roche meant that, in times of trouble, he was rarely singled out for comment and criticism, and could elegantly side-step unpleasant issues that sometimes faced the company. He could, for instance, when questioned about the ugly Stanley Adams affair – in which a former Roche employee blew the whistle on the company for price-fixing – avoid further discussion of the issue by simply responding, 'I didn't even know him.'

Hoffmann-La Roche's presidents were important to Sacher's success strategy, and he saw to it that his steering from the back row was done with enormous tact, so that he never appeared to impose. This is confirmed by statements made by Fritz Gerber, in 1988 and in 1993.

'Paul has a very strong will, and he's able to express his ideas, but I never experienced him as being dictatorial, and I wouldn't have stood for that. He's certainly someone who doesn't give up his ideas easily, but he wasn't prejudiced. He never pushed me into anything. We understood each other well. But he did give me a great deal of advice. I was very often able to say to him, "Listen,

I'm considering the following. What would you do?" But there it ended. He never tried to impose himself.'

Because of Sacher's unwillingness, and also that of company members, to speak clearly about his control, it has been difficult to estimate accurately the true extent of his influence. Only when Peyer's Roche chronicle, itself tactful and understated, was published in 1996, was there any real clarity on the extent to which Sacher had influenced the company, especially in the three decades following the Second World War.

For instance, by the time former company president Emil Barell returned from his six-year absence (1940-46) in the USA, Sacher had taken steps to establish a new management structure which would allow more control to others, without posing a clear threat to Barell's position. He had also installed on the board a financial expert, Dr Albert Caflisch, who was clearly planned as Barell's successor. This meant that when Barell died in 1953, all the necessary preparations had already been made for the company to move on with a strong management team under Caflisch's presidency.

Four years later, it was again Sacher who decided that he needed to install a potential new president in the company. He persuaded the lawyer and former general director of the Union Bank of Switzerland, Dr Adolf Walter Jann, to join the Hoffmann-La Roche board, passing over to him as additional leverage the vice-presidency, which he himself had held since 1952. In 1965, Jann was elected president. And when it became clear in the 1970s that a new figure was needed to lead the company out of its growing difficulties, it was Sacher who found and wooed Fritz Gerber, who replaced Jann as president in spring 1978.

'I always say that he seduced me,' said Fritz Gerber in 1988. 'During the autumn of 1977 we had many intensive discussions, and he then suggested that I take over the presidency. I hesitated because I had other obligations, but for me he was such a fascinating personality that I finally accepted his offer.'

As in his work with composers and musicians, Sacher managed to pass on many of his ideas and visions without ever giving the impression that he was steering.

'I would say,' recalled Gerber, 'that he explained things to me that I hadn't understood before from a more philosophical, personal point of view. The enrichment I received from him also came from his enormous tolerance and generosity. [With his help] I found the courage to think in larger dimensions.'

Seven months before his death in May 1999, I asked Sacher once again about the true extent of his impact on the fortunes of Hoffmann-La Roche, observing that it seemed he had had a full-time job. 'We don't talk about that' was his response. 'Maybe one can fit things together if one reads the Peyer book. But it's simple. I was responsible for Roche. You can't do that with just the left hand.'

As he told me in June 1998, 'I brought Roche to its golden age.'

★★★

In the 1970s, however, Hoffmann-La Roche paid a high price for its self-absorption and secrecy. Adolf Jann had initially impressed Sacher and his colleagues on the board with his vision of a new level of integrated medicine in which companies like Hoffmann-La Roche would play a central role. Yet, despite his huge interest in and promotion of pharmaceutical and medical research, he ultimately allowed the complacency created by the success of Librium and Valium to stop him accomplishing the diversification he had planned. Jann's motto, often publicly expressed, that 'We are not the greatest but the finest company' worked well in the first half of his reign as president, when the tranquillizers' success created company euphoria. In the 1970s, however, it became markedly clear that the company had lost touch with the changes in the general attitude towards health and the environment. Because Sacher had ensured Jann's installment, however, he was loathe to remove him, and in this connection has been criticized by former board members, including his step-son, Lukas Hoffmann. It took the worldwide adverse publicity that resulted from the Stanley Adams affair in the early 1970s and the Seveso incident in 1976 to catalyze the beginning of change in the company's attitude towards divulging information.

Stanley Adams, a former Roche executive and product manager, had informed the European Economic Commission's competition directorate in 1973 that Roche and several other multinational companies were breaking EEC free-trade rules by vitamin price-fixing. Adams left Roche shortly afterwards, but his identity was leaked to Roche while proceedings against the company were in train. On 31 December 1974, when Adams tried to enter Switzerland with his family, he was arrested at the border, and later charged with breaching trade secrets and giving economic information to a foreign power (to prove his case against Roche, Adams had passed on confidential business reports, which is against Swiss law). While he was in prison awaiting trial, Adam's wife committed suicide after apparently being told he would serve twenty years. Adams was sentenced to a conditional twelve months' imprisonment and five years' banishment from Switzerland, and later left the country. After Hoffmann-La Roche was fined by the EEC for its illegal trading practices (the fine was later reduced by the European high court to a mere £150,000), Adams himself was awarded damages of around half a million pounds sterling against the European Commission, which had revealed his identity.

This incident, in which the international press clearly sided with Adams, served to compound public distrust of a company so reluctant to divulge information, and that distrust grew to the level of public protest after the Seveso incident eighteen months later.

On 10 July 1976, human error at the production works of the firm Icmesa S.p.A. (a subsidiary of the Roche-owned perfume company Givaudan) in Seveso, Italy, led to the release into the atmosphere of a cloud of chemicals, including the highly poisonous dioxin. According to Roche statistics, there was environmental damage to an area of fifteen square kilometres, 447 people suffered short-term skin damage from the leaked chemicals, and another 193 suffered from chemically-induced acne.*

At the time of the incident, Roche management believed that it could handle the crisis with the same disdain that it had displayed in the Adams affair, but the consumer climate had changed, and the public had become more demanding. Criticism of the company escalated, and in spring 1978 Jann had to go. He was replaced by Fritz Gerber.

With Gerber, a new Roche era began. He provided the leadership which allowed Roche to maintain its prominent position in

---

* Official Roche reports claimed that no long-term adverse physical effects had been established by the mid-1980s.

the pharmaceutical industry, clearly recognizing the necessity for increased cost-consciousness after the fat years of the tranquillizer boom. The know-how for a major financial re-structuring of the company in the late 1980s was supplied by the company's head of finance, Henri Meier. The overall success of Gerber's reign is attested to by a comparison of Roche's market capitalization at two dates. In 1978, when he took up his presidency, it was SFr 6.3 billion; in 2000, the year before his retirement, it was SFr 165 billion.

Sacher had read his new president accurately, recognizing that Gerber, with his breezy, confident manner, was the right man to open up the company's services to the public, and to deal with the complex legacy of decades of secrecy. And yet that legacy remained, as could be seen from Gerber's response to questions during an interview in 1993 about the Adams affair.

The facts of the Adams' affair show clearly that a fair measure of responsibility for the death of Adam's first wife lay with Roche, which had hounded Adams after his identity was leaked, and who had alerted the police to arrest him on his re-entry into Switzerland. One board member later defended Roche's behaviour in an interview by saying, 'First Adams turned the police and the public against us. We had to defend ourselves.' When Gerber himself was asked about Roche's involvement in the events leading to the suicide of Adam's first wife, he first tried to discredit Adams by showing me newspaper reports of the latter's arrest in England in May 1993 for hiring another man to murder his second wife, and then insisted that any further discussion of the matter continue off the record. When I returned to the issue later in the interview, his cordial tone changed abruptly: 'Now we are on thin ice.' The subject was dropped.

★★★

And the price for Sacher's involvement in the affairs of Roche?

In April 1996, as part of the celebrations for his ninetieth birthday, Paul Sacher gave several interviews. During one for the leading Swiss newspaper, the *Neue Zürcher Zeitung*, he was asked whether he had ever felt a conflict between his life as an artist and his activities as a member of the board of Hoffmann-La Roche. In response, Sacher – after discussing all that his dealings with the company had brought him – stated categorically, 'This activity never led to conflict. It also never deterred me from my musical activities.'[70]

Perhaps what Sacher meant was that he had never allowed his activities with Roche to stop him accepting an engagement which pleased him, or to get in the way of his activities with his orchestras and institutions. Whatever he really meant, the question was a complex one, and the words Sacher spoke in that interview were the words of the public Paul Sacher, a living legend speaking to a public for whom he had no intention of lowering his mask or showing his true feelings.

In a discussion with me four years earlier, however, the same question had elicited a very different response from the private Paul Sacher. 'For everything you do in your life which leads to success, there is also a shadow side, and for that you have to pay.

'If I'm just a conductor, and never dirty my hands with Hoffmann-La Roche, I'm much better off as an artist. I dirtied my hands with this work. There's not exactly blood on them, but there's money on these hands, and naturally this side of my life story detracts from my artistic success, sometimes even to a very great degree. For instance, earlier, it was seldom that I was referred to as "a patron". I was referred to as "a conductor".

'Then, for a time, people said, "the conductor and patron". Then they said, "the patron and conductor". Now it's only "patron". So you get pushed into a role in which you don't want to be, and which you certainly don't see as your main role.

'People realized that, in order to do everything I wanted in music, I needed money. That money had to come from somewhere, and it came from my work for Roche. Of course that detracts from my career as a conductor, and from my reputation as a conductor. People say, "Yes, of course. Simple, easy, with so much money" – even when a performance is good, an artistic success! That's the price you pay. You pay a price for everything. And I have paid the price heavily.

'Besides that, I had no choice. I didn't choose it at all. It was simply the circumstances of my life, which were determined by my marriage with Maja. I knew that I would pay because of this wealth. That was always absolutely clear. And my life – with its

'The Grand Old Man of Roche', 1996

sunshine and its shadows – that was not only completely clear, but also completely conscious. It did me a lot of damage. Artistically it hurt me a great deal, but I can't change it. That's just the way it was after I married Maja. Those are the consequences, and there's nothing more to say.

'Today,' Sacher ended with a sigh on that quiet grey day in September 1992, 'today I'm the Grand Old Man of Roche.'

22

Nothing but Age

Paul Sacher's life was once described by his elder daughter, Katharina von Faber-Castell, as 'fifty lives...full of secrets'. Conductor, musician, benefactor, businessman, innovator – all in their time and their season describe Paul Sacher. But how would he describe himself?

When asked this question in 1993, he answered, 'That's an important question. Don't call me a businessman. I was never a businessman. I was able to do good business – I had to, in order to manage Maja's fortune. But the centre of my life is music. That's my life. I'm a conductor, and perhaps something else as well which people no longer know: I am a pioneer. I created a chamber orchestra when there were no chamber orchestras. I gave commissions when it was not fashionable to give commissions. I set up the Schola Cantorum Basiliensis when no such institution existed – it was quite new and unique in the world. And then there was the Sacher Foundation. What I did throughout my life was pioneering.'

A few months before Sacher made this statement, another era of his life as a musician had come to an end. On 7 September 1992, after fifty years of activity, the Society of the Collegium Musicum Zurich was officially disbanded.

The Collegium had played an important role in Sacher's musical development. From 1942 to 1992, it had performed over seven hundred works, around three hundred of which were contemporary pieces selected from a hundred and five twentieth-century composers. Of these composers, a full third were Swiss. Beginning with Frank Martin, Arthur Honegger and Willy Burkhard, followed by Armin Schibler, Rudolf Kelterborn and Klaus Huber, and then with Heinz Holliger, Josef Haselbach and Matthias Bamert, Sacher had introduced his public to, and educated its taste for, three generations of Swiss composers.

The core of the orchestra had been made up of some of the finest string players in Switzerland, many of whom, like Brenton Langbein, the viola player Ottavio Corti, or the cellist Raffaele Altwegg, remained with the ensemble for decades (Langbein joined the orchestra in 1954, and was its leader from 1956 until it disbanded in 1992). The orchestra's reputation as an elite ensemble was considerable, and the group had performed worldwide.

The Collegium's last concert, on 13 June 1992, was a celebration of both early and new music – the ensemble's original *raison d'être*. It consisted of the world première of a contemporary work, and two works by Mozart, the composer who had always been Sacher's greatest love. 'There is no music which moves me so deeply as that of Mozart,' he had pronounced in 1956.[71]

As a conductor in the twentieth century, Sacher remained unrivalled (with the possible exception of the Salzburg Mozart specialist Bernhard Paumgartner) in the number of Mozart (and Haydn) works he performed. He had turned his attention to the revival of the unknown works of these masters with total dedication at a time when creating the necessary materials to perform them was a huge task. Over the years, he performed around forty works by Haydn, and at least ninety by Mozart, many of the latter with the Collegium Musicum Zurich in its annual Mozart Serenade concerts within the framework of the Lucerne Music Festival. Initiated in 1944, these concerts originally consisted of all-Mozart programmes, a tradition which, from 1971, was altered to include at least one work by another composer. At these concerts and elsewhere, Sacher often presented the public with little-known or completely unknown Mozart works – divertimenti, serenades and nocturnes – many of which are in today's general repertoire.

The contemporary work selected for Sacher's final Collegium concert was Wolfgang Rihm's *Gesungene Zeit* (Time Chant) for violin and orchestra, a Sacher commission for the violinist Anne-Sophie Mutter, who premièred the work.

Sacher's relationship with Mutter is a good example of the synergy and influence he could bring to his relationships with artists. Described once by Herbert von Karajan as one of the 'greatest young musical talents since the young Menuhin', Mutter has openly conceded that it was Sacher who awoke her interest in contemporary art and music. While introducing her to Pierre Boulez, Krzysztof Penderecki and others, Sacher avuncularly explained to her that, as a modern young woman, she must concern herself with modern music. 'You can't go on playing the Romantic classics for ever. You're a young woman of our time,' he reportedly told her. An introduction to Witold Lutoslawski at a dinner party at Schönenberg in the 1980s led to Lutoslawski composing *Chain 2* for violin and orchestra for Mutter, and she gave its first performance with Sacher and the Collegium in Zurich in 1986.

★★★

In contrast to the disbanding of the BKO, which ended without Sacher having designated a successor, Sacher had decided during the late 1980s that when he retired from conducting the Collegium it should continue under Brenton Langbein.

Despite his repeated comments to this effect, however, the Collegium disbanded in 1992. But, as in Basle, its end was quickly followed by an initiative to carry on Sacher's work, and to benefit from the momentum he had created. At the end of 1992 a number of Collegium board members and concert-goers, as well as the Zurich city government department responsible for cultural affairs, decided to continue the tradition of performing international contemporary classical music in Zurich. A new ensemble under the name of Collegium Novum Zurich was established, with that as its primary aim. A fair guage of Sacher's personal importance to his public was revealed by the new ensemble's first attempt at a subscription initiative.

As Dr Christoph Krayenbühl explained, 'When the initiative was launched, we wrote to all Collegium Musicum subscribers, somewhere between two hundred and fifty and three hundred people. Only fifteen positive answers came back. The subscription audience seemed to be "Paul-centered". Many of them were of a similar age and had grown old with Paul. He had an immense circle of friends and acquaintances. Suddenly, for really modern programmes [directed by other conductors], there was far less interest.'

Krayenbühl's comment that Sacher's subscription audience was 'Paul-centred' is an over-simplification of the facts. The success of Sacher's Collegium concerts was hardly solely reliant on his person. He had earned the devotion of his subscription public over decades by educating its members to negotiate the new sounds and structures of contemporary composers, embedding the most difficult works between compositions which were more accessible. His choice of programmes, too, had been an important factor in maintaining the interest of his public. Not only that, but he offered his audiences regular opportunities to hear and see top international soloists in his concerts. As in Basle, for years he had paid the orchestra's considerable deficit himself, without receiving a penny of support from the machinery in Zurich that subsidized the orchestras of his peers. The Collegium received no official financial support from the state until it was approaching its thirtieth year. The tiny sum of SFr 5000 was paid in 1970 and 1971, rising to SFr 7000 in 1972 and 1973. Although this sum was increased to SFr 20,000 in 1973-85, and to SFr 40,000 in 1985-92, it remained modest, especially when compared to the first yearly subsidy given in 1993 to the new Collegium Novum Zurich (no less than SFr 200,000).

Whether Sacher's success with the Collegium was driven by his personality, his subtle but effective education of his audiences, or by the high calibre of his guest artists, it is clear that when he finally left the Collegium's podium an era in contemporary music was over.

★★★

By the end of his life, Sacher's wealth and generosity had become legendary. In 1973 he was listed in *Forbes* magazine as the third richest man in the world, and in 1990 the Swiss magazine *BILANZ* described him as the richest or second richest man in Switzerland. Sacher himself described the misunderstandings surrounding his wealth as 'a bit fatal'.

'I want to tell you something. If I were the owner of Hoffmann-La Roche, when I appeared on the front page as the richest man in Switzerland, I'd say, "Well, good. I'm the owner of Hoffmann-

La Roche." But it's a bit fatal when that happens and I'm not. The money went from Fritz Hoffmann to Emanuel, and from there to Lukas and Vera. The money is in the legitimate place where it belongs, and that's not me. The misunderstanding is excusable because I was the Hoffman family's representative at Hoffmann-La Roche. ... Hoffmann-La Roche have twelve or thirteen billion [Swiss francs] in reserves, and people think that's me! That's a pity. If I was…'

A straight answer about Sacher's financial status was never forthcoming in all the years I knew him. Once, when asked about his wealth in a public interview by Gerd Albrecht, former musical director and conductor of the Zurich Tonhalle Orchestra, Sacher responded, 'You see, Mr Albrecht, in Switzerland there are two things that people don't talk about. One is love, the other is money.' All the same, despite the fact that he proved early in his career that he could succeed without readily available resources, money always played a huge role in Sacher's equation for success.

In spite of this, he often seemed unable to accept the fact of his money without qualification. In many conversations in my presence, he played down his wealth, once telling his daughter Katharina that moderate wealth was fine, but that one should not become so wealthy so as to stand out from others. In sharp contrast, it was Sacher himself who loved to tell the story about Igor Stravinsky's relationship to money.

At one point during a New York society dinner party attended by Stravinsky, the conversation turned to money. The hostess complained that this was not an agreeable topic for the dinner table. Stravinsky strongly disagreed, exclaiming loudly, 'I love money. It's already in my name.' He proceeded to write out his first initial *I* (for Igor), then crossed it with the letter *S* (for Stravinsky), forming a *$*.

Sacher's relationship to money was characteristically more complex. On one hand, he could sincerely and accurately claim that 'My life is rich because of what I do, not because I have money,' while on the other he could recognize the true value of his immense wealth.

'You know, I don't believe in material things, nor do I believe in possessions, nor do I believe in money,' he claimed in October 1992.

'But I like all those things because with them I live very comfortably. Money is a means to freedom. It allows me to do things I couldn't do without it.'

Nevertheless, for Sacher, there was always a price attached to money. 'Money doesn't make you happy, and possessions don't make you happy. I realized very quickly that money and possessions are always a burden. One has to busy oneself with them. One has to take care of them. One has to take responsibility for them.'

Sacher's sense of that responsibility was evident in his founding in 1962 of Sacher Compagnie Basel AG (SCOBAG AG), a most private of private banks. Established primarily to manage the Sacher, Hoffmann and Oeri fortunes, Scobag also offered lucrative investment possibilities to members of other well-established Basle families.

According to Ernst Würmli, however, Sacher's care of his billions began with small details. Würmli recalled being summoned to Sacher's study shortly after his employment at Schönenberg began in autumn 1975: 'The entire window-sill was full of bills and invoices. "What is this?" Sacher asked, pointing to one of the bills. "And this? Do we have to have that? Why do we need this? We already have one of those in the garage." He was as hard as nails.

'Some people have said he's mean, but one can't say that. He has to check. He can't simply give out money. He has to know what he's paying for. I mean, just for the garden we have ten or twenty suppliers – one for manure, another for earth, another for machines. One has to know if the things are really delivered. It doesn't mean that he doesn't trust the people, but it's possible for someone to write a bill for something that hasn't been delivered. So every bill is inspected. Every bill comes to him. He inspects it. Then he gives them to me. I check them, then sign them. Then they are paid.'

Sacher's diligent and detailed control of domestic expenditures stood in sharp contrast to his legendary generosity. For instance, a young colleague of Sacher's was invited to lunch at Schönenberg in the week of her thirtieth birthday in June 1983. As she was about to leave, Sacher pulled out of his pocket a long string of perfect pearls, complete with a diamond clasp, and casually tucked them into the pocket of her coat. That birthday present was later valued at more than SFr 40,000.

Professor Edgar Bonjour claimed in 1985 that 'countless people live from Paul'. Although Sacher refuted this claim as exaggerated, it is true that at any given time there were a number of people, including family members, who were wholly supported by him, as well as a multitude of others who received occasional or regular financial help.

'There are certainly many people who would live badly without my money,' Sacher said in 1988, 'all sorts of composers, or artists, but I don't keep all that at the top of my head. But my support doesn't always last for ever, usually just for a certain time. For instance, a person can suddenly have great success, and get a great deal of money, or he marries money. Then he doesn't need my money any more. But it's not true that countless people would go hungry without me.

'Then there are people whom I might have given a beautiful violin, one which still belongs to me. I haven't actually given it to them … But since nobody knows about it, whether or not they give it back when I die is a very different matter…

'And then there are people who I just give something to … Or others, like a woman in St Gallen who writes to me regularly. She says it's the last time; I should give her fifteen hundred francs … Then she writes again a week later. That time it's seven hundred. There are a lot of such people. And in many cases I pay. It doesn't hurt me, and that's a poor person [who has written to me].

'One wrote to me from Aarau. She had a sick daughter and lived needily as a journalist. I thought, "How terrible, if someone can't help their own daughter." I sent her the money – rather a lot – and she said she wouldn't ask again. Three years later, she asked again. Life is like that.

'That's normal charity. Everyone who can do things like that without suffering themselves should do it. I don't suffer for it. And I don't have the idea that I should save my money. I never thought like that. I think that I have money and can live well, and as many people as possible should have a share. I mean, when they're in trouble, or are poor, or when I like the people, or when I think, "He needs a bit of freedom in order to develop himself," I do that. But I never write it down.

'Every week I receive at least ten requests. I'm just a first address.'

The number of people helped directly or indirectly by Paul Sacher is impossible to establish. Sacher never kept any records, and the sheer numbers meant that he could not remember all of them.

'Not even Paul himself can recall all those he helped,' said Ernst Würmli in the late 1980s. 'For instance, he had a small statue of Buddha, which is now in the display case. He said I should take it to the Museum of Natural History and see if they could restore it. Then a Mr So-and-So came along [to look at it], and said, "Oh, from Dr Sacher. Yes, of course [we can restore it]. He always gives us so much for our village in Bali" – or wherever it was. Nobody knows about things like that. He does such a lot which doesn't have anything to do with the arts.'

★★★

By 1998, Sacher had received dozens of awards in recognition of his services to music. On seven occasions he was awarded medals, including the Béla Bartók Memorial Medal from Hungary and the First Class Cross of Honour from Vienna. He was inducted into a number of honorary societies, including the Legion of Honour in France, the Order of Merit of the Republic of Italy, and the Royal Philharmonic Society. He received eight honorary doctorates for his work in music from institutions including the Eastman School of Music in the USA, the Franz Liszt Hochschule for Music in Budapest, and Oxford University. In 1992, he even received an honorary doctorate in medicine and surgery from the University of Genoa for his role in the creation of the former Roche-funded Institute for Immunology; at the award ceremony he said that he was 'very pleased to accept this degree' because 'medicine is a human activity for which I have the highest regard'.

Sacher's speeches on such occasions were sincere reflections of service and appreciation. And yet his relationship to awards, like so many aspects of his life and character, was complex and frequently ambivalent. On one hand, as late as 1997 at the age of ninety-one, he could fly halfway across the world to receive an award, appearing greatly to enjoy the attention he received. On the other hand, he could make disparaging comments about them. 'To tell the truth, they are of no importance – really no

Paul with his son, Georg Schmid, and Lesley Stephenson at the presentation of his honorary doctorate at Babson College, Massachusetts, 1993

importance. Maybe it's nice to have it, and maybe for a moment it gives you a little joy, but it's of no importance. And all these things always come too late. Always too late. Honegger once said something about this. He got a wonderful decoration in the year he lived with us at Schönenberg. And [when I congratulated him], he said, *"Mon pauvre Paul. C'est l'âge. Ce n'est rien que l'âge* [My poor Paul. It's age. Nothing but age]."

'You have to be old to be decorated,' Sacher reflected. '*C'est la vérité, pure et simple* [That's the truth, pure and simple].'

Although it is true that the majority of Sacher's awards came after his seventieth birthday, his claim that awards 'always came too late' was not entirely accurate in his own case. He received his first honorary doctorate for his services to music from the University of Basle in 1951, when he was a mere forty-five. The Schoenberg Medal from Vienna and the Mozart Medal from Salzburg were both awarded before he turned fifty.

When reminded of these facts, he retorted bluntly, 'A medal? A medal? What does a medal mean? For me it means much more to be in love with a beautiful girl than to have a doctorate. [To be in love] is life. The other is only paper.'

When I asked whether his awards and doctorates might not have a special importance for him because he had not attained any formal academic status beyond high-school matriculation, Sacher simply laughed. 'I did my matriculation. That's all. And afterwards no examination. Life is my great examiner. Giving a concert or making love to a wonderful girl – that's an examination!'

★★★

There were many women in Paul Sacher's life. Both the photographs in his 'Ladies' Album', and his own testimony bear witness to the fact that, besides the three major relationships of his adult life, there had been many others, even if they were sometimes fleeting. Some, like that with Els Havrlik, were intense but platonic. Others, like that with Romana Segantini, were neither platonic nor fleeting.

Looking back at these relationships in interviews in the mid-1990s, Sacher could sometimes speak of them with candour and circumspection. His initial rationalization of this maverick behaviour was that in each relationship he found relief from the depression which periodically descended on him. 'In every relationship,' he said in 1996, 'a door opened, leading away from the dark.' But he did once admit that either he was not the man to share a fifty-year love story with one woman, or he simply hadn't found the woman with whom that was possible.

'When you turn and look back, then you look for motives. You ask yourself, "Why did you do all that? Why dozens of women instead of one or two? What were you thinking?" Apparently the number is unavoidable. But whoever has the strength to concentrate on one person is better off. Sometimes I see old couples who are happy, and I think, "Goodness, that's enviable, that's enviable. They haven't taken all the bypaths, they haven't lost all that time" – although I never looked on that time as lost.'

★★★

One might have expected Sacher, aged eighty-six, to retire after the Collegium's closure. Instead, he remained active and productive, conducting the orchestra (despite its official disbandment) once a year for another three years in its annual Mozart Serenade concerts in Lucerne. He also continued to conduct the Basler Schlagzeug Ensemble until in his early nineties. He remained on the board of Hoffmann-La Roche until 1996. He continued to oversee the development and growth of the Sacher Foundation. In fact, he remained so busy that he failed to notice the passing of the years. 'It's strange,' he told me quizzically in January 1993, 'but I never realized I was growing old.'

As the 1990s wore on, however, and Sacher's health became more fragile, he slowly began to withdraw from public life. After 1996, it became increasingly rare for him to be found in his apartment above the Sacher Foundation at Münsterplatz. More and more often he sought the solace, comfort and memories of Schönenberg.

'At this house I feel as if I'm on holiday,' he explained, 'and I'm protected. I don't need many people around me. I know the artists whose works are here. [I used to talk to the artists,] now I talk to their pictures. It's a type of solitude I like.'

But not all was solitude.

In his final years, Sacher again felt the need for support and a companion. He had been extremely lonely, and Maja's and Irma's illnesses had left their marks. Nina, too – with whom he had had no regular contact for several years – had died in 1994. He became increasingly dependent on Margrit Hahnloser, a competent and ambitious Swiss art-historian whom he had met some years earlier. She became his close companion for the last eight years of his life. But Hahnloser was wary of anyone whose relationship to Sacher might threaten her own, and in the mid-1990s doors began to close in the faces of those who had previously had direct and easy access. Sacher, for so long the controller, was at last being controlled.

All his life, Sacher had avoided conflict with those he was close to. Although he was aware of the changes Margrit was making, he was unwilling to resist them openly for fear of being left alone. But he did resist on his own terms, and continued to meet in private those people he wanted to see. When he thought that a meeting – like those required for this book – might lead to domestic conflict, he relied on his trusted staff to time events precisely, so as to avoid confrontation. And when the occasional encounter could not be avoided, Sacher relied on his ingenuity and the understanding of his guests to see him through.

★★★

The symphony of dreams that was Sacher's life did not end with his slow withdrawal from the management of his former projects. There was yet another dream on the horizon, a dream which occupied him for years: the setting up of the Museum Jean Tinguely in Basle.

The artist Jean Tinguely had been a close friend and protégé of Maja Sacher. At first, Sacher had been more than sceptical about some of Tinguely's work, particularly his mobile machine sculptures.

'I had problems understanding all that rusty iron,' he later confessed. 'I always put up resistance. ... When I saw how enthralled [Maja] was by Tinguely's work, I told her that "No work of art has ever been created from junk and rusty metal. It will fall apart in ten years. It's like a book printed on inferior paper." But my arguments were counterproductive. She knew she was right.'[72]

As Maja's health began to fail in the 1980s, Sacher increasingly assumed the role of intermediary in her communications with Tinguely. Understanding grew between the two men and, with it, Sacher's understanding of the sculptures. (Later, when asked about the beginnings of his friendship with Tinguely, he used to say, 'I've inherited him from Maja.')[73]

The idea of establishing a museum to house Tinguely's work originated during a visit to Tinguely's workshop in Neyruz near the Swiss-French city of Fribourg in 1986. Sacher had been invited by Tinguely to see his extraordinary multi-component mobile sculpture, *Dance of Death*, created out of remnants from a nearby farm which had burnt down. Less than three months later, Sacher returned to Neyruz with Fritz Gerber, and they agreed to buy two sections of the work. But it was Tinguely's dream to have the entire group kept together and, if possible, kept in Basle. He suggested that *Dance of Death* in its entirety should be set up at Schönenberg.

Discussions were still under way when Tinguely died suddenly, on 30 August 1991. His widow, Niki de Saint Phalle, offered to donate works from his estate to Hoffmann-La Roche, on condition that a museum be built and that the sculptures' machines be kept in running order. Sacher and Gerber agreed. Not only would building a museum to house Tinguely's treasures preserve the artist's work, but the museum could also serve as a centenary gift from Hoffmann-La Roche to the public.

The idea of building the museum at Schönenberg was later abandoned, and the Museum Jean Tinguely, designed by the Swiss-Italian architect Mario Botta, was built in Solitude Park in Basle on land overlooking the Rhine.

With typical ambivalence, Sacher discussed his own role in the creation of the museum with me in 1993. 'I am an *éminence grise*. That's what I like to be most. Then the others have to do everything. Me? I've done nothing at all. I'm nothing. But without me it wouldn't be happening.'

★★★

It was to Jean Tinguely that Sacher had turned when Irma Schmid died in November 1988. Sacher wanted Tinguely to create a sculpture for the gravesite that Irma and he would eventually share.

Tinguely set to work, but his first two attempts seemed wrong. A third solution incorporated the construction of an iron fence round the grave, with a mobile gate which opened quietly. But Sacher was not convinced: he wanted no noise or movement at his graveside. He wrote to Tinguely, 'As you know, this grave for Irma is also to be my grave. I am concerned about the work of art that is to embellish it. After death everything is silent. Nothing moves. That's why I feel that the construction you contribute should be still, and should not make any sound.'[74]

Tinguely, however, did not live long enough to complete the project. Today a wrought-iron sculpture by the artist Oscar Wiggli overlooks the grave.

In the end, Sacher did not share Irma Schmid's resting place. Perhaps arising from a conflict of loyalties, he suddenly informed his son in the year or so before his own death that he had bought a gravesite for himself in the Friedhof am Hörnli cemetery in Basle, a few metres from the Hoffmann family grave in which Maja Sacher had been buried alongside her first husband and young son.

There he rests alone.

Paul Sacher, 1985

Coda:
Con Grazia

'Talk to us about grace.'

When Paul Sacher was approaching his ninetieth birthday in 1996, and making preparations for large-scale celebrations, he decided that part of those celebrations should be a concert and thanksgiving service in Basle Cathedral. He asked the Rev. Theophil Schubert, a family friend who had given the address at Maja Sacher's funeral in 1989, to preach the sermon. Schubert agreed, and then asked if there were a particular theme he should address. Sacher replied, 'Talk to us about grace.'

★★★

The subject of grace had arisen periodically in our personal conversations over the years, particularly when Sacher was in a more introspective, melancholy mood. For him, grace was a God-given 'power working in my [life] and other lives, which can be described only with this concept'.[75] He believed that it was thanks to grace that he had been able to fulfil his multi-faceted vision, and that it was grace which had helped him negotiate the complex paths through his relationships. It was grace, too, that had helped him confront and deal with the inner conflicts which were such a strong part of his character; '*ganz schlimm*' (really bad) was how he described them to me in 1998.

Sacher had expressed his awareness of these inner conflicts in his teens, when he wrote to Lili Streiff about his battle with 'the beast' inside himself,[76] which sometimes arrived unannounced. These conflicts were a source of the lifelong discrepancies in his behaviour, and created the siege mentality into which he could easily slip. But no matter where Sacher was on his path, grace –

he believed – always accompanied him. So it was no surprise that he should want to dwell for a few minutes on the force that he believed had helped him to negotiate the challenges, successes and inner turbulence of his long life.

Sacher's belief in the presence of grace, however, neither excuses nor contradicts his shadow side, or the lapses from personal integrity that it caused. Nor does it in any way diminish the significance and breadth of his accomplishments – they are undeniable, contested only by those who do not know, or who cannot appreciate, the circumstances under which his pioneering began. Few critics or assessors writing today were alive in the 1920s or 1930s. Moreover, even if they had been alive, it is unlikely that they would be old enough to remember the environment in which Sacher began his work. It is difficult for those of us born in the middle or latter part of the twentieth century to grasp the significance of what he accomplished, largely because we never knew the environment in which he set about fulfilling his mission.

Sacher grew up in a world in which armchair access to the media and electro-technology was the stuff of futurists' dreams. His initial access to music came only through books or the occasional concert. The spirit of innovation and entrepreneurism which the young Sacher needed in order to move first a city and, later, the general listening public out of its distaste for contemporary music can barely be imagined.

Paul Sacher was a pioneer. Beginning with the BKO, he envisaged, founded and developed orchestras and music institutions which today still serve as prototypes. He commissioned music at a time when nobody else was interested in doing so. And perhaps his most remarkable musical achievement was that he never stood still. It would have been easy for him to 'retire' after his successes with luminaries like Bartók, Honegger and Stravinsky, commissioning simpler works from composers who imitated them. But instead, Sacher moved on in the 1950s and 1960s to the work of Britten, Henze and Sándor Veress, and then to Berio, Lutoslawski and Birtwistle. He was still giving commissions in his nineties, still conducting, still educating. There is little to support the claim made by some that his significance and influence faded after the Second World War.

In a complete assessment of Sacher, however, we must not only take into account the institutions and ensembles he created and led, but also recognize the catalytic quality of his life's work. The work and lives of many composers were profoundly influenced by their direct contact with Paul Sacher, and they, in turn, affected indirectly the lives of those who heard their music or studied with them. Sacher's orchestras, and his own aesthetic and instrumental preferences, ultimately influenced the development of twentieth-century classical music after the First World War to an extent which cannot be overestimated. And his influence continued: many musicians were, like Anne-Sophie Mutter, persuaded by Sacher to embrace contemporary music, and consequently also won the support of their audiences for the voices of their own age. Younger composers, such as the German Wolfgang Rihm, are today materially supported in their development by the Sacher Foundation.

Of all Paul Sacher's successes, many consider his crowning achievement to be the celebration of music itself, on one hand through creating and inspiring the revival of early music, on the other by promoting contemporary music at a time when it was generally scorned. Paul Sacher helped to bring about the creation of nearly one hundred and fifty works in the twentieth-century classical repertoire.

Many see these actions as befitting some grand scheme, but for Sacher it was all much simpler. 'As far as a man can think in the future, I did what I thought necessary, and what was possible for me.'

An appraisal of Sacher would be incomplete without an acknowledgement of his leadership and successes in the service of Hoffmann-La Roche, one of the most prosperous companies of the last century. Taken alone, Sacher's accomplishments at Roche would have been a full life's work for anyone. For him, they were a source of power and pride, and a respite from his other tasks.

Yet, for all his accomplishments, there were flaws. Sacher was a complex, whimsical man who could be overbearing, manipulative, and downright rude. He could be arrogant and insensitive to others. He could be stubborn, often to a fault. His attitude towards fidelity to the women in his life could at best be described as fluid. While some of these characteristics may be attributed to his singleness of purpose in pursuit of his goals, they are far more likely to have been the all-too-human excesses of a driven man. And if, for some, they mar the grandeur of his accomplishments, they also remind us – as Sacher was often reminded by Katja Rasumovsky, the mother-in-law of Lukas Hoffmann – that he was still 'only a man'. A man who overcame opposition and obstacles to raise himself among the giants of business and music; a man who lived his life doing that which he must do, and that which he wanted to do.

The last century was too large and sprawling to be dominated by any single person or institution in any given field, but if anyone came close to dominance in the field of contemporary classical music, it was Paul Sacher.

★★★

'Talk to us about grace,' Paul Sacher had urged the Rev. Schubert when discussing his thanksgiving service. 'Talk to us about the power working in my [life] and other lives that can be described only with this concept.' Paul Sacher's life stands as a tribute to the power of 'grace' as he understood it, the power he believed had given him a mission to discover and promote the voices of his time. It was the power of grace that allowed him to break the law of stones, to reach beyond the limitations of his dream-filled youth to enter the *'Basler Daig';* and it was the power of grace that helped him live with the demons inside.

'There are people who cannot, and will not, speak about grace,' the Rev. Schubert said in his sermon. 'They speak of their own endeavours, and success is attributed solely to their clever use of their talents and the skilful employment of people and methods.'[77]

When he was younger, Paul Sacher, too, may have made such claims. Later, however, he believed that it was the power of grace which had led him to conduct his life as he did, as a Symphony of Dreams realized and fulfilled.

Paul Sacher died on 26 May 1999.

Notes, Sources, Bibliography and Index

Notes

1 The *c* in the early records was later often changed to a *k*.
2 The first official record of the name Dürr in the Pratteln church registers is that of Hans Jacob Dürr's first child, Samuel, whose birth was registered on 21 January 1664.
3 Probate inventory of Basle city, No. 411, 1899.
4 Paul Sacher to Lili Streiff, 7 May 1924.
5 Paul Sacher to Lili Streiff, 7 June 1924
6 *Neue Basler Zeitung* newspaper, No. 229, 29 September 1924.
7 Paul Sacher to Lili Streiff, 26 January 1925.
8 *Schweizerische Musikzeitung* newspaper, No. 6, 12 February 1927, p. 72.
9 *Basler Nachrichten* newspaper, 24 January 1927, supplement 1, No. 23.
10 *National Zeitung* newspaper, 24 January 1927, supplement to evening edition, No. 39.
11 Paul Sacher to Lili Streiff, 8 November 1925.
12 *Basler Anzeiger* newspaper, 6 June 1929.
13 Paul Sacher, *Maja Sacher-Stehlin: 7 Februar 1896 – 8 August 1989* (private publication commemorating the life of Maja Sacher-Stehlin), Pratteln, 1989, p. 18.
14 Paul Sacher, *Reden und Aufsätze* (Speeches and Essays), Zurich, 1986, p. 35.
15 Bernard Geller, 'Paul Sacher et l'association des musiciens suisses: un demi-siècle d'activité (Paul Sacher and the Society of Swiss Musicians: Half a Century of Activity), in Veronika Gutmann, ed., *Paul Sacher als Gastdirigent* (Paul Sacher as Guest Conductor), Zurich, 1986, p. 113.
16 *Basler Zeitung* newspaper, 12 March 1993, p. 3.
17 Paul Sacher to Romana Segantini, 19 November 1925.
18 Romana Segantini to Paul Sacher, 9 November 1944.
19 Paul Sacher to Romana Segantini, January 1945.
20 Romana Segantini to Paul Sacher, March 1975.
21 Peter Reidemeister and Veronika Gutmann, eds., *Alte Musik, Praxis und Reflexion* (Early Music in Practice and Reflection), Winterthur, 1983, p. 24.

22 Ibid, p. 36.
23 Ina Lohr, 'Zur Programmgestaltung' (Making Programmes), in *Alte und Neue Musik I: 25 Jahre Basler Kammerorchester* (Early and Contemporary Music Vol. 1: 25 Years Basle Chamber Orchestra), Zurich, 1952, p. 27.
24 Heinrich Strobel, 'Alte Musik: wie sie sein soll. Besuch in der Schola Cantorum Basiliensis' (Early Music: How it Should Be. A Visit to the Schola Cantorum Basiliensis), in Reidemeister and Gutmann, *Alte Musik*, p. 76.
25 Walter Nef, 'Paul Sacher. Ein Beitrag zu seiner Biographie' (Paul Sacher: A Contribution to His Biography), in *Reden und Aufsätze*, p. 137.
26 Sacher, *Maja Sacher-Stehlin*, p. 12.
27 Vera Oeri-Hoffmann to the author, 11 November 1995.
28 Igor Stravinsky to Paul Sacher, May 1930; Stravinsky-Sacher correspondence, Paul Sacher Foundation, Basle.
29 Béla Bartók to Boosey & Hawkes, 29 January 1937.
30 Béla Bartók to Béla Bartók, Jr., 18 August 1939.
31 Ibid.
32 Hans Conrad Peyer, *Roche: Geschichte eines Unternehmens, 1896-1996* (Roche: History of an Enterprise, 1896-1996), Basle 1996, p. 43.
33 Ibid., p. 80.
34 Ibid.
35 Ibid.
36 Dale Carnegie, *How to Stop Worrying and Start Living*, London 1996, p. 151.
37 Béla Bartók to Paul Sacher, 14 October 1940.
38 Paul Sacher to Karl Naef, November 1947.
39 Protocol of the Pro Helvetia Executive Committee meeting, 18 October 1948.
40 Paul Sacher to Conrad Beck, 26 November 1951.
41 Béla Bartók to Ralph Hawkes, 30 May 1942.
42 Paul Sacher, 'Béla Bartók zum Gedächtnis' (In Memory of Béla Bartók), in *Alte und Neue Musik, I: 25 Jahre Basler Kammerorchester* (Early and Contemporary Music, Vol. I: 25 Years Basle Chamber Orchestra), Zurich, 1952, p. 187.

43. Bohuslav Martinů, 'Toccata e due Canzoni', in *Alte und Neue Musik I: 25 Jahre Basler Kammerorchester* (Early and Contemporary Music 1: 25 Years Basle Chamber Orchestra), Zurich, 1952, p. 171.
44. *Sonntags Zeitung* newspaper, 13 December 1992, p. 19.
45. Sacher to Werner Reinhart, 24 June 1941.
46. *Ex libris* magazine, No. 6, June 1984, p. 21.
47. Willi Schuh, 'Der Dirigent Paul Sacher' (The Conductor Paul Sacher), in Collegium Musicum Zurich Society, *Zwanzig Jahre Collegium Musicum Zürich* (Twenty Years of the Collegium Musicum Zurich), Zurich, 1962, p. 21.
48. Mstislav Rostropovich, ed., *Dank an Paul Sacher* (Thanks to Paul Sacher), Zurich, 1976, p. 5.
49. Hans Oesch, 'Paul Sacher: Versuch einer Würdigung' (Paul Sacher: An Attempted Assessment), in *Alte und Neue Musik II: 50 Jahre Basler Kammerorchester* (Early and Contemporary Music II: 50 Years Basle Chamber Orchestra), Zurich, 1977, p. 25.
50. *Die Welt* newspaper, Hamburg, 27 February 1975.
51. Paul Sacher, Introduction to catalogue of the exhibition *Musikhandschriften in Basel aus verschiedenen Sammlungen* (Music Manuscripts in Basle from Various Collections), Basle Art Museum, 31 May–31 July 1975; quoted in *Alte und Neue Musik II*, p. 329.
52. Paul Sacher's acceptance speech on receiving the Basle Arts Prize in 1972; in Sacher, *Reden und Aufsätze*, p. 62.
53. Oesch, 'Paul Sacher', p. 17.
54. Paul Sacher, letter to the members of the Basler Kammerorchester (BKO), 6 December 1975; quoted in *Paul Sacher an die Mitglieder des Basler Kammerorchester* (Paul Sacher to the Members of the Basle Chamber Orchestra), 27 November 1986.
55. Oesch, 'Paul Sacher', p. 32.
56. *National Zeitung* newspaper, 2 February 1972, morning edition, p. 5.
57. Paul Sacher in Paul Sacher Foundation, *Paul Sacher Foundation*, Basle 1986, p. 5/6.

58 Albi Rosenthal, 'Die Paul Sacher Stiftung am Wendepunkt: Der Ankauf des Nachlasses von Igor Strawinsky' (The Turning-Point of the Paul Sacher Foundation: The Purchase of the Igor Stravinsky Legacy), in *Paul Sacher in memoriam*, Basle 2000, p. 32.
59 *The Observer*, 4 May 1986; quoted in Hoffmann-La Roche, *80 Jahre Paul Sacher, 28 April 1986: Erinnerungen an den Geburtstag* (Paul Sacher at 80, 28 April 1986: Memories of the Birthday), Basle, 1986, p. 168.
60 Paul Sacher's speech at the opening of a Stravinsky exhibition in Basle, printed in *Igor Strawinsky: Sein Nachlaß: Sein Bild* (Igor Stravinsky: His Legacy: His Portrait), the exhibition programme and speeches, Basle Stadttheater, Basle, 1984, p. 16.
61 Paul Sacher to the members of the BKO, 27 November 1986.
62 *Tages Anzeiger* newspaper, 28 November 1986.
63 Basle City Government decree No. 5284 B, 10 August 1982.
64 Speech by Fritz Gerber; printed in Hoffmann-La Roche, *80 Jahre Paul Sacher*, p. 37.
65 *Tages Anzeiger* newspaper, 24 January 1996, p. 33.
66 Robert Ball, 'The Secret Life of Hoffmann-La Roche', *Fortune* magazine, August 1971, p. 134.
67 Ibid.
68 Ibid, p. 130.
69 Ibid, p. 134.
70 *Neue Zürcher Zeitung* newspaper 27 April 1996, p. 65.
71 Willi Schuh, Der Dirigent Paul Sacher (The Conductor Paul Sacher), in Collegium Musicum Zurich Society, *Zwanzig Jahre Collegium Musicum Zürich* (Twenty Years Collegium Musicum Zurich), Zurich, 1962, p. 17.
72 Margrit Hahnloser, ed., *Briefe von Jean Tinguely an Paul Sacher und gemeinsame Freunde* (Letters from Jean Tinguely to Paul Sacher and Mutual Friends), Berne, Pratteln and Fribourg, 1996, p. 11.
73 Ibid, p. 11.
74 Ibid, p. 30.
75 Rev. Theophil Schubert, sermon, 28 April 1996.
76 Paul Sacher to Lili Streiff, 7 May 1924.
77 Rev. Theophil Schubert, sermon, 28 April 1996.

Sources and Bibliography

Archives

Amtsblatt des Kantons Basel-Landschaft (Official Gazette of Canton Basle Country), 1853–1861

Basler Adreßregister (Basle Address Books) 1860–1925/1920–1930. Staatsarchiv, Kanton Basel-Stadt (State Archive, Canton Basle City)

Bezirksschreiberei Liestal, Hypotheken-Protokolle (Mortgage Protocolls) 1825–1868, Vol. 682: p. 410; 683: p. 153, 301; 684: p. 120, 165, 306; 685: p. 492. Staatsarchiv Kanton Basel-Landschaft (State Archive, Canton Basle Country).

Ehe- und Todesregister von Pratteln (Marriage and Death Registers of Pratteln), 1690–1906. Gemeinde Pratteln (Municipality of Pratteln)

Erbschaftsinventare von Basel Stadt (Probate Inventories of Basle City), 1899, No. 411. Staatsarchiv Basel-Stadt (State Archive, Canton Basle City)

Erziehungs-Akten (Education Records), Spalenschulhaus (Spalen Primary School) 1912–1916, K/9a Knaben (Boys) Staatsarchiv, Kanton Basel-Stadt (State Archive, Canton Basle City)

Erziehungs-Akten (Education Records), Provisorische Schülerverzeichnisse der Unteren Realschule (List of provisional students of the Lower Realschule): T15 1914–1919. Staatsarchiv, Kanton Basel-Stadt (State Archive, Canton Basle City)

Erziehungs-Akten (Education Records), Zeugnistabellen der Unteren Realschule (School Reports of the Lower Realschule): T9a: 1916–1917, 1917–1918, 1918–1919, 1919–1920; T9b: 1920–1921, 1921–1922, 1922–1923. Staatsarchiv Kanton Basel-Stadt (State Archive, Canton of Basle City)

Erziehungs-Akten (Education Records), Zeugnistabellen der Oberen Realschule (School Reports of the Upper

Realschule) 1920–1924. Staatsarchiv, Kanton Basel-Stadt (State Archive, Canton Basle City)

Erziehungs-Akten (Education Records), Schülerverzeichnis Obere Realschule (List of students at the Upper Realschule), T22 1918–1930. Staatsarchiv, Kanton Basel-Stadt (State Archive, Canton Basle City)

Erziehungs-Akten (Education Records), Zeugnistabellen der Oberen Realschule (School Reports of the Upper Realschule) 1920–1924. Staatsarchiv, Kanton Basel-Stadt (State Archive, Canton Basle City)

Familienregister der Gemeinden Payerne und Zuzgen (Family registers of the municipalities of Payerne and Zuzgen)

Kirchen-Akten (Church Records E9, Pratteln Familienregister (Pratteln Family Register), 1759–1859, Vol. 9. Staatsarchiv Kanton Basel-Landschaft (State Archive, Canton Basle Country)

Maps of Basle City, 1880, 1900, 1910

Protokolle der Allgemeinen Gesellschaft für Speiseanstalten in Basel (Protocols of the General Society for Eating Houses in Basle) Vol. 1: 12 April 1901–13 October 1925; Basle University Library

Protocols of Pro Helvetia meetings, 1943–1959; Paul Sacher Private Archive, Pratteln

Schülerverzeichnis der Unteren Realschule (List of students at the Lower Realschule), 1917–1918. Staatsarchiv, Kanton Basel-Stadt (State Archive, Canton Basle City)

Totenregister (Register of Deaths) Staatsarchiv Kanton Basel-Stadt (State Archive Canton Basle City) (Civilstand N1, 1899, No. 25)

Universität Basel – Personalverzeichnis WS 1924–SS 1932 (List of teaching staff from Basle University between winter semester 1924 and summer semester 1932), Basle University

Verzeichnisse der Gebäudeversicherung: Brandversicherung C3 (Inventory of building insurance premiums: fire insurance), Pratteln 3.0/1552–1877. Staatsarchiv Kanton Basel-Landschaft (State Archive, Canton Basle Country)

Correspondence

Béla Bartók Letters, Bartók Archives, Tampa, Florida
Conrad Beck – Paul Sacher, Paul Sacher Foundation, Basle
Anny Dürr – Laura Estermann, Family Estermann, Payerne
Dr Henri B. Meier – the author, 23 June 1994
Karl Naef – Paul Sacher, November 1947, Paul Sacher, Pratteln
Vera Oeri-Hoffmann – the author, 11 November 1995
Lili Roth-Streiff – Paul Sacher, 1924–6, Mrs Lili Roth-Streiff, Zurich
Paul Sacher – Béla Bartók, Paul Sacher Foundation, Basle
Paul Sacher – Werner Reinhart, Musikkollegium Winterthur Archive, Winterthur City Library, Winterthur
Paul Sacher – Members of the Basle Chamber Orchestra, 6 December 1975, Paul Sacher, Pratteln
Paul Sacher – Members of the Basle Chamber Orchestra, 15 May 1976, Paul Sacher, Pratteln
Paul Sacher – Members of the Basle Chamber Orchestra, 27 November 1986, Paul Sacher, Pratteln
Romana Segantini – Paul Sacher, Mrs Gioconda Leykauf-Segantini, Hof, Germany
Igor Stravinsky – Paul Sacher, Paul Sacher Foundation, Basle

Interviews

Bartók, Peter, 10 October 1993
Bielser, Alice, August 1994, February 1995
Beck, Conrad, 16 July 1987
Beck, Friedl, 29 June 1993, January 1996
Birtwistle, Harrison, 3 February 1999
Bodmer, Andrea, 25 January 1996
Bornstein, Lotte, March 1995
Boulez, Pierre, 30 August 1985
Cavelti, Elsa, 17 June 1996
Döbelin, August, September 1995
Dürr, Hedi, April 1994
Estermann, Charles, October 1993

Faber-Castell, Andreas von, 11 April 1993
Faber-Castell, Count Anton Wolfgang von, 17/18 July 1993
Faber-Castell, Cornelia von, 27 April 1987
Faber-Castell, Katharina von, 24 March 1987
Fackler, Willi, September 1993
Forrestier, Jean-Claude, 13 January 2002
Frey-Sacher, Nelly, May, December 1993; March, November 1994; April 1995
Frommlet, Hedwig, 2/5 June 1995, October 1995
Fueter, Daniel, May 1999
Galli, Dorothea, April 2001
Gerber, Fritz, 16 November 1988, 7 June 1993
Haldemann, Hugo, 20 September 1995
Hartmann, Hans, September 1993, 12 July 1995
Havrlik, Els, 3 February 1991
Herwarth, Michaela von, 9 July 1992
Hoffmann, Lukas, June 1993
Honegger, Pascale, May 1988
Honegger, Rudolf, 9 August 1993
Janz, Curt Paul, 24 July 1995
Keller, Christoph, June 1993
Krayenbühl, Dr Christoph, 1 September 1993
Langbein, Brenton, May 1991
Leykauf-Segantini, Gioconda 2/3 August 1993, October 1995
Majer, Marianne, 27 July 1995, 9 October 1995
Meier, Dr Henri B., February 2000
Manz-Tanner, Dr Matthias, 1994, 1995
Martz, Dr Georg, September 1993
Miescher, Otto, September 1988
Mueller, Hannelore, September 1995
Müller-Lhotska, Dr Urs A., 28 February 2000; 1 March 2000
Müry, Dr Alfred, 15 August 1995
Oeri-Hoffmann, Vera, September 1994
Oeri-Hoffmann, Dr Jakob, August 1994
Pellmont, Tibor, March 1995
Rosenthal, Albi, 8 March 1993
Rüti, Marie-Louise, 28 March 1995

Sacher, Paul:
  August, October, November 1985;
  February, April, May, October, December 1986;
  June 1987; February, April, October 1988;
  February, June, October 1989; February, April, June 1990;
  February 1991; February, September 1992;
  January, February, April, October, December 1993;
  June 1995; October 1998
Salis, Flandrina von, September 1985
Salis, Professor Jean Rudolf von, October 1988
Sarasin, Lukas, October 1999
Schaub-Tschopp, Else, April 1994
Schweizer, Hanna, August 1994
Segantini, Romana, 11 February 1991
Staehelin, Margrit, May 1994
Striebel, Mrs, March 1995
Thierstein, Mr G., April, May 1994; April 1995
Vortisch, Elisabeth September 1995
Vortisch, Madeleine, September 1995
Vortisch, Sybille, September 1995
Wenzinger, August, September 1995
Würmli, Ernst, April 1990
Wyttenbach, Jürg, 5 March 1998

Publications

Basle Chamber Orchestra Society, *Alte und Neue Musik I: 25 Jahre Basler Kammerorchester 1926–1951* (Early and Contemporary Music: 25 Years Basle Chamber Orchestra), Zurich, 1952
Basle Police Force, *Die Basler Polizei, 1905–1980: 75 Jahre Polizeibeamten-Verband des Kantons Basel-Stadt* (The Basle Police Force, 1905–1980: 75 Years of the Police Officers' Society in Canton Basle City), Basle, 1980
Basler Anzeiger newspaper, 6 June 1929
Basler Zeitung newspaper, 12 March 1993, 24 January 1996
Berliner Tagblatt newspaper, 1 June 1935

Bielser, Alice, *Bielser von Pratteln* (The Bielsers of Pratteln), Basle, 1988

BILANZ magazine, November 1990

Birkner, Othmar, and Rebsamen, Hanspeter, *Inventar der neueren Schweizer Architektur 1820–1850* (Inventory of Newer Swiss Architecture 1820–1850), Berne, 1982

Collegium Musicum Zurich Society, *Zehn Jahre Collegium Musicum Zürich 1941–1951* (Ten Years Collegium Musicum Zürich 1941–1951), Zurich, 1951

Collegium Musicum Zurich Society, *Zwanzig Jahre Collegium Musicum Zürich 1941–1961* (Twenty Years Collegium Musicum Zürich 1941–1961), Zurich, 1962

Collegium Musicum Zurich Society, *Dreissig Jahre Collegium Musicum Zürich 1941–1971* (Thirty Years Collegium Musicum Zürich 1941–1971), Zurich, 1971

Die Welt newspaper, 27 February 1975

Ehrismann, Sibylle, ed., *Fünfzig Jahre Collegium Musicum Zürich 1941/42–1991/92* (50 Years Collegium Musicum Zurich 1941/42–1991/92), Zurich, 1994

Ex Libris magazine, No. 6, June 1984

Fehr, Hans, *3 mal 25 Jahre: Fragmente aus der Roche-Geschichte* (3 times 25 Years: Fragments from the History of Hoffmann-La Roche), Basle, 1971

Financial Times newspaper, 1 May 1993, 27 May 1999

Fortune magazine, August 1971

Gauss, D. K., Freivogel, L., Gaff, O., and Weber, K., *Geschichte der Landschaft Basel und des Kantons Basel Landschaft* (History of the Basle Countryside and the Canton of Basle Country), Vol. 2, Liestal 1932

Graf, Walter, *Die Selbstverwaltung der fricktalischen Gemeinden im 18. Jahrhundert* (Self-government of the Fricktal Municipalities in the 18th Century), dissertation, Zurich University, 1965.

Gruner, Erich, *Arbeiterschaft und Wirtschaft in der Schweiz: 1880–1914* (The Working Classes and Economy of Switzerland 1880–1914), Vol. 1, Zurich, 1987

Gutmann, Veronika, ed., *Alte und Neue Musik II: 50 Jahre Basler Kammerorchester 1926–1976* (Early and Contemporary Music II: 50 Years Basle Chamber Orchestra), Zurich, 1977

Gutmann, Veronika, ed., *Paul Sacher als Gastdirigent – Dokumentation und Beiträge zum 80. Geburtstag* (Paul Sacher As Guest Conductor – Documentation and Contributions to his 80th Birthday), Zurich, 1986

Hahnloser, Margrit, ed., *Briefe von Jean Tinguely an Paul Sacher und gemeinsame Freunde* (Letters from Jean Tinguely to Paul Sacher and Mutual Friends), Berne, Pratteln and Fribourg, 1996

Hasler, Eveline, *Anna Göldin: Letzte Hexe* (Anna Göldin: The Last Witch), Zurich and Cologne, 1982

Hoffmann-La Roche, *Zwanzigster Geschäftsbericht des Verwaltungsrates, 1938* (Twentieth Business Report of the Executive Board, 1938), Basle, 1939

Hoffmann-La Roche, *70 Jahre Paul Sacher* (Paul Sacher at 70), programme and speeches for Sacher's seventieth birthday celebrations, Pratteln, 1979

Hoffmann-La Roche, *80 Jahre Paul Sacher, 28. April 1986: Erinnerungen an den Geburtstag* (Paul Sacher at 80, 28 April 1986: Memories of the Birthday), Basle, 1986

Hoffmann-La Roche, *Verbrennung dioxinhaltiger Abfälle aus Seveso. Schlußbericht der Expertenkommission vom 7. Mai 1986 zuhanden der Behörden des Bundes und des Kantons Basel-Stadt* (The burning of waste material containing dioxin from Seveso. Final Report of the Expert Commission of 7 May 1986 for the authorities of the Federal Council and the canton of Basle City), Berne, 1986

Hoffmann-La Roche, *New Corporate and Financial Structure. Information for the Holders of our Stocks*, Basle, May 1989

The Independent newspaper, 1 May 1993

Jegge, Emil, *Die Geschichte des Fricktals bis 1803* (The History of the Fricktal until 1803), Laufenburg, 1943

Koussevitzky Music Foundation, *1967 Edition of the Catalogue of Works commissioned by the Koussevitzky Music Foundation*, Boston, MA, 1967

Kuehl, Karen, *Faber-Castell: Das Faber-Castell Schloß in Stein bei Nürnberg* (Faber-Castell: The Faber-Castell Castle in Stein near Nuremberg), 1985

Kuhn, Heinrich, ed., *Neue Musik in Basel: Paul Sacher und sein Mäzenatentum* (Contemporary Music in Basle: Paul Sacher and His Patronage), Basle, 1987

Künssberg, Freiherr E. von, *Grenzrecht und Grenzzeichen* (Border Law and Border Markings), Freiburg im Breisgau, 1940

Kutter, Markus, ed., *100 Jahre BBG, Basler Baugesellschaft* (100 Years of the BBG, Basle Building Society), Basle, 2000

MAGMA magazine, Zurich, June 1983

Neue Basler Zeitung newspaper, 29 September 1924

Neue Zürcher Zeitung newspaper, 24 January 1961, 27/28 April 1996

Oesch, Hans, ed., *Paul Sacher Stiftung II: Quellenstudien I* (Paul Sacher Foundation II: Source Studies I), Winterthur, 1991

Passavant, Nicolas, and Wanner, Gustav Adolf, *Hundertfünfzig Jahre DANZAS 1815–1965* (One Hundred and Fifty Years of DANZAS 1815–1965), Basle, 1965

Paul Sacher Foundation, *Paul Sacher Foundation*, Basle, 1986

Paul Sacher Foundation, *Komponisten des 20. Jahrhunderts in der Paul Sacher Stiftung* (Twentieth-Century Composers at the Paul Sacher Foundation), Basle, 1986

Paul Sacher Foundation, *10 Jahre Paul Sacher Stiftung. Erinnerungen an den Festakt vom 27 April 1996 im Stadtcasino Basel* (Ten Years of the Paul Sacher Foundation: Memories of the Celebrations of 27 April 1996 in the Stadtcasino, Basle), Basle, 1996

Paul Sacher Foundation, *Mitteilungen der Paul Sacher Stiftung* (Paul Sacher Foundation News), No. 2, Basle, January 1989; No. 12, Basle, April 1999; No. 13, Basle, April 2000

Paul Sacher Foundation, *Paul Sacher und die Musik des zwanzigsten Jahrhunderts: Auftragswerke, Widmungskompositionen, Uraufführungen, 1926–1990* (Paul Sacher and the Music of the Twentieth Century: Commissions, Dedicated Works and World Premières 1926-1990), Winterthur, 1991

Paul Sacher Foundation, *Settling New Scores: Music Manuscripts from the Paul Sacher Foundation,* documentation for the Paul Sacher Foundation exhibition of music scores at the Pierpont Morgan Library in New York, Basle, 1999.

Paul Sacher Foundation, *Trauerfeier für Dr.h.c. Paul Sacher* (Programme of Paul Sacher's Funeral), Basle, 1999

Paul Sacher Foundation, *Zur Erinnerung an Dr. h.c. Paul Sacher* (In Memory of Dr Paul Sacher), Basle, 1999

Paul Sacher Foundation, *Paul Sacher in memoriam*, Basle, 2000

Pauli, Hansjörg, *Hermann Scherchen, 1891–1966*, Zurich 1993

Peyer, Hans Conrad, *Roche: Geschichte eines Unternehmens 1896–1996* (Roche: History of an Enterprise, 1896–1996), Basle, 1996

Pro Helvetia Foundation, *Stiftung Pro Helvetia: Botschaften des Bundesrates, Bundesbeschluß, Geschäftsordnung* (Pro Helvetia Foundation: Message of the Federal Council, Federal Decree, Standing Orders), 1956

Pro Helvetia Foundation, *Jahrbuch der Stiftung Pro Helvetia 1939–1964* (Yearbook of the Pro Helvetia Foundation 1939–1964), Zurich, 1964

Reidemeister, Peter, and Gutmann, Veronika, eds., *Alte Musik: Praxis und Reflexion* (Early Music: Practice and Reflection), Winterthur, 1983

Roche Group, *Annual Report and Group Accounts 1997*, Basle, 1997

Rostropovich, Mstislav, ed., *Dank an Paul Sacher* (With Thanks to Paul Sacher), Zurich, 1976

Sacher, Paul, *Maja Sacher-Stehlin: 7 Februar 1896 – 8 August 1989*, Pratteln, 1989

Sacher, Paul, *Reden und Aufsätze* (Speeches and Essays), Zurich, 1986

Schaffner, Martin, *Die Basler Arbeiterbevölkerung im 19. Jahrhundert* (The Basle Working Classes in the 19th Century), Basle, 1972

Schweizer, Klaus, ed., *Alte und Neue Musik III – 60 Jahre Basler Kammerorchester 1976–1987* (Early and Contemporary Music: 60 Years Basle Chamber Orchestra), Zurich, 1988

SonntagsZeitung newspaper, 14 June 1992

Stohler, Hans, *Die Basler Grenze* (Basle's Borders), Basle, 1964. Neujahrsblatt der Gesellschaft für das Gute und Gemeinnützige, 142 (Periodical 142, Society for Public Benefit)

Straumann, Agathe, ed., *Igor Strawinsky: Sein Nachlaß, Sein Bild* (Igor Stravinsky: His Legacy, His Portrait), exhibition programme and speeches, Basle Stadttheater, Basle, 1984

Sulzer, Peter, *Zehn Komponisten um Werner Reinhart: Briefwechsel* (Ten Composers around Werner Reinhart: Correspondence), Vol. 1, Winterthur, 1979; Vol. 2, Winterthur, 1980

Suter, Paul, *Die Gemeindewappen des Kantons Baselland* (Municipal Coats-of-Arms in the Canton of Basle Country), Liestal, 1952

Tages Anzeiger newspaper, 30 November 1986, 17 September 1993, 24 January 1996

Tages Anzeiger newspaper supplement, *Das Magazin* No.26, 1 July 2000

Teuteberg, René, *Basler Geschichte* (The History of Basle), Basle, 1988

The New Yorker magazine, 10 April 2000

Türler, Heinrich, ed., *Historisch-Biographisches Lexikon der Schweiz* (Historical–Biographical Encyclopaedia of Switzerland), Vol. 3, Neuenburg, 1926

Wanner, Gustav Adolf, *Hundert Jahre Schneider & Cie. AG Internationale Transporte* (100 Years of Schneider & Cie. AG International Transport), Basle, 1964

Wanner, Gustaf Adolf, *Fritz Hoffmann-La Roche 1868–1920* (Fritz Hoffmann-La Roche 1868–1920), Basle, 1968

Zeugin, Ernst, *'Bilder aus Prattelns Vergangenheit'* (Pictures from Pratteln's Past), *Prattler Heimatschriften*. No. 6, Pratteln, 1974

Zinsser, William, ed., *Extraordinary Lives: The Art and Craft of American Biography*, Boston, MA, 1988

Photographic Sources

1. Paul Sacher, Pratteln, Switzerland 47
2. Paul Sacher, Pratteln, Switzerland 52
3. Paul Sacher, Pratteln, Switzerland 54
4. Paul Sacher, Pratteln, Switzerland 55
5. Paul Sacher, Pratteln, Switzerland 59
6. Charles Estermann, Payerne, Switzerland 75
7. Charles Estermann, Payerne, Switzerland 76
8. Lili Roth-Streiff, Zurich, Switzerland 81
9. Lili Roth-Streiff, Zurich, Switzerland 82
10. Paul Sacher, Pratteln, Switzerland 83
11. Hans Hartmann, Baden, Switzerland 86
12. Willi Fackler, Basle, Switzerland 88
13. Else Schaub-Tschopp, Basle, Switzerland 98
14. Paul Sacher, Pratteln, Switzerland 128
15. Paul Sacher, Pratteln, Switzerland 136
16. Paul Sacher, Pratteln, Switzerland 151
17. Paul Sacher, Pratteln, Switzerland 152
18. Paul Sacher, Pratteln, Switzerland 160
19. Paul Sacher, Pratteln, Switzerland 189
20. Private collection, Zurich, Switzerland 199
21. Private collection, Zurich, Switzerland 200
22. Paul Sacher, Pratteln, Switzerland 209
23. Paul Sacher, Pratteln, Switzerland 213
24. Paul Sacher, Pratteln, Switzerland 225
25. Keystone photograph agency, Zurich, Switzerland 241
26. Christian Vogt (photographer), Basle, Switzerland 261
27. Keystone photograph agency, Zurich, Switzerland 286
28. Gustav Freedman (photographer), Massachusetts, USA 297
29. Christian Vogt (photographer), Basle, Switzerland 303

Cover photograph: Claude Giger, Basle, Switzerland.
Author photograph: Christian Vogt, Basle, Switzerland.

Index

Adam, Max 109
Adams, Stanley 280, 282–284
Anda, Géza 184
André, Maurice 263
Ansermet, Ernest 159, 216
Arp, Hans 150

Bach, Johann Sebastian 58, 96, 99, 100, 144, 182
Bächtold, Susi 149
Baldegger, Hedwig 234
Ball, Robert 278
Barell, Dr Emil C. 167–172, 175, 276, 281
Barth, Wilhelm 117
Bartók, Béla 117, 120, 139, 161–163, 178, 179, 181, 191–195, 214, 217, 244, 246, 248, 296, 308
Bartók, Béla junior 162
Bartók, Ditta 162
Bartók, Peter 11, 192–194
Bavier, Helene von 115
Beck, Conrad 106, 119, 120, 145, 156, 161, 163, 164, 179, 187, 188, 217, 218, 227, 268
Beck, Friedl 164, 180, 218
Beecham, Sir Thomas 94
Beethoven, Ludwig van 85, 92–95, 157, 158, 183, 229
Berg, Alban 144, 211, 212
Berio, Luciano 233, 244, 257, 308
Bielser, Alice 11, 146
Bielser, Anna 27
Birtwistle, Harrison 308
Blauenstein, Barbara 35
Blum, Andreas 247
Blum, Robert 156
Bodmer, Andrea 183
Bodmer, Dr Hans Conrad 183

Boissonnas, Luc 11, 184
Bonaparte, Napoleon 21, 30, 38
Bonjour, Professor Edgar 13, 157, 232, 252, 295
Bornstein, Sarah 53
Bornstein-Laufer, Moritz 56
Bornstein-Laufer, Tauba 56
Botta, Mario 301
Boulez, Pierre 163, 212, 215, 233, 257, 291, 308
Bourdelle, Antoine 116
Bourgeois, Joe 150
Bourquard, Jenovefra 39
Brahms, Johannes 93, 95, 96, 227
Braque, Georges 150, 234
Britten, Benjamin 224, 239, 308
Bruckner, Anton 95, 96, 227
Burckhardt, Carl Jakob 138
Burckhardt, Jacob 252
Burkhard, Willy 161, 181, 186, 217, 230, 289
Busch, Fritz 158

Caflisch, Dr Albert 281
Carnegie, Dale 177
Carter, Elliot 257
Cavelti, Elsa 223, 230
Celibidache, Sergiu 158
Chagall, Marc 117, 150
Craft, Robert 255, 256

Dali, Salvador 164
Denissow, Edison 266
Döbelin, August 236
Durigo, Ilona 161
Dürr, Anna *see* Sacher, Anna
Dürr (née König), Anna Maria 'Nanny Dürr' 38, 41, 50, 51, 77
Dürr, Elisabeth 35

Dürr, Friedrich i (1746–1804) 26, 28, 31, 147
Dürr Friedrich ii (b. 1772) 31, 32, 34
Dürr Friedrich iii (1800–1864) 34, 35, 37
Dürr, Friedrich iv (1851–1934) 38, 45, 46, 62, 73, 77
Dürr, Fritz 49
Dürr, Hans Jacob 26, 27
Dürr, Hedi 77, 78, 87
Dürr, Louise 51, 58
Dürr, Jacob 27
Dürr, Johannes i (1703–1781) 27
Dürr, Johannes ii (b. 1845) 37
Dürr, Maria 73, 74
Dürr, Niklaus (cousin of Friedrich Dürr ii) 34
Dürr, Niklaus (son of Friedrich Dürr ii) 34
Dürr, Samuel 27
Dürr-König see Dürr

Ehinger, Hans 109
Eptinger family 25, 26
Erni, Jürg 247
Ernst, Markus 268
Ernst, Max 116, 117
Estermann, Carl Baptist 73, 74
Estermann, Charles (son of Maria Dürr, 1884–1962) 74
Estermann, Charles (grandson of Maria Dürr) 73
Estermann, Laura 74
Estermann, Maria see Dürr, Maria

Faber, Lothar von 197
Faber-Castell, Anton, Count von 197, 198, 202, 259
Faber-Castell, Andreas von 198, 201, 202, 204, 205
Faber-Castell, Cornelia von 203, 204, 262
Faber-Castell, Katharina von 201–204, 260, 262, 289, 293

Faber-Castell, Nina, Countess von 195–197, 199–205, 232, 236, 259, 260, 262, 264, 265, 270, 300
Faber-Castell, Roland, Count von 197, 198, 201–205
Fischer, Edwin 118
Forrestier, Jean-Claude 268
Fortner, Wolfgang 106, 156
Frey-Sacher, Nelly see Sacher, Nelly
Frommlet, Elisabeth 'Bethli' 64, 65
Frommlet, Eugen 64
Frommlet, Hedwig 64–65
Fueter, Daniel 246
Furtwängler, Wilhelm 94, 118

Galway, James 263
Gerber, Fritz 273, 275, 280–284, 301
Geyer, Stefi 161, 178, 182, 193, 246, 248
Gysler, Paul 60

Hahnloser, Margrit 300, 316, 323
Halffter, Christóbal 266
Hamm, Adolf 100, 110, 111, 157, 179
Handel, George Frederick 96, 97, 99, 100, 144, 182, 230
Haselbach, Josef 266, 289
Havrlik, Els 19, 20, 92, 100, 112, 166, 274, 298
Hawkes, Ralph 161, 193
Haydn, Joseph 95–97, 99, 108, 157, 182, 230, 246, 290
Henze, Hans Werner 239, 248, 267, 308
Herwarth, Michaela von 94, 107, 130, 139, 140, 158, 218
Hindemith, Paul 95, 104, 107, 117, 120, 144, 178, 224, 226, 230
Hoffmann, Alfred 170, 171
Hoffmann, Andreas 26, 271
Hoffmann (née Merian), Anna Elisabeth 166
Hoffmann, Emanuel 113, 116, 125, 127, 146, 154, 170–172, 271, 293
Hoffmann, Fritz 116, 158, 165–171, 276, 277, 293

Hoffmann, Lukas 125, 126, 153, 154, 163, 203, 279, 282, 293, 310
Hoffmann, Vera 126, 154, 181, 191, 203, 218, 227, 277, 293
Hoffmann (née La Roche], Adèle 116, 165
Holliger, Heinz 217, 266, 267, 269, 289
Honegger, Arthur 108, 117–120, 125, 163, 178, 179, 181, 209–211, 214, 215, 217, 229, 230, 247, 289, 298, 308
Honegger, Pascale 163, 181, 196, 208, 210, 218, 227, 232, 233
Honegger, Rudolf 80, 85, 87
Hürlimann, Dr Martin 184
Hutchins, Robert Maynard 177

Jann, Dr Adolf Walter 276, 279, 281–283
Janz, Curt Paul 94, 97, 103, 104, 119, 157, 158
Jespers, Floris 117
Jespers, Oscar 117
Jünger, Patricia 216, 268

Kaegi, Professor Werner 252, 253
Karajan, Herbert von 158, 290
Keller, Christoph 247
Kelterborn, Rudolf 266, 268, 269, 289
Klee, Paul 150
Kleiber, Erich 118
Klemperer, Otto 118
Kocher, Werner 153
Koechlin-Hoffmann, Albert 171
Kopelent, Marek 266
Koussevitzky, Serge 120, 192, 193, 240
Krayenbühl, Dr Christoph 183, 184, 291
Krayenbühl, Dr Hugo 184
Křenek, Ernst 239
Krétlov, Walter 58
Kunz, Ernst 106

Langbein, Brenton 229, 247–249, 267, 290, 291
Leykauf-Segantini, Gioconda 134, 138
Ligeti, György 266

Lipatti, Dinu 163, 208
Lippmann, Walter 14
Liszt, Franz 93, 296
Lobeck, Otto 143, 144, 221
Lohr, Ina 122, 141, 142, 155, 157, 219
Luginbühl, Max 196
Lutoslawski, Witold 233, 257, 291

Mahler, Gustav 93
Majer, Marianne 11, 104, 105, 107, 108, 112, 116, 120, 123, 135, 140, 142, 164, 214
Mann, Thomas 244
Martin, Frank 144, 213, 235, 289
Martinů, Bohuslav 120, 163, 181, 182, 195, 217, 230
Martz, Dr Georg 153
Mascioni, Anita 122, 123, 130
Meerwein, Carl 166
Meier, Dr Henri 174, 275, 284
Meier, Theo 220
Meili, Max 142
Melchers, Dr Fritz 271
Melchers, Ursula 271
Menuhin, Yehudi 193, 291
Merian, Christoph, 21, 166
Miescher, Otto 69, 70, 84, 91
Mihalovici, Marcel 120, 230
Mintz, Schlomo 263
Miró, Joan 117
Modigliani, Amedeo 116
Moeschinger, Albert 156
Mohr, Ernst 109
Moret, Norbert 266, 268
Moser, Rudolf 79, 85, 93, 100, 104, 106, 120
Monteverdi, Claudio 106, 143
Mozart, Amadeus 95–97, 99, 100, 108, 124, 157, 179, 182, 210, 230, 246, 290, 298, 299
Mueller, Hannelore 155, 156, 219, 220
Mühll, Alfred Von der 104, 105
Mühll, Dora Von der 113, 125
Mühll, Hans Von der 113

Müller von Kulm, Walter 181, 220, 221
Müller, Paul 186
Münch, Hans 158
Münch, Charles 210
Müry, Dr Albert 104, 105, 111
Mutter, Anne-Sophie 290, 291, 309

Naef, Dr Karl 187
Nef, Professor Karl 92, 93, 141, 143
Nef, Walter 142, 155
Oeri, Dr Jakob 277, 279
Oeri-Hoffmann, Vera *see* Hoffmann, Vera
Oesch, Professor Hans 240, 242, 244
Paumgartner, Bernhard 290
Pears, Peter 224, 233
Pellmont, Béla 57
Pellmont, Elise 57, 126
Pellmont, Géza 57, 58
Pellmont, Ilia 57
Pellmont, Karl junior 60, 126
Pellmont, Karl senior 57
Pellmont, Tibor 57, 58, 126
Penderecki, Krzysztof 267, 291
Pereira, Alexander 207
Peyer, Hans Conrad 169, 276, 281, 282
Picasso, Pablo 117, 150, 234
Planck, Max 221, 222
Portner, Charlotte 134
Preiswerk, Eduard 135
Pulawski, Adalbert 56

Rampal, Jean-Pierre 263
Rasumovsky, Katja 310
Rebmann, Elisabeth 31
Regamey, Constantin 186
Reichenbach, François 14, 97, 233, 260
Reinhard, Walter 187
Reinhart, Werner 110, 142, 159, 212, 216, 224, 226
Remy, Dr Sigismund 245
Richelieu, Cardinal 138
Rihm, Wolfgang 258, 268, 290, 309
Rosenthal, Albi 255–257
Rosenwald, Julius 177

Rostropovich, Mstislav 'Slava' 163, 233, 239, 263, 270
Roth, Emil 80

Sacher, Adele 49, 50, 66
Sacher (née Holer [Hohler]), Adelheid 37–42, 49
Sacher, Adolf 40
Sacher, Anna 'Anny' 41, 45–51, 53, 55–58, 60–63, 65–70, 73, 77–79, 84, 85, 100, 101, 111, 112, 118, 126, 149, 154, 219, 234
Sacher, Anton 39
Sacher, August 37–40
Sacher, Fridolin 39
Sacher, Fritz 49
Sacher (née Stehlin), Maja 113–117, 125–130, 135, 140, 146, 149, 150, 152–155, 162–165, 167, 179, 181, 196, 203, 204, 208, 211, 215, 217, 218, 220, 232–235, 250, 259, 260, 262, 264–266, 270, 271, 285, 287, 289, 300–302, 307
Sacher, Nelly 45, 53, 57, 58, 59, 61, 63, 64, 66, 67, 70, 77, 78, 83, 84, 111, 112, 126, 134, 135, 204, 249
Sacher, Oswald 39
Sacher, Oswald August 'Gusti' 41, 46–51, 56–58, 61, 63, 65, 66, 70, 77, 154, 234–236
Sacher, Paul
  Personal life:
  childhood and early life 50–61, 63–65, 70–78
  academic education 53, 60, 67–70, 78–80, 84, 92, 93
  musical education 58, 78, 79, 85, 92–95
  influence of Payerne 71, 74
  health 50, 53, 80, 235, 236
  tendency to depression 66, 92, 299, 307
  belief in astrology 196, 223, 231, 232
  character 84, 87, 89, 91, 92, 95, 97,

101, 103, 105, 111, 112, 145, 167, 214, 243, 245–250, 253, 270–272, 274–276
views on poverty and wealth 64, 79, 149, 258, 293–295
relationship with mother 53, 68, 69, 100, 112, 234
relationship with father 66, 70, 236
relationship with grandmother 49, 51, 57
courtship Maja Hoffmann-Stehlin 112, 113, 116, 125–130
relationship with Romana Segantini 130, 133–139
relationship with Countess Nina von Faber-Castell 195, 201–205, 259, 264
relationship with Irmtraut Schmid 260–266, 269, 270, 272, 301, 302
father-role 153, 154, 260, 265
relationship with daughters 202, 260, 262
relationship with son 265, 266, 270, 271
charitable works 295, 296
Professional life:
early goals 68, 70, 78, 85, 95–99, 104
high-school orchestra 85–87
dislike of piano 78, 94
Orchester Junger Basler 96, 97, 99
making Basle his base 118, 119
Basler Kammerorchester (BKO) founding 99; financing 104, 105, 123, 139, 140, 267
Gruppe der Fünf (Group of Five) 109
International Society of Contemporary Music 109, 142, 161, 179
Basle Men's Choir 110
Basle Chamber Choir 111
Schola Cantorum Basiliensis 141–144, 219
acquiring Lobeck's early-instrument collection 143, 144, 221
Collegium Musicum Zürich founding 181, 182;

financing 183, 184, 292
work with Pro Helvetia 184–188
founding of Basle Music Academy 219–221
purchase of Igor Stravinsky legacy 255–257
creation of Paul Sacher Foundation 251, 254, 257, 258
work with Basle Percussion Ensemble 268, 269
Hoffmann-La Roche 165–175 *passim*, 273–287 *passim*, 301
creation of Museum Jean Tinguely 300, 301
conducting style 108, 156, 228, 229
musical tastes 78, 94, 95, 107, 124, 144, 196, 211, 212
programme planning 156, 157
audience education 144, 145
commissioning 105–107, 124, 139, 144, 211, 216, 217, 242, 243
love of Mozart 290
overall assessment 308–310
Sacher, Wilhelmine 48
Sacher-Dürr *see* Sacher
Saint Phalle, Niki de 301
Salis, Professor Jean Rudolf von 129, 175, 186, 253
Salis, Flandrina von 227
Sarasin, Alfred 253
Sarasin, Lukas 252, 253
Satie, Erik 109, 120
Schmid, Alfred 'Fred' 121
Schmid, Irmtraut 260–266, 269–272, 300–302
Schmid, Georg 262–266, 270–272, 302
Schmid, Siegfried 268
Schneider, Dr Gustav 80
Schneider, Karl Erhard 48
Schaub-Tschopp, Else 97, 130, 140
Scherchen, Dr Hermann 109, 224, 226
Schoeck, Othmar 188
Schoenberg, Arnold, 95, 144, 178, 211, 212, 298

Schubert, Revd Theophil 307, 310
Schuh, Dr Willi 184, 188, 190, 228
Schulthess, Walter 181, 182, 246
Schwarzenberg, Annette 181
Segantini, Romana 130, 133–139, 249, 298
Segantini, Gioconda *see* Leykauf-Segantini, Gioconda
Segantini, Giovanni 134
Segantini, Gottardo 134
Senn, Otto 104, 105, 109, 183
Senn, Willy 109
Serkin, Rudolf 157, 239
Smet, Gustav de 117
Speich, Dr Rudolf 174
Staehelin, Margrit 130, 218
Staehelin, Dr Max 130
Steel, Ronald 14
Steffensen-Burckhardt, Maria 252
Stehlin, Dr Hans Georg 153
Stehlin, Fritz 115
Stehlin, Johann Jakob 115, 167
Steib, Katharina 254
Steib, Wilfred 254
Steiner, Dr Georg 80
Sternbach, Dr Leo 277
Stockhausen, Karlheinz 217, 218
Strauss, Richard 188, 190
Stravinsky, Igor 107, 117, 120, 144, 159, 161, 190, 195, 211–214, 216, 217, 230, 244, 254–258, 268, 293, 308
Stravinsky, Vera 255, 256
Streiff, Revd. Fritz 80
Streiff, Lili 11, 80, 103, 307
Strobel, Heinrich 143, 215

Täuber, Sophie 150
Tinguely, Jean 150, 207, 233, 300–302
Tippett, Michael 224
Traub, Max Carl 165
Tschopp, Annie 96–98, 112, 130, 135, 139–141
Vaurabourg, Andrée 208
Veress, Sándor 308

Von Sprecher, family 196, 259
Vortisch, August 'Gusti' 122, 123, 135, 155
Vortisch, Elisabeth 123
Vortisch, Madeleine 122
Vortisch, Sybille 122

Wagner, Richard 93
Wasserman, Alfred 111
Webern, Anton 144, 211, 212, 257
Weingartner, Felix 93–95, 108, 112, 113, 117, 118, 158, 228
Wenzinger, August 109, 142, 156
Wernli, Andreas 247
Whitman, Walt 224
Wiggli, Oskar 302
Wilde, Oscar 80
Wildenstein, Baroness 115
Winterstein-Bosshard, Heny 184
Würmli, Ernst 263, 266, 271, 294, 296
Wyttenbach, Jürg 269
Yun, Isang 266
Zäslin, Johannes 30, 147

Works Commissioned
by Paul Sacher
1926-1999

Performances were world premières and conducted by Sacher, unless indicated otherwise. The list of 146 works commissioned by Paul Sacher, and in many cases dedicated to him and his orchestras, is as complete as published sources, research, and information from the Paul Sacher Foundation in Basle, Switzerland, render possible.

Abbreviations: BKO: Basler Kammerorchester; CMZ: Collegium Musicum Zürich; BSE: Basler Schlagzeug Ensemble; BOG: Basler Orchestergesellschaft

Alessandro, Raffaele d' (1911-59)
Bassoon Concerto, op. 75 (1956); Henri Bouchet (bn), BKO, Basle, 22 February 1957

Ammann, Benno (1904-86)
Frammento per vibrafono e clarinetto basso [Fragments for vibraphone and bass clarinet] (1981); BOG-serenade, Basle, 11 September 1983

Bäck, Sven-Erik (1919-94)
Serenade *Sumerki* (1977); CMZ, Lucerne, 21 August 1977
Signos for six percussionists (1980); BSE, BOG-serenade, Basle, 7 September 1980

Bartók, Béla (1881-1945)
Music for Strings, Percussion and Celesta (1936); BKO (10th anniversary concert), Basle, 21 January 1937
Divertimento for strings (1939); BKO, Basle, 11 June 1940

Beck, Conrad (1901-89)
Largo for String Orchestra (1928); BKO (study performance organised by the Group of Five), Basle, 23 March 1929
Symphony No. 5 (1929-30); BKO, Basle, 2 October 1930
Kleine Suite for strings (1930); BKO, Colmar (Société Philharmonique), 29 October 1931
Oratorium after verses by Angelus Silesius for soloists, choir, orchestra and organ (1933-4); Ria Ginster (sop), Maria von Basilides (con), Fritz Lechner (bass), Adolf Hamm (organ), BKO, Basle, 7 June 1934
Serenade for flute, clarinet and strings (1935); Joseph Bopp (fl), Oskar Gerstner (cl), BKO, Basle, 2 October 1935
Rhapsodie (Concertino No. 2) for piano and small orchestra (1936); Adrian Aeschbacher (pf), BKO, Basle, 21 January 1937
Chamber Cantata on sonnets by Louïze Labé, for soprano, flute,

piano, and string orchestra; Ginevra Vivante (sop), Orchestre
de la Société Philharmonique de Paris, Paris, 8 November 1937

Concerto for Violin and Small Orchestra (1940); Rodolfo
Felicani (vn), BKO, Basle, 24 January 1941

Chamber Concerto for harpsichord and string orchestra (1942);
Eduard Müller (hpd), BKO, Basle, 27 November 1942

Suite No. 2 for string orchestra (1945); BKO, Basle, 15 February 1946

Viola Concerto (1949); first Basle performance, Walter Kägi (va),
BKO, Basle, 14 December 1951

Concertino for clarinet, bassoon and orchestra (1953-4); Louis
Cahuzac (cl), Henri Bouchet (bn), Sinfonie Orchester des
Hessischen Rundfunks, Frankfurt, 17 June 1954

Sonatina for orchestra (1957-8), composed for the 500th
anniversary of Basle University); BKO, Basle, 2 July 1960

Hommages: two pieces for orchestra (1965); BKO, Basle,
12 May 1966

Fantasie for orchestra (1968-9); BKO, Basle, 19 March 1970

Elegie [Elegy]: solo cantata on fragments of 'The Muse' by
Friedrich Hölderlin for soprano and orchestra (1971-2);
Hanneke van Bork (sop), BKO, 14 December 1973

Lichter und Schatten [Lights and Shadows]: three movements for
two horns, percussion and string orchestra (1982); CMZ,
Zurich, 18 November 1982

Berio, Luciano (1925-2003)

Il ritorno degli snovidenia [The Return of the Snovedians] for
cello and small orchestra (1976); Mstislav Rostropovich (vc),
Gérard Wyss (pf), BKO 50th anniversary concert, Basle,
20 January 1977

Chorale (on Sequenza VIII) for violin, two horns, and strings
(1981); Carlo Chiarappa (vn), CMZ, Zurich, 17 January 1982

Binet, Jean (1893-1960)

Trois Pièces for string orchestra (1937-9); BKO, Basle,
24 January 1941

'*L'Or perdu*' [The Lost Gold]: poem for voice and orchestra
(Jean Cuttat), (1953); Irma Kolassi (sop), BKO, Basle,
29 January 1954

Birtwistle, Harrison (b. 1934)
Endless Parade for trumpet, vibraphone and strings (1986-7); Håkan Hardenberger (tr), CMZ, Zurich, 1 May 1987

Blacher, Boris (1903-75)
Dialog for flute, violin, piano and string orchestra (1951); Joseph Bopp (fl), Rodolfo Felicani (vn), Valerie Kägi (pf), BKO, Basle, 14 December 1951

Blum, Robert (1900-94)
Der Streiter in Christo Jesu [The Warrior in Christ Jesus]. Cantata for soprano and chamber orchestra on texts from the epistles of St Paul (1943); Elsa Scherz-Meister (sop), Valerie Kägi (pf), BKO, Basle, 15 October 1943

Tropi e canzoni. Three fantasies for string orchestra (1968); CMZ, Zurich, 25 April 1969

Boulez, Pierre (b. 1925)
sur Incises (1996-8); according to the Paul Sacher Foundation, this work for solo piano, 2 pianos, 3 harps, 2 vibraphones, marimba, 3 clarinets and 3 percussion originated from a Sacher commission which the composer later declined, preferring to offer the work to Sacher as testimony to their friendship

Anthèmes 3 (work in progress); announced as a violin concerto for Anne-Sophie Mutter; commissioned by Sacher before his death in May 1999. First performance expected in 2006 to mark the centenary of Sacher's birth and the Paul Sacher Foundation's 20th anniversary.

Brun, Fritz (1878-1959)
Variationen über ein eigenes Thema [Variations on an Original Theme] for piano and string orchestra (1944); Max Egger (pf), BKO, Basle, 13 October 1944

Burkhard, Willy (1900-55)
Ewige Brausen [Eternal Roar] for bass and chamber orchestra on text by Knut Hamsun, op. 46 (1936); Felix Loeffel (bass), BKO, 21 January 1937

Concerto for String Orchestra, op. 50 (1937); BKO, Basle, 28 January 1938

Hymnus for orchestra, op. 57 (1939); Winterthurer Stadtorchester, Winterthur, 13 December 1939

Genug ist nicht genug [Enough is not Enough]. Cantata on poems by C. F. Meyer for mixed choir with string orchestra, two trumpets, and timpani], op. 53 (1938-9); BKO, 11 June 1940

Das Jahr [The Year]. Oratorio for mixed chorus, soloists and orchestra, on text by Hermann Hiltbrunner, op. 62 (1940-41); Helene Fahrni (sop), Elisabeth Gehri (alto), Felix Loeffel (bass), BKO, Basle, 19 February 1942

Violin Concerto No. 2, op. 69 (1943); Stefi Geyer (vn), CMZ, Zurich, 26 January 1945

Sinfonie in einem Satz [Symphony in One Movement], op. 73 (1944); Winterthurer Stadtorchester, Winterthur, 20 December 1944

Piccola sinfonia giocosa, op. 81 (1949); CMZ, Zurich, 6 May 1949

Toccata for four wind instruments, percussion and string orchestra, op. 86 (1951); CMZ (10th anniversary concert), Zurich, 7 December 1951

Concertino for two flutes, harpsichord, and string orchestra, op. 94 (1954); CMZ, Edinburgh, 2 September 1954

Carter, Elliott (b. 1908)

Oboe Concerto (1986-7); Heinz Holliger (ob), John Carewe, CMZ, Zurich, 17 June 1988

Casella, Alfredo (1883-1947)

Concerto for Piano, Timpani, Percussion and Strings, op. 69 (1943); Valerie Kägi (pf), BKO, Basle, 22 March 1945

Ciry, Michel (b. 1919)

Dolor y paz [Pain and Peace] for string orchestra, op. 47 (1950); Studioorchester Beromünster, Zurich, 8 March 1951

Dutilleux, Henri (1916-94)

Mystère de l'instant [Mystery of the Moment] for 24 strings, cimbalom and percussion, (1989); CMZ, Zurich, 22 October 1989

Fortner, Wolfgang (1907-87)
Nuptiae Catulli [Catullus's Wedding]. Cantata for tenor, six-part chamber choir, and chamber orchestra on words by Catullus (1937); Salvatore Salvati (ten), BKO, Basle, 11 February 1939
The Creation for baritone (or mezzo) and orchestra, to text by James Weldon Johnson (1953-4); Dietrich Fischer-Dieskau (bar), BKO, Basle, 18 February 1955
Ballet blanc for two violins and string orchestra (1958); Heribert Lauer and Walter Henrich (vn), Wolfgang Fortner, CMZ, Zurich, 5 December 1958
Triplum for orchestra with three obbligato pianos (1965-6); Klaus Linder, Rolf Mäser and Ulrich Sandmeier (pf), BKO, Basle, 15 December 1966
Prismen [Prisms] for flute, oboe, clarinet, harp, percussion and orchestra (1974); Aurèle Nicolet (fl), Heinz Holliger (ob), Peter Rieckhoff (cl), Ursula Holliger (hp), Jean-Claude Forestier (perc), BKO, Basle, 13 February 1975
Variationen for large chamber orchestra (1978); BKO, Basle, 27 March 1980

Geiser, Walther (1897-1993)
Fantasy I for piano, strings and timpani, op. 31 (1941-2); Valerie Kägi (pf), BKO, Basle, 27 November 1942
Concerto da camera for two violins, harpsichord, and string orchestra, op. 50 (1957); Doris Baumgartner and Rodolfo Felicani (vn), Eduard Müller (hpd), BKO, Basle, 13 December 1957

Ghedini, Giorgio Federico (1892-1965)
Concerto detto 'L'Alderina' for flute, violin, timpani, cello and orchestra (1951); Orchestra Alessandro Scarlatti, Naples, 17 April 1951
Concentus basiliensis for violin and chamber orchestra (1954); Rodolfo Felicani (vn), BKO, Basle, 8 December 1955

Gubaydulina, Sofiya (b. 1931)
Violin Concerto for Anne-Sophie Mutter (work in progress); commissioned before Sacher's death in May 1999

Guyonnet, Jacques (b. 1933)
Lucifer photophore: Five pieces for chamber orchestra (1974-5); Jacques Guyonnet, BKO, Basle, 6 June 1975

Halffter (Jiménez), Cristóbal (b. 1930)
Double Concerto in two movements for violin, viola and orchestra (1984); Christiane Edinger (vn), Tabea Zimmermann (va), Cristóbal Halffter, BKO, Basle, 6 February 1986

Haselbach, Josef (1936-2002)
Cantata No. 2, '*Büchner-Kantate*', for soprano, speaking chorus, mixed choir and orchestra, on texts by Georg Büchner (1977-80); Kathrin Graf (sop), Karl Scheuber, CMZ, Zurich, 30 January 1981

Concerto for Vibraphone, Piano, and Chamber Orchestra (1982-3); Jean-Claude Forestier (vib), Gérard Wyss (pf), CMZ, Zurich, 4 May 1984

Leporellos Traum [Leporello's Dream] for chamber orchestra (1989); CMZ, Zurich, 19 January 1991

Haug, Hans (1900-67)
Kammero-Kantate for soloists, choir, string orchestra, and piano, on composer's own text for BKO ('Kammero') celebration (1931); BKO, Basle, 25 September 1931

Henze, Hans Werner (b. 1926)
Sonata per archi (1957-8); CMZ, Zurich, 21 March 1958

Cantata della fiaba estrema for soprano, chamber choir and thirteen instruments, on text by Elsa Morante (1963); Ingeborg Hallstein (sop), CMZ, Zurich, 26 February 1965

Double Concerto for oboe, harp, and strings (1966); Heinz Holliger (ob), Ursula Holliger (hp), CMZ (25th anniversary concert), Zurich, 2 December 1966

Compases para preguntas ensimismadas for viola and 22 musicians (1969-70); Hirofumi Fukai (va), BKO, Basle, 11 February 1971

Violin Concerto No. 2 for bass-baritone, violin, 33 instrumentalists and tape, with text by Magnus Enzensberger (1971);

Brenton Langbein (vn), Kurt Widmer (bass-bar), Pitt Linder
(sound production), BKO, Basle, 2 November 1972
Symphony No. 10 (1998-2000); Sir Simon Rattle, City of
Birmingham Symphony Orchestra, Lucerne, 17 August 2002

Hindemith, Paul (1895-1963)
Symphony *'Die Harmonie der Welt'* [The Harmony of the World]
(1951); BKO (25th anniversary concert), Basle, 24 January 1952

Holliger, Heinz (b. 1939)
Atembogen [Arc of Breath] for orchestra (1974-5);
Heinz Holliger, BKO, Basle, 6 June 1975

Honegger, Arthur (1892-1955)
La Danse des morts [The Dance of the Dead]. Oratorio on text
by Paul Claudel for soloists, chorus and string orchestra (1938);
Ginevra Vivante (sop), Lina Falk (alto), Hughes Cuénod (ten),
William Aguet (narrator), Eduard Müller (organ), BKO, Basle,
1 March 1940
Symphony No. 2, *'Symphonie pour cordes'*, for string orchestra and
trumpet (ad libitum) (1941); CMZ, Zurich, 18 May 1942
Symphony No. 4, *'Deliciae basiliensis'* (1946); BKO (20th anniversary concert), Basle, 21 January 1947
Une cantate de Noël [A Christmas Cantata] for solo baritone, choir,
children's choir, orchestra, and organ (1953); Derrik Olsen
(bar), Eduard Müller (organ), BKO, Basle, 18 December 1953

Ibert, Jacques (1890-1962)
Symphonie concertante for oboe and string orchestra (1948-9);
Edgar Shann (ob), BKO, Basle, 23 February 1951

Jünger, Patricia (b. 1951)
Vibrazioni for 37 drums (1981); BOG-serenade, Basle,
13 September 1981
Oh, You My Sweet Evening Star for six percussionists (1982); BSE,
Geneva, 30 August 1982
Machine's Party for chamber orchestra (1985); Patricia Jünger,
CMZ, 12 June 1987

Heller Schein [Bright Gleam]. Ländler variations on text by
  Elfriede Jelinek for mezzo-soprano, bass clarinet, percussion,
  and chamber orchestra (1988); Eva Csapò (mez), Hilmar
  Koitka (bass cl), Patricia Jünger, CMZ, Zurich,
  22 October 1989

Kelterborn, Rudolf (b. 1931)
Traummusik [Dream Music]. Six pieces for small orchestra (1971);
  CMZ, Zurich, 28 January 1972
Gesänge zur Nacht [Night Songs] for soprano and chamber
  orchestra on poems by Ingeborg Bachmann und Erika
  Burkart (1978); Edith Wiens (sop), CMZ, Zurich, 2 March 1979
Visions sonores [Resonant Visions] for six percussionists and six
  obbligato instruments (1979)]; Primoz Novsak (vn), Ernest
  Strauss (vc), Felix Manz (fl, piccolo), Antony Morf (cl, bass cl),
  Frantisek Vlasak (tr), Bruno Gutknecht (bass trombone), BSE,
  BKO, Basle, 4 June 1980
Musik für sechs Schlagzeuger [Music for Six Percussionists] (1983-4);
  BSE, BOG-serenade, Basle, 2 September 1984
Annäherungen. Musik für Horn und Schlagzeugensemble
  [Approaches: Music for Horn and Percussion Ensemble] (1998);
  Josef Brejza (hn), Kelterborn, BSE, Basle, 17 September 1998

Kopelent, Marek (b. 1933)
Symphony (1982); Heinz Holliger, BKO, Basle, 17 February 1983

Kovách, András (b. 1915)
Symphony No. 3 (1956-7); BKO, Basle, 6 November 1959

Křenek, Ernst (1900-91)
Symphonisches Stück [Symphonic Piece] for string orchestra,
  op. 86 (1939); BKO, Basle, 11 June 1940
Kette, Kreis und Spiegel. Sinfonische Zeichnung [Chain, Circle and
  Mirror. Symphonic Design], op. 160 (1956-7); BKO, Basle,
  23 January 1958
Statisch und ekstatisch. Zehn kurze Orchesterstücke [Static and
  Ecstatic. Ten short pieces for orchestra], op. 214 (1972);
  Křenek, CMZ, Zurich, 23 March 1973

Lutoslawski, Witold (1913-94)
Double Concerto for oboe, harp and chamber orchestra (1979-80); Heinz Holliger (ob), Ursula Holliger (hp), CMZ, Lucerne, 24 August 1980

Chain II. Dialogue for violin and orchestra (1984-5); Anne-Sophie Mutter (vn), CMZ, Zurich, 31 January 1987

Malipiero, Gian Francesco (1882-1973)
Symphony No. 6 for string orchestra (1947); BKO, Basle, 11 February 1949

Marescotti, André-François (1902-95)
Concert Carougeois II (1958-9); Rodolfo Felicani and Petru Manoliu (vn), Walter Kägi (va), Ernest Strauss (vc), BKO, Basle, 11 February 1959

Martin, Frank (1890-1974)
Der Cornet [The Cornet]. Ballad after Rainer Maria Rilke, 'Die Weise von Liebe und Tod des Cornets Christoph', for alto and chamber orchestra (1942-3); Elsa Cavelti (alto), BKO, Basle, 9 February 1945

Petite symphonie concertante for harp, harpsichord, piano, and two string orchestras (1944-5); CMZ, Zurich, 17 May 1946

Etudes for string orchestra (1955-6); BKO, Basle, 23 November 1956

Cello Concerto (1965-6); Pierre Fournier (vc), BKO, Basle, 26 January 1967

Trois danses for oboe, harp, string quintet, and string orchestra (1970); Heinz Holliger (ob), Ursula Holliger (hp), Brenton Langbein, Curt Conzelmann (vn), Ottavio Corti (va), Mischa Frey (vc), Hermann Voerkel (double bass), CMZ, Zurich, 9 October 1970

Martinů, Bohuslav (1890-1959)
Double Concerto for two string orchestras, piano and timpani (1938); Valerie Kägi (pf), BKO, Basle, 9 February 1940

Concerto da camera for violin, piano, timpani, percussion and string orchestra (1941); Gertrud Flügel (vn), Valerie Kägi (pf), BKO, Basle, 23 January 1942

Toccata e due canzoni for chamber orchestra (1946);
  BKO (20th anniversary concert), Basle, 21 January 1947
Sinfonia concertante No. 2 for violin, oboe, bassoon, violoncello,
  and orchestra (1949); Petru Manoliu (vn), Alexander Gold
  (ob), Henri Bouchet (bn), Louis Fest (vc), Valerie Kägi (pf),
  BKO, Basle, 8 December 1950
The Epic of Gilgamesh. Oratorio for soloists, choir, and orchestra
  to text by Martinů adapted from *The Epic of Gilgamesh* (1954-5);
  BKO, Basle, 23 January 1958

Meale, Richard (b. 1932)
Evocations for oboe and chamber orchestra with violin obbligato
  (1973); Heinz Holliger (ob), Brenton Langbein (vn), CMZ,
  Zurich, 8 March 1974

Mieg, Peter (1906-90)
Combray for string orchestra (1977); CMZ, Zurich,
  24 January 1978

Mihalovici, Marcel (1898-1985)
Sinfonia giocosa for orchestra, op. 65 (1951); BKO, Basle,
  14 December 1951

Moeschinger, Albert (1897-1985)
Concerto for Violin, String Orchestra, Timpani and Small Drum,
  op. 40 (1935); Walter Kägi (vn), BKO, Basle, 2 October 1935
Concerto No. 3 for piano and chamber orchestra, op. 42 (1938);
  Franz Josef Hirt (pf), BKO, Basle, 22 March 1939
Concerto lyrique for saxophone and chamber orchestra, op. 83
  (1958); Hans Ackermann (sax), BKO, Basle, 23 January 1959
Consort for Strings, op. 99 (1965); BKO, Basle, 26 January 1967
Variations mystérieuses for chamber orchestra (1975-6); BKO,
  Basle, 31 March 1977

Moret, Norbert (1921-98)
Hymnes de silence [Hymns of Silence] for organ, strings, trombones, and percussion (1976-7); Heiner Kühner (org), BKO,
  Basle, 12 January 1978

Two Love Poems for soprano, violoncello, and orchestra, on text by Walt Whitman (1978-80); Phyllis Bryn-Julson (sop), Mstislav Rostropovitch (vc), BKO, Basle, 19 January 1984

Double Concerto for violin, cello and chamber orchestra (1981); Romana Pezzani (vn), Luciano Pezzani (vc), CMZ, Zurich, 18 November 1982

Visitations for soprano, mezzo-soprano, tenor, organ, piano and percussion, text adapted by Norbert Moret from Aeschylus, Shakespeare, the Bible (1981-2); Phyllis Bryn-Julson (sop), Julia Juon (mez), Heiner Hopfner (ten), Rudolf Scheidegger (org), Gérard Wyss (pf), Peter Solomon (portative org), Kathi Jacobi (regal), Markus Ernst, Jean-Claude Forestier, Gerhard Huber, Siegfried Kutterer, Siegfried Schmid, Hans Wäber (perc/BSE), BKO, Basle, 20 January 1983

Sacher-Serenade for quartet (1981-2); Felix Genner (bass cl), Peter Solomon (portative org), Kathi Jacobi (regal), BSE, BOG-serenade, Basle, 11 September 1983

Triple Concerto for flute, oboe, harp, and string orchestra (1984); Aurèle Nicolet (fl), Heinz Holliger (ob), Ursula Holliger (hp), CMZ, Zurich, 17 June 1985

Cello Concerto (1985); Mstislav Rostropovitch (vc), Brenton Langbein, CMZ, Zurich, 30 October 1988

Moser, Rudolf (1892-1960)

Concerto grosso for string orchestra and harpsichord, op. 32 (1927); BKO, Basle, 26 June 1927

Müller von Kulm, Walter (1899-1967)

Musik für Streichorchester [Music for String Orchestra], op. 42 (1939); BKO, Basle, 9 February 1940

Müller-Zürich, Paul (1898-1993)

Symphony in C for string orchestra, op. 40 (1944-5); CMZ, Zurich, 26 January 1945

Oboussier, Robert (1900-57)

Introitus für Streichorchester [Introit for String Orchestra] (1945-46); CMZ, Zurich, 14 February 1947

Petrassi, Goffredo (1904-2003)
Concerto for Orchestra No. 2 (1951); BKO (25th anniversary concert), Basle, 24 January 1952

Regamey, Constantin (1907-82)
4 x 5. Concerto for four quintets (1963); BKO, Basle, 28 May 1964
Lila. Double Concerto for violin, cello, and orchestra (1976); Primoz Novsak (vn), Susanne Basler (vc), BKO, Basle, 31 March 1977

Reimann, Aribert (b. 1936)
Chamber opera (work in progress); 1996 commission for a chamber opera for David Freeman's Opera Factory Zurich and Opera Factory London, based on Federico García Lorca's play *El público* [The Public]; co-funded by Paul Sacher on behalf of Opera Factory Zurich

Rihm, Wolfgang (b. 1952)
Gebild for string orchestra, high trumpet, and two percussionists (1982); Marc Ullrich (tr), CMZ, Zurich, 15 May 1983
Dunkles Spiel for 4 percussionists and 16 instruments (1988-90); Rainer Günther, Frithjof Koch, Pierre Böboux, Daniel Zoller (perc), CMZ, Zurich, 16 June 1990
Gesungene Zeit. Musik für Violine und Orchester [Time Chant: Music for violin and orchestra] (1990-91); Anne-Sophie Mutter (vn), CMZ, Zurich, 15 June 1992

Ringger, Rolf Urs (b. 1935)
Shelley-Songs for tenor, harp, and strings (1976-7); Peter Pears (ten), Ursula Holliger (hp), CMZ, Zurich, 28 May 1980

Strauss, Richard (1864-1949)
Metamorphosen [Metamorphoses], for 23 solo strings (1945); CMZ, Zurich, 25 January 1946

Stravinsky, Igor (1882-1971)
Concerto in D for string orchestra (1946); BKO, Basle, 21 January 1947

A Sermon, a Narrative and a Prayer. Cantata for soloists, narrator, choir and orchestra on texts from the Bible and by Thomas Dekker (1960-61); Jeanne Deroubaix (alto), Hugues Cuénod (ten), Derrik Olsen (narrator), concert to celebrate Stravinsky's 80th birthday, BKO, Basle, 22 February 1962

Suter, Robert (b. 1919)
Sonata per orchestra (1967-9); BKO, Basle, 22 February 1968
Trois nocturnes for viola and orchestra (1968-9); Hirofumi Fukai (va), BKO, Basle, 19 March 1970
Conversazioni concertanti for saxophone, vibraphone and 12-part string orchestra] (1978); Iwan Roth (sax), Jean-Claude Forestier (vib), CMZ, Zurich, 2 March 1979

Takemitsu, Toru (b.1930)
Eucalypts for flute, oboe, harp and strings (1970); Aurèle Nicolet (fl), Heinz Holliger (ob), Ursula Holliger (hp), CMZ, Tokyo, 16 November 1970

Tamás, János (1936-95)
Wartender Frühling for string sextett (1991); Kammermusiker Zürich, Zurich, 13 December 1992

Tippett, Michael (1905-98)
Divertimento on Sellinger's Round for chamber orchestra (1953-4); CMZ, Zurich, 5 November 1954

Veress, Sándor (1907-92)
Concerto for Piano, Strings and Percussion (1950-52); Veress (pf), Sinfonieorchester des Südwestfunks Baden-Baden, Baden-Baden, 19 January 1954
Concerto for String Quartet and Orchestra (1960-61); Végh Quartet, BKO, Basle, 25 January 1962

Vogel, Wladimir (1896-1984)
Komposition für Kammerorchester [Composition for Chamber Orchestra] (1976); BKO, Basle, 12 January 1978
Variationen über Tritonus und Septime [Variations on the Tritone

and the Seventh] (1978); Brenton Langbein, CMZ, Zurich, 27 February 1981

Wyttenbach, Jürg (b. 1935)
Exécution ajournée. Gesten für Musiker [Stayed Execution. Jokes for Musicians] (1969-1970); Jürg Wyttenbach, BKO, Basle, 20 June 1970

Paul Sacher conducted the first performances of many other contemporary works dedicated to him. Details of these can be found in the published sources for the commissions list given below.

Published Sources

Basle Chamber Orchestra Society, *Alte und Neue Musik 1: 25 Jahre Basler Kammerorchester 1926-1951* [Early and Contemporary Music: 25 Years of the Basle Chamber Orchestra 1926-1951], Zurich, 1952

Ehrismann, Sibylle, ed., *Fünfzig Jahre Collegium Musicum Zürich 1941/42-1991/92* [50 Years of the Collegium Musicum Zurich 1941/42-1991/92], Zurich, 1994

Gutmann, Veronika, ed., *Alte und Neue Musik II: 50 Jahre Basler Kammerorchester 1926-1976* [Early and Contemporary Music II: 50 Years of the Basle Chamber Orchestra 1926-1976], Zurich, 1977

Gutmann, Veronika, ed., *Paul Sacher als Gastdirigent-Dokumentation und Beiträge zum 80 Geburtstag* [Paul Sacher as Guest Conductor: Documentation and Contributions to his 80th Birthday], Zurich, 1986

Müller-Märki, Ruth, *Paul Sacher: Champion of New Music,* DMA thesis, Manhattan School of Music, 2002

Paul Sacher Foundation, *Paul Sacher und die Musik des zwanzigsten Jahrhunderts: Auftragswerke, Widmungskompositionen, Uraufführungen, 1926-1990* [Paul Sacher and the Music of the Twentieth Century: Commissions, Dedicated Works and World Premières 1926-1990], compiled by Klaus Schweizer, Winterthur, 1991

Paul Sacher Foundation, *Inventare der Paul Sacher Stiftung I: Sammlung Paul Sacher/Musikmanuskripte* [Paul Sacher Foundation Inventory I: Paul Sacher Collection/Music Manuscripts], Mainz, 2000

Schweizer, Klaus, ed., *Alte und Neue Musik III: 60 Jahre Basler Kammerorchester 1976-1987* [Early and Contemporary Music: 60 Years of the Basle Chamber Orchestra 1976-1987], Zurich, 1988

The author wishes to thank Dr Felix Meyer (director), and Mr Robert Piencikowski (curator of music manuscripts) at the Paul Sacher Foundation for their assistance in compiling this list.

Paul Sacher's Family Tree

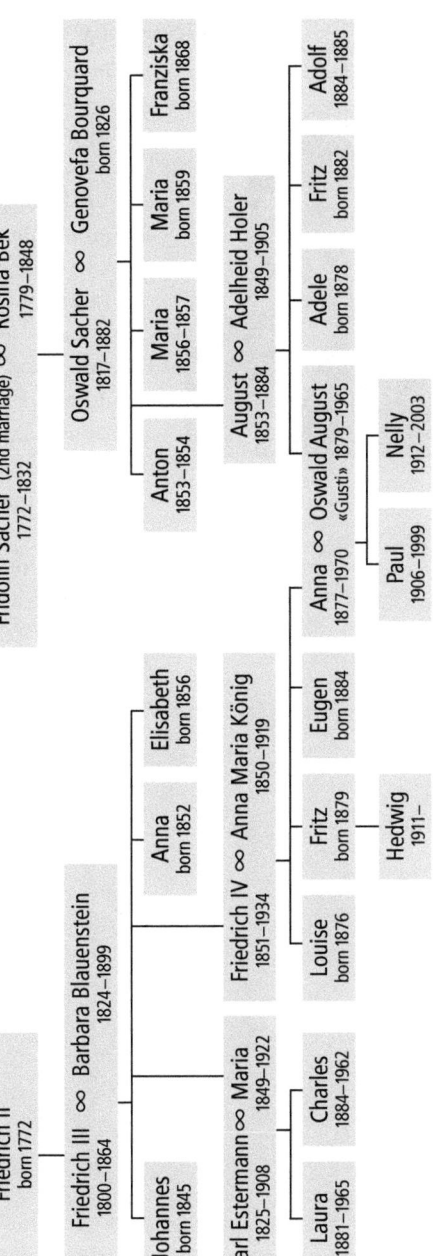

Biography of the author

Lesley Stephenson was born in New Zealand and grew up in Australia. She studied law and languages at Sydney University and graduated with a Bachelor of Arts degree. In the 1980s she made a career as an opera and concert singer, working with conductors and producers such as Pierre Boulez, Paul Daniel, François Rochaix and David Freeman.

Today Lesley Stephenson is a freelance writer for several newspapers such as *The (London) Times,* and also works as an editor for several international firms. She is a certified teacher of the F.M. Alexander Technique, and director of the Centre for Personal Performance Enhancement in Zurich.